AUSTRALIAN MUSICAL THEATRE

Australian Musical Theatre: Never Been Better? is the first sustained scholarly analysis of the Australian musical in the twenty-first century. In the past, the Australian musical has been much maligned: plagued by the sceptre of 'The Great Australian Musical' and dogged by recurring concerns about the content and quality of the genre. In this book, Mara Davis Johnson assesses these concerns and argues that they are unfounded.

Through detailed analysis of six musicals, she showcases the breadth and diversity of contemporary Australian musical theatre productions. The book demonstrates how these performances stage a repertory of tropes, characters, places, stories, fixations, and myths that produce a national imaginary for Australia. Methodologically, the book takes a holistic and multi-disciplinary approach that honours the hybrid nature of the musical and its broad cultural appeal.

This makes for an accessible, wide-ranging discussion that will appeal to scholars in diverse fields. The book will be an essential resource for scholars and students of musical theatre, theatre and performance studies, and Australian cultural studies and history.

Mara Davis Johnson is Lecturer in Creative and Performing Arts at the University of Wollongong, Australia. She is a musician, composer, vocal coach, and dramaturg whose research centres on musical theatre in all its forms.

AUSTRALIAN MUSICAL THEATRE

Never Been Better?

Mara Davis Johnson

Routledge
Taylor & Francis Group

LONDON AND NEW YORK

Designed cover image: The cast of *Muriel's Wedding: The* Musical performing 'Sunshine State of Mind.' Photo: Jeff Busby ©

First published 2026
by Routledge
4 Park Square, Milton Park, Abingdon, Oxon OX14 4RN

and by Routledge
605 Third Avenue, New York, NY 10158

Routledge is an imprint of the Taylor & Francis Group, an informa business

British Library Cataloguing-in-Publication Data
A catalogue record for this book is available from the British Library

ISBN: 978-1-032-96599-4 (hbk)
ISBN: 978-1-032-96595-6 (pbk)
ISBN: 978-1-003-59008-8 (ebk)

DOI: 10.4324/9781003590088

Typeset in Galliard
by Apex CoVantage, LLC

For Luke, my greatest convert.

CONTENTS

FIGURES

ABOUT THE AUTHOR

Mara Davis Johnson is Lecturer in Creative and Performing Arts at the University of Wollongong, Australia, where she teaches music and theatre. She is a musician, composer, vocal coach, and dramaturg whose research centres on musical theatre in all its forms. She holds a Bachelor of Creative Arts (Honours) from the University of Wollongong, a Bachelor of Music Studies from the University of Sydney, and a PhD in Musical Theatre from the University of New South Wales, Sydney. Her writing has been published in journals such as *AI & Society*, *Critical Stages/Scénes Critique*, and *Antithesis*, in edited collections such as *Barrie Kosky's Transnational Theatres* (Springer, 2021), and for media outlets such as *The Conversation*. Mara is a member of the Australasian Association for Theatre, Drama, and Performance Studies and the International Federation of Theatre Research. She is a co-author of *Performing Data: Theatre Practice and Research*, which is forthcoming with Bloomsbury Press.

ACKNOWLEDGEMENTS

I commenced this research as a doctoral candidate. My PhD was completed at the University of New South Wales, with the support of an Australian Postgraduate Award. It would not have come to fruition had it not been for the guidance of my exceptional supervisor Jonathan Bollen, who encouraged me to think about publication early in the piece and gave valuable advice on the proposal. Jonathan has a rare gift for giving the kind of feedback that motivates you to keep going, and I am grateful for his rigour, care, and generosity throughout the candidature and beyond. I also thank co-supervisor Michael Hooper for his guidance throughout my candidature. Examiners Ian Maxwell and Elizabeth Wollman gave me thought-provoking feedback and the much-needed confidence to push the work to the next level and pursue publication.

Dear colleagues Joanne Tompkins, Charlotte Farrell, Izabella Nantsou, and Sarah Thomasson provided generous and insightful feedback on select chapters. In addition, I am grateful to the Australasian Association for Theatre, Drama, and Performance Studies (ADSA) for providing such a warm and welcoming community for early-career researchers to join.

The University of Wollongong facilitated access to research funding to include images in the book. I thank Jo Law and Peter Kelly for their support of this project and Stephanie Perrett for all her help in navigating the financial services of the University of Wollongong. Photographers Jeff Busby, Meredith O'Shea, and Pia Johnson generously gave their permission to include images as part of the book and bring the productions to life for readers.

While I saw all the productions in this book live on stage, archival video recordings, scores, and scripts have played an invaluable role in the depth of the analysis. This access was supported by Judith Seeff at the Sydney Theatre

Company, Stevie Bryant at Belvoir, Jeremy Rice at Melbourne Theatre Company, the staff at Global Creatures, Iain Grandage, Kate Miller-Heidke, Keir Nuttall, Marilen Tabacco, and Eddie Perfect.

My husband Luke accompanied me to several of these productions, and his insights were always immensely valuable and appreciated. Without his support, I would not have embarked upon and could not have completed this project. I am lucky to have such an intelligent and perceptive life partner and interlocutor at my disposal.

Our children – Emile, Ottavio, and Josephine – were carried and born in conjunction with this research and so have literally lived and breathed it alongside me. I hope one day they might read this book and gain some insight into the intellectual life of their mother.

I am sure that my parents, Joseph Davis and Inga Lazzarotto, did not realise when they bought me the tickets to see my first musical that musical theatre would become such an important feature of their family life. I thank them from the bottom of my heart for the many sacrifices they have made to nurture my interest in the arts. More tangibly, without the many hours of childcare they have provided in recent years, this book simply could not have been written. Our 'big kids,' Harriet and Albury, were also extremely helpful in entertaining their younger siblings throughout the PhD and publication process and helping our household run smoothly.

The artists whose works feature in this book – Eddie Perfect, Lally Katz, Kate Miller-Heidke, Keir Nuttall, Ursula Yovich, and Alana Valentine – all generously provided their permission to quote their work. In the course of this process, I was fortunate to be able to communicate with some of them directly. My correspondence with Eddie Perfect was particularly touching. He spoke about the gratitude he felt that someone had taken the time to grapple so deeply with his work and that it so rarely felt like this was the case: 'Honestly, 99% of the time it feels like the things I'm trying to say, or the ideas I'm interested in wrestling with, float by in an unexamined blur.'

It can often feel like academic work suffers a similar fate. What keeps me going is the desire to genuinely understand and convey how a performance has affected me, and what I think an artist is trying to say. I am so glad that, at least in this one case, it seems that I achieved my goal. Who could ask for anything more?

INTRODUCTION

Beyond Quest, Crisis, and the Great Australian Musical

When most people think about musical theatre, their minds are immediately drawn to Broadway, or perhaps the West End. But what happens in these theatre districts is just part of the story of a form that is produced, and beloved, all around the world. Australia is an emerging force in this global theatrical landscape. Since the beginning of the twenty-first century, Australian musicals and producers have found their way to international stages. *Moulin Rouge*, produced by the Australian-based company Global Creatures, received fourteen nominations at the 2020 Tony Awards, more than double any previous Australian production. The Michael Cassel Group is currently producing work in Australia, on Broadway and the West End, and touring in Asia and the Middle East. Composers and lyricists, like Tim Minchin (*Matilda* and *Groundhog Day*) and Eddie Perfect (*Beetlejuice*), and performers, like Caroline O'Connor and Anthony Warlow, are forging international careers. Barrie Kosky, an expatriate theatre director, has been presenting musicals left, right and centre at the Komische Oper in Berlin.

This burgeoning industry has taken some time to develop, and consequently, the domestic environment that has produced these recent successes has been little explored and little understood, even in Australia itself. Described evocatively by Steve Dow as an 'understudy in the wings, struggling for the spotlight in competition with Disney lions, British boots, and Mormons on a mission,' Australian musicals have always played second fiddle to the Broadway and West End hits and classic revivals that still dominate the Australian musical theatre landscape.[1] This study brings Australian musical theatre into the well and truly into the spotlight, arguing that it is a sophisticated and diverse national body of performance.

DOI: 10.4324/9781003590088-1

Of the Australian musicals that have made it to the stage in recent decades, it is remarkable how many are concerned with representation of nation's history, culture, and socio-political life. This book interrogates the relationship between Australian musicals and the nation, and the way in which contemporary Australian musicals negotiate, contest, and reimagine national identity. The forthcoming chapters explore six musicals that function as critical sites of enquiry: *Muriel's Wedding* (2017), *Shane Warne: The Musical* (2008/2013), *Songs from the Middle* (2010), *The Rabbits* (2015), *Barbara and the Camp Dogs* (2017), and *Vivid White* (2017) demonstrate how recent musical theatre produces and reproduces a repertory of themes, tropes, characters, places, stories, fixations, and myths that form a national imaginary for Australia. Not merely set in Australia, nor merely created by Australians, these works ask questions that are central to the nation's conception of itself in a post-colonial and increasingly globalised world, offering multivalent, contested perspectives on questions of national belonging.

Although the Australian musical's focus on the nation is not unique to the current century, I place my attention squarely on the recent past. I do so because this is a body of work, and a cultural moment, that I experienced synchronously, having attended performances of each of these musicals. This study is the culmination of a project that has spanned my adolescent and adult life. My passion for musicals about Australia did not begin in the library or at the researcher's table, but rather, derived from an intuitive feeling generated in the moment of performance. The period examined in this book spans my transition from fan to scholar, tracing the period in which my interested matured from merely enthusiastic to academic. I honour this in my approach by taking care to highlight the affective dimensions of musical theatre as they intersect with the nation.[2] I do so by considering the impact of these musicals – what Angharad Closs Stevens describes as the 'sensations, affects, intensities' that they produce, and by drawing out how, as John Gillis argues, the nation is not something we think *about* but think *with*.[3] Or, as Eddie Perfect, the author of several musicals featured in the subsequent chapters remarks: 'people like to see their own stories reflected back at them.'[4]

Yes, they do. To explicate these ideas, in this introduction, I first draw out the connections between musical theatre and the representation of national identity. I then situate and contextualise Australian musical theatre by detail the persistent economic and cultural forces that have worked against the development and production of Australian musicals, and the rhetoric of crisis and inadequacy that has predominated. I introduce and dispense with the sceptre of the 'Great Australian Musical,' a notion that has plagued discussion of the form. Before this, however, it is necessary to address a definitional question: what is an Australian musical?

Defining the Australian Musical

Discussion of the Australian musical has been plagued by anxieties about what exactly constitutes or qualifies as such. Much of this commentary has centred on whether the nationality of the artist/s or the work's subject matter is paramount. In 2004, Peter Wyllie Johnston outlined a taxonomy of the Australian musical that assessed the 'Australian-ness' of various elements – music, lyrics, book, story, director, producer, place of first production, and principal cast.[5] On this basis, he produced a schema of six categories: no Australian music or lyrics; Australian music and principal cast; more than half 'Australian'; 'All-Australian' except for the story; 'All-Australian'; 'All-Australian' including Indigenous Australians, and argued that 'it is possible to place every musical ever written by an Australian' into one of these.[6] This analysis revealed that works with Australian stories or subject matter are in the minority. In *The Australian Musical: From the Beginning*, Wyllie Johnston and Peter Pinne's subsequent book on the subject, the authors take a broad view, defining the Australian musical as one 'created entirely or partly by Australian composers and writers.'[7] John Senczuk, who also attempted a taxonomy of the form, offered a comparable but slightly expanded definition, where he defined an Australian musical as being

> conceived, written, composed, or *auteured* by Australian creative artists. Australian musicals do not necessarily demand Australian subject matter, but the very act of bringing the work before an audience, providing it with an Australian sensibility, a unique view of the world, or an Australian style or idiom, qualifies its inclusion in the canon.[8]

Senczuk goes onto give the example of *Matilda: The Musical*, proffering that it should be eligible 'for at least partial inclusion in the canon' due to the fact its score is composed by the Australian comedian Tim Minchin.[9] But the logic of this argument – Tim Minchin is Australian, ergo *Matilda* is an Australian musical – doesn't pass the 'pub test,' to use a very Australian expression. This book develops the argument that this is not enough, but that Australian musicals are those that are distinctively, observably engaged in the production and reproduction of the national imaginary. My first act in doing so is to define an Australian musical as a work with an Australian story, an Australian-composed score, and Australian artists in key creative roles. The musicals discussed in the forthcoming chapters adhere to these parameters. Additionally, I argue that, in all the musicals in this book, the audience is distinctively addressed as a bounded community: what Janelle Reinelt terms a 'national citizenry.'[10] This definition accounts for how these works specifically function as sites of national cultural production.

Formally, the Australian musical is as varied as its international counterparts, spanning the book musical, the sung through musical, the jukebox musical, the rock musical, and the song cycle/revue. Sonically, these works employ a wide musical palate, including opera, jazz, American popular song, rock, funk, soul, blues, and hip-hop. Some Australian musicals are large-scale productions with big choruses; others are small, intimate works. They frequently use dance as a storytelling technique. They adopt conventions like 'I want' songs, stirring, anthemic finales, and metatheatrical songs about singing, that will be familiar to observers of the Broadway musical. Due to the absence of clearly defined central theatre districts, Australian musicals are produced in a wide range of theatres and spaces.[11] While historically Australian musicals have largely been produced by commercial organisations like the Michael Cassel Group, Global Creatures, and John Frost Enterprises, they have increasingly become the purview of the state-funded opera and theatre companies.[12] As such, Australian musicals are funded through a range of economic models. This means that the boundary between opera, musical theatre and dramatic theatre in Australia is, as John Senczuk notes, 'blurry.'[13] Such dynamics play out in the chapters of this book.

Who We Are: Musical Theatre and the Nation

The stuff of Australian musicals is that of the national imaginary, a term that encompasses a repertory of themes, tropes, characters, places, stories, fixations, anxieties, and myths that are regarded as connected to a particular nation-state. My conception builds on the idea of the 'social imaginary' as theorised by the sociologist Charles Taylor.[14] Taylor, who acknowledges his debt to Benedict Anderson's conception of the nation as an 'imagined community,' defines the social imaginary as a 'common understanding that makes possible common practices and a widely shared sense of legitimacy'; 'the ways we are able to think or imagine the whole of society.'[15] As Paul James, summarising Taylor's theory, observes, the social imaginary 'is not the particular ideas or beliefs held by people, but the collation of those ideas in a larger social frame.'[16] James goes onto to explain that

> while an imaginary can be informed by theoretical developments and it can be analysed by theorists, it is not primarily an intellectual schema. . . . Rather it is a lived and generalising sensibility held by the many – from those who do not have the words to articulate its meaning to those who seek to analyse its condensing discourses.[17]

This notion of a 'lived' sensibility iterates, as Anderson insisted, that 'imagined' does not mean false or 'not real.'[18] National imaginaries are embodied and enacted through the lives of citizens: they form a '"repertory" of collective actions at the disposal of a given group of society.'[19] This is a productive (and appropriately theatrical) metaphor for thinking through the national imaginary. But, as James points out, an imaginary is not a totalising force. Instead, it is better understood as 'a cultural dominant, layered across prior and emerging imaginaries,' one that is 'determined by current ideas *and* practices constituted in relation to meanings and practices of the past.'[20] National imaginaries are not fixed but instead are produced and reproduced in multivalent ways. This will become perspicuous in the ensuing chapters.

My inquiry is grounded in the fact that the musical is understood as being intertwined with the nation. In *The American Musical and the Formation of National Identity*, the foremost text on the subject, Raymond Knapp argues that 'defining America' has been '*the* central theme in American musicals' and that they are 'always concerned, on some level, with constructions of America.'[21] This tradition continues to the present day, with musicals like *The Scottsboro Boys* (2010), *Giant* (2012), and the blockbuster *Hamilton* (2015) continuing to interrogate this theme, while canonical musicals like *Oklahoma!* and *West Side Story* continue to be revived and revised, offering new perspectives on the state of the nation.[22] Moreover, the connection between musical theatre and the nation is not a uniquely American phenomenon. Recent scholarship examining national musical theatres in countries other than the United States has observed similar phenomena while also seeking to unseat perceptions of an American stranglehold on the genre. In their history of British musical theatre, Gordon, Jubin and Taylor state that 'by focusing on what makes British musicals uniquely *British*,' they set out to 'challenge the historically inaccurate and culturally biased view of the British musical as a second-rate imitation of a superior Broadway model.'[23] Similar scholarship emerging from Britain, South Korea, and Canada explores the ways in which the musical has been developed in these contexts.[24] Millie Taylor and Adam Rush's recent book *Musical Theatre Histories: Expanding the Narrative* considers the multiple, intersecting, global histories of the form.[25] By surveying the particularities of Australian musicals, as well as by considering the transnational forces that are affecting the musical more broadly, my aim in this book is to bring Australia more firmly into this developing conversation.

Why do musicals provide a particularly apt site for examination of the national imaginary? One theory is because of the way in which they imagine their audience. David Walsh and Len Platt see the musical as an 'open, direct, and ideologically unapologetic expression of the ideals, dreams, anxieties, feelings, fulfillments, and frustrations of its audience.'[26] David Savran describes the musical as a form of 'urban folk culture,' one where the songs become 'monuments of a shared participatory culture.'[27] Knapp argues that musicals were particularly suited for this task because they

> not only brought a specific community together within a constructed community, but also sent that audience out into a larger community armed

with songs to be shared, providing at least some basis for achieving a sense of unity among the increasingly varied peoples of a country expanding rampantly both geographically and through immigration.[28]

In this aspiration, as Walsh and Platt suggest, musicals 'can become powerful vehicles of popular collective expression' because they '[articulate] symbolically, in the patterns of their narrative, lyrical harmonies, and dance, the tensions and reconciliation of everyday relations between individuals and society.'[29] This is a highly utopian pursuit. But as Richard Dyer, writing about musicals as entertainment, argues, the musical's 'utopian sensibility' is derived from

> the real experiences of the audience. Yet to do this, to draw attention to the gap between what is and what could be, is, ideologically speaking, playing with fire. What musicals have to do, then, (not through any conspiratorial intent, but because it is always easier to take the line of least resistance, i.e. to fit in with prevailing norms) is to work through these contradictions at all levels in such a way as to 'manage' them, to make them seem to disappear. They don't always succeed.[30]

Dyer's account of the tension between what 'is' and what 'could be' illustrates the way that audiences of musicals participate in an imaginative process, one that privileges affective experience. As he observes, utopianism 'presents, head-on as it were, what utopia would *feel* like rather than how it would be organized. It thus works at the level of sensibility,' which he clarifies as an 'affective code.'[31] A comparable process features in the construction of the national imaginary in that Australian musicals reveal the national imaginary as a continually contested, re-imagined space, both '*instituted* and instituting: broadly, both passively found or encountered as conditions for experiencing the world, and actively and innovatively transformed as they are re-experienced.'[32] Australian musicals both reflect and seek to shape the world that they inhabit.

Does this focus on the national imaginary risk reifying the category of 'nation'? In 2010, the noted theatre reviewer Alison Croggon published an impassioned polemic titled 'How Australian Is It?' in which she argued that Australian theatre's continued focus on the nation, bolstered by funding institutions like the Australia Council for the Arts (now Creative Australia), is politically problematic. She described appeals to national identity and Australian stories as 'inevitably part of a larger nationalist project, however loosely defined,' one that 'at its worst, expresses itself in the parochial, xenophobic, and colonial.'[33] Profiling directors Barrie Kosky and Benedict Andrews, playwrights Daniel Keene and Wesley Enoch, and a host of independent theatre companies, she concluded that 'the best of our contemporary theatre' has judiciously done away with the nation and that 'perhaps the genie is well and truly out of the bottle, and our theatre has grown past the need to merely perform its national identity.'[34] Croggon is right that engagement with the national imaginary should not define the value of a theatre production, and her frustration with an environment that she sees as overvaluing performance that focuses on the nation is palpable. But implicit in her argument is not only that some of Australia's best artists do not care about the nation – and that whatever they produce is Australian enough and that should be the end of the matter – but also audiences shouldn't either, and if audiences are unhappy about this, they should perhaps reconsider their prejudices.

Unlike Croggon, I am reluctant to dismiss the importance of Australian stories so readily. I am equally reluctant to conceive of theatre and performance that interrogates the national imaginary as inherently immature, a line of enquiry that we will out-grow of in due course. I situate my work through the category of nation because following Craig Calhoun, I argue that nations matter: they matter historically; they matter socio-politically; and they matter to their citizens. They continue to 'command . . . profound emotional legitimacy.'[35] While it is necessary to pay 'critical attention to [the nation's] limits, illusions, and potential for abuse,' as Calhoun notes, we should take care not to dismiss it.[36] There is great value, as Kathleen Lennon states, in interrogating the highly affective, contested space occupied by these national imaginaries: 'given the emotional pull such imaginings generate it is important to consider how they are assessed, how we are to reflect on their legitimacy.'[37] Australian musicals have much to offer in this regard. The Australian musicals studied in this thesis, rather than kowtowing to a jingoistic nationalist agenda, ask valid, timely, thorny questions about who we are, where we live, where we have come from, and where we are headed. In foregrounding this, I demonstrate the productive nature of analysis of the national imaginary.

So far in this introduction, I have sought to position Australian musical theatre as a vibrant site of inquiry, contextualising it as a body of work that engages thoughtfully with the national imaginary. But this is not how discussions of Australian musical theatre are generally approached. In fact, the history of Australian musical theatre has been, to this point, mired in fears of parochialism and marked by a rhetoric of crisis. In the next section, I engage with this discourse and its effects on the production and reception of new Australian musicals.

Reassessing the Crisis in Australian Musical Theatre

In 2001, Peter Fitzpatrick published an article in the journal *Australasian Drama Studies* entitled 'Whose Turn to Shout? The Crisis in Australian Music Theatre.'[38] Despite the recent success of two new Australian musicals – *The Boy from Oz* (1998) and *Shout! The Legend of the Wild One* (2000) – in this paper Fitzpatrick described what he saw as an industry in crisis, and a cultural landscape in which Australian musicals were underfunded and underappreciated. This crisis rhetoric, sustained by the media, can be characterised as operating on three fronts: as a crisis of attention, a crisis of economics, and a crisis of aesthetics.

The Crisis of Attention

The crisis of attention is one of public awareness. It is the view that Australian musicals have been unduly ignored and, as Peter Wyllie Johnston states, have 'seldom been close to centre stage in analyses of Australian cultural life.'[39] There were several attempts to ameliorate this, such as the 1994 concert, *Once in a Blue Moon: A Celebration of Australian Musicals*, a compilation of songs from various Australian musicals televised on the ABC, the national broadcaster.[40] A decade later, in 2004, the Melbourne Arts Centre presented an exhibition entitled *Making a Song and Dance: The Quest for the Australian Musical*, which aimed to draw to the history of Australian musicals and to inform the public about the history of the genre. In the exhibition catalogue, co-curator Simon Plant wrote that '[e]veryone can name an Australian novel, an Australian painting, an Australian play. But an Australian musical? Faces go blank. Eyes blink. The idea does not compute.'[41] *Making a Song and Dance* was intended to negate the 'myth,' as noted by the playwright and librettist Hilary Bell, 'that musical theatre in Australia is a kind of terra nullis [*sic*], without heritage or history,' or as Fitzpatrick describes it, the 'one performative area' where the 'myth of emptiness' remains.[42]

Fitzpatrick also conceived the crisis of attention as an academic one, derived from the fact there was limited published research on the Australian musical. In 2004, Peter Wyllie Johnston noted that in the twentieth century 'not a single book' on the subject of Australian musical theatre had been published.[43] The first book, titled *The Australian Musical: From the Beginning*, was published by Johnston and Peter Pinne in 2019. By cataloguing 324 Australian musicals written over the past 100 years, the book sought to dispel the myth of emptiness and negate the crisis of attention.[44] In addition to there being a lack of published academic material, Fitzpatrick was also concerned that the criticism that did exist lacked the necessary historical context and disciplinary expertise. He attributed what he called the 'extraordinary academic neglect' of the Australian musical as reflecting a wider failure of attention, one that dismissed musical theatre as a

> creature of its own popularity, offering predictable escapist entertainment rather than challenge, its form as inimical to serious argument as it was to emotional authenticity. It could not belong in the academy, because any art so dependent on gross box office, a range of industries and (generally) hefty capital investment was by definition a tainted form, born of compromise and market manipulation, in contrast to the supposedly purer mechanism of literary production. And even when popular culture came academically

into its own in the 1980s, musical theatre, in Australia as elsewhere, largely failed to accompany it.[45]

However, in the two decades since Fitzpatrick published his article, musical theatre scholarship internationally has undergone a profound transformation. Up until the beginning of the twenty-first century, scholars still felt the need to rise to the defence of the musical and assert that it was worthy of serious academic criticism.[46] At the time I am writing, two decades later, there is an extensive body of academic writing about musical theatre available. In the context of the United States, one can confidently say that the academic crisis is over: the musical requires no further defence as a serious subject for academic criticism. Australian scholarship, while growing, is still relatively sparse.[47] This book is a significant next step in addressing the crisis of attention.

The Economic Crisis

The economic crisis that befalls the Australian musical is less easily remedied. The financial demands of musical theatre production are a challenge that cannot be solved inside the academy. The current state of play is that commercial production companies are reluctant to take a gamble on new Australian work, as it is a much safer investment to import already successful Broadway or West End shows and so, overwhelmingly, this is what occurs. With millions of dollars invested in bringing musicals from elsewhere, it has been very difficult for homegrown productions to compete. Compounding this difficulty is the view that the Australian market is far too small for an investment to be satisfactorily recouped. As art forms based in spectacle, musicals historically have large casts, orchestras, production teams, and budgets; ergo, they require an enormous amount of money to be staged. These economic concerns have material effects on the kinds of musicals that are produced: as David Savran writes, 'the aesthetic is always – and unpredictably – overdetermined by economic relations and interests.'[48] The production contexts of the musicals featured in this thesis reflect these realities. The large casts and elaborate sets of certain musicals were achieved through a combination of government funding as well as commercial investments. Some artists have problem solved these financial limitations by producing works on a very small scale, thereby limiting costs and facilitating touring seasons.[49] The only musical in this study that was created and performed in a wholly commercial production context (*Shane Warne*) failed to recoup its investments, demonstrating the profound economic challenges that befall new work.

A vocal critic of this economic climate has been the director, writer, and designer John Senczuk. In his 2015 essay, *Is the Time Ripe for the Great Australian Musical?*, Senczuk used the language of crisis when he wrote that 'we fund other art forms at both national and state level as a matter of course, and yet fail to financially support and encourage the art form that fuses all three disciplines (music, theatre and dance).'[50] Artists have frequented lamented the dearth of opportunities to stage original Australian musical theatre. This debate came to the fore in June 2017, when the Australian actor, musician, and composer Eddie Perfect called attention to the lack of Australian music theatre works receiving nominations for Helpmann Awards. He posted a series of tweets proclaiming that 'one look at the noms [nominations] confirm the obvious; original Australian music theatre is in real crisis.'[51] Other tweets elaborated on Perfect's frustrations: 'We have a multi-million dollar commercial industry with negligible interest in developing our own works'; 'Unlike EVERY other art form, MT [Musical Theatre] is entirely imported'; 'Commercial producers have no imperative to develop new work, even after receiving millions from state govs to "win" Oz Broadway premieres.'[52]

The unfortunate consequence of this is that while productions of new Australian musicals struggle to be produced and then patronised, Australian audiences are more enthusiastic than ever about musical theatre. At grassroots level, the nation has a thriving community theatre culture, with prolific societies staging many musicals each year, often with comparatively large budgets and high-quality performers, who are often recent graduates from training institutions.[53] State governments view the acquisition of big musicals as lucrative economic events, with cities like Sydney and Melbourne competing for the right to host these events, sometimes spending tens of millions of dollars to secure the latest hit. In May 2016, *The Sydney Morning Herald* reported that the New South Wales government refused to disclose how much money it had spent to obtain the current run of *Beautiful: The Carole King Musical.*[54] State governments are only willing to put in large amounts of money when the show in question is a known quantity that has already enjoyed success in the highly competitive Broadway or West End market. When the show is successful, the economic benefit can be enormous. In 2018, musical theatre was the second largest category of live performance in Australia – 18.5% of revenue overall, 38.4% in New South Wales, and 32.6% in Victoria.[55] In that year, the industry generated over $400 million for the Australian economy. But new Australian work is not responsible for these kinds of returns. In response to Perfect's tweets about the 2017 Helpmann nominations, the veteran producer John Frost weighed in, espousing that Australian content will never be a big winner at the box office, and so producers are best placed to import overseas productions. He also advised young composers to move overseas in search of greater opportunities. He remarked that 'no, I don't think there will be a Great Australian Musical. I think that because the minute you use the word "Australian" I think it sort of makes it sound very parochial.'[56] He did not mean this as a compliment.

The Aesthetic Crisis

This is the aesthetic crisis: the idea that Australian stories and national sensibilities might be incompatible with the musical. This view, encapsulated by Hilary Bell, is the perception that 'the Musical is meaningless to Australians, that on a fundamental level we resist the idea that the protagonist arrives at a point where they must sing.'[57] Journalist Ben Neutze views this as symptomatic of the economic crisis, arguing local writers are disadvantaged by the saturation of the market with overseas works and, as a result, can often find it difficult to locate the right tone:

> Most of us don't balk at, say, *Wicked*, with its overt sentimentality; we can relate to the struggles of its outsider protagonist, even if she expresses herself in ways that most of us would never dream of. We can entirely invest in Elphaba's self-determination in *Defying Gravity*, even if we'd never burst into such an assertive and personal expression. You put that song into the mouth of most Australian characters? It'd become a joke.[58]

Neutze contends that the problem is one of imitation and that Australian writers need to be provided with further opportunities, to 'build our own style of musical theatre from the ground up, almost as if it were an entirely new art form.'[59] Reviewing *Once in a Blue Moon* in 1994, the journalist and radio presenter Michael Cathcart echoed this observation, conveying his disappointment that the showcased songs 'sounded as if they had been written to conform to some generic musical ideal . . . [seeming] to emulate American models rather than find a new Australian voice.'[60] The anxiety that Australian musical theatre writing is derivative (and therefore lacking) is bolstered by the fact that works are rarely produced again after their original runs, even if they have been successful. The aversion to staging new works also extends to the amateur musical theatre scene. As David Spicer, manager of the foremost company licensing the rights to Australian musicals, remarked, Casey Bennetto's musical *Keating!* has only been licensed a handful of times, despite being a commercial and critical success.[61] I engage substantially with these arguments and, through close analysis, reveal that they are unfounded. Australian musicals are aesthetically sophisticated and are rendering Australian stories and people in song effectively, making meaningful interventions into the national imaginary.

The aesthetic crisis and the economic crisis are deeply entangled, as Frost's remarks indicate, mired in a chicken-and-the-egg quandary. Frost's argument is that there simply is just not enough money to be made to justify the investment, and Australian content is just too difficult a sell. Others, like Senczuk, argue the exact opposite, that the musicals are ready and waiting to be produced, but the problem is that the systems are not in place to support them. The apotheosis of this three-front crisis is Australia's 'failure' to produce what is referred to as the 'Great Australian Musical.'

The 'Great Australian Musical'

The 'Great Australian Musical' is the idea that there could be a musical with an Australian score, an Australian narrative, and an Australian cast, that enjoys enormous critical and financial success both domestically and internationally. It is a utopian idea that what the Australian musical theatre industry needs to resolve the economic, academic and aesthetic crises once and for all is, as Neutze writes, for one amazing musical to 'break through, change our attitudes to new work, give us international recognition and begin an age where home-grown work stands alongside imports.'[62] The notion of the 'Great Australian Musical' has irrevocably shaped the development of new Australian musical theatre. Journalist Chris Boyd recalled that 'in the late 1980s and early 90s, there was an anxious and increasingly desperate search for a Great Australian Musical. It was as if, as a culture, we were a *Les Mis* short of real pride. The most ambitious projects were often the biggest failures.'[63] Most new Australian musicals created in the last thirty years have been measured against this ideal, and as Pinne and Wyllie Johnston describe, the 'Great Australian Musical' continues to be a 'persistent part of Australia's cultural conversation.'[64]

One difficulty with actually finding a 'Great Australian Musical' is that 'great' and 'Australian' are, as if by definition, incompatible. *The Boy from Oz*, the first Australian musical to appear on Broadway, premièred on Australian stages in 1998 and was received with great enthusiasm and acclaim. Gale Edwards, the director, said about the project that 'I have taken on one of the biggest challenges in Australian show biz history: to create the great Australian musical.'[65] In 1999, writing in *The Age*, Helen Thomson wondered: 'Is *The Boy from Oz* the Great Australian Musical – at last? Well that may depend on your definition of musical, but it's certainly a great show.'[66] Why the hesitation? As Tim Lloyd wrote in the Adelaide Advertiser in 2001, 'I don't want to look a gift horse in the mouth, but the trouble with [The Boy From] *Oz* and *Shout!* is that they are not really Australian musicals.'[67] This 'un-Australian-ness' was attributed to their use of jukebox musical format and the fact that there were no additional songs written for the production.[68] Additionally, in the case of *The Boy from Oz*, by the time the musical had its much-anticipated opening on Broadway in 2003, according to Peter Fitzpatrick, there was 'little left that was distinctively Australian' with the new production having significantly diminished the contributions of the musical's Australian librettist, Nick Enright.[69] When *The Boy from* Oz returned to Australia in 2006 with Hugh Jackman at the helm, however, 'the local jokes and vernacular were restored for Australian audiences, and with them Nick Enright's credit as writer of the show.'[70] The other contenders that have made the transfer to Broadway – *Priscilla, Queen of the Desert, Moulin Rouge!*, and *King Kong* – can have similar claims levelled at them. *Priscilla* has an Australian story and Australian characters, but not an Australian score. *Moulin Rouge*, based on the movie of the same name, has an Australian director in Baz Luhrmann but is set in Paris and adopts a transnational style. *King Kong* does not have an Australian story and only had one Australian creative (Eddie Perfect, writing lyrics) working on the score, which featured music by a cluster of artists as diverse as The Avalanches, Sarah McLachlan, and the English composer Marius de Vries.

Yet even those that seemingly have ticked all the boxes still not risen to the status of the 'Great Australian Musical.' Why did the search not stop with Jimmy Chi's *Bran Nue Dae* (1990), a landmark work hailed as the first Indigenous Australian musical, and that has enjoyed enduring success, being both adapted for film and revived on stage? The answer, for Peter Casey, is that it never toured internationally.[71] An overt attempt to claim the title was *Eureka!* (2004), a dramatisation of the 1854 Eureka Rebellion, a revolt against the British colonial authority by gold miners in Ballarat, which was backed by significant money and much hope. Director Gale Edwards was once again at the helm, describing it as 'the best story in the world,' 'a many-layered, sophisticated work with as many challenging issues that are still relevant to Australia: multiculturalism, Aborigines, the notion of being a tool of a foreign land . . . how topical is that?'[72] Its advertising, plastered on the side of trams and buses, proclaimed it 'The Great Australian Musical.'[73] It had an appropriately Australian plot, Australian creators and, as Senczuk, who along with Edwards had written book and lyrics, outlined, it was 'appropriately financed,' with seven million dollars invested; it had also undergone an extensive workshop period.[74] Nevertheless, as Raymond Gill observed, it 'failed to penetrate the public consciousness.'[75] The musical closed in Melbourne without playing a run in Sydney. It has never been produced since.

Various initiatives to remedy these crises have been attempted over the years. Some potentially transformative developments have fallen by the wayside. The Pratt Prize for musical theatre, a large cash-prize was only awarded three times, while *Kookaburra: The National Music Theatre Company*, an ambitious project founded by the Australian performer Peter Cousens, launched in 2006 and collapsed just three years later due to intractable financial problems.[76] Tertiary institutions like the Victorian College of the Arts (VCA) and the Western Australian Academy of Performing Arts (WAAPA) have had various programs to encourage the development of new work. In 2015, the VCA held a National Music Theatre Symposium 'to bring together key artists and practitioners from across the country to form a national network for new music theatre development.'[77] These initiatives, while worthy, have not resulted in regular, organised systems for fostering new writing. In Senczuk's essay, he proposed an ambitious plan for the resolution of the situation: first, the creation of a body called the Australian Music Theatre Foundation (AMTF) modelled on Screen Australia (a federally funded film production industry body), and second, what he termed 'The Perth Solution.' In this model, Perth would become a hub for large-scale music theatre projects and Australian premieres. Perth's proximity to Asia, argues Senczuk, rendered the location 'commercially strategic,' as well as having other benefits.[78] Senczuk's suggestions have not been implemented.

Schemes through national- and state-based funding bodies are gradually beginning to bear fruit. In 2009, the Australia Council for the Arts announced a three-year initiative to fund new musical theatre works.[79] This was then merged with New Musicals Australia, an organisation created to support, develop, and promote new Australian work. New Musicals Australia has since been subsumed into The Hayes Theatre, located in Sydney's Potts Point, which has become a hub for new Australian musicals. Independent companies like Squabbalogic and the Melbourne-based theatre Chapel off Chapel, along with the Hayes, were important players in facilitating new works in the early years of the twenty-first century. Home Grown, an organisation and website that support artists and composers, sells sheet music, runs events and concerts, and provides young writers with development opportunities.[80] In 2018, in collaboration with Home Grown, Trevor Jones started compiling YouTube playlists of recordings of the songs of new Australian musical theatre writers with the aim of raising awareness of their work.[81] While still engaging with this notion of the 'crisis,' in 2018 Jones published a piece for *The Conversation* in which he argued that the field was prospering like it never had before. By cataloguing several successful productions from 2017, as well as focusing on emergent initiatives and development programs, his article represented an important shift in the discourse towards a more positive tone, one that this study develops.[82] This will be further addressed in the conclusion.

To proceed, it is imperative that, as writer Peter Casey implores, we dispense with the baggage of the 'Great Australian Musical,' which he describes as a 'horrible, counter-productive notion' and 'nonsense':

> See, the Brits and the Americans aren't worried about any 'Great British/ American Musical.' They know they've written great shows, and they enjoy arguing about which one is the greatest. We, on the other hand, apply vague, ever-shifting criteria to every musical we write, and judge that each effort fails to match some ideal we've never fully discussed or defined.[83]

Casey implores us to '[strike the term] from our parlance, and instead focus on a Great Many Australian Musicals, of a Great Many Kinds.'[84] In the subsequent chapters, I follow Casey's appeal, examining a set of musicals that are formally diverse and distinctively Australian in their engagement with the national imaginary.

This discussion of the crisis in Australian musical theatre has established the persistence of the perception of musical theatre as a national project. It has revealed anxieties around the levels of Australian content and summarised the economic realities of funding new musicals in a country with a relatively small, spread-out population. It is against this backdrop that this book begins its work. While we can say that the academic and the aesthetic crisis have substantially subsided, many of the economic arguments are ongoing issues and will not form the basis of the enquiry herewith. Instead, the study focuses on dispelling the aesthetic concerns. It does so by undertaking detailed, sustained analysis of contemporary Australian musical theatre productions that explicates their engagement with the questions most central to the national imaginary, and their aesthetic merit and innovation.

Structure and Approach

The book is structured around a series of key questions that constitute an Australian national imaginary: Who are we? Where are we? Where have we come from? Where are we are now? Where are we headed?

The first three chapters examine who we are and where we're from. Chapter 1 examines Kate Miller-Heidke and Keir Nuttall's *Muriel's Wedding* and how it imagines 'who we are' from an international perspective. The musical set its sights overseas from the beginning and navigates a split focus between its actual domestic audience and its prospective international one. The chapter situates the production as transnational 'Broadway-style' musical. Rather than retaining the early 1990s setting of the film upon which it is based, the musical re-envisions the story for the twenty-first century, integrating social media into the plot. Harnessing the social media aesthetic is a key feature of the musical's transnational strategy as it works to mitigate the Australian-ness of the story. A similar but inverted strategy is used for the production's representation of place, where the cities of Sydney and the Gold Coast are rendered through the 'tourist gaze,' familiar enough to be recognisable to Australians but generic enough to appeal to an international market. *Muriel's Wedding* uses the forms of both the jukebox musical and the 'movical' to strike a fine balance between the familiar and the new, a strategy formulated to balance sure economic returns with artistic creativity. Ultimately, I argue that *Muriel's Wedding* assumes an ambassadorial role, acting as a branded product for the nation ready to represent Australia abroad.

Like *Muriel's Wedding*, *Shane Warne: The Musical*, Chapter 2 asks, 'Who are we?' but it does so from a domestic vantage point, taking as its subject the interplay of nation, sport and masculinity. Eddie Perfect's first full-length musical is a largely faithful staging of the life of its eponymous protagonist, one that interrogates the primacy of sport in Australian culture, how Warne complicates lofty ideals around the role of the sporting celebrity, and the relationship between beer, sport, male bonding, and citizenship. Its narrative sees Warne progress through the repertory of national characters: everyman, battler, underdog, anti-authoritarian rebel, and tall poppy. The modus operandi for the humour in the production is an approach known as 'taking the piss.' As a counterpoint to the noxious male camaraderie involved in such humour, the musical explores two instances of mateship, one between Warne and his coach and the other between Warne and Perfect. The chapter argues that while in Australian cultural discourse the arts and sport have often been pitted against one another, in *Shane Warne* Perfect complicates this view by aestheticising the moment that Warne bowled the 'ball of the century.' The musical celebrates the centrality of sport and masculinity to the national imaginary by examining the crossovers between art and sport as definers of national character.

Chapter 3 focuses on Eddie Perfect's song cycle, *Songs from the Middle*, which considers 'Where are we?' by representing the iconic Australian landscapes of suburbia and the beach. Perfect expands the 'stigmatise or mythologise' binary associated with suburbia through four different approaches to the site: an ironic yet playful approach that appropriates tropes of the suburban gothic in 'The Way It Was'; a melancholy, nostalgic narrative in 'My Sister Worked at Bunnings'; a comic, ambivalent yet affectionate relationship in 'What Are We to Do'; and the final number, 'Nepean Highway,' explores the tension between leaving suburbia and returning home. Perfect's treatment of the beach, a landscape considered metonymic of the nation, is explored through analysis of two songs set on the beach: 'The Middle of the World' and 'There's a Beach Somewhere.' These songs represent the temporality of the beach experience, characterised by repetition and a sense of timelessness, by utilising features of musical impressionism to weave subtle connections with nineteenth-century impressionist paintings of the beach. The 'beach songs' construct the landscape as a simultaneously spiritual and ordinary site. I aver that the cycle highlights the affective dimensions of the iconic Australian landscapes of suburbia and the beach by representing their dual role in the national imaginary as mythic sites and everyday places where ordinary people live.

The second half of the book grapples with past, present, and future. In Chapter 4, *The Rabbits* confronts the question: 'Where have we come from?' Based on the picture book by John Marsden and Shaun Tan, the musical adaptation responds to fraught political debates about how to interpret Australian history. *The Rabbits* stages an anthropomorphic allegory of colonisation where the British colonisers are represented as rabbits and the Indigenous population represented as marsupials. The production uses different musical genres to delineate character groups – popular music styles for the Marsupials, opera for the Rabbits, and a hybrid for the Bird. I argue that this instructs the audience how to read the power dynamics of the plot, encouraging an empathetic response to the plight of the Marsupials. *The Rabbits* stages the utopian aspirations of reconciliation through its anthemic finale, 'Where?' The chapter details how these aspirations are undermined by the way that the character of the Bird mirrors the subject position of the audience, creating 'white witnesses' who observe the events of colonisation, full of 'settler shame' but powerless to intervene. The production induces a sense of 'feeling bad' which its utopian finale transforms into 'feeling good,' figuring its audience as 'sorry people,' 'white witnesses,' who can go on home, purged of their shame and with their faith in reconciliation renewed. Through this performance of apology, *The Rabbits* conceptualises the theatre as a site where a national citizenry can gather to have their shame transformed and their faith in the nation renewed.

Ursula Yovich's *Barbara and the Camp Dogs*, Chapter 5, assesses the question 'Where are we now?' by staging an Indigenous perspective on race relations in contemporary Australia. A monodrama cross rock musical, *Barbara* is a portrait of a nation struggling to reconcile with the effects of colonisation. The production sets itself apart from conventional musical theatre and drama by framing the performance as a rock gig set in a pub. Placing a narrative that centres Indigenous women in a pub is a subversive act that reclaims a space that has historically excluded this group. In the production, the coexistence of comedy and anger is figured as a coping mechanism for intergenerational trauma. Ultimately, the rock music-fuelled anger of *Barbara and the Camp Dogs* lacerates the national imaginary, urging audiences to listen from the heart to the Indigenous experience of the ongoing effects of colonisation.

Finally, Chapter 6 examines Eddie Perfect's *Vivid White*, a musical which turns its gaze to the future, asking 'Where are we headed?' A satire of the Australian housing market, the musical exploits the national obsession with homeownership to impress upon its audience the need for action on climate change. The musical examines the exclusivity of the topos of the owner-occupied home and the nation's penchant for renovation. In doing so, it draws attention to discourses of whiteness, Indigenous sovereignty, and the implications of a culture that is, rather ironically, obsessed with property ownership in the context of stolen land. The production magnifies the pre-existing and intense undercurrents of the debate around housing by situating renters as a persecuted underclass. The *deus ex machina* ending transposes the local crisis of the housing market onto the global crisis of climate change, bringing together a highly secure, most deeply held fiction with a reality that is both contested and frightening. Through its pastiche of musical theatre styles and conventions, *Vivid White* subverts the musical's 'middlebrow horizon of expectations' to offer a politically charged satire. By rendering the two male protagonists as satirical musical comedians, Perfect metatheatrically reflects on the efficacy of satire as a mode for political change. *Vivid White* proffers that climate change, a global problem, must first be addressed with attention to the material effects of the loss of home. The musical ends with the Australian dream of property ownership in tatters.

In the conclusion to the book, I draw out the transformation to the national imaginary produced by these six musicals. I then address the profound shift that the Australian musical underwent in the first decades of the twenty-first century more broadly, taking stock of the present moment and reflecting on other works that engage with the national imaginary in both familiar and new ways. In addition, it addresses the 'female turn' in Australian musical theatre, addressing the way that female creators and audiences are becoming central to the future direction of the form.

Two aspects of the approach to studying musical theatre are worth foregrounding. As is no doubt evident, the chapters are organised thematically, rather than chronologically. To analyse the way that Australian musical theatre produces and re-produces the national imaginary, I adopt an extensive and varied body of theoretical material, spanning a diverse range of disciplines. The approach takes on Stacy Wolf's assertion that 'study of Broadway musical theatre fosters a richly multivalent, multidisciplinary approach to U.S. history, culture, and society' to an Australian context.[85] Like Andy Medhurst, who, in his study of Britishness in comedy, writes that he has been neither able nor willing 'to stay within the docile parameters of one academic discipline,' this study adopts a similarly multi-disciplinary approach, engaging with as many fields of scholarship as relevant and needed for the particular case study at hand, which results in some unusual bedfellows. For example, the analysis of *The Rabbits* draws from settler-colonial theory, Australian history, Indigenous studies, scholarship on theatrical witnessing, and affect theory, while *Vivid White* calls for a combination of housing and urban studies, cultural studies, geography, theory of satire, and climate change communication. Each chapter has its own distinct mix of critical discourses, offered to foreground the 'explicitly reflexive relationship' between musical theatre and culture.[86]

Detailed analysis is the most effective counter to the crisis discourse. While *The Australian Musical: From the Beginning* has the distinction of being the first published book about Australian musical theatre, its nature as a historical chronology (1901–2018) means it is unable to discuss any one production in detail. This study illustrates the richness of these recent productions by giving them sustained analytic attention. As the book is a detailed analysis of six works, some relevant works have been excluded. However, as Knapp reflects (criticising the survey-style coffee-table books that abound on the American musical), 'aesthetic merit' is more effectively 'established and explored within more specific context than a belaboured chronology permits.'[87]

Conclusion

The book's subtitle, 'Never Been Better,' is drawn from the lyrics of the opening song of *Muriel's Wedding*, 'Sunshine State of Mind.' In the song, in their roles as inhabitants of the fictional Porpoise Spit (based on the city of the

Gold Coast), the chorus dance around the stage in bikinis and board shorts to offer a representation of Australia as a place characterised by perfect weather and a 'no worries' attitude. As the discussion of the crisis in Australian musical theatre has revealed, there are recurring concerns about the content and quality of Australian musicals: whether they truly represent us. I trust you will see that they do; that contemporary Australian musicals explore multivalent national imaginaries. From celebrities to ordinary people, to urban and natural landscapes, to our conflicted past, troubled present, and uncertain future, these musicals reflect the richness and heterogeneity of contemporary Australian musical theatre productions. Structurally, musically, and aesthetically, these musicals are very different from one another. What unites them is their concern with engagement with what it means to be Australian. These musicals are vibrant, exciting, arresting, affective, fun, confronting, and playful explorations of who we are, and they have never been better.

Notes

1 Steve Dow, 'How to Make the Australian Musical: From The Sapphires to Strictly Ballroom,' *The Guardian*, June 15, 2017, https://www.theguardian.com/stage/2017/jun/15/how-to-make-the-australian-musical-from-thesapphires-to-strictly-ballroom.

2 I acknowledge that the term 'affect' is used in multiple, divergent ways across many different fields. Throughout the book, my use of this term is in service of connecting the way that affect is conceptualised in scholarship around national identity and cultural geography, and the way that musical theatre scholars like Stacy Wolf invoke it to talk about the way musicals produce 'pleasure, affect, and visceral engagement.' Wolf, 'In Defence of Pleasure: Musical Theatre History in the Liberal Arts [A Manifesto],' *Theatre Topics* 17, no. 1 (2007): 51–60, https://doi.org/10.1353/tt.2007.0014. Angharad Closs Stephens makes the connect between performance, nation, and affect explicitly, writing that engagement with the arts offers her the opportunity to 'expand my routes into addressing the affective force of nationality.' Stephens, *National Affects: The Everyday Aspects of Being Political* (Bloomsbury, 2022), 9.

3 Stephens, *National Affects*, 10; John Gillis, *Commemorations: The Politics of National Identity* (Princeton University Press, 1995), 5, my emphasis.

4 Jo Roberts, 'Rehearsals in Full Swing for King of Spin Musical,' *The Sydney Morning Herald*, July 31, 2008, 9.

5 Peter Wyllie Johnston, '"Australian-ness in Musical Theatre": A Bran Nue Dae for Australia?,' *Australasian Drama Studies* 45 (2004): 157–179.

6 Wyllie Johnston, '"Australian-ness in Musical Theatre,"' 157.

7 Peter Wyllie Johnston and Peter Pinne, *The Australian Musical: From the Beginning* (Allen and Unwin, 2019).

8 John Senczuk, 'Is the Time Ripe for the Great Australian Musical?,' *Platform Paper* 42 (2015): 6. Senczuk's 2017 taxonomy of Australian musicals is by scale/size. While his categories are rather idiosyncratic, he paints a reasonable picture of the landscape. John Senczuk, 'SWOT Analysis of Musical Theatre – the Australian Musical,' *Music in Australia*, November 2, 2017, accessed January 27, 2022, https://www.musicinaustralia.org.au/swot-analysis-of-musical-theatre-the-australian-musical/.

9 Senczuk, 'Is the Time Ripe,' 6.

10 Janelle Reinelt, 'The Role of National Theatres in an Age of Globalization,' in *National Theatres in a Changing Europe*, ed. S. E. Wilmer (Palgrave Macmillan, 2008), 228.

11 In Melbourne, the six theatres in the CBD are officially known as the East End District, but this district does not quite function as a Broadway or West End equivalent in practice. Swim, 'Why Melbourne's East End theatre district is no West End,' *Daily Review*, July 8, 2014, accessed November 19, 2021, https://dailyreview.com.au/why-melbournes-eastend-theatre-district-is-no-west-end/. In late 2021, planning was underway for such a theatre district to be created in Sydney's Haymarket, but at the time of writing in 2025, discussions are still underway.

12 Research has found that not-for-profit – as opposed to commercial theatre – is playing an ever-increasing role in the development of new plays and musicals in the United States too. Tim Donahue and Jim Patterson, *Stage Money: The Business of the Professional Theater* (The University of South Carolina Press, 2010).

13 This is both in terms of both substance (content) and place of performance. Senczuk, 'Is the Time Ripe,' 3

14 Charles Taylor, *Modern Social Imaginaries* (Duke University Press, 2004); Charles Taylor, *A Secular Age*, (Harvard University Press, 2007).

15 Taylor, *Modern Social Imaginaries*, 25; Taylor, *A Secular Age*, 153; Benedict Anderson, *Imagined Communities: Reflections on the Origins and Spread of Nations* (Verso, 1983).

16 Paul James, 'The Social Imaginary in Theory and Practice,' in *Revisiting the Global Imaginary: Theories, Ideologies, Subjectivities*, ed. Chris Hudson and Erin K. Wilson (Palgrave Macmillan, 2019), 41.

17 Here James is parsing the work of both Taylor and Manfred Steger. While Steger explicitly uses the term 'national imaginary,' in his work, he does so to analyse the ways in which the national imaginary is mobilised by political ideologies, such as liberalism and fascism. For the context of this study, the more general definition of the social imaginary given by Taylor, with the addition of the nation as framing device, is more apt. James, 'The Social Imaginary,' 41. Manfred Steger, *The Rise of the Global Imaginary: Political Ideological from the French Revolution to the Global War on Terror* (Oxford University Press, 2009).

18 Anderson, *Imagined Communities*.

19 Taylor, *Modern Social Imaginaries*, 25.

20 James, 'The Social Imaginary,' 41, original emphasis.

21 Raymond Knapp, *The American Musical and the Formation of National Identity* (Princeton University Press, 2005), 8, 103.

22 Donatella Gallela, 'Redefining America, Arena Stage, and Territory Folks in a Multiracial "Oklahoma!",' *Theatre Journal* 67, no. 2 (2015): 213–233, https://www.jstor.org/stable/24582593. Daniel Fish's 2018 Broadway revival of *Oklahoma!* is another good example.

23 Robert Gordon, Olaf Jubin and Millie Taylor, *British Musical Theatre since 1950* (Bloomsbury, 2016), 6, original emphasis.

24 David Savran, *Tell it to the World: The Broadway Musical Abroad* (Oxford, 2024); Adrian Wright, *A Tanner's Worth of Tune: Rediscovering the Post-war British Musical* (The Boydell Press, 2010); Robert Gordon and Olaf Jubin (eds.), *The Oxford Handbook of the British Musical* (Oxford University Press, 2016); Ethan Mordden, *Pick a Pocket or Two: A History of British Musical Theatre* (Oxford University Press, 2021); Mel Atkey, *Broadway North: The Dream of a Canadian Musical Theatre* (Dundurn Press, 2006); Ji Hyon Yun, ' "Are they supposed to be Heugin?": Negotiating Race, Nation, and Representation in Korean Musical Theatre,' (PhD diss., City University of New York, 2018).

25 Millie Taylor and Adam Rush, *Musical Theatre Histories: Expanding the Narrative* (Bloomsbury, 2023).

26 David Walsh and Len Platt, *Musical Theatre and American Culture* (Prager Publishers, 2003), 1.

27 David Savran, 'Towards a Historiography of the Popular,' *Theatre Survey* 45, no. 2 (2004): 215, https://doi.org/10.1017/S004055740400016X.

28 Knapp, *The American Musical*, 8.

29 Walsh and Platt, *Musical Theatre*, 1.

30 Richard Dyer, *Only Entertainment* (Routledge, 2002), 27.

31 Dyer, *Only Entertainment*, 20, my emphasis.

32 Kathleen Lennon, *Imagination and the Imaginary* (Routledge, 2015), 74, original emphasis.

33 Alison Croggon, 'How Australian Is It?,' *Overland* 200 (2010): 57.

34 Croggon, 'How Australian Is It?, 62.

35 Anderson, *Imagined Communities*, 4.

36 Craig Calhoun, *Nations Matter: Culture, History and the Cosmopolitan Dream* (Routledge, 2007), 1.

37 Lennon, *Imagination and the Imaginary*, 73.

38 Peter Fitzpatrick, 'Whose Turn to Shout? The Crisis in Australian Musical Theatre,' *Australasian Drama Studies* 38 (2001): 25.

39 Wyllie Johnston, '"Australian-ness", 157.

40 The performance is available on YouTube: OzLive, 'Once in a Blue Moon – A Celebration of Australian Musicals,' *YouTube*, September 18, 2016. Accessed November 17, 2021. https://www.youtube.com/watch?v=ABwnQV__rPc. A recording was also produced: *Once in a Blue Moon: A Celebration of Australian Musicals*, ABC Music, 1994, cast recording.

41 Simon Plant, 'Big Show Off,' *Making a Song and Dance*, exhibition catalogue (Victorian Arts Centre, 2004), 3.

42 Hilary Bell, 'Song and Dance,' *Storyline* 11 (2005): 27; Fitzpatrick, 'Whose Turn to Shout?,' 25. *Terra nullius* is a Latin phrase describing a principle in international law that if territory is considered to be unclaimed and unused, it is able to be seized. It was applied by the British to the many Aboriginal lands of Australia at the time of colonisation, and it took centuries for this to be overturned in Australian courts. The landmark 1992 Mabo Decision determined that *terra nullius* had been incorrectly applied.

43 Wyllie Johnston, '"Australian-ness in Musical Theatre"', 157.

44 John Thomson claims to have found 530 examples, but these have never been published in full. John Thomson, 'Ned, Juanita and the Gang,' *National Library of Australia News* 13, no. 8 (2003): 3–6.

45 Fitzpatrick, 'Whose Turn to Shout?,' 26. He is critical of the reviews of both *The Boy from Oz* and *Shout!* for this reason.

46 For these defences of the form, see Knapp, *The American Musical*, xvi; Savran, 'Towards a Historiography'; Wolf, 'In Defence of Pleasure.'

47 Australian theatre performance that uses music and/or song as a substantive element has not been referred with consistent terminology. The field has often been conceptualised broadly, collapsing many different types of performance, like opera, music theatre, and musicals, into a singular category. In 2004, a special issue of the journal *Australasian Drama Studies*, edited by Keith Gallasch and Laura Ginters focused on music theatre in this broadest sense. Scholarship that examines 'music theatre' – the term Corinna Bonshek defines as being 'situated across the disciplinary boundaries of new music performance, sound-art, digital musics, opera, music-theatre, installation art, new media art, film, theatre, performance art' and that often requires bespoke hybrid descriptions, 'installation-performance, multimedia opera, through-scored play, theatricalised concert and video-opera,' has been addressed by Bonshek, and also Rainer and Linz. Corinna Bonshek, 'Interdisciplinarity and Vocal Performance in Australian Contemporary Music Theatre,' *Contemporary Music Review* 25, no. 4 (2006): 341–351, https://doi.org/10.1080/07494460600761013; John Jenkins and Rainer Linz, *Arias: Recent Australian Music Theatre* (Red House Editions, 1997).

48 Savran, 'Towards a Historiography,' 213.
49 Peter Gotting, 'Big Spenders: Australian Musicals Must Downsize to Survive,' *The Guardian*, August 29, 2014, https://www.theguardian.com/stage/australia-culture-blog/2014/aug/29/australian-musicals-strictly-struggling-blog.
50 Senczuk, *The Time is Ripe*, 31–32.
51 Patrick McDonald, 'Cabaret Festival Co-director Eddie Perfect Tweets after Helpmann Award Nominations,' *The Adelaide Advertiser*, June 21, 2017, accessed June 24, 2025, https://www.adelaidenow.com.au/entertainment/arts/australian-musical-theatre-in-crisis-adelaide-cabaret-festival-codirector-eddie-perfect-tweets-after-helpmann-award-nominations/news-story/6f531bf95474df8063c68c5f4e018bf1. The Helpmann awards were established in 2001 and are an annual awards ceremony for Australian live performance.
52 McDonald, 'Cabaret Festival Co-director.'
53 Senczuk discusses both the amateur and the tertiary context in the platform paper. *The Time is Ripe*, 38–44.
54 Andrew Taylor, 'NSW Government Refuses to Disclose How Much It Paid to Lure Carole King Musical to Sydney,' *The Sydney Morning Herald*, May 11, 2016, http://www.smh.com.au/entertainment/musicals/nsw-government-refuses-to-disclose-how-much-it-paid-to-lure-carole-king-musical-to-sydney-20160511-gosjc3.html.
55 I have used the 2018 report since the 2019–2020 figures are adversely affected by the COVID-19 pandemic. 'LPA Ticket Attendance and Revenue Report 2018,' *Live Performance Australia*, accessed June 24, 2025, http://reports.liveperformance.com.au/ticket-survey-2018/category/musical-theatre.
56 Matthew Smith, 'Is the Australian Musical Dead?,' *ABC News*, October 24, 2016, accessed September 18, 2018, http://www.abc.net.au/news/2017-10-24/is-the-australian-musical-dead/9082118.
57 Bell, 'Song and Dance,' 27.
58 Ben Neutze, 'There's a Crisis in Australian Musical Theatre – and It's about More than Funding & Support,' *Daily Review*, June 21, 2017, accessed August 17, 2022, https://dailyreview.com.au/australian-musical-theatre-crisis/61397/.
59 Neutze, 'There's a Crisis.'
60 Michael Cathcart, 'Taking a Stroll Down Memory Lane to the Dinky-Di Sound of Music,' *The Age*, April 27, 1994, 23.
61 Senczuk, *The Time is Ripe*, 42–43. In *The Guardian*, Peter Gotting described *Keating!* as having 'raked it in for Belvoir St.' Gotting, 'Big Spenders.'
62 Ben Neutze, 'The Search for the Great Australian Musical,' *Daily Review*, March 24, 2014, accessed November 6, 2021, https://dailyreview.com.au/the-search-for-the-great-australian-musical/.
63 Chris Boyd, '*Prodigal* Returns as Leader of Great Australian Musical Pack,' *The Australian*, January 24, 2011, 14.
64 Wyllie Johnston and Pinne, *The Australian Musical*, ix.
65 Joyce Morgan, 'Not Just One of the Boys,' *The Sydney Morning Herald*, January 30, 1998, 15.
66 Helen Thomson, 'No Need to Go to Rio for a World-Class Show,' *The Age*, May 24, 1999.
67 Tim Lloyd, 'The Sound of Australian Musicals Still Not Home-Grown,' *The Adelaide Advertiser*, January 13, 2001, 22.
68 Joyce Morgan argued this explicitly in relation to *The Boy from Oz*. Joyce Morgan, 'Not Just One of the Boys,' *The Sydney Morning Herald*, January 30, 1998, 15.
69 Peter Fitzpatrick, 'Life or a Cabaret?: Nick Enright and *The Boy from Oz*,' in *Nick Enright: An Actor's Playwright*, ed. Susan Pender and Anne Lever (Rodopi, 2008), 30.
70 Fitzpatrick, 'Life or a Cabaret?,' 31.

71 Peter Casey, 'About That Great Australian Musical,' *ArtsHub*, February 10, 2015, accessed February 4, 2018, http://performing.artshub.com.au/news-article/opinions-and-analysis/performing-arts/peter-j-casey/about-that-great-australian-musical--247109. Writing in 1992, Helen Gilbert stated that the production was 'soon to go to London,' but I have been unable to find any evidence that this eventuated. Helen Gilbert, '"Bran Nue Dae" by Jimmy Chi & Kuckles (Book Review),' *Australasian Drama Studies* 20 (1992): 134.

72 Michael Shmith, 'Eureka! This May Well Be the One,' *The Age*, October 3, 2004, 13.

73 Michael Shmith, 'Arts About,' *The Age*, October 17, 2004, 33.

74 Senczuk, *The Time is Ripe*, 12–17.

75 Raymond Gill, 'The Final Stage Culture Vulture,' *The Age*, August 26, 2006, 5.

76 The Pratt Prize for Musical Theatre, August 17, 2022, http://www.paramountgraphics.com.au/sites/production_company_2008/pratt_prize/background.html. *Kookaburra's* most significant contribution was the development of James Miller and Peter Rutherford's *The Hatpin*, which premiered in Sydney in 2008 and travelled to the New York Music Theatre Festival the same year.

77 Richard Watts, 'Towards New Australian Musicals,' *ArtsHub*, September 28, 2015, accessed November 14, 2021, https://www.artshub.com.au/news/news/towards-new-australian-musicals-249418–2349944; 'The VCA: A New Force in Australian Music Theatre,' *Stage Whispers,* accessed February 1, 2018. http://www.stagewhispers.com.au/articles/198/vca-force-new-australian-music-theatre?page=7.

78 Senczuk, *The Time is Ripe*, 57–58.

79 'Funding for New Music Theatre Announced,' *Australia Council for the Arts*, April 3, 2009, accessed March 18, 2018, http://www.australiacouncil.gov.au/news/media-centre/media-releases/funding-for-music-theatre-announced/.

80 *Home Grown Musicals Australia*, http://www.homegrownaus.com/, accessed May 12, 2025, https://www.homegrownaus.com.

81 Trevor Jones, 'Call for Australian Musicals – YouTube Playlist and Sheet Music – Submissions Now Open,' *Aussie Theatre*, March 3, 2018, accessed March 14, 2021, 3https://aussietheatre.com.au/features/home-grown-aussietheatre-com-australian-musicals-youtube-playlist-call-submissions.

82 Trevor Jones, 'Where Are the New Australian Musicals? Waiting in the Wings,' *The Conversation*, June 22, 2017, https://theconversation.com/were-are-the-new-australian-musicals-waiting-in-the-wings-79831; Trevor Jones, 'Far from Being in Crisis, 2017 Was a Great Year for Australian Musical Theatre,' *The Conversation*, December 27, 2017, https://theconversation.com/far-from-being-in-crisis-2017-was-a-great-year-for-australian-musical-theatre-89237; Trevor Jones, 'Is Australian Music Theatre in Crisis?,' *Theatre People*, January 3, 2018, http://www.theatrepeople.com.au/Australian-musical-theatre-crisis/.

83 Casey, 'About That Great Australian Musical.'

84 Casey, 'About That Great Australian Musical.'

85 Wolf, 'In Defence of Pleasure,' 53.

86 Walsh and Platt, *Musical Theatre*, 1.

87 Knapp, *The American Musical*, 6.

References

Anderson, Benedict. *Imagined Communities: Reflections on the Origins and Spread of Nations*. Verso, 1983.

Atkey, Mel. *Broadway North: The Dream of a Canadian Musical Theatre*. Dundurn Press, 2006.

Australia Council for the Arts. 'Funding for New Music Theatre Announced.' April 3, 2009. Accessed March 18, 2018. http://www.australiacouncil.gov.au/news/media-centre/media-releases/funding-for-music-theatre-announced/.

Bell, Hilary. 'Song and Dance.' *Storyline* 11 (2005): 26–29.

Bonshek, Corinna. 'Interdisciplinarity and Vocal Performance in Australian Contemporary Music Theatre.' *Contemporary Music Review* 25, no. 4 (2006): 341–351. https://doi.org/10.1080/07494460600761013.

Boyd, Chris. 'Prodigal Returns as Leader of Great Australian Musical Pack.' *The Australian*, January 24, 2011, 14.

Calhoun, Craig. *Nations Matter: Culture, History and the Cosmopolitan Dream.* Routledge, 2007.

Casey, Peter. 'About That Great Australian Musical.' *ArtsHub*, February 10, 2015. Accessed February 4, 2018. http://performing.artshub.com.au/news-article/opinions-and-analysis/performing-arts/peter-j-casey/about-that-great-australian-musical–247109.

Cathcart, Michael. 'Taking a Stroll Down Memory Lane to the Dinky-Di Sound of Music.' *The Age*, April 27, 1994, 23.

Croggon, Alison. 'How Australian Is It?' *Overland* 200 (2010): 57–62.

Donahue, Tim, and Jim Patterson. *Stage Money: The Business of the Professional Theater.* The University of South Carolina Press, 2010.

Dow, Steve. 'How to Make the Australian Musical: From the Sapphires to Strictly Ballroom.' *The Guardian*, June 15, 2017. https://www.theguardian.com/stage/2017/jun/15/how-to-make-the-australian-musical-from-thesapphires-to-strictly-ballroom.

Dyer, Richard. *Only Entertainment.* Routledge, 2002.

Fitzpatrick, Peter. 'Whose Turn to Shout? The Crisis in Australian Musical Theatre.' *Australasian Drama Studies* 38 (2001): 23–35.

Fitzpatrick, Peter. 'Life or a Cabaret?: Nick Enright and The Boy from Oz.' In *Nick Enright: An Actor's Playwright*, edited by Susan Pender and Anne Lever. Rodopi, 2008, 29–44.

Gallasch, Keith, and Laura Ginters, eds. *Australasian Drama Studies* 45 (2004).

Gallela, Donatella. 'Redefining America, Arena Stage, and Territory Folks in a Multiracial "Oklahoma!".' *Theatre Journal* 67, no. 2 (2015): 213–233. https://www.jstor.org/stable/24582593.

Gilbert, Helen. '"Bran Nue Dae" by Jimmy Chi & Kuckles (Book Review).' *Australasian Drama Studies* 20 (1992): 133–135.

Gill, Raymond. 'The Final Stage Culture Vulture.' *The Age*, August 26, 2006, 5.

Gillis, John. *Commemorations: The Politics of National Identity.* Princeton University Press, 1995.

Gordon, Robert, and Olaf Jubin, eds. *The Oxford Handbook of the British Musical.* Oxford University Press, 2016.

Gordon, Robert, Olaf Jubin, and Millie Taylor. *British Musical Theatre Since 1950.* Bloomsbury, 2016.

Gotting, Peter. 'Big Spenders: Australian Musicals Must Downsize to Survive.' *The Guardian*, August 29, 2014. https://www.theguardian.com/stage/australia-culture-blog/2014/aug/29/australian-musicals-strictly-struggling-blog.

Home Grown Musicals Australia. http://www.homegrownaus.com/.

James, Paul. 'The Social Imaginary in Theory and Practice.' In *Revisiting the Global Imaginary: Theories, Ideologies, Subjectivities*, edited by Chris Hudson and Erin K. Wilson. Palgrave Macmillan, 2019, 29–50.

Jenkins, John, and Rainer Linz. *Arias: Recent Australian Music Theatre.* Red House Editions, 1997.

Jones, Trevor. 'Where Are the New Australian Musicals? Waiting in the Wings.' *The Conversation*, June 22, 2017. https://theconversation.com/were-are-the-new-australian-musicals-waiting-in-the-wings–79831.

Jones, Trevor. 'Far from Being in Crisis, 2017 Was a Great Year for Australian Musical Theatre.' *The Conversation*, December 27, 2017. https://theconversation.com/far-from-being-in-crisis-2017-was-a-great-year-for-australian-musical-theatre–89237.

Jones, Trevor. 'Is Australian Music Theatre in Crisis?' *Theatre People*, January 3, 2018. Accessed October 22, 2020. http://www.theatrepeople.com.au/Australian-musical-theatre-crisis/.

Jones, Trevor. 'Call for Australian Musicals – YouTube Playlist and Sheet Music – Submissions Now Open.' *Aussie Theatre*, March 3, 2018. Accessed March 14, 2021. https://aussietheatre.com.au/features/home-grown-aussietheatre-com-australian-musicals-youtube-playlist-call-submissions.

Knapp, Raymond. *The American Musical and the Formation of National Identity*. Princeton University Press, 2005.

Lennon, Kathleen. *Imagination and the Imaginary*. Routledge, 2015.

Live Performance Australia. *LPA Ticket Attendance and Revenue Report 2018*. Accessed November 21, 2021. http://reports.liveperformance.com.au/ticket-survey-2018/category/musical-theatre.

Lloyd, Tim. 'The Sound of Australian Musicals Still Not Home-Grown.' *The Adelaide Advertiser*, January 13, 2001, 22.

McDonald, Patrick. 'Cabaret Festival Co-director Eddie Perfect Tweets after Helpmann Award Nominations.' *The Adelaide Advertiser*, June 21, 2017. Accessed June 24, 2025. https://www.adelaidenow.com.au/entertainment/arts/australian-musical-theatre-in-crisis-adelaide-cabaret-festival-codirector-eddie-perfect-tweets-after-helpmann-award-nominations/news-story/6f531bf95474df8063c68c5f4e018bf1.

Mordden, Ethan. *Pick a Pocket or Two: A History of British Musical Theatre*. Oxford University Press, 2021.

Morgan, Joyce. 'Not Just One of the Boys.' *The Sydney Morning Herald*, January 30, 1998, 15.

Neutze, Ben. 'The Search for the Great Australian Musical.' *Daily Review*, March 24, 2014. Accessed November 6, 2021. https://dailyreview.com.au/the-search-for-the-great-australian-musical/.

Neutze, Ben. 'There's a Crisis in Australian Musical Theatre – and It's about More than Funding & Support.' *Daily Review*, June 21, 2017. Accessed August 17, 2022. https://dailyreview.com.au/australian-musical-theatre-crisis/61397/.

Once in a Blue Moon: A Celebration of Australian Musicals. ABC Music, 1994, cast recording.

OzLive. 'Once in a Blue Moon – A Celebration of Australian Musicals.' *YouTube*, September 18, 2016. Accessed June 30, 2025. https://www.youtube.com/watch?v=ABwnQV__rPc.

Plant, Simon. 'Big Show Off.' In *Making a Song and Dance*, exhibition catalogue. Victorian Arts Centre, 2004.

The Pratt Prize for Musical Theatre. Accessed June 30, 2025. http://www.paramountgraphics.com.au/sites/production_company_2008/pratt_prize/background.html.

Reinelt, Janelle. 'The Role of National Theatres in an Age of Globalization.' In *National Theatres in a Changing Europe*, edited by S. E. Wilmer. Palgrave Macmillan, 2008, 215–232.

Roberts, Jo. 'Rehearsals in Full Swing for King of Spin Musical.' *The Sydney Morning Herald*, July 31, 2008, 9.

Savran, David. 'Towards a Historiography of the Popular.' *Theatre Survey* 45, no. 2 (2004): 211–217. https://doi.org/10.1017/S004055740400016X.

Savran, David. *Tell it to the World: The Broadway Musical Abroad.* Oxford, 2024.

Senczuk, John. 'Is the Time Ripe for the Great Australian Musical?' *Platform Paper* 42 (2015): 1–64.

Senczuk, John. 'SWOT Analysis of Musical Theatre – the Australian Musical.' *Music in Australia*, November 2, 2017. Accessed January 27, 2022. https://www.musicinaustralia.org.au/swot-analysis-of-musical-theatre-the-australian-musical/.

Shmith, Michael. 'Eureka! This May Well Be the One.' *The Age*, October 3, 2004, 13.

Shmith, Michael. 'Arts About.' *The Age*, October 17, 2004, 33.

Smith, Matthew. 'Is the Australian Musical Dead?' *ABC News*, October 24, 2016. Accessed September 18, 2018. http://www.abc.net.au/news/2017-10-24/is-the-australian-musical-dead/9082118.

Steger, Manfred. *The Rise of the Global Imaginary: Political Ideological from the French Revolution to the Global War on Terror.* Oxford University Press, 2009.

Stephens, Angharad Closs. *National Affects: The Everyday Aspects of Being Political.* Bloomsbury, 2022.

Swim. 'Why Melbourne's East End Theatre District is No West End.' *Daily Review*, July 8, 2014. Accessed November 19, 2021. https://dailyreview.com.au/why-melbournes-eastend-theatre-district-is-no-west-end/.

Taylor, Andrew. 'NSW Government Refuses to Disclose How Much It Paid to Lure Carole King Musical to Sydney.' *The Sydney Morning Herald*, May 11, 2016. http://www.smh.com.au/entertainment/musicals/nsw-government-refuses-to-disclose-how-much-it-paid-to-lure-carole-king-musical-to-sydney-20160511-gosjc3.html.

Taylor, Charles. *Modern Social Imaginaries.* Duke University Press, 2004.

Taylor, Charles. *A Secular Age.* Harvard University Press, 2007.

Taylor, Millie, and Adam Rush. *Musical Theatre Histories: Expanding the Narrative.* Methuen, 2023.

Thomson, Helen. 'No Need to Go to Rio for a World-Class Show.' *The Age*, May 24, 1999.

Thomson, John. 'Ned, Juanita and the Gang.' *National Library of Australia News* 13, no. 8 (2003): 3–6.

'The VCA: A New Force in Australian Music Theatre.' *Stage Whispers.* Accessed February 1, 2018. http://www.stagewhispers.com.au/articles/198/vca-force-new-australian-music-theatre?page=7.

Walsh, David, and Len Platt. *Musical Theatre and American Culture.* Prager Publishers, 2003.

Watts, Richard. 'Towards New Australian Musicals.' *ArtsHub*, September 28, 2015. https://www.artshub.com.au/news/news/towards-new-australian-musicals-249418-2349944.

Wolf, Stacy. 'In Defence of Pleasure: Musical Theatre History in the Liberal Arts [A Manifesto].' *Theatre Topics* 17, no. 1 (2007): 51–60. https://doi.org/10.1353/tt.2007.0014.

Wright, Adrian. *A Tanner's Worth of Tune: Rediscovering the Post-war British Musical.* The Boydell Press, 2010.

Wyllie Johnston, Peter. '"Australian-ness in Musical Theatre": A Bran Nue Dae for Australia?' *Australasian Drama Studies* 45 (2004): 157–179.

Wyllie Johnston, Peter, and Peter Pinne. *The Australian Musical: From the Beginning.* Allen and Unwin, 2019.

Yun, Ji Hyon. '"Are they Supposed to be Heugin?": Negotiating Race, Nation, and Representation in Korean Musical Theatre.' PhD diss., City University of New York, 2018.

1

BROADWAY AS TRANSNATIONAL BRAND IN *MURIEL'S WEDDING: THE MUSICAL*

To be a contender for the title of the 'Great Australian Musical' a new musical must not only have an original Australian score and an authentically Australian story, but it must also appeal to international markets. *Muriel's Wedding: The Musical* (2017), based on P.J. Hogan's 1994 film of the same name, epitomises these aspirations. *Muriel* pitches itself as authentically Australian by engaging with the repertory of the national imaginary, yet it is careful not to do this at the expense of its future international prospects. While staying true to the original film, the musical makes just enough changes to market itself as a fresh, new proposition. These are canny business and marketing strategies indicative of a musical theatre marketplace where economic factors have significant impacts on artistic decisions.

Muriel opened in November 2017 at the Roslyn Packer Theatre in Sydney. It was a co-production between Global Creatures and Sydney Theatre Company, with book by Hogan, music and lyrics by Kate Miller-Heidke and Keir Nuttall, and direction by Simon Phillips. For a new Australian musical, it boasted a large cast – twenty-nine performers accompanied by a nine-piece musical ensemble. It played a critically acclaimed, nine-week sell-out season, and a cast recording of the production was released in January 2018.[1] Before the initial season had closed, Global Creatures announced that the production would play a return season in July 2019 at the Lyric Theatre in Sydney. This second iteration of the work was produced independently from the Sydney Theatre Company, and some changes were made, including new cast members. The revised production toured to Her Majesty's Theatre in Melbourne and the Queensland Performing Arts Centre (QPAC).

In *Muriel*, the national imaginary is situated within a global imaginary. The production's international focus underscores questions that are central to the

DOI: 10.4324/9781003590088-2

national imaginary: What is our place in the world? And how do Australian musicals – and Australians – look from afar? In this chapter I show how *Muriel* adopts what David Savran terms the transnational, 'Broadway-style,' or what can also be understood as Broadway as 'global brand.'[2] *Muriel*'s adoption of the conventions of the transnational musical is conceptualised as a form of codification, rather than standardisation. The chapter examines three areas of 'branding' evident in the musical. First, I describe how setting the production contemporaneously (rather than retaining the early 1990s era of the original film) allows *Muriel* to integrate social media into the narrative and the aesthetic, facilitating a blurring of the lines between the marketing strategy and the musical. Second, I examine how the cities of the Gold Coast and Sydney are branded through song, demonstrating the ways in which these representations are filtered through a transnational tourist gaze. Third, I argue that, as a combination of a jukebox musical and a movical (musical based on a film), *Muriel* codifies the familiarity and international brand recognition of the original film and its ABBA soundtrack in order to capitalise on an existing community of fans. The effect of all this is that *Muriel* functions in an ambassadorial role, as a prospective representative for Australia on the world stage.

While *Muriel* is not the only musical in this book for which producers have harboured aspirations of international success, it is the one for which these aspirations were most prominent. As its name suggests, the producer, Global Creatures, has an explicitly international outlook and, while owned and based in Australia, also has offices in London and New York. In 2020, with their production of *Moulin Rouge!*, the company achieved the feat of being the first Australian-owned entity to open a show on Broadway. This vision is largely attributable to Chief Executive Officer Carmen Pavlovic, who remarked to *Limelight* magazine that she 'set the company up to tell . . . stories that have international appeal.'[3] Before taking the helm at Global Creatures in 2008, Pavlovic had accrued extensive experience working in Europe. As Director of the International Production Department for Stage Entertainment (an international live performance production company based in the Netherlands), she had been involved in expanding their operations to Russia, Italy, and France. While Global Creatures has traditionally developed their new musicals in Australia, their goal has then been to bring those works to international markets.[4] In a 2018 article in the *Australian Financial Review*, Gerry Ryan, founder and co-owner of the company, stated that 'we've basically developed product not for the Australian market, because you'll never get your return from an Australian tour. We're doing it for the international tour.'[5]

Muriel's sights were set beyond Australia's shores from the beginning, and in May 2017, before the production had even opened in Sydney, it was reported that the musical would have its North American premiere in Toronto in 2018.[6] A few months later, in September, the North American plans were delayed.[7]

Then, in February 2020, a twelve-day development culminating in a private reading was held in New York.[8] The production was due to open on the West End in 2021, but this did not eventuate, most likely as a result of the effects of the COVID-19 pandemic.[9] In 2025, it finally achieved its international debut. The UK production of *Muriel* opened at the Curve Theatre in Leicester on April 11 and ran for four weeks. It was positively reviewed, with Lindsay Johnson of *The Telegraph* giving it five stars.[10]

These international ambitions were noted by reviewers at the time of the musical's Sydney opening, even though they had yet to be realised. Steve Dow described the production as having 'an eye to domestic and international success . . . with better-than-even odds of kicking up its uggs from the West End to Broadway,' while Richard Watts characterised its new ending (different from that of the original film) as 'more fitting of Broadway – whose theatres this production is clearly aiming for.'[11] Ben Neutze remarked on the production's dual focus between its domestic and, at that time, imagined international audience, stating that while *Muriel*'s producers may have had the 'ambition to turn it into an international property . . . the creative team have clearly focused all of their energies into crafting a show that embraces and speaks directly to an Australian musical theatre audience.'[12] These remarks demonstrate that *Muriel*'s international focus had a discernible impact on the production, one which is well worth analysing.

Given the history recounted in the introduction to this book, if *Muriel*'s international reach eventually extends beyond Leicester, this will be regarded as a vote of confidence in the quality, prestige, and relevance of the Australian musical. But underpinning this is the assumption – and the reality – that the musical must also be a financial success. As such, the idea of an international season is a fundamentally economic decision. In her work on musical theatre historiography and the role of flops (musicals that fail to recoup their investments, sometimes spectacularly), Elizabeth Wollman argues that musical theatre scholarship has paid insufficient attention to the aesthetic effects of the commercial imperatives on the musical theatre business, which has resulted in a 'tendency to downplay the very commercial trappings the industry relies on to survive.'[13] Wollman notes that

> in so obscuring the way Broadway actually works, the industry – and, then, its gatekeepers, historians, and scholars – cloud the fact that the failure or success of a show can have less to do with art than with money, institutional support, and who is or is not granted access to those things.[14]

Analysing how *Muriel*'s dramaturgy is affected by its international and economic aspirations – by paying 'closer attention to the ways its machinery influences its artistic output' – reveals the ways in which artists are producing new musicals within these parameters.[15]

In doing so, I focus on the concept of branding as an illustration of the kind of 'machinery' to which Wollman refers. If in the twenty-first century, Broadway has become, as David Savran claims, 'first and foremost a marketing tool, a megabrand,' how does this manifest aesthetically?[16] How does the idea of branding permeate the dramaturgy? Some of the significant ways in which the ethos of branding can be seen in *Muriel* are: the integration of social media into the narrative; the production of the city brands of the Gold Coast and Sydney; and the way that it capitalises on the brand recognition of both Hogan's movie and its ABBA soundtrack.

The Broadway Musical as Transnational Cultural Product

Muriel is a product of an increasingly transnational musical theatre industry. While scholarship has predominantly centred on the American musical and its relationship to American history and culture, as Jessica Sternfeld notes, the advent of the (predominantly) British phenomenon of the megamusical in the 1980s complicated this.[17] The geographic shift initiated by the megamusical has precipitated a rethinking of the American claim over the genre. After all, the largest producer of musicals in the world is in fact the aforementioned Stage Entertainment, a company which has headquarters in the Netherlands – not in New York.[18] Adding to this, the megahits of the last thirty years, like *Les Misérables* or *The Lion King*, have all become difficult to characterise in terms of their national origins. Is *Les Misérables*, for example, best characterised as 'a French musical, a British megamusical, or a Paris-West End-Broadway hybrid?'[19]

This decentring of the American claim over the musical has occurred in tandem with broader forces of globalisation. The megamusical brought with it a new breed of commercial producers, like Andrew Lloyd Webber's The Really Useful Group and Cameron Mackintosh, whose operations were structured with an international scale and scope. Australia is an emerging regional market in this musical theatre landscape. In the 1980s and 1990s Mackintosh was the only international producer operating in Australia, but as producer Rob Brookman observed, 'now pretty much all major international producers of successful musical theatre productions see the Australian market as having great potential.'[20] The exorbitant costs of mounting Broadway musicals in the United States means that producers have, as Savran has described, 'begun to look overseas for coproducers in countries that hunger for musicals but in which labour costs are significantly lower than in the United States.'[21] Australia has 'cheaper advertising costs, pay rates, theatre hire and building costs,' all of which contribute to its appeal.[22] Sydney has become an attractive option for out-of-town tryouts, with musicals like *An Officer and a Gentleman*, which opened in Sydney in 2012, and *Doctor Zhivago*, which played Sydney, Melbourne, and Brisbane in 2011, as examples of this phenomenon.[23]

Savran argues that these factors have not only changed the conditions of production but also have seen the emergence of a new subgenre: the 'Broadway-style' musical, which he defines as a syncretic form where 'global and local, commercial and esoteric, orthodox and avant-garde' meet.[24] He states that 'as a result of its flexibility, and despite its US-Americanness, the Broadway-style musical has succeeded in saturating theatrical genres around the world.'[25] Using South Korea and Germany as case studies, Savran explicates the two-way traffic between these nations and Broadway and how the transnational flow of capital (and the impact of Disney and other large producers) has reshaped the Broadway musical.

It is important to note, as Savran does, that transnational does not mean *a*national. The point is that the national imaginary sits inside a wider frame, which we might call a *global* imaginary. For example, as Savran observes, in South Korea,

> along with K-pop, [musicals] represent an attempt at both consolidating and disseminating a hip Korean cosmopolitanism that is in fact bankrolled by vast sums of both private and public capital. But the investment is paying off insofar as Koreans have become extremely adept at producing and performing foreign musicals and crafting their own for local consumption and export.[26]

This is the model *Muriel* aspires to, and in this schema, Broadway becomes a brand, a strategy employed to pursue national distinctiveness only as far as the national can be marketed on the global stage. Savran quotes Simone Genatt, Chair of Broadway Asia, who stated that 'Broadway is an incredibly powerful brand. Much more powerful [abroad] . . . than in the American system,' and that when a new musical theatre economy emerges, whether it be in 'Latin America or China or Dubai . . . they tend to brand themselves with Broadway to show that they are a market to be reckoned with and a market that has clout and money.'[27] In this light, *Muriel*'s embrace of transnational, Broadway-style features can be read as attempt to assist an Australian musical to succeed on an international stage.

Muriel's use of the conventions of the transnational musical can be understood as part of a process of codification. Following Luc Boltanski and Eve Chiapello, Savran proposes the notion that transnational musicals are better understood as engaging in a process of codification, rather than standardised reproduction.[28] In *The New Spirit of Capitalism*, Boltanski and Chiapello outline that

> whereas standardization consisted in conceiving a product from the outset, and reproducing it identically in as many copies as the market could absorb, codification, element by element, makes it possible . . . to introduce

variations in such a way as to obtain products that are relatively different, but of the same style.[29]

This is an excellent way of conceptualising *Muriel*'s use of the conventions of the transnational musical. Codification is a way of balancing two economic imperatives: one where consumers prize and demand authenticity, the other for products to be transposable and reproducible. In the case of *Muriel*, it allows the musical to retain an Australian accent, for example, but for much of the music to be sung in a generic, pseudo-American Broadway style. It allows it to keep its strong female protagonists but corral the ending of the story into a recognisable boy-meets-girl scenario. It also means the musical can profit from the familiarity of ABBA music by using it as a mechanism that facilitates the integration of new compositions into the score.

This process of subsummation to the Broadway brand might be considered negatively, as a missed opportunity to create something wholly and authentically Australian. Savran is dismissive of this line of argument, which he describes as the 'cultural invasion' thesis. This is the notion that the transnational musical is a standardised, soulless, mass-produced theatrical product, the bastion of what a 'sizable group of Anglophone critics,' in Savran's words, call McTheatre.[30] For Savran, this characterisation is misguided because it fails to recognise that musicals performed outside the United States 'are inevitably mediated by local producers, directors, actors, and performance traditions' and that local cultures 'adopt, adapt, and transform the conventions of the Broadway-style musical to perform global citizenship.'[31] This process is manifest in *Muriel*.

The role ABBA plays in the musical is a useful illustration of how codification – a tailoring to local tastes and circumstances – operates in the context of the transnational musical. An iconic feature of the original film was its soundtrack. The character of Muriel is obsessed with the music of ABBA and in the film, ABBA songs are used diegetically at key points: Muriel and Rhonda win a talent quest on Hibiscus Island with their performance of 'Waterloo,' and Muriel walks down the aisle to 'I Do, I Do, I Do, I Do, I Do.' For Hogan, the retention of the ABBA music for the musical was a non-negotiable part of the process. Obtaining the rights was a lengthy process, and it took Pavlovic over eighteen months to secure a meeting with ABBA's management, until eventually Benny Andersson and Bjørn Ulvaeus agreed to meet, and the deal was struck.[32]

Accounting for the role of ABBA in *Muriel* may, on the surface, seem like a straightforward argument about transnational cultural products and globalisation. However, Australia has a particular relationship with the band, one that renders its role in *Muriel* more significant. As music journalist Molly Meldrum observed, the pairing of ABBA and Australia 'has been one of music's most enduring love affairs.'[33] After failing to follow up their 1974 Eurovision winner, 'Waterloo,' with an equally big hit, ABBA's appeal had waned, until

Meldrum began to play their music on the television programme *Countdown*. Their popularity exploded: 'Fernando' was the number one song on the Australian popular-music charts for fourteen weeks in 1976, a record that has never been exceeded. Their 1977 tour was such a success that they decided to film the drama-documentary *ABBA: The Movie* in Australia. Australia has also produced *Björn Again*, an ABBA tribute band who have been performing since 1988, and who, as Benny Andersson of ABBA noted, 'are still working and have been together three times as long as we were.'[34] Therefore, in the *Muriel* musical, ABBA's music is best understood as part of the national repertory and also embedded within a global market as a transnational product.

Bringing *Muriel* into the Twenty-First Century

While the original film was set in the early 1990s (the time of the film's making), the musical re-envisions the story for the 2010s. Hogan's rationale for the update was that:

> Back in 1994 Muriel had a problem that seemed peculiar to her . . . how do you become famous (that is loved/admired/envied by all) when you have no discernible talent, no achievements, and when no one believes in you except you? The new millennium has provided the tools for dreamers afflicted by obscurity: Twitter, Facebook, Instagram, You Tube [sic], not to mention that Hogwarts for the irrelevant, Reality TV. Muriel was born to be a Millennial. So a Millennial she has become.[35]

The musical uses social media as a thematic device, as a visual aesthetic, and as a bridge between the world-of-the-play and real-world marketing campaigns. In the musical, Muriel's odyssey through the bridal shops of Sydney is now documented on Instagram, which is also the platform where, on stage, she announces her engagement to Alexander Shkuratov, a Russian swimmer in need of Australian residency.

The new century is conveyed through the set design, with the proscenium arch studded with small screens that look like smart phones, and which change as the story progresses, flashing through selfies, emojis, and social media posts. The visual language of social media is integrated choreographically and physically. In the scene in the first act at the Breakers Nightclub, Tania and her friends record a 'boomerang,' a feature of the Instagram platform. Their tilted heads, forward shoulders and pouted lips are mainstays of social media posts published by young women. The song 'Shared, Viral, Linked, Liked,' performed by the girls when they discover Muriel's engagement to Alexander has made her 'Insta-famous,' sees them perform actions like swiping their screens and taking selfies in the choreography. The frenetic hemiola and changing time signature of the chorus conveys the speed of the updating feed and their insatiable appetite for new content, while the tight harmonies convey the uniformity of their point of view. By using the globalised aesthetic of social media, which does not differ from country to country (the Instagram platform looks the same whether you are in Sydney, London, New York, or Singapore), *Muriel* aims to make itself an accessible and attractive proposition around the world. This spills over into the representations of the characters, their manner of speech, vocal style, and body language. For example, the gaggle of mean girls who treat Muriel poorly in Porpoise Spit are a relatively generic group of young women for whom social media is a constant fixture in their lives. Apart from their accents, there is little to distinguish them from a comparable group in London or New York.

In its incorporation of social media within the plot, *Muriel* follows in the footsteps of *Dear Evan Hansen* (2015), a work described as the first 'digital age' musical.[36] A noteworthy feature of *Dear Evan Hansen* is its community of committed and enthusiastic fans, known as 'Fansens.'[37] Updating the era from the early 1990s to the present day immediately made *Muriel* more relevant to this generation of so-called digital natives. Additionally, as Chandler and Scheuber-Rush observe, 'savvy commercial producers have long been conscious of the fact that musical theatre audiences want to advertise their fandom and allegiance.'[38] By using social media in the plot, and incorporating it into the visual design and lexicon, *Muriel* aims to encourage and ennoble fans to do just this. Although *Muriel* has not generated its own version of the Fansens, its marketing aims to facilitate a situation in which such a devoted transnational fan community could emerge.

Muriel actively promoted the production of paratexts. Audiences were encouraged to pose in front of a bright yellow backdrop that was set up in the foyer, featuring the #imwithmuriel hashtag, and holding cutout signs in the shape of a speech bubble with choice quotes from the production. These photos were then posted to the production's various social media channels. Moreover, *Muriel* was merchandised, and audiences were able to buy a range of items at the performance, including tote bags, t-shirts, tea towels, keyrings, and customised mugs. Blurring the offstage/onstage commodification of the musical, audience members could also become part of the performance proper by purchasing an 'Onstage Wedding Guest Ticket,' which meant that just before the wedding scene they were invited onstage and seated in the pews as if wedding guests.[39] These participants were also given a bonbonniere as a token of their involvement.

These strategies for situating *Muriel* firmly in the twenty-first century both indicate the pursual of a younger demographic but also the trend towards integrated marketing strategies that engage these audiences in the production of paratexts. This fine line between 'branding' and the musical itself continues in its portrayal of Australia's cities.

Place Branding: Producing Sydney and the Gold Coast in Song

Muriel is set in two distinctly drawn places, one fictional and one real: Porpoise Spit, Muriel's hometown, based on the city of the Gold Coast, and Sydney, her adopted home. In the musical, both cities are branded through song. In 'Sunshine State of Mind,' the Gold Coast is figured as a paradise where sun, sand, surf, and a 'no worries' attitude prevails. In the song 'Sydney,' Australia's largest city is represented as a queer metropolis, a welcoming, diverse city with a vibrant nightlife. These city brands are well established, having been reinforced and reiterated in national and international advertising campaigns. The brands provide stable anchoring points for *Muriel's* prospective international audience, producing an Australia seen through what John Urry describes as 'the tourist gaze.'[40]

The opening song of the musical, 'Sunshine State of Mind,' reproduces aspects of Australia that are ubiquitous to the nation's tourist advertising. The fictional Porpoise Spit stands in for the Gold Coast, a fifty-seven-kilometre stretch of southeast Queensland and Australia's sixth largest city. The city, and its most iconic locale, Surfers Paradise, is famous for its 'long stretches of white sandy beaches, a skyline of resort skyscrapers, an enduring legacy of such gimmicks as the gold lamé bikini-clad Meter Maids, and the now century-old figure of the tanned and carefree surfer.'[41] All of these tropes are present in the song, which frames the Gold Coast as an idyllic place, characterised by perfect weather and friendly, attractive people, the combination of which engenders a 'no worries' attitude. There is no narrative reason to set the song on the beach, as the landscape is not an important scenographic or thematic element of Hogan's film or the musical adaptation. 'Sunshine State of Mind' is set on the beach because it is a way of opening the musical with a clear evocation of what might be referred to as 'Brand Australia.'

The song encapsulates how the Gold Coast is the part of Australia that 'most clearly epitomises sun, surf, and sex.'[42] The stage is set with a single door, slightly upstage, and a brightly green-lit floor. To the sound of an exuberant accented A major chord, followed by a set of repeated notes bowed detaché by the violin, a young man holding a surfboard bounds onto the stage. Soon after, he is joined by a blond woman in a hot pink swimsuit. They sing in question-and-answer fashion: he stands as if looking at the ocean and proclaims that 'today the sea is gentle as can be,' to which she responds, 'like a newborn baby sleeping.' He continues by noting that the water is a balmy temperature: 'sweet at twenty-eight degrees,' to which she adds, 'and all the fish are leaping.' As they sing, more couples begin to populate the stage, marvelling at the perfection of their surroundings. In harmony, and in alternating groups of men and women, they sing: 'Take a breath of morning air, everything's perfect. Rays of light to dry your hair, everything's perfect.' A painted backdrop flies in at the back of the stage, resplendent with palm trees and high-rise buildings in the distance. The ensemble's voices energetically crescendo to arrive at the bouncy chorus:

You say "How's the weather?"
I say "Never been better"
Perfect everyday
Let's stay here forever

Not only is the landscape stunningly beautiful but so are all the people: 'Sun, sand, surf, no worries, Suntan, sexy bodies,' the cast sing. Everyone in Porpoise Spit is in possession of a 'beach body.' The women are lithe, blonde, blue-eyed, bikinied, and toned; the men tanned and barrel-chested, sporting board shorts and thongs. The choreography is highly stylised: the performers run with wide, energetic strides, like they are in an advertisement; the women repeatedly fluff their hair and pose with popped knee. They gaily dance around the men who spin, lift, and ride their surfboards.

Visually and musically, the song conveys brightness, recalling the 2004 'Australia – A Different Light' tourist campaign. Designer Gabriela Tylesova selected 'bold' colours for the set pieces and costumes for 'Sunshine State of Mind' and described the song as '[k]ind of the perfect postcard for tropical Queensland.'[43] The bright E major tonality mirrors the bright colours of the set. The song is incessantly upbeat; its crisp offbeat hand claps reminiscent of an advertising jingle. The music draws on elements of the surf-pop sound – a simple chord progression, rich vocal harmonies, distorted electric guitar and a 'doo-wop' influence – but with twenty-first-century production values, resulting in a slick, highly produced pop track.

The 'sunshine state of mind' is epitomised by a 'no worries' attitude, the conduit for which is unwaveringly excellent weather and unfettered access to the beach. The plain-speaking lexicon of the song eschews witty phrases, internal rhymes, or profound sentiments and promotes an uncomplicated, easy lifestyle: 'Everybody knows everybody and everything is great,' conclude the lyrics of the chorus. Cliff Goddard notes that a phrase like 'no worries,' which acts as an 'unofficial "national motto,"' highlights the 'value placed on efforts to suppress or ignore bad feelings' in Australian culture.[44] At the end of each chorus, there is an eight-bar section during which the male performers sing a rhythmic figure using a 'doo' sound, and the women sing 'ooo, livin' in a sunshine state of mind.' These melismatic sounds convey an ineffable ease: things here are so good that they do not need to be put into words. These sentiments are drawn directly from Queensland tourism advertising campaigns. The title of the song references Queensland's slogan, 'The Sunshine State,' a tagline that appears on car numberplates and in advertising. A long-running advertising campaign run by the State Government has been the 'Beautiful

One Day, Perfect the Next' strategy.[45] Lyrics like 'never been better,' 'perfect every day,' and 'everything is great' clearly play on these familiar turns of phrase.

Sydney, on the other hand, is inscribed in the musical as a place of liberation and self-discovery, as the place where Muriel goes to remake herself. She flees her hometown, Porpoise Spit, for Sydney after her family learns that she stole her mother's credit card to pay for a holiday on Hibiscus Island. When she arrives home to an ambush, she makes a split-second decision to escape to Sydney in search of Rhonda, the old classmate with whom she reconnected on her holiday. In Sydney, with Rhonda's help, Muriel's self-confidence starts to blossom. Free of the shackles of her critical father and the friends that continually exclude her, she gets a job, changes her name to Mariel, and starts her first romantic relationship. Sydney is figured as the catalyst for all these positive changes in her life.

This is all brought together in the song 'Sydney.'[46] As Muriel stands on the stage, suitcase in hand, preparing to leave, she hears a group of voices sing to her, slowly and dreamily 'When you get to Sydney,' offering her the encouragement she needs. Rhonda's voice is heard calling out 'Oh Muriel, my life started in . . .' – a throwback to a previous scene – but this time the sentence is completed by the ensemble, who jubilantly cry out 'Sydney' as they spin onto the stage. Set pieces start to fly in, revealing the Harbour Bridge and, in the distance, the Sydney Opera House. The music increases in intensity as a scalic figure played by strings weaves its way to a climax along with the gradual build of synthesised sound, and then the arrival of the song's chorus:

When you get to Sydney
You will never never wanna go home
When you get to Sydney
You won't ever have to feel alone
When you get to be what you wanna be, do what you wanna do
Say what you wanna say, screw who you wanna screw
When you get to Sydney
You will finally get to be you

In other words, Sydney is a city ready to receive you, whomever you might be.

This vision of the city is also derived from its official branding as a tourist destination. These ideals of freedom, inclusion, and self-expression can be linked to a formal rebranding process that the city had undergone a decade earlier. As former Chief Executive Officer of Events NSW Geoff Parmenter recounts, in 2008, on the back of a series of reports conducted by the businessman John O'Neill, 'a broad group of Sydney stakeholders joined in a major city-wide collaboration to unite, align and inspire the city to market itself far more strongly.'[47] Four key points of distinction emerged from this process: Sydney's natural beauty, its 'can do' attitude, its uninhibited outlook, and its sense of progressiveness. Parmenter observed that these qualities were 'seen as emanating from the way the city embraces its diversity. Sydney does not *tolerate* different perspectives; Sydney *celebrates* them.'[48]

The song 'Sydney' emphasises how the city welcomes outsiders, irrespective of their status or background. In the latter half of the number, the company huddles around Muriel to expound on Sydney's diversity. The citizens of Sydney are variously straight, Asian, high on drugs, and queer: 'Nothing is exotic here,' as the lyrics say. Sydney is also multicultural: 'black or yellow or beige or brown,' and socio-economically diverse, 'the down and the up and the up and down.' Earlier in the song, a few Sydneysiders share what brought them there. 'I ran away from home,' announces one woman; 'Stole a car and hit the road,' confesses a man. We do not learn any of these Sydneysiders' names, reflecting the possibilities of living in a global urban centre. In Sydney, under this cloak of anonymity, there is the possibility to remake yourself: be able to 'do what you wanna do, be what you wanna be, screw who you wanna screw.'[49]

The 'screw who you wanna screw' line and the characterisation and costuming of the number also represents 'Sydney' as a queer city (Figure 1.1). This is an element of the production that is endogenous to the stage adaptation. While in relation to the film, some critics had read the relationship between Muriel and Rhonda as queer, the portrayal of the city in Hogan's film is distinctly different from that of the musical.[50] The visual aesthetic of the song 'Sydney' recalls the Sydney Gay and Lesbian Mardi Gras, an annual festival of queer pride celebrated since 1978. The cast of characters who populate the stage are dressed in all manner of outlandish attire: assless chaps, feathers, corsets, leather, glitter, and sequins adorn the costumes. Several performers are in drag. At one point, a woman dressed in a short sparkly lycra dress and giant platform shoes comes forward to tell the audience that she 'left everything I know to get to the end of the rainbow.'

All this taps into the city's existing brand as a queer tourist destination.[51] While the carnivalesque celebration of Mardi Gras did not originate in Australia, Kevin Markwell argues that its Sydney iteration is distinctively Australian in its 'mélange of flamboyant theatricality, costume, and parody embodying what might be called a "larrikin spirit" eager to test authority,' noting that 'the gay pride marches of many European and North American cities do not seem to have such a defining effect on the character of these cities as Mardi Gras does on Sydney.'[52] The Mardi Gras therefore acts as a point of distinction, a way that Sydney sells itself to the world.

The mobilisation of the Mardi Gras within the musical is part of a strategy to cast Sydney as a world city, one that is modern, exciting, and dynamic, with a vibrant nightlife culture. The song is written in an Electronic Dance

FIGURE 1.1   The cast of *Muriel's Wedding: The Musical* performing 'Sydney.'
Photo: Jeff Busby ©

Music (EDM) genre, a style that is associated with partying, dancing, and nightclubs. It features a strong electronic bass beat from a drum machine, and the voices are mixed using delay effects. Other EDM production techniques like high pass filters and tape-stop transitions are used throughout the song. The choreography is angular and references nightclub dancing, while the use of intelligent lighting in fluorescent colours communicates a party atmosphere. The addition of the backdrop of the bridge suggests New Year's Eve on the foreshore. All this aims to position Sydney as a modern, global, vibrant city: a 'metropolis that is part of a global consciousness.'[53]

A model for *Muriel*'s engagement in this process of city-branding-through-song is John Kander and Fred Ebb's 'New York, New York,' which originally appeared in Martin Scorsese's 1977 film of the same name. While it was sung by Liza Minnelli for the film, Frank Sinatra's cover became the iconic version of the song. 'New York, New York' has become an anthem for the city, played as baseball games, celebrations, and used in advertising. Miriam Greenberg writes that by 1985, when the Sinatra version was crowned 'New York's Official Song' by Mayor Ed Koch, 'the anthem's poignancy had been replaced with triumphalism, as the city's brand name became synonymous with the indomitable spirit of the individual, and of the free market itself.'[54] To read 'Sydney' with 'New York, New York' in mind is to highlight the way that transnational musical theatre can become enmeshed with the economy of a city.

Destination New South Wales, the tourism arm of the NSW State Government, stated in their 2017–2018 Annual Report that 'securing major Australian and world premiere, first-run musicals remains a major focus . . . due to their ability to attract ex-Sydney visitors and deliver significant economic benefits to Sydney and NSW.'[55] And, as Global Creatures announced in a media release, Destination NSW invested in *Muriel*. The company stated that it was

> thrilled to be partnering with Destination New South Wales to premiere this new musical in Sydney. Muriel's Wedding is an exciting fit as so much of the story takes place in this wonderful city. Muriel's dreams of freedom, inclusion and self-expression go to the heart of what Sydney has to offer.[56]

This partnership between the tourism arm of the NSW government and Global Creatures demonstrates the way in which musical theatre is an economically significant industry, one that can act as a brand ambassador for Australia.

Brand Recognition: *Muriel* as Jukebox Movical

In the transnational musical theatre industry, brand recognition is valuable currency. It is considered economically prudent for producers to invest in known quantities and familiar stories. Two common strategies in this vein are to produce movicals (musicals adapted from films) and jukebox musicals (musicals that include existing songs, rather than bespoke compositions).[57] *Muriel* combines both these strategies and, through the codification of these forms, strikes a balance between the familiar and the new, transforming itself from an idiosyncratic Australian film to a transnational, Broadway-style musical. *Muriel* is a successful realisation of these subgenres, both of which have frequently attracted criticism for their derivative tendencies.

The fact that *Muriel*'s producer, Global Creatures, has based all four of its original productions on films is evidence of the appeal of the movical to producers. While this is not in and of itself a new phenomenon – musicals are the form of adaptation *par excellence*, and films have often served as source texts for musicals – the exponential surge in movicals over the past twenty-five years is noteworthy. According to Rachael Munro's 2016 analysis, the number of movicals peaked in 2012 at 88% of Broadway productions.[58] This has led some to argue that the growth in movicals is being driven by primarily by economic factors. Judith Sebesta, for example, argues that as the cost of production for musicals continues to rise, musicals 'based on new material' have become 'risky commodities,' and subsequently, 'revivals and adaptations' are increasingly the norm.[59]

Familiarity was certainly a factor in Global Creatures' decision to pursue a *Muriel* musical. While Hogan's film had had a rocky path to the screen, it was ultimately a huge success, boasting the distinction of being one of the most profitable Australian films ever made.[60] The film grossed $57 million, 'an almost unthinkable amount for a relatively low-budget Australian film today,' as Jake Wilson observed.[61] Pavlovic's reasoning put familiarity at the forefront of the decision-making process, stating that

> the film is reasonably well known internationally . . . the story is really identifiable, the quirkiness and irreverence of it is an aspect of Australian culture that people are fond of internationally, and the ABBA music obviously is very recognisable worldwide. The whole package has a lot of potential to appeal internationally.[62]

Here, Pavlovic sketches out the promise of *Muriel* as a transnational, Broadway-style musical, and the company's confidence that they can capitalise on the success and familiarity of the original film.

While making a movical is considered a prudent financial decision, it is not a guarantee of success. As Richard Watts encapsulated in his review, 'for every triumphant *Billy Elliot* there's a leaden *King Kong*, but producers – including . . . Global Creatures – persist. Get the formula right and the millions will flow.'[63] The 'formula' is a finely tuned balance of the familiar and the new, as movicals have often been criticised for their slavish reproduction of the source text. But *Muriel* is more than just an exercise in nostalgic mimicry. Rather, the musical uses the familiarity of the original film to its advantage, as a strategy that offers audiences a balance of what they know and love, as well as some surprises. Its inventiveness can be attributed at least in part to Hogan, who was uninterested in replicating his film on stage: 'That seemed to me just a waste of time,' he told *The Sydney Morning Herald*.[64] One of the most significant changes is the deeper integration of the ABBA music into the dramaturgy, which distinguishes *Muriel* from a standard jukebox musical.

Alongside the ABBA songs, *Muriel* has a new, Australian-composed score by Miller-Heidke and Nuttall. This is significant because the lack of an original Australian-composed score has been perceived to be the missing element of several otherwise successful Australian musicals. Ben Neutze, for example, made this criticism when he stated that '*Priscilla*, like much of *Strictly Ballroom*, is a jukebox musical with little Australian music, so it doesn't feel like a worthy recipient of the title. The Great Australian Musical should have a Great Australian Score, after all.'[65] Moreover, *Muriel* is the only one of the Global Creatures musicals in possession of such a score. It was a bold decision to embark upon a production with so much original music, since this is often seen as a liability for a new musical, and even more so because the company had had mixed success with the scores of their previous works. The music of both *King Kong* and *Strictly Ballroom* had been roundly criticised. For *Strictly Ballroom*, they had attempted a semi-jukebox format where the iconic songs from the soundtrack were surrounded by new music composed by a broad range of different artists coming from very diverse musical backgrounds. This aspect of the production was received very poorly, with Jason Blake writing that 'Luhrmann should have made a genuine jukeboxer out of *Ballroom* and saved everyone a lot of time and trouble.'[66] This is eventually what came to pass, and it is now performed as a jukebox musical with no original material. Their most recent production, *Moulin Rouge!*, is a standard jukebox musical. In the case of *Muriel*, its score was seen as even more of a 'gamble,' as the journalist Joyce Morgan put it, because the new songs were competing with ABBA's. Adding to this pressure was the famous line from the film, spoken by Muriel when she reflects on how her life as changed in Sydney: 'Since I've met you [Rhonda] and moved to Sydney, my life is as good as an ABBA song.' Nuttall commented that this pressure was felt deeply by him and Miller-Heidke, saying that they felt very conscious that their new songs were going 'to sit beside some of the most well-known and highly successful songs in the history of popular music.'[67]

With *Muriel*, Global Creatures found a way to make this semi-jukebox format work to their advantage. Its success lies in the process of codification, with the familiarity of the ABBA music working to enhance the reception of Miller-Heidke and Nuttall's new songs.[68] Miller-Heidke and Nuttall, using characteristically Australian underdog humour, were thrilled that the reception of the original songs was overwhelmingly positive: 'no one has said our music sucks next to ABBA, which is incredible.'[69] The semi-jukebox format is therefore a canny strategy that allows the production to have a new, Australian-composed score and to reap the benefits of the jukebox musical, where familiarity and brand recognition reassures and recruits audiences.

Muriel therefore extends the capabilities of the jukebox form, which has often been maligned as a kind of 'comfort food.'[70] It lives up to the promise of the jukebox musical as articulated by John Severn in his defence of the form, when he contends that the jukebox musical's 'lure of familiarity' is offset

> by the lure of the new, by a curiosity as to the unfamiliar territory on which the familiar will be encountered. If the lure of the familiar plays a part in attracting audiences, it is also likely to be accompanied by a willingness to see what can be done with the familiar by others, and an openness to finding new interpretations for familiar material oneself.[71]

Muriel's success is partly attributable to the way that the musical embeds the ABBA music into the fabric of the narrative.

The musical brings the four members of ABBA to life on the stage (Figure 1.2). Benny, Bjorn, Agnetha, and Frida, visible only to Muriel, pop in and out of the action, acting as her 'spirit guides and guardian angels,' as Jason Blake remarked.[72] ABBA make their first appearance in the musical after Muriel's embarrassing ejection from Tania and Chook's wedding because the

FIGURE 1.2   The cast of *Muriel's Wedding: The Musical* performing 'Money Money Money.'

Photo: Jeff Busby ©

dress she is wearing turns out to be shoplifted. Back at home, as her father tries to broker a deal with the policeman, Muriel begins to sing the opening lines of 'Dancing Queen' to herself as a comforting coping mechanism. Safe in her room, with her ABBA poster on the wall, ABBA emerge from the wardrobe to sing with her. She asks them if they think she has talent, and if they think she's attractive, to which ABBA respond with a chorus of 'Ja's,' dancing all the while. Muriel asks them if she will ever get her 'chance,' just like the protagonist of the song, at which point her bedroom furniture disappears to reveal a fantasy husband with a single rose in hand. Here 'Dancing Queen' and Muriel's earlier 'I want' song, 'The Bouquet,' are combined as a mashup. As the time-signature changes from 4/4 to 6/8, half the chorus sing the first line of the chorus, while the other half sing the lyrics from the 'The Bouquet' in harmony. The time-signature snaps back to 4/4 for the last four bars, where the tune of 'Dancing Queen' is sung to the final word of 'The Bouquet' (love).

A similar mashup of ABBA songs occurs in Act Two, in the scene where Rhonda exposes Muriel's fraudulent marriage in the bridal shop. ABBA, hiding in plain sight as mannequins wearing bridal gowns, vocalise 'Dancing Queen' as Muriel and Rhonda argue. Rhonda, who has been unwell with cancer, and is in a wheelchair, gives Muriel the bad news that the tumour is back. Muriel, spooked by the prospect of continuing to have to look after her friend, has ABBA in her ear, encouraging her to focus on herself. While Muriel tries to engage in conversation with Rhonda, ABBA are distracting her with matches from a dating site, underscored by the melody of 'Take a Chance on Me,' repurposed as the bass line for a reprise of the song 'True Friend,' a statement of friendship sung in earlier in Act Two by Muriel and Rhonda. Under Rhonda's triumphant final note, ABBA repeat the final line, showing that despite her promises to Rhonda, Muriel has moved on. ABBA reappear at pivotal emotional moments throughout the musical. The combination of the physical realisation of ABBA as characters, and the integration of the ABBA music not only into the narrative but also into the score, is a very effective strategy for reaping the benefits of the familiarity of the ABBA music while still offering audiences original songs.

Conclusion: Ambassador Muriel

This idea of the *Muriel* musical as Australia's representative on the global stage has currency. Ben Neutze's review, praising the production, stated that

> it feels like we've finally been seen, heard, and validated. If Australian musical theatre audiences are Muriel, then this show is our very own Rhonda, putting its arm around us and declaring to Broadway and the West End: 'I'm not alone, I'm with Muriel.'[73]

In this reading, Broadway and the West End are figured as international stages, platforms where Australia competes for recognition, excellence, and validation. Neutze's conceptualisation of the national citizenry as a united front, ready to support 'our' representatives, recalls other international competitions when the nation bands together in this way: sporting events like the Olympics; or, more pertinently, another cultural event in which transnational and national imaginaries coalesce – the Eurovision Song Contest.

As strange as it may seem, in the twenty-first century Eurovision has become a celebrated event on the Australian calendar. In 2013, Australia entered the competition: first as a guest performer, then as a wild-card entrant, and finally, as a competitor proper in 2015. The song contest offers each entrant an opportunity to engage in a process of nation branding with each country determining a way of presenting itself to the world through song, dance, and spectacle. But, just like in *Muriel*, this nation branding is 'complicated by the fact that each nation's domestic audiences are also consuming the projected image. This means that those constructing the image must also incorporate an inward-looking aspect in its idea of the nation.'[74]

More than this, though, Australia's participation in Eurovision cultivates a sense of global belonging. Describing her experience of the song contest, the singer Jessica Mauboy, Australia's 2018 representative, commented that what

Eurovision does is 'really [make] you feel part of the world.'[75] Carniel notes that while 'Eurovision offers Australian audiences and fans a sense of transnational connection to the world and belonging to global society,' Mauboy's ostensibly positive statement belies a much

> deeper Australian fear or anxiety: a sense of disconnection from the rest of the world. This anxiety can be alleviated by participation in and a feeling of belonging to global events such as the Olympics, the FIFA World Cup, and the Eurovision Song Contest.[76]

We could, following Neutze, add to this list a presence on Broadway and/or the West End.

The legacy of the Great Australian Musical is an anxiety that Australian musical theatre has not proven itself to the world. *Muriel* engages with this thematically by presenting Australia as a modern, outward looking nation, open for business and ready to participate on the world stage. As *Muriel* the musical travels the world as Australia's musical ambassador, she makes the journey with ABBA, our transnational cheer squad, cheering her – and thereby, us – on. As spectators, we wish her well and want her to succeed and, in the process, the national citizenry is bound together as we barrack for 'our' Muriel. In the next chapter, we will see a different sort of ambassador, one that comes in the form of a sporting celebrity.

Notes

1 Kate Miller-Heidke and Keir Nuttall, *Muriel's Wedding: The Musical*, Sony Music, sound recording, 2018. It is also available via Spotify.
2 David Savran, 'Trafficking in Transnational Brands: The New "Broadway-Style" Musical,' *Theatre Survey* 55, no. 3 (2014): 318–342, https://doi.org/10.1017/S0040557414000337; David Savran, 'Broadway as Global Brand,' *Journal of Drama in English* 5, no. 1 (2017): 24–37, https://doi.org/10.1515/jcde-2017-0003; David Savran, *Tell it to the World: The Broadway Musical Abroad* (Oxford, 2024).
3 Jo Litson, 'Carmen Pavlovic: Yes, She Can-Can,' *Limelight*, July 26, 2021, https://limelightmagazine.com.au/features/carmen-pavlovic-yes-she-can-can/
4 *King Kong*, their first musical opened in Melbourne 2013 and underwent many years of development before its eventual Broadway première in 2018. *Strictly Ballroom* premièred in 2014 in Sydney, and four years later opened on the West End. *Moulin Rouge!* had a reverse trajectory and was workshopped in New York, had an out-of-town tryout in Boston, and premièred on Broadway in 2019, transferring to London and Australia in 2021.
5 Andrew Burke, 'Michael Cassel and the High Risk Business of Musical Theatre,' *Australian Financial Review*, July 20, 2018, https://www.afr.com/life-and-luxury/arts-and-culture/michael-cassel-and-the-high-risk-business-of-musical-theatre-20180718-h12to4
6 'Exclusive: *Muriel's Wedding The Musical* Has Found its Muriel,' *Daily Review*, May 22, 2017, accessed January 4, 2018, https://dailyreview.com.au/muriels-wedding-musical-found-muriel/60081/

7 Adam Hetrick, '*Muriel's Wedding* Musical Delays North American Premiere,' *Playbill.com*, September 26, 2017, accessed June 30, 2025, https://www.playbill. com/article/muriels-wedding-musical-delays-north-american-premiere

8 Olivia Clement, '*Muriel's Wedding* Will Have Private Lab Reading in N.Y.C in 2020,' *Playbill.com*, December 27, 2019, accessed May 7, 2021, https://www.playbill. com/article/muriels-wedding-to-receive-developmental-lab-in-nyc-in-2020.

9 'Muriel's Wedding: The Musical,' *Westendtheatre.com*, accessed December 16, 2021, https://www.westendtheatre.com/46946/shows-coming-soon/muriels-wedding-the-musical/

10 Lindsay Johns, 'Muriel's Wedding, Leicester Curve, Review: A Triumphant Adaptation of the Breezy Aussie Romcom,' *The Telegraph*, May 1, 2025, https://www.telegraph. co.uk/theatre/what-to-see/muriels-wedding-leicester-curve-review-abba/

11 Stephen Dow 'How to Make the Australian Musical: From *The Sapphires* to *Strictly Ballroom*,' *The Guardian*, June 15, 2017, https://www.theguardian.com/stage/2017/ jun/15/how-to-make-the-australian-musical-from-the-sapphires-to-strictly-ballroom; Richard Watts, 'Review: *Muriel's Wedding The Musical*, Her Majesty's Theatre,' *ArtsHub*, April 2, 2019, https://www.artshub.com.au/news/reviews/ review-muriels-wedding-the-musical-her-majestys-theatre-257652-2362740/.

12 Ben Neutze, '*Muriel's Wedding* The Musical Review (Roslyn Packer Theatre),' *Daily Review*, November 19 2017, accessed December 14, 2021, https://dailyreview. com.au/muriels-wedding-musical-review-roslyn-packer-theatre/.

13 Elizabeth Wollman, 'How to Dismantle a [Theatric] Bomb: Broadway Flops, Broadway Money, and Musical Theater Historiography,' *Arts* 9, no. 66 (2020): 3, https://doi.org/10.3390/arts9020066.

14 Wollman, 'How to Dismantle,' 3.

15 Wollman, 'How to Dismantle,' 12.

16 Savran, 'Trafficking in Transnational Brands,' 338.

17 Jessica Sternfeld, *The Megamusical* (Indiana University Press, 2006), 1.

18 Savran, 'Trafficking in Transnational Brands,' 328.

19 Savran, 'Trafficking in Transnational Brands,' 325.

20 Maryann Wright, 'Australia Beats Broadway to Host World Premieres of Up-And-Coming Musical Classics,' *News.com.au*, September 23, 2011, https://www. news.com.au/entertainment/music/australia-beats-broadway-to-host-world-premieres-of-up-and-coming-musical-classics/news-story/0874c65342bd60648e 0de178395964bb?sv=38d13dfecd86950cd48a9eecfa837b2c.

21 Savran, 'Trafficking in Transnational Brands,' 320.

22 Wright, 'Australia Beats Broadway.'

23 *An Officer and a Gentleman*, produced by John Frost and Sharleen Cooper Cohen, was a flop and closed just after eight weeks. *Doctor Zhivago* fared better, playing a season in Seoul in 2012 before opening on Broadway in 2015.

24 Savran, *Tell it to the World*, 4.

25 Savran, *Tell it to the World*, 3.

26 Savran, 'Broadway as Global Brand,' 31.

27 Savran, *Tell it to the World*, 56.

28 Savran, *Tell it to the World*, 29.

29 Luc Boltanski and Eve Chiapello, *The New Spirit of Capitalism* (Verso, 2005), 445.

30 Savran, *Tell it to the World*, 26.

31 Savran, *Tell it to the World*, 25, 33.

32 Karl Quinn, 'Where's Muriel? P.J. Hogan on the Agony of Casting Australia's Daggiest Bride, Again,' *The Sydney Morning Herald*, September 10, 2018, https://www.smh.com.au/entertainment/musicals/muriel-and-me-pj-hogans-journe y-with-australias-daggiest-bride-20180907-h152vy.html.

33 Molly Meldrum, 'The Eurovision Winner Takes It All,' *The Big Issue* 5, May 18, 2017, 15.

34 Helen Barlow, 'ABBA's Benny Andersson Reflects on Eurovision Win and the Credit He Still Gives to "Countdown",' *SBS Movies,* May 20, 2015, https://www.sbs.com.au/movies/article/2015/05/20/abbas-benny-andersson-reflects-eurovision-win-and-credit-he-still-gives-countdown.

35 Ben Neutze, 'Kate Miller-Heidke's "Muriel's Wedding" Musical to Premiere at Sydney Theatre Company,' *Daily Review,* September 8, 2016, accessed May 19, 2021, https://dailyreview.com.au/kate-miller-heidkes-muriels-wedding-musical-premiere-sydney-theatre-company/.

36 Lindsey R. Barr, '"Waving through a Window": Nostalgia and Prosthetic Memory in *Dear Evan Hansen,*' *Studies in Musical Theatre* 14, no. 3 (2020): 314, https://doi.org/10.1386/smt_00044_1.

37 Bethany Doherty, '"Tap, Tap, Tapping on the Glass": Generation Z, Social Media and *Dear Evan Hansen,*' *Arts* 9, no. 68 (2020), https://doi.org/10.3390/arts9020068; Adam Rush, '#YouWillBeFound: Participatory Fandom, Social Media Marketing and *Dear Evan Hansen,*' *Studies in Musical Theatre* 15, no. 2 (2021): 119–132, https://doi.org/10.1386/smt_00063_1. A similar phenomenon has occurred with the musical *Hamilton.* Jessica Hillman-Mccord, 'Digital Fandom: Hamilton and the Participatory Spectator,' in *iBroadway: Musical Theatre in the Digital Age* (Palgrave Macmillan, 2017), 119–144.

38 Clare Chandler and Simon Scheuber-Rush, '"Does Anybody Have a Map?": The Impact of "Virtual Broadway" on Musical Theater Composition,' *The Journal of Popular Culture* 54, no. 2 (2021): 278, https://doi.org/10.1111/jpcu.13013.

39 This was also a feature of the U.K. season.

40 John Urry and Jonas Larsen, *The Tourist Gaze 3.0* (Sage Publications, 2011).

41 Aysin Dedekorkut-Howes, Caryl Bosman and Andrew Leach, 'Considering the Gold Coast,' in *Off the Plan: The Urbanisation of the Gold Coast* (CSIRO Publishing, 2016), 1.

42 Hilary Winchester, Pauline McGuirk and Kathryn Everett, 'Schoolies Week as a Rite of Passage: A Study of Celebration and Control,' in *Embodied Geographies: Space Bodies and Rites of Passage,* ed. Elizabeth Kenworthy Teather (Routledge, 1999), 59. See also Kelly Palmer, 'Challenging the Beach as Paradise in Fiction and Memoir: The Gold Coast's Bathing Beauties,' *Writing the Australian Beach: Local Site, Global Idea,* ed. Elizabeth Ellison and Donna Lee Brien (Springer International Publishing, 2020), 143–163.

43 John Bailey, 'Strong Light and Colours Integral to Design of *Muriel's Wedding: The Musical,*' *The Sydney Morning Herald,* March 17, 2019, https://www.smh.com.au/entertainment/m16mcoverbox-20190308-h1c69z.html

44 Cliff Goddard, *Ethnopragmatics: Understanding Discourse in Cultural Context* (De Gruyter, 2006), 72.

45 This slogan ran for twelve years before being replaced in 2010. Andrew Heasley, 'A Beautiful Slogan One Day . . . Gone the Next,' *Traveller.com.au,* September 11, 2010, https://www.traveller.com.au/a-beautiful-slogan-one-day-x2026-gone-the-next-1551j. It was then revived in 2018. Toby Crockford, '"Beautiful One Day, Perfect the Next": Slogan Gets Second Wind for Comm Games Tourism Push,' *The Brisbane Times,* April 1, 2018, https://www.brisbanetimes.com.au/national/queensland/beautiful-one-day-perfect-the-next-slogan-gets-second-wind-for-comm-games-tourism-push-20180401-p4z7a3.html.

46 A performance of this song is available on YouTube. Let Me Entertain You – LMEYpodcast '"Sydney," *Muriel's Wedding: The Musical* – Sydney Lyric Theatre, Media Call,' *YouTube,* July 4, 2019, accessed May 9, 2021, https://www.youtube.com/watch?v=czxj-UEimvc.

47 Geoff Parmenter, 'The City Branding of Sydney,' in *City Branding: Theory and Cases,* ed. Keith Dinnie, (Palgrave Macmillan, 2011), 199.

48 Parmenter, 'The City Branding of Sydney,' 202, original emphasis.

49 These lines could also be read as a play on the song 'Because I Love You' by the Australian rock band The Masters Apprentices.

50 John Champagne, 'Dancing Queen? Feminist and Gay Male Spectatorship in Three Recent Films from Australia,' *Film Criticism* 21, no. 3 (1997): 84, https://www.jstor. org/stable/44018887; Jill Mackey, 'Subtext and Countertext in "Muriel's Wedding",' *NWSA Journal* 13, no. 1 (2001): 87, https://www.jstor.org/stable/4316784; Andy Medhurst, 'But I'm beautiful,' *Sight and Sound* 12, no. 7 (2002): 33.

51 For the domestic audience, queering Sydney has a different resonance. Leigh Boucher reads it as a response to the 2016 same-sex marriage plebiscite, a divisive moment in recent Australian political history where a voluntary postal survey was used to gain the public's support for the legalisation of gay marriage. Leigh Boucher, '*Muriel's Wedding: The Musical* is a Deeply Satisfying Tribute to Australia's Most-Loved Dag,' *The Conversation*, November 23, 2017, https://theconversation. com/muriels-wedding-the-musical-is-a-deeply-satisfying-tribute-to-australias-most-loved-dag–87855. An alternate reading is that a queer Sydney is a statement of support for LGBTIQ rights given the intensification of Muriel's heterosexuality (through her relationship with Brice) in the musical.

52 Kevin Markwell, 'Mardi Gras Tourism and the Construction of Sydney as an International Gay and Lesbian City,' *GLQ* 8, no. 1–2 (2002): 85, https://muse. jhu.edu/article/12201.

53 John Connell, *Sydney: The Emergence of a World City* (Oxford University Press, 2000), 16.

54 Miriam Greenberg, *Branding New York: How a City in Crisis was Sold to the World* (Routledge, 2008), 228.

55 Destination NSW, *Annual Report 2017–2018*, accessed July 4, 2022, https:// www.destinationnsw.com.au/about-us/annual-reports, 32.

56 'Sydney to Host World Premiere of *Muriel's Wedding: The Musical*,' *Destination NSW*, September 9, 2016, accessed May 5, 2021, https://www.destinationnsw. com.au/news-and-media/media-releases/sydney-host-world-premiere-muriels-wedding-musical.

57 Martin Kohn, 'The Celluloid Source,' *Detroit Free Press*, March 17, 2002.

58 Rachael Munro, writing about *King Kong*, performed a corpus analysis of 900 musicals using the Internet Broadway Database (IBDb) and concluded that 400 are preceded by a film. She also observed a discernible increase in the number of movicals produced from the 2000s onwards. Rachel Munro, *King Kong: A Music Theatre Event and the Dawn of the Megamovical*, (Masters diss., University of Melbourne, 2017), 32.

59 Judith Sebesta, 'From Celluloid to Stage: The "Movical," *The Producers*, and the Postmodern,' *Theatre Annual* 56 (2003): 99.

60 It was turned down by everyone Hogan approached, and the only reason that it was eventually made by the French company CiBY was that the noted director Jane Campion, an old friend, vouched for him. Stephen Lowenstein, 'P.J. Hogan: *Muriel's Wedding*,' in *My First Movie: Twenty Celebrated Directors Talk about Their First Film* (New York: Pantheon Books, 2000), 382–410.

61 Jake Wilson, 'You're Not So Terrible Muriel: Why We Still Love *Muriel's Wedding*, 20 Years On,' *The Sydney Morning Herald*, November 14, 2014, https:// www.smh.com.au/entertainment/movies/youre-not-so-terrible-muriel-why-we-still-love-muriels-wedding-20-years-on-20141111–11k77s.html.

62 Quinn, 'Where's Muriel?'

63 Watts, 'Review: *Muriel's Wedding*.'

64 Lenny Ann Low, '*Muriel's Wedding The Musical* Brings Porpoise Spit to the Stage,' *The Sydney Morning Herald*, September 7, 2016, https://www.smh. com.au/entertainment/theatre/muriels-wedding-the-musical-20160905-gr8ybg.html.

65 Ben Neutze, 'The Search for the Great Australian Musical,' *Daily Review*, March 24, 2014, accessed November 4, 2021, https://dailyreview.com.au/the-search-for-the-great-australian-musical/.

66 Jason Blake, '*Strictly Ballroom The Musical* Sparkles but Falls Short,' *The Sydney Morning Herald*, April 13, 2014, https://www.smh.com.au/entertainment/musicals/strictly-ballroom-the-musical-sparkles-but-falls-short-20140413–36kxg.html. The one aspect that was almost universally praised was Eddie Perfect's musical contributions – so much so that after the original Sydney season, he was commissioned to write a brand-new opening number in an attempt to rescue the beleaguered production.

67 Keir Nuttall, *I'm With Muriel: Applying a Persona-Centred Songwriting Technique to the Creation of a New Australian Musical* (PhD diss., Queensland University of Technology, 2021), 22.

68 ABBA's music has layers of familiarity, not only because of the band's status as global supergroup, but because their music had been previously featured in both musical theatre and film. *Mamma Mia!*, described by Malcolm Womack as 'without hyperbole, the most successful musical in the world,' is a jukebox musical that weaves a narrative around ABBA's catalogue. Malcolm Womack, '"Thank You For the Music" Catherine Johnson's Feminist Revoicings in *Mamma Mia!*,' *Studies in Musical Theatre* 3, no. 2 (2009): 202, https://doi.org/10.1386/smt.3.2.201/1.

69 Jane Albert, 'Muriel's Not So Terrible After All,' *Broadsheet*, November 23, 2017, accessed June 30, 2025, https://www.broadsheet.com.au/sydney/entertainment/article/muriels-not-so-terrible-after-all.

70 John Severn, *Shakespeare as Jukebox Musical* (Routledge, 2019), 9. One of the jukebox musical's most strident opponents has been the American composer and lyricist Michael John LaChiusa, who argued that the familiarity of the existing music gives a jukebox musical a huge advantage in that audiences are able to enter the theatre already humming the tunes. Michael John LaChiusa, 'Open Season,' *Opera News* 79, no. 1 (2014), accessed August 18, 2022, https://www.operanews.com/Opera_News_Magazine/2014/8/Features/Open_Season.html.

71 Severn, *Shakespeare as Jukebox Musical*, 17.

72 Jason Blake, '*Muriel's Wedding* The Musical Review: Maggie McKenna's Dream Debut,' *The Sydney Morning Herald*, November 20, 2017, https://www.smh.com.au/entertainment/muriels-wedding-the-musical-review-maggie-mckennas-dream-debut-20171119-gzodmb.html.

73 Neutze, '*Muriel's Wedding* The Musical.' 'I'm not alone, I'm with Muriel,' is a famous line from the film and musical, marking the moment when Rhonda sticks up for Muriel on Hibiscus Island and at which the friendship of the women is cemented.

74 Jessica Carniel, 'Nation Branding, Cultural Relations and Cultural Diplomacy at Eurovision: Between Australia and Europe,' in *Eurovisions: Identity and the International Politics of the Eurovision Song Contest since 1956*, ed. Julie Kalman, Ben Wellings and Keshia Jacotine (Palgrave Macmillan, 2019), 160.

75 Jessica Carniel, '"It Really Makes You Feel Part of the World": Transnational Connection for Australian Eurovision Audiences,' in *Eurovision and Australia: Interdisciplinary Perspectives from down Under*, ed. Chris Hay and Jessica Carniel (Springer International, 2019), 213.

76 Carniel, '"It Really Makes You Feel,"' 213.

References

Albert, Jane. 'Muriel's Not So Terrible After All.' *Broadsheet*, November 23, 2017. Accessed June 30, 2025. https://www.broadsheet.com.au/sydney/entertainment/article/muriels-not-so-terrible-after-all.

Bailey, John. 'Strong Light and Colours Integral to Design of *Muriel's Wedding: The Musical.' The Sydney Morning Herald*, March 17, 2019. https://www.smh.com.au/entertainment/m16mcoverbox-20190308-h1c69z.html

Barlow, Helen. 'ABBA's Benny Andersson Reflects on Eurovision Win and the Credit He Still Gives to "Countdown."' *SBS Movies*, May 20, 2015. https://www.sbs.com.au/movies/article/2015/05/20/abbas-benny-andersson-reflects-eurovision-win-and-credit-he-still-gives-countdown.

Barr, Lindsey. '"Waving through a Window": Nostalgia and Prosthetic Memory in *Dear Evan Hansen.' Studies in Musical Theatre* 14, no. 3 (2020): 313–320. https://doi.org/10.1386/smt_00044_1.

Blake, Jason. '*Strictly Ballroom The Musical* Sparkles but Falls Short.' *The Sydney Morning Herald*, April 13, 2014. https://www.smh.com.au/entertainment/musicals/strictly-ballroom-the-musical-sparkles-but-falls-short-20140413-36kxg.html.

Blake, Jason. '*Muriel's Wedding* The Musical Review: Maggie McKenna's Dream Debut.' *The Sydney Morning Herald*, November 20, 2017. https://www.smh.com.au/entertainment/muriels-wedding-the-musical-review-maggie-mckennas-dream-debut-20171119-gzodmb.html.

Boltanski, Luc, and Eve Chiapello. *The New Spirit of Capitalism*. Verso, 2005.

Boucher, Leigh. '*Muriel's Wedding: The Musical* is a Deeply Satisfying Tribute to Australia's Most-Loved Dag.' *The Conversation*, November 23, 2017. https://theconversation.com/muriels-wedding-the-musical-is-a-deeply-satisfying-tribute-to-australias-most-loved-dag-87855.

Burke, Andrew. 'Michael Cassel and the High Risk Business of Musical Theatre.' *Australian Financial Review*, July 20, 2018. https://www.afr.com/life-and-luxury/arts-and-culture/michael-cassel-and-the-high-risk-business-of-musical-theatre-20180718-h12to4.

Carniel, Jessica. '"It Really Makes You Feel Part of the World": Transnational Connection for Australian Eurovision Audiences.' In *Eurovision and Australia: Interdisciplinary Perspectives from Down Under*, edited by Chris Hay and Jessica Carniel. Springer International, 2019.

Carniel, Jessica. 'Nation Branding, Cultural Relations and Cultural Diplomacy at Eurovision: Between Australia and Europe.' In *Eurovisions: Identity and the International Politics of the Eurovision Song Contest Since 1956*, edited by Julie Kalman, Ben Wellings and Keshia Jacotine. Palgrave Macmillan, 2019.

Champagne, John. 'Dancing Queen? Feminist and Gay Male Spectatorship in Three Recent Films from Australia.' *Film Criticism* 21, no. 3 (1997): 66–88. https://www.jstor.org/stable/44018887.

Chandler, Clare, and Simon Scheuber-Rush. '"Does Anybody Have a Map?": The Impact of "Virtual Broadway" on Musical Theater Composition.' *The Journal of Popular Culture* 54, no. 2 (2021): 276–300. https://doi.org/10.1111/jpcu.13013.

Clement, Olivia. '*Muriel's Wedding* Will Have Private Lab Reading in N.Y.C in 2020.' *Playbill.com*, December 27, 2019. Accessed May 7, 2021. https://www.playbill.com/article/muriels-wedding-to-receive-developmental-lab-in-nyc-in-2020.

Connell, John. *Sydney: The Emergence of a World City*. Oxford University Press, 2000.

Crockford, Toby. '"Beautiful One Day, Perfect the Next": Slogan Gets Second Wind for Comm Games Tourism Push.' *The Brisbane Times*, April 1, 2018. https://www.brisbanetimes.com.au/national/queensland/beautiful-one-day-perfect-the-next-slogan-gets-second-wind-for-comm-games-tourism-push-20180401-p4z7a3.html

Dedekorkut-Howes, Aysin, Caryl Bosman, and Andrew Leach, eds. *Off the Plan: The Urbanisation of the Gold Coast*. CSIRO Publishing, 2016.

Destination NSW. *Annual Report 2017–2018*. https://www.destinationnsw.com.au/about-us/annual-reports.

Doherty, Bethany. "'Tap, Tap, Tapping on the Glass": Generation Z, Social Media and *Dear Evan Hansen.*' *Arts* 9, no. 68 (2020). https://doi.org/10.3390/arts9020068.

Dow, Steve. 'How to Make the Australian Musical: From *The Sapphires* to *Strictly Ballroom.*' *The Guardian*, June 15, 2017. https://www.theguardian.com/stage/2017/jun/15/how-to-make-the-australian-musical-from-the-sapphires-to-strictly-ballroom.

'Exclusive: *Muriel's Wedding The Musical* Has Found its Muriel.' *Daily Review*, May 22, 2017. Accessed January 4, 2018. https://dailyreview.com.au/muriels-wedding-musical-found-muriel/60081/.

Goddard, Cliff. *Ethnopragmatics: Understanding Discourse in Cultural Context.* De Gruyter, 2006.

Greenberg, Miriam. *Branding New York: How a City in Crisis was Sold to the World.* Routledge, 2008.

Heasley, Adam. 'A Beautiful Slogan One Day . . . Gone the Next.' *Traveller.com.au*, September 11, 2010. https://www.traveller.com.au/a-beautiful-slogan-one-day-x2026-gone-the-next-1551j.

Hetrick, Adam. '*Muriel's Wedding* Musical Delays North American Premiere.' *Playbill.com*, September 26, 2017. Accessed June 30, 2025. https://www.playbill.com/article/muriels-wedding-musical-delays-north-american-premiere.

Hillman-Mccord, Jessica, ed. *iBroadway: Musical Theatre in the Digital Age.* Palgrave Macmillan, 2017.

Johns, Lindsay. 'Muriel's Wedding, Leicester Curve, Review: A Triumphant Adaptation of the Breezy Aussie Romcom.' *The Telegraph*, May 1, 2025. https://www.telegraph.co.uk/theatre/what-to-see/muriels-wedding-leicester-curve-review-abba/

Kohn, Martin. 'The Celluloid Source.' *Detroit Free Press*, March 17, 2002.

LaChiusa, Michael John. 'Open Season.' *Opera News* 79, no. 1 (2014). https://www.operanews.com/Opera_News_Magazine/2014/8/Features/Open_Season.html.

LetMe Entertain You – LMEYpodcast. "'Sydney," *Muriel's Wedding: The Musical* – Sydney Lyric Theatre, Media Call.' *YouTube*, July 4, 2019. Accessed June 30, 2025. https://www.youtube.com/watch?v=czxj-UEimvc.

Litson, Jo. 'Carmen Pavlovic: Yes, She Can-Can.' *Limelight*, July 26, 2021. https://limelightmagazine.com.au/features/carmen-pavlovic-yes-she-can-can/.

Low, Lenny Ann. '*Muriel's Wedding The Musical* Brings Porpoise Spit to the Stage.' *The Sydney Morning Herald*, September 7, 2016. https://www.smh.com.au/entertainment/theatre/muriels-wedding-the-musical-20160905-gr8ybg.html.

Lowenstein, Stephen. 'P.J. Hogan: *Muriel's Wedding.*' In *My First Movie: Twenty Celebrated Directors Talk about Their First Film.* New York: Pantheon Books, 2000.

Mackey, Jill. 'Subtext and Countertext in "Muriel's Wedding."' *NWSA Journal* 13, no. 1 (2001): 86–104. https://www.jstor.org/stable/4316784.

Markwell, Kevin. 'Mardi Gras Tourism and the Construction of Sydney as an International Gay and Lesbian City.' *GLQ* 8, no. 1–2 (2002): 81–99. https://muse.jhu.edu/article/12201.

Medhurst, Andy. 'But I'm Beautiful.' *Sight and Sound* 12, no. 7 (2002): 32–34.

Meldrum, Molly. 'The Eurovision Winner Takes It All.' *The Big Issue*, May 18, 2017, 5.

Miller-Heidke, Kate, and Keir Nuttall. *Muriel's Wedding: The Musical.* Sony Music, sound recording, 2018.

Munro, Rachael. *King Kong: A Music Theatre Event and the Dawn of the Megamovical.* Masters diss., University of Melbourne, 2017.

'Muriel's Wedding: The Musical.' *Westendtheatre.com.* Accessed June 30, 2025. https://www.westendtheatre.com/46946/shows-coming-soon/muriels-wedding-the-musical/

Neutze, Ben. 'The Search for the Great Australian Musical.' *Daily Review*, March 24, 2014. Accessed November 4, 2021. https://dailyreview.com.au/the-search-for-the-great-australian-musical/.

Neutze, Ben. 'Kate Miller-Heidke's "Muriel's Wedding" Musical to Premiere at Sydney Theatre Company.' *Daily Review*, September 8, 2016. Accessed May 19, 2021. https://dailyreview.com.au/kate-miller-heidkes-muriels-wedding-musical-premiere-sydney-theatre-company/.

Neutze, Ben. '*Muriel's Wedding* The Musical Review (Roslyn Packer Theatre).' *Daily Review*, November 19 2017. Accessed December 14, 2021. https://dailyreview.com.au/muriels-wedding-musical-review-roslyn-packer-theatre/.

Nuttall, Keir. *I'm With Muriel: Applying a Persona-Centred Songwriting Technique to the Creation of a New Australian Musical.* PhD diss., Queensland University of Technology, 2021.

Palmer, Kelly. 'Challenging the Beach as Paradise in Fiction and Memoir: The Gold Coast's Bathing Beauties.' In *Writing the Australian Beach: Local Site, Global Idea*, edited by Elizabeth Ellison and Donna Lee Brien. Springer International Publishing, 2020, 143–163.

Parmenter, Geoff. 'The City Branding of Sydney.' In *City Branding: Theory and Cases*, edited by Keith Dinnie. Palgrave Macmillan, 2011.

Quinn, Karl. 'Where's Muriel? P.J. Hogan on the Agony of Casting Australia's Daggiest Bride, Again.' *The Sydney Morning Herald*, September 10, 2018. https://www.smh.com.au/entertainment/musicals/muriel-and-me-pj-hogans-journey-with-australias-daggiest-bride-20180907-h152vy.html.

Rush, Adam. '#YouWillBeFound: Participatory Fandom, Social Media Marketing and *Dear Evan Hansen*.' *Studies in Musical Theatre* 15, no. 2 (2021): 119–132. https://doi.org/10.1386/smt_00063_1.

Savran, David. 'Trafficking in Transnational Brands: The New "Broadway-Style" Musical.' *Theatre Survey* 55, no. 3 (2014): 318–342. https://doi.org/10.1017/S0040557414000337.

Savran, David. 'Broadway as Global Brand.' *Journal of Drama in English* 5, no. 1 (2017): 24–37. https://doi.org/10.1515/jcde-2017-0003.

Savran, David. *Tell it to the World: The Broadway Musical Abroad.* Oxford University Press, 2024.

Sebesta, Judith. 'From Celluloid to Stage: The "Movical," *The Producers*, and the Postmodern.' *Theatre Annual* 56 (2003): 97–112.

Severn, John. *Shakespeare as Jukebox Musical.* Routledge, 2019.

Sternfeld, Jessica. *The Megamusical.* Indiana University Press, 2006.

'Sydney to Host World Premiere of *Muriel's Wedding: The Musical.*' *Destination NSW*, September 9, 2016. Accessed May 5, 2021. https://www.destinationnsw.com.au/news-and-media/media-releases/sydney-host-world-premiere-muriels-wedding-musical.

Urry, John, and Jonas Larsen. *The Tourist Gaze 3.0.* Sage Publications, 2011.

Watts, Richard. 'Review: *Muriel's Wedding The Musical*, Her Majesty's Theatre.' *ArtsHub*, April 2, 2019. https://www.artshub.com.au/news/reviews/review-muriels-wedding-the-musical-her-majestys-theatre-257652-2362740/.

Wilson, Jake. 'You're Not So Terrible Muriel: Why We Still Love *Muriel's Wedding*, 20 Years On.' *The Sydney Morning Herald*, November 14, 2014. https://www.smh.com.au/entertainment/movies/youre-not-so-terrible-muriel-why-we-still-love-muriels-wedding-20-years-on-20141111-11k77s.html.

Winchester, Hilary, Pauline McGuirk, and Kathryn Everett. 'Schoolies Week as a Rite of Passage: A Study of Celebration and Control.' In *Embodied Geographies: Space Bodies and Rites of Passage*, edited by Elizabeth Kenworthy Teather. Routledge, 1999.

Wollman, Elizabeth. 'How to Dismantle a [Theatric] Bomb: Broadway Flops, Broadway Money, and Musical Theater Historiography.' *Arts* 9, no. 66 (2020): 1–13. https://doi.org/10.3390/arts9020066.

Womack, Malcolm. '"Thank You For the Music" Catherine Johnson's Feminist Revoicings in *Mamma Mia!*' *Studies in Musical Theatre* 3, no. 2 (2009): 201–211. https://doi.org/10.1386/smt.3.2.201/1.

Wright, Maryann. 'Australia Beats Broadway to Host World Premieres of Up-And-Coming Musical Classics.' *News.com.au*, September 23, 2011. https://www.news.com.au/entertainment/music/australia-beats-broadway-to-host-world-premieres-of-up-and-coming-musical-classics/news-story/0874c65342bd60648e0de178395964bb?sv=38d13dfecd86950cd48a9eecfa837b2c.

2

SPORT, MASCULINITY, AND NATION IN *SHANE WARNE: THE MUSICAL*

In 2012, a three-part television documentary entitled *Sporting Nation* aired on the ABC, the national broadcaster. Narrated by the late satirist and lover of sports John Clarke, its opening remarks encapsulated Australia's deep sense of itself as sports mad. 'It is a truth universally acknowledged,' Clarke espoused, 'that Australia is a sporting nation. In Australia, in order to be a properly accredited member of society, with human rights and so on, you've got to either play sport or watch sport. Ask anyone. Australians love sport.'[1] While there are good reasons to question the simplicity of such a proposition, sport remains one of the pre-eminent contexts in which, as Catriona Elder notes, 'Australian-ness is produced and marketed.'[2] Eddie Perfect's *Shane Warne: The Musical* (2008/2013) is a work that actively engages with the notion of Australia as a sporting nation. It stages the life of the legendary late Australian cricketer Shane Warne.[3] Warne's achievements as a spin bowler, according to Gideon Haigh, rendered him our 'best-known sportsman; perhaps even the most recognised Australian.'[4] At the same time, Warne was also a polarising figure, one who stayed in the spotlight long after retiring from the game, and who continued to make news headlines until his unexpected death at the age of 52 on 4 March 2022 in Thailand, reportedly of a heart attack. His death prompted an outpouring of national grief, with the Great Southern Stand at the Melbourne Cricket Ground renamed the SK Warne Stand as a tribute to his cricket career.

In a feature about the musical televised on *The 7.30 Report* Perfect characterised the work as a 'very Australian hero story because we like our heroes chipped and a bit tarnished and not perfect.'[5] Rebecca Harkins-Cross' review described the production as exhibiting an 'irreverence' that 'particularly appeals to our sensibility,' asserting that it was 'difficult to imagine any other country' making a musical about such a figure.[6] Neil Armfield, the director,

DOI: 10.4324/9781003590088-3

made a similar remark when he described the musical as being 'actually about something very specific in the Australian character.'[7] This chapter accounts for and interrogates these observations by analysing the way in which the musical produces and reproduces the repertory of the national imaginary.

Shane Warne interrogates 'who we are' by staging the interplay between nation, sport, and masculinity in the national imaginary. I do so by outlining the centrality of sport to Australian culture and then exploring the ways in which sporting heroes like Warne are figured as emblematic of the nation. The chapter then demonstrates how Warne embodies a sequence of Australian male archetypes. He begins the narrative as an underdog, transforms into a maverick anti-authoritarian who refuses to be tamed by rigid institutions, and then falls victim to the so-called tall poppy syndrome. Following this, I analyse the 'mateship' evident in the relationships between the male characters, as well as the extratextual manifestation of mateship in the relationship that developed between Perfect and Warne. The musical's approach to humour, 'taking the piss,' is considered in this light. Finally, the chapter explores the often-antagonistic relationship between art and sport in Australian society, arguing that what Perfect attempts in *Shane Warne* is a levelling of the divide between art and sport. I argue that the musical seeks to unify these apparently opposite cultural spheres, using dramatic expression to convey the significance of sport to the national imaginary.

The version of Australia into which Warne's life and career provides a window is one that is male dominated. This is unsurprising, since sport in Australia has typically been characterised as a male domain, one that operates as a 'major means through which ascendant forms of masculinity are asserted, promoted, tested and defended.'[8] While there are female characters in *Shane Warne*, they conform to recognisable archetypes associated with secondary characters: the mother, the wife, and the whore, as Fiona Scott-Norman observed.[9] The musical was criticised for its perceived maltreatment of Warne's ex-wife, Simone Callaghan. While Rosemarie Harris, who played Callaghan in the 2008 production, was at pains to assure audiences that she would be treated kindly by the production, for many reviewers these admirable intentions were ultimately in vain. While Jason Blake commended Harris for her attempt to '[invest] Simone with considerable dignity,' he criticised the script for presenting her 'as a bit of a dingbat.'[10] Warne's mother, Brigitte, is similarly not given much depth or stage time. The focus in *Shane Warne* is squarely on the experiences of men and the bonds between them, and the forthcoming analysis proceeds on this basis.

From Cricket Pitch to Stage

The idea for a musical about Warne was originally conceived in jest. In 2005, Perfect was on tour performing in *The Big Con* with the comedian Max Gillies and kept seeing Shane Warne's name all over the newspapers. He made an offhand comment in a phone call to his manager, Michael Lynch, that someone should write a musical about Warne, and, to his great surprise, Lynch (a great cricket fan) encouraged him to pursue such a project.[11] It was, from the outset, an auteur project, with Perfect composing music, lyrics, and book and also performing the titular role. It had an unofficial première at the 2007 Adelaide Cabaret Festival, where a work-in-progress version of the show was presented. The following year, a short segment was performed at the Melbourne International Comedy Festival.[12] A full production opened in Melbourne at the Athenaeum Theatre on 10 December 2008, and in 2009 the production went on tour, playing seasons at the Regal Theatre in Perth and the Enmore Theatre in Sydney.

While *Shane Warne* was well reviewed by critics and won several awards, the production did not perform as well as expected at the box office. It had a successful five-month season in Melbourne, but when the production transferred to Sydney, it played for just two-and-a-half weeks, not the three months that it had been slated to run.[13] It was, in Perfect's words, a 'commercial flop,' one where 'everybody who invested . . . lost their money. I invested three years of my life on it, so I lost money in that respect, too.'[14] However upon reflection some years later he stated that he was pleasantly surprised by the strength of the work. As a result, *Shane Warne* received a second life when in 2013 the work was revised and presented in a revamped concert version at Hamer Hall, Melbourne, directed by Simon Phillips. The revised production featured a twenty-four-piece orchestra, markedly larger than the original four-piece band, and was conducted and orchestrated by Iain Grandage. This iteration added new material covering Warne's retirement from international cricket, his dramatic weight loss, and his high-profile relationship with the actress Elizabeth Hurley. The latter half of the work underwent major revisions, resulting in a 'new beginning and new ending, new scenes and new structure, four new songs and new characters.'[15]

The musical is a generally faithful treatment of Warne's biography. It opens with Warne as a teenager, struggling to realise his ambition to be a professional AFL player. AFL, a code of Australian rules football, is played throughout the nation but particularly popular in Warne's home state of Victoria. A fast rock number, entitled 'Run,' recounts the failure of this venture and Warne's time spent in menial jobs like delivering pizza before he was accepted into the Australian Institute of Cricket in Adelaide. It is here that we meet future teammate and friend, Michael Slater, and his coach, Terry Jenner, whom Warne credited for his transformation from undisciplined young man to a formidable athlete who eventually made his test cricket debut against India in 1992, the same year that he met his first wife, Simone. The plot builds towards the match that made Warne famous throughout the world: the 1993 Ashes match at Old Trafford in which he bowled a leg-break that was immediately dubbed 'the ball of the century.' The next scene dramatises the moment Shane and Simone met (at a celebrity golf tournament, where she was promoting Foster's beer) and eventually transforms into a staging of their wedding. The song's tongue-in-cheek title, 'Dancing with the Stars,' foreshadows Simone's stint some years later on the reality television programme of the same name. From here, things start to unravel for Warne, both personally and professionally, with the R&B styled 'The Away Game' staging Warne and his teammates drinking and womanising in a club (and generally behaving badly) after a big win in India. Act One concludes with one of his most notorious scandals, when Warne and fellow teammate Mark Waugh accepted an offer from an Indian bookmaker, known only as John, to provide information about the pitch and weather for cash. This Bollywood number, 'My Name Is John,' provides a jubilant climax for the end of the act.

In Act Two, the scandals continue to mount. 'What an S.M(ess)S I'm In,' set in a supermarket, satirises Warne's repeated extramarital affairs. The first of these was with a British nurse named Donna Wright, for which he was removed as Vice-Captain of the Australian Cricket Team. The scandal, which involved lewd phone calls and text-messages, is narrated in a short number sung by the character of Wright immediately afterwards. This is then followed by a right of reply for Simone, a short ballad entitled 'Is the Sun the Moon?' After his career suffers because of his infidelity (and other scandals), Warne objects to the condition of modern celebrity and the way that personal and professional lives have been collapsed. In the Motown-inspired 'Shine Like Shane,' Warne defends himself against his detractors, refusing to apologise for his actions. Yet, shortly after, the musical acknowledges that he will also benefit from his notoriety. Following his announcement about his impending retirement from international cricket is the number 'Spin Spin Spin,' which recounts what happens next. While Warne's sporting career might be ending, his career as a celebrity will continue.[16] The title uses the dual meaning of 'spin' to draw a parallel between Warne's career as one of cricket's greatest spin bowlers and the way that he was always focused on how to wrest control of the media narrative – the 'spin.' The show ends with a short, slow playout tacked onto the end of 'Dancing with the Stars,' where Warne sings:

> There's nothing left to prove
> Just enjoy the lovely view
> It's such a lovely view

This ending expands on the argument made in 'Shine Like Shane' that, however one might feel about Warne, he has earned his place as a national sporting icon.

Sporting Nation

Cricket was the first team sport played in the Australian colonies by British settlers, which leads historian Bill Mandle to suggest that it was as key to the cultivation of a sense of national identity as the motifs of the bush, the goldfields, or the city.[17] A striking feature of the history of the sport is that from 1877 national teams were playing matches, which gave the appearance of a unified nation prior to Federation in 1901.[18] This, for Brett Hutchins, explains how cricket earned the mantle of the national game (in comparison with state-based varieties of football). Cricket, he states, has 'consistently announced Australia as an independent and successful country to the world, or at least the Empire,' and the sport and its players 'create the vision of a glorious history and a unified and triumphant nation.'[19]

The association between cricket and nation continued after Federation and into the present. Australia's inaugural Prime Minister, Sir Edmund Barton, enjoyed umpiring a cricket match, and as Elizabeth Bernays observes, 'most of his successors have shared his passion for the game.'[20] Former Prime Minister Sir Robert Menzies in particular was saw himself 'as the nation's leading spectator-sportsman.'[21] More recently, Former Prime Minister John Howard (who modelled himself on Menzies, and who was in power for a large part of Warne's career) publicly stated that he held cricket in high regard and that he viewed being 'captain of the Australian cricket team as the absolute pinnacle of sporting achievement and really the pinnacle of human achievement almost, in Australia.'[22] The Howard government held the view that knowledge of cricket was so important that when it introduced a citizenship test in 2007, one of the sample questions provided on the website asked migrants to name Australia's greatest cricketer from the 1930s: the answer to which was Sir Donald Bradman. A batsman so revered that he had a knighthood bestowed upon him in 1945, Bradman embodied the vision cricket espoused above and, according to Hutchins, became 'idealised as the human character of Australian nationhood.'[23]

The extent to which greatness on the sporting field is valued highlights the eminence of the sporting celebrity in Australian society. Richard Cashman argues that the sportsman is as potent a figure in the national imaginary as the bushman, the bushranger, and the soldier.[24] In contemporary Australian society, sports personalities play a cultural role that extends far beyond their performance on the field. They are perceived as national ambassadors (a term that invokes the language of diplomacy) and as role models. The sporting hero, as Gill Lines notes, is supposed to '[epitomise] social ideals and masculine virtues,' with the hope that the values they display 'on the playing fields will readily transfer into everyday life.'[25] Consequently, more stringent standards of behaviour apply to sporting heroes than to other celebrities. Scrutiny of their lives is seen as relevant to the public interest, and their achievements and indiscretions alike reflect upon the nation as a whole.

Lofty ideals like virtue, purity, and public decorum are particularly present in the discourse around cricket, which is often characterised as a gentlemen's game, associated with style, grace under pressure, sportsmanship, courage, and good temperament. Douglas MacQueen-Thomson evocatively expressed the moral dimension of cricket when he remarked that it is a sport particularly conducive to the creation of heroes as it is

> often characterised as pure, driven by principles of fairness and honour. 'It's just not cricket' implies far more than simple adherence to the rules. Instead, it suggests acting within an unarticulated code of decency and proper behaviour. It is as though the game (as opposed to the known lives of the players) takes place in a more rarefied sphere which is incorrupt, almost sanctified. Dressed in pristine white, the players could possibly be mistaken for participants in some peculiar national religious ritual.[26]

'It's just not cricket,' the phrase invoked here, is an oft-cited idiom that embodies the importance of good conduct and a strong sense of morality and fairness to the game.[27] While this 'myth of purity' is not, as MacQueen-Thomson acknowledges, 'historically grounded,' it persists nonetheless.[28]

In the opening number of the musical, 'The Tale of Warne,' Perfect proposes that it is Warne's failure to live up to these ideals that has made him such a captivating figure. As the earlier plot synopsis illustrates, Warne had been implicated in scandals over the course of his career: accepting bribes, failing drug tests, numerous instances of infidelity, sexual indiscretions, and so forth and, as such, problematises the 'myth of purity.' 'The Tale of Warne' articulates the contradiction between Warne as, on one hand, lionised national sporting hero and, on the other, disappointingly fallible human being. The lyrics begin with an unequivocal statement of Warne as an 'all-Australian hero,' one who 'held the hopes of a nation in the palm of his right hand.' But while the first verse praises him for his sporting prowess ('he slayed the Poms'), it balances this with a caveat ('although he smoked and carried several extra kilos') recognising that it is not only Warne's behaviour that renders him an unlikely hero but that he also does not look like a professional sportsman ought to. Far from the image of a lithe, lean, sculpted athlete, Warne was stocky and renowned for his drinking, smoking, and poor eating habits; yet this seemed to have little effect on his extraordinary ability to bowl. The music interprets these contradictions through two distinct idioms. The number begins with some stately fanfare-style orchestral material in C minor, featuring a fast semiquaver string ostinato and long brass tones, its instrumentation and the texture resembling the 'Wide World of Sports' theme music for cricket which played on Australian television station Channel Nine.[29] However, after twelve bars, the music abruptly changes to a funky, syncopated electric guitar riff that underpins the first verse. When these two styles coalesce, in the latter half of the song, the music reinforces that Warne is both heroic and 'just a guy.'[30]

The way the musical tussles with these two sides of Warne mirrors a tension in the Australian national imaginary, where the nation's convict past is privileged, thereby casting the descendants of settlers as continuing the proud tradition of anti-authoritarianism. In reality, as journalist Waleed Aly argues, 'the mythology of the carefree larrikin, thoroughly informal in manners and sceptical of power' reflects 'the Australia of Ned Kelly and Waltzing Matilda, which captures much of how we talk about ourselves, but very little of how we actually behave.'[31] Aly argues that Australians are in actuality, extremely deferent to authority. Warne, in this sense, practised what he preached and, thereby, presents a captivating figure, a living, breathing manifestation of what the nation tells itself it is all about.

National Characters

In the musical, Warne embodies a cast of archetypal characters from the repertory of the national imaginary: battler, underdog, everyman, anti-authoritarian rebel, and tall poppy. These figures are mobilised frequently in Australian cultural life, advertising, and media. Warne's life provides fertile ground for examination of these characters because he embodied so many of them over its course.

The first character embodied by Warne is the underdog, a term that has its origins in the convict experience and that describes a figure who is not expected to triumph due to not having the advantages of their competitor (a 'top dog').[32] 'Run,' a fast rock number sung by Warne, establishes Warne's status as such. The lyrics of the first verse portray him as a no-hoper for whom life is not going as planned, detailing his failed attempt at an AFL career by referring to Warne's time playing for the St Kilda Saints: 'Would you take a look at me, Saints jumper number twenty-three.' The coach is 'going mental in the stands' because Warne cannot run fast enough to catch his opponent. In the chorus, Warne and the coach, Gary Colling, sing in harmony:

> Run! Put your head down Shane and
> Run! Pull your finger out and
> Run! Or you're never gonna make it

Eventually Warne concedes that 'I didn't make it.' He takes a menial job delivering pizzas, where he similarly is cajoled to 'run' by another authority figure, the manager: 'take the pizza Shane and run, get your arse in gear and run, or you're never gonna make it.' As in the opening, the members of the chorus function as fellow citizens: they shift from AFL players to Pizza Hut employees, to commentators who write him off. In the final chorus, as he laments his plight, these citizens sing in harmony with him. Warne opines 'what a loser I've become, boy I thought that I would make it,' with the chorus exchanging his 'I' for the third person pronoun 'he.'

Warne continues to play the role of underdog even after he is accepted into the Australian Cricket Academy. His aversion to authority is seen in his interactions with coaches, about whom he was 'famously dismissive.'[33] The song 'AIS,' which stages his arrival at the Academy, establishes the rigid training environment against which Warne would rebel and ultimately triumph.[34] 'AIS,' which is performed by the character of Jack Potter, a coach at the institute, and a chorus of other cricket players, situates the institution as a hierarchical, masculine domain. In the first verse, Potter lays down the law, addressing the young men with 'Morning ladies,' indicating that through their training at the institution, they will *become* men, endowed with the particularly masculine qualities necessary for careers as sports star. Potter continues by denigrating the young men, characterising them as 'recruits' – engendering a comparison with another highly masculinised setting, the armed forces – and continuing on to tell them that 'you little shits are not yet fit to lick my boot.' The hierarchy is reinforced when he threatens them with corporal punishment if they do not behave as they should: 'Gonna work you hard, I won't spare the rod, You can call me sir, but I prefer you call me God!' All this is reinforced by the music, which is composed in a 1980s electro idiom, with an unrelenting electronic drumbeat, and featuring synthesisers. The verse utilises a repetitive eight bar chord progression that varies very little, further emphasising the inflexibility of the training institute. Later in the song, Potter counsels the new recruits that no bad behaviour will be accepted. He treats all the aspiring cricketers with contempt but singles out Warne, sensing that he may not be as compliant as some of the others. Rebelling will not pay dividends, and submission is the only strategy: 'So fall in line, Show us your form, Put in or piss off, and that includes you Warne.'

Warne's antipathy towards authority figures aligns him with national heroes like the bushranger Ned Kelly, who is the prime representative of the anti-authoritarian spirit that suffuses the national imaginary. The spirit of Ned Kelly is explicitly invoked in the song 'Hollywood,' which is set just prior to Warne bowling of the ball of the century. In this power ballad in the style of Jon Bon Jovi, Perfect sings with a deep and resonant tone timbre, and with a low tessitura, Warne bucks himself up with the opening lines:

Oh did Ned Kelly back down at Glenrowan?
Go run and hide just so he could fight another day?
No he simply said, 'No drama. I'll just make some kick ass armour.'
And he blew those coppers away.

Perfect likened Warne to Kelly when he commented in a newspaper interview that he was 'a maverick in a stuffy gentleman's game. He changed the way the game was played and had that larrikin, anti-authoritarian character that Aussies love. Like all our heroes from Ned Kelly on he had chips and flaws and said "fuck you" to authority.'[35] Warne's identification with the outlaw is vindicated when his unconventional approach to bowling results in such a triumphant victory.

Warne's appeal as an 'iconic Australian Everyman' (as described by Neil Armfield) or 'every-bloke' (to borrow Christine Beasley's turn of phrase) is explored in the number 'Payin' Attention Now.'[36] The joyous gospel-inspired number that immediately segues from 'That Ball' (the musical's homage to the infamous bowl) charts the intense media coverage that he received afterwards ('You couldn't open up a single publication without finding Warney on ev'ry page'); the sponsorship deals he was offered ('Just Jeans and Nike, Oakley sunnies and fifty grand to drink Powerade'); and the profound impact that his particular style of bowling had on the game ('And soon ev'ry little nipper was bowling googlies and flippers'). The song pitches Warne as just like you or me: 'We all put our pants on each day the same way,' as the lyrics say. In the middle section, Warne's manager, Tony, is contemplating how to pitch him to advertisers and the public, saying that 'we can't just stick a can of beer or zinc cream in his hand,' but that 'we need to try to qualify the essence of his brand.' In the bridge section, he continues by saying

> Sure, the kid's got skill and talent
> Sure, the boy's got fame
> Sure, he's got a million women calling out his name
> But still, he's a suburban boy
> Yes deep down we're the same
> Take away my P.H.D.
> Warney's just the same as me

The music changes and becomes more swing than gospel for eight bars as Tony searches for a phrase that encapsulates what he is looking for. He finally arrives at 'Ev'ryone's a little bit like Shane,' a phrase that encapsulates that Warne's real strength, cricketing aside, is his relatability, his ordinariness, the sense that if he has been able to achieve this level of fame, anyone can. Reviewer Jason Blake recounted that at the performance Warne himself attended, before the show started, the Emerson, Lake, and Palmer version of Aaron Copland's *Fanfare for the Common Man* played in the auditorium – a paratextual feature that underscores this point.[37]

In reality, though, Warne's appeal is to a very specific segment of Australian society: the white, working-class man. In the song, Warne is described as a 'suburban boy,' one who has to 'fight to rise above' the fray, a line which conjures images of the Aussie battler. What 'everyone' eats are 'pies and chips,' quintessentially Anglo-Australian food, and the title of the song is, as the lyrics say, 'perfect slogan for the cashed-up bogan.'[38] If you're 'a loner from Altona with no diploma' (someone without higher education from the outer fringes of a major city), you should 'try to be a little bit like Shane.' In this section of the song, the ensemble echoes Tony in a call-and-response fashion, like a jubilant gospel choir exalting their saviour. From this point, every repetition of the refrain moves up a key by semitone, heightening the euphoric, celebratory aspect of the number.

Later in the work, as his career progresses and things start to spiral out of control, the media and the public start to turn against him, and Warne is forced to make the transition from rebel underdog to tall poppy: an term rooted in the notion of Australian egalitarianism that describes person who has achieved great success in their field, but who is perceived to have let said success go to their head, and is subsequently attacked and criticised.[39] In 'Shine Like Shane,' a Motown-inspired number, Warne chastises the public for what he views as fickleness: 'You all want vanilla, would another flavour kill ya? Or is boring old conformity the rage?' He describes himself as a 'tall poppy' in the bridge section, which has a half-time feel:

Yes success has cost me
I'm just another lopped tall poppy
That's what they do when you're an Aussie
Someone chops you down to size

Here he draws attention to the redressive element of Australian culture, that once someone is perceived to have gone above their station in life, or transgressed cultural norms, the people need to cut them down again. Warne refuses to accept this and instead continues to celebrate his life and career, reinforcing his status as a man unwilling to submit. He reserves the right to dictate the terms of his career and his public profile, reflecting an antagonism to institutional authority that is deeply embedded in the national imaginary.

Taking the Piss

If engagement with sport is a pre-requisite for inclusion in the imagined community that is Australia, then 'using and appreciating (or at least tolerating) humour' is a close second.[40] The musical takes an approach to humour known as 'taking the piss,' a quintessentially Australian phrase that refers to the act of sending someone up. It thrives in male homosocial contexts, like the pub, and in male homosocial dynamics, like sporting teams and clubs. Jessica Milner Davis notes that its underpinnings are egalitarian, as it is traditionally performed 'without retribution, or offence being taken, whether victims are friends or strangers, equals or superior.'[41]

'Taking the piss,' rather than out-and-out hero worship, is the *modus operandi* for the humour in *Shane Warne*. Greg Baum, describing the production, states that it 'not so much satirises Warne as takes the piss out of him, in the great Australian tradition. It is genuinely clever, genuinely funny, genuinely affectionate and too madcap to cause more than passing offence.'[42] Harkins-Cross also uses this same phrasing in her review, observing 'an abiding affection [for Warne] behind all the piss-taking, and that's why it works so well: for every barb about Warnie's weight problems, hedonism and mobile phone misdemeanours, there's a real reverence for the cricketer's innate talent and larger-than-life personality.'[43] While the musical evinces empathy and respect for Warne, Perfect does not shy away from presenting all aspects of Warne's life and career. While he describes his position as 'fairly firmly in the Warne camp,' he states that *Shane Warne* is more homage than hagiography.[44] It is even evident in the approach to the composition of the music, which pairs anachronistic musical genres with unlikely subject matter, such the R&B styled 'The Away Game,' which casts Warne as a smooth, slick operator who croons as he pursues women while on tour, or the gospel 'We're Going There' (to be discussed forthwith).

Shane Warne also stages the antisocial dimensions of 'taking the piss,' drawing attention to its reliance on male bravado and a group-think mentality. The song 'We Never Cross the Line,' which begins as a rousing oom-pah number in 4/4 time, sends up the bad behaviour of sports teams that occurs with regrettable frequency. A chorus of men bellow that 'We never cross the line, calling somebody a maggot or a filthy faggot is fine' and that 'isolating weakness is a skill that must be honed.' This reflects what Milner Davis describes as the 'aggressively normative and socialising function' of taking the piss, and its coercive properties.[45] The men acknowledge that it might '[seem] inappropriate but calling someone's Mum a slut is in the spirit of the game.' They abdicate responsibility for the effects of their actions by asserting that 'if the spineless prick can't take it, that's no fault of mine' and reiterate that 'we never cross the line.' The lyrics at the end of the song, a comic list of rhyming words, subtly indicates that this may not be the most noble course of action, or perhaps even that amusing: 'But we never, hardly ever, rarely only barely maybe if it's clever, mostly, seventy percent of the time, we never cross the line.'

The lyrics of 'We Never Cross the Line' are very crude, recalling that 'taking the piss' delights in flouting 'civilised conventions on obscenity and filth.'[46] Apt examples are 'when you hit that pitch we're gonna give you shit about ev'ry bitch you've boned,' 'it seems inappropriate but calling someone's Mum a slut is in the spirit of the game,' and 'try saying "your wife seemed well but it was hard to tell cos she was sucking on my cock!"' While Perfect takes advantage of 'taking the piss' throughout the musical, this song is demonstrative of Perfect's understanding of the way this form of Australian humour is mobilised within the male homosocial setting known as mateship.

Mateship

As a counterpoint to the noxious male camaraderie detailed above, *Shane Warne* explores male relationships defined by care, tenderness, and encouragement. In Australian parlance, as Nick Dyrenfurth writes, mateship refers to the 'bonds of loyalty and equality, and feelings of solidarity and fraternity that Australians, usually men, are typically alleged to exhibit.'[47] Dyrenfurth notes that while many nations hold notions about male brotherhood or solidarity, '[o]nly in Australia is mateship regarded as the lynchpin of the national character.'[48]

In the song 'We're Going There,' sport acts as an important catalyst for mateship and male bonding, as well as a marker of citizenship. Warne and his teammates are in the middle of a training session when he abruptly ceases completing his drills. 'Screw this,' he says, announcing he is leaving to go and watch the Saints play Hawthorn at the pub. One of his teammates says, 'You can't do that. Coach'll kill you,' to which Warne replies, 'he's not here, is he? Come on. . . .' The comic song that ensues frames the transgression humorously, summoning narratives of convicts breaking free of oppressive colonial masters. While the football game (the sport) is the catalyst, the pub, and more importantly, beer, is the lubricant for these male relationships. In the song, an impassioned Warne asks his teammates to imagine what they will find if they leave with him: 'Can you see it? In the distance?' he asks, 'Liquid amber, rich and rare.' This elevated description of beer as 'rich and rare,' quoting the grandiloquent language of the Australian national anthem, foregrounds the metonymy of the drink to the nation. In a later verse, this connection is made more explicit: 'You're Australian,' he says, 'you deserve it,' suggesting that drinking beer is a citizen's birth right.

'We're Going There' frames the experience of watching sport with one's mates, beer in hand, as a spiritual experience (Figure 2.1). 'Though they oppress us,' Warne sings, 'there is salvation, and it's beer, beautiful beer.' The mention of 'salvation' recalls Varda Burstyn's observation that sport is a kind of secular sacrament, one that approximates 'the experience of religion more than any other form of human cultural practice.'[49] Beer drinking too has been conceived of as such by writers like Cyril Pearl, who declared in 1969 that beer was a 'religion in Australia.'[50] In 'We're Going There,' 'heaven' is the pub and 'salvation' is located in what Wenner and Jackson refer to as the 'holy trinity'[51] of sport, beer, and male bonding. Musically, the song is a cross between a national anthem and a church hymn or spiritual, with Perfect's ostentatious riffing calling to mind the over-embellished versions of the 'Star-Spangled Banner' often heard at American football games. As the number progresses, Warne assumes the role of prophet: 'Follow me,' he freely riffs as the song builds to a climax. Such are his powers of persuasion that from this point (after the requisite exultant key change from B-flat major up a tone to C major) he is joined in song by the other men, who have been moved to sing by his oratory.

FIGURE 2.1   The cast of *Shane Warne: The Musical* performing 'We're Going There.'
Photo: Meredith O'Shea ©

The end of the song draws all these threads – sport, male bonding, beer, and citizenship – together. The ensemble are an exalted version of what Catherine Palmer and Kirrily Thompson term the 'grog squad.'[52] The men, first singing in unison, then splitting into harmony in three parts, conclude that 'man's purpose' is to 'stand man to man with a beer in his hand, watching the game on a muted TV.' The importance of this phrase is emphasised by the music through the introduction of triplets and an altered time signature, as well as emphatic chords that punctuate the acapella harmonies. 'We're Going There' elevates the ordinarily rowdy, uncouth, inelegant practice of men drinking and watching sport in the pub together and, through religious and political allusions to heaven, the national anthem, and salvation, casts it as a civic ceremony of national allegiance and mateship.

The most meaningful relationship of mateship represented in the musical is that between Warne and his coach, Terry Jenner, played by Shane Jacobson. Jenner and Warne met at the Australian Academy of Sport in 1990, the same year that Jenner was released from prison, where he had served a term stealing funds from his employer to pay a gambling debt. His association with Warne reinvigorated his career, and their friendship was maintained over the years via long telephone calls, with Warne describing him as 'my Dr Phil on all matters and levels – wherever I was around the world we would call and chat.'[53] When Jenner passed away in April 2011, Warne wrote that 'Cricket has lost a true character and champion – the world is a lesser place without Terrence James Jenner! Mate, I will miss you so much.'[54]

In the musical, Jenner is afforded two solo numbers that demonstrate the depth of his relationship with Warne. In 'Piss It All Away,' a simple G major ballad in Broadway style reminiscent of a Jerry Herman song like 'I Won't Send Roses' from *Mack and Mabel*, Jenner implores Warne not to make the same foolish mistakes that he did. The lyrics, which begin using third person address, establish a commonality between himself and Warne: 'Long ago, too long ago, a fella like yourself, had it all, could turn the ball, but never half as well.' The simple melody, rhythmically constructed to closely mimic the rhythm of speech, contains hints of melancholy chromaticism and a gentle rubato as he laments his arrogance and inability to stop himself from making a costly mistake. Warne's talent has given him hope where he thought there was none. Speaking about himself in the third person, he sings: 'Thought that prison had crushed his soul, but it came back when he saw you bowl.' In the final verse, as the music swells, Perfect creates a sense of immediacy by switching the address to first person. Jenner turns the tables onto Warne, imploring him not to waste his talent:

Well I guess what I'm trying to say
Is if you wanna piss your life away
You're fucking crazy if you think I'll stay
And watch you make all of the same mistakes
I won't watch while you piss it all away

The song is a testament to the importance of male bonding. Through their shared experience of being somewhat outsiders, Jenner's counsel has the potential to really make an impact on Warne. This is seen at end of the song, where in the space created by the fermata on the final chord of the song Jenner suddenly speaks rather than sings – 'Now go home Shane and do the fucking work' – before the button note brings the song to its conclusion. This abrupt switch to spoken, forthright dialogue has the effect of jolting Warne into action. In the next scene, Jenner receives a phone call from Warne's mum, Brigitte, where she tells him 'whatever you said, it worked. He's jogging. Shane is actually jogging.' The musical then segues to a fitness montage, which shows Warne taking himself seriously, putting in the hard work and applying himself to his training regime. The latter part of this montage includes a reprise of 'Run,' reconfigured to demonstrate Warne's successful acceptance into the Australian cricket team. This sequence of events reinforces the power and importance of the mateship provided by a male mentor, in the sense that Jenner was able to achieve what Warne's mother had been unable to accomplish.

Jenner's second song, 'Pick Up Shane,' stages a tender moment when he offers Warne emotional support after a personal and professional disappointment. Like

'Piss It All Away,' it is a conventional Broadway ballad with an ABA structure and an orchestration that features strings. In a YouTube clip promoting the 2013 production, Perfect recounted how he was taken with the anecdote that Warne gifted Jenner a bottle of red wine when he graduated from the cricket academy. Jenner had the idea that he would not drink it immediately, but that he would save it until the pair had something special to celebrate.[55] In 1999, after returning to cricket too soon after shoulder surgery, Warne was dropped from the Australian team for the first and only time in his career. Jenner took the bottle of wine and flew to the West Indies, where Warne had been playing, and arranged to meet him in a hotel lobby at midnight. This is staged in the musical amid of a scene between Warne and Malcolm Speed, the Chief Executive Officer of the International Cricket Council, where Warne is told he is losing the vice-captaincy. The lights come up on Jenner at a restaurant table, sitting alone with an unopened bottle of red wine:

Waiter: You asked for a phone, sir?
Terry Jenner: Yes. Thanks.
Waiter: Is it just yourself, sir?
Terry Jenner: No. I'm expecting someone. A mate.

But Warne never arrives. Jenner calls his hotel room, and the call goes unanswered, so he leaves a message on Warne's voicemail. This moment reflects how, in Perfect's words, this 'incredibly generous' and 'wildly symbolic' gesture was 'left completely unrequited.'[56] The sombre pealing of the unanswered phone between verses poignantly articulates this, and while Jenner expresses hope that they one day will get to drink it together, they never did. In the last verse, Jenner gently tells Warne not to be proud and that he'll be there all that night if he needs him: 'if you decide to change your mind' and 'I've got wine and I'm alone.' The tenderness expressed here is unparalleled in the rest of the work; certainly, it does not feature in any of the scenes with either of Warne's love interests.

An unexpected relationship of mateship developed between Perfect and Warne as a result of the production. Perfect had decided to play the role of Warne himself in part because the two men bear a striking resemblance to each other. In her review, Alison Croggon described Perfect as looking 'more like Shane Warne than Shane Warne does,' with his 'vertical uber-blonde hair and slightly stocky body.'[57] But the similarities between Warne and Perfect run deeper than looks; in fact, they hail from the same part of Melbourne. Perfect grew up in Mentone; Warne in Black Rock, just a few suburbs away. Warne went to school in Mentone, attending Mentone Grammar School on a sports scholarship. Fiona Gruber notes that while Warne is eight years older than Perfect, the result of their common upbringing is that they share an '[adolescence] that involved the same beaches and pubs, and the same backyard sports culture.'[58] Perfect believes that there is a congruence in the way that their careers have played out: 'I fell arse backwards into writing and performing my own songs, just as Shane Warne fell arse backwards into cricket.'[59] Rebecca Harkins-Cross, in her review of the show, noted that the two men seem to share a similar disposition, stating that '[l]ike Warnie himself, Perfect can get away with the most vulgar of on-field sledges or sordid gags about the sportsman's various affairs with his impish charm.'[60]

Promotional photographs published in *The Herald-Sun* for the 2013 production illustrate the camaraderie of the two figures and are powerful visual documents of their relationship (Figure 2.2). While surely staged, these photos exude genuine friendship – Perfect and Warne look happy to be in each other's company. This cordial relationship took time to develop. Warne was initially very unhappy when he heard that there was a musical being staged about him, and the production was vetted by lawyers to avoid potential defamation suits.[61] Warne had a tetchy relationship with the media and often felt aggrieved about their coverage of him, going as far as to say that it should be illegal to write

FIGURE 2.2 Promotional photograph of Shane Warne and Eddie Perfect.

Photo: Ellen Smith ©

about someone's life without their permission.[62] In keeping with this, despite being publicly invited by Perfect to come and view a performance of *Shane Warne*, there was no indication that he would attend.[63] Perfect tried often in the media to assure audiences (and Warne) that the show was not intended as a merciless attack on the cricketer:

> A lot of people think it's going to be this all-singing, all-dancing attack on Shane Warne, which I just don't think would be interesting. What's interesting is not to justify Shane Warne's actions but lead people to a point where they see how a human would react in those situations. And possibly go 'wow, if that was me I don't know if I would have made a better choice.'[64]

Eventually, these arguments managed to cut through, and Perfect's attempts to woo Warne opening night succeeded. Warne attended and, ever the media personality, even came up on stage to bow with the cast after the curtain call (Figure 2.3). Shortly afterwards, he published a review endorsing the production. He admitted that he had felt rather nervous sitting in the audience – 'More edgy, even, than facing Pakistani quickie Shoaib Akhtar on a green, seaming deck, I reckon' – but that the production had won him over by the end, saying that 'I think Eddie and his team have written the musical in a respectful and sympathetic way, and that they have captured my fun, larrikin side.'[65] It is notable here that Warne describes himself as a larrikin, a term with explicit national associations.[66] It is this cultural archetype that they both seem to be enacting in the second photograph, epitomising Clem Gorman's description of the larrikin as

> almost archly self-conscious, too smart for his or her own good, witty rather than humorous, exceeding limits, bending rules and sailing close to the wind, avoiding rather than evading responsibility, playing up to an audience, mocking pomposity and smugness, taking the piss out of people, cutting down tall poppies . . . larger than life, sceptical, iconoclastic, egalitarian yet suffering fools badly, insouciant and, above all, defiant.[67]

According to Jo Casamento, these two larrikins even shared a beer together after Warne viewed the musical.[68] The strong sense of admiration that Perfect felt for Warne emerges powerfully through the remarks quoted above, and while Warne was sceptical at first, his eventual turn-around exhibits a reciprocal feeling of goodwill towards Perfect.

Culture Wars: Art versus Sport

The coming together of Perfect and Warne – artist and sportsman – is at odds with the oft-invoked dichotomy between art and sport in the national

FIGURE 2.3   Curtain call for Shane Warne and Eddie Perfect at the premiere of *Shane Warne: The Musical.*

Photo: Craig Borrow

imaginary of Australia. Christopher McAuliffe opens his essay on the subject with a quote from the playwright David Williamson, known for his engagement with sport in plays like *The Club* (1977). Williamson recounts how in the early 1970s 'it was believed that anyone with talent in writing, theatre or film should leave the country immediately and work elsewhere before they were stifled by the deadly distrust of creativity in sports-obsessed Australia.'[69] Lamentations about the privileged position of sport in comparison to the arts, particularly when it comes to government funding, are recurring refrains. This means that, as McAuliffe writes, 'from behind ramparts, the cultivated Australian sees sport suffering none of the attacks that it does and, worse, usurping art's role as the definer of national character.'[70] However, the distinction between art and sport is, in fact, less pronounced than the critical reviews intimate. Sport (including cricket) is no stranger to the theatre and has appeared periodically on Australian stages.[71]

Perfect attempted to downplay this schism when publicising the work, telling *The Sydney Morning Herald* that 'if you enjoy a laugh, if you enjoy musicals, if you enjoy cricket, you'll love it.'[72] However, these embattled cultural positions were evident in reviews of *Shane Warne*. Anne-Marie Peard included a note at the bottom of her reviews for the 'patrons more used to stadiums' who

> didn't get the concept of live theatre. It's not like the MCG. Getting up in the middle of the first half (or 'act') and coming back into the theatre with beer for your mates isn't acceptable 'theatre' behaviour – and it just encouraged other blokes to do the same. Please wait for half time (or 'interval') and don't do it again in the second half. Or, at least, come back with enough beers for the people sitting near you![73]

Further disdain was expressed in Michael Ruffles' *Canberra Times* review, which claimed

> Bogans have overtaken the theatre. A snobbish reaction, but a natural one for cultural elitists appalled by the idea of a musical based on the life of a sports star. And a smoking, drinking, pizza-loving one at that. But it is perfectly appropriate that the audience be armed with stubbies and pies when they swill into Melbourne's Athenaeum, having just stubbed out their ciggies. This is no ordinary show, it's a musical for the masses, equally appropriate for the bogans of Bay 13 as those who secretly absorb every word of sport-related scandal.[74]

These reviews paint a picture of a society divided by class: the middle-class theatre-going audience, who are polite and well behaved and understand the rules, and the sports fans, who are loud, uncouth, and uncultured. In 2010, when assessing why the production had not been successful as he had hoped, Perfect mused that perhaps these differences were more intractable than he had thought:

> Going to the theatre is still an act of featuring yourself as being cultured . . . sport is anti-intellectual and it's populist and it's what everyone does, and so theatre people didn't feel like seeing a show about sport because it didn't make them feel elevated and smart. . . . And a lot of people didn't like laughing at the same jokes as the bogan down the aisle.[75]

Danny Katz's satirical review of *Shane Warne* was more optimistic about the potential power of the musical to bridge such divides.[76] Katz draws attention to the perceived incongruity between form (musical theatre) and content (Warne/cricket) by reversing gender and cultural norms. The persona in the piece is a musical theatre loving Aussie bloke with no interest whatsoever in cricket: 'Like probably just about every other average red-blooded all-Aussie bloke who grew up in the suburbs during the 1970s and '80s, I'd only ever go and see a show called *Shane Warne the Musical* for one reason: because I love music theatre.'[77] While the premise of the review rests upon the logic of the incongruity between men, cricket, and musical theatre, Katz subverts this by demonstrating his knowledge of the musical theatre canon through reference to several musicals. The review concludes with an ironic statement of discovery:

> When I got home, I was even inspired to find out a bit more about this quaint, obscure little game called 'cricket,' so I got on the net and found out what a silly mid-on was, learned about cover-drives, and spent 10 minutes Googling a googly.[78]

The inference here is that maybe, just maybe, someone who went to see *Shane Warne* might, to their surprise, develop an enjoyment and appreciation for musical theatre and that perhaps the pairing is not as odd as it might seem.

One way that Perfect communicates the commonalities between the two forms is by drawing on metaphors of sport as art. Such metaphors are evident in descriptions of Warne's bowling, which refer to literature, painting, or classical music. Louis Nowra likens Warne's talent as 'approach[ing] the sublime beauty of a piece of music or poetry.'[79] He also offers a comparison between Warne and Mozart:

> In the film *Amadeus* the envious and bland composer Salieri is astonished by Mozart's ineffable music but can't fathom how someone who is so childish, simple, delighted by scatology and sex, and incapable of articulating his own genius, should be the possessor of such a gift. It is as if God is channelling music through the simple human container that is Mozart. In a similar way one can look at Warne and ask oneself – how did a boofhead like him achieve such a rare and wondrous ability?[80]

Billington, too, sees Warne's abilities in this way, describing him as the 'Maria Callas of leg spin' and characterising his playing style as the 'enigma variations' (a reference to the composition by Elgar).[81] Perfect captures the spirit of these sport-as-art metaphors in the song 'That Ball,' which aestheticises the moment that Warne bowled the 'ball of the century.'

Told from the perspective of ordinary spectators, 'That Ball' is a slow, august ballad. Its tonality is reminiscent of the music of Stephen Sondheim, particularly something like 'Johanna' from *Sweeney Todd*, which adds a semi-operatic weightiness. The chordal rhythm that underpins it is stately and majestic, and the vocal tone of the performers shifts from the contemporary styles evident in the previous number to a more operatic style of singing, with long legato phrases and plenty of vibrato, immediately signifying the gravitas of the number. The scene is described with effusive poetic detail, but with an ironic awareness of the incongruity of form and content. A lyric like 'he ambled shambolic, kind of graceless with a swirl of arms' casts Warne's rather ungraceful movements as almost balletic. The male singer crisply over-articulates when he describes how Warne bowled with a 'rip and fizz and a hiss and grunt.' The legato melody mimics the smooth movement of the ball, describing the way that it 'left his fingers arching down leg stump.'

'That Ball' presses pause on the narrative to extend and explore a moment that was over in the in the blink of an eye. Watching the footage of Warne bowling 'that ball,' one is struck by its brevity. The title of the song recalls the philosopher John Dewey's notion of '*an* experience,' the process by which a situation is transformed into an event of significance: *that* shot, *that* race, *that* ball.[82] In the second verse, as more chorus members join in, the tempo slightly accelerates as they describe history being made: 'Someone was talking, I said "shut up one sec!" and the hairs stood up on the back of my neck.' This description intimates that watching sport is as profound an experience as what any work of art could provide. The song understands the profundity of such a sporting achievement, what it means for individuals, for a nation, and how it lingers in collective memory: 'I remember that ball like it was yesterday and never will forget.' It does not write such an event off as a jingoistic exercise of nation-building, but rather frames it as a moment of magnificent beauty and supreme skill: 'it was like the moon landing, I remember just where I was standing and I couldn't believe it could turn that far.'

In 'That Ball,' Perfect highlights how great sporting achievements, just like great works of art, approach the sublime. Despite the aggrandised musical idiom, the song does not take the piss at all. It is a genuinely beautiful number that captures the significance of spectator sport to Australians, conveying the deep significance of the moment Warne bowled that ball and how it has lodged itself in the national imaginary. 'That Ball' is a defining moment of sporting achievement and national pride.

Conclusion: Who We Are

In *Shane Warne*, Perfect argues that for different strata of the nation, sport and the theatre have essentially the same function. Sport is 'the regular theatre for ordinary Australians, or as historian Manning Clark put it, when referring to Australian football, it is the ballet for the ordinary person.'[83] Earlier, I quoted McAuliffe's diagnosis that the tension between art and sport is to do with the perception that sport has unseated art as 'definer of a national character.' *Shane Warne*'s contribution to Australian musical theatre is that it takes on this task with aplomb. In its approach to humour and the music, it 'takes the piss,' reflecting how Australia thinks of itself as a culture that does not take itself too seriously. It relishes the opportunity to stage the tropes and characters of the national imaginary, refusing to submit to what McAuliffe identifies as a 'deep anxiety about the shallowness or hollowness of Australian character.'[84] In doing so, the musical locates Australian-ness in the confluence of sport, masculinity, and nation, tracing it through the repertory of national archetypes, like the battler, and by articulating relationships of mateship. In *Shane Warne*, we see a levelling between art and sport: a meeting in the middle. In the next chapter, we will see the idea of the Australian 'middle' further interrogated.

Notes

1 Episode 1, *Sporting Nation*, ABC Television, 2012. The genesis of this remark is from the seminal Australian text *The Lucky Country*, in which a similar sentiment is stated. Donald Horne, *The Lucky Country* (Penguin Books, 1964), 40.

2 Catriona Elder, *Being Australian: Narratives of National Identity* (Allen & Unwin, 2007), 288.

3 I attended a performance of the 2008 production in Melbourne. Access to a score and libretto has been obtained through David Spicer Productions. These archival documents correspond to the revised version of the work, and thus the analysis mostly refers to the later version. There is some visual documentation of the 2013 performance, available on Perfect's Vimeo channel. Eddie Perfect, 'My Name Is John (*Shane Warne The Musical*),' *Vimeo*, August 22, 2014, accessed May 18, 2025, http://vimeo.com/104073352; Eddie Perfect, 'Pick Up Shane (*Shane Warne The Musical*, 2013),' *Vimeo*, August 22, 2014, accessed May 18, 2025, http://vimeo.com/104073354; Eddie Perfect, 'Run (*Shane Warne The Musical*),' *Vimeo*, August 22, 2014, accessed May 18, 2025, http://vimeo.com/104073355; Eddie Perfect, 'Shine Like Shane (*Shane Warne The Musical*),' *Vimeo*, August 22, 2014, accessed May 18, 2025 http://vimeo.com/104073356; Eddie Perfect, 'The Ashes (*Shane Warne The Musical*),' *Vimeo*, August 22, 2014, accessed May 18, 2025, http://vimeo.com/104073357, accessed August 24, 2022. The cast recording is available on Spotify.

4 Gideon Haigh, *On Warne* (Hamish Hamilton, 2012), 5.

5 Tracee Hutchison, '*Shane Warne The Musical*,' *7.30 Report*, ABC Television, November 11, 2008, accessed November 17, 2017, https://www.abc.net.au/local/videos/2008/11/12/2417241.htm.

6 Rebecca Harkins-Cross, 'Shane Warne: The Musical,' *The Sydney Morning Herald*, June 21, 2013, https://www.smh.com.au/entertainment/shane-warne-the-musical-20130621–2oms0.html.

7 Hutchison, '*Shane Warne The Musical*.'

8 Jim McKay et al, 'Gender Equity, Hegemonic Masculinity and the Governmentalisation of Australian Amateur Sport,' in *Culture in Australia: Policies, Publics and Programs*, ed. Tony Bennett and David Carter (Cambridge University Press, 2001), 233.

9 Fiona Scott-Norman, 'Right Note for Wronged Wife,' *The Age*, December 5, 2008, https://www.theage.com.au/entertainment/art-and-design/right-note-for-wronged-wife-20081205-ge7k1q.html.

10 Jason Blake, '*Shane Warne The Musical*,' *The Sydney Morning Herald*, May 22, 2009, https://www.smh.com.au/entertainment/art-and-design/shane-warne-the-musical-20090522-gdtjnk.html.

11 There are several slightly different versions of this story, but this is the one detailed by Perfect in a short documentary made about the work. This documentary, entitled *Shane Warne The Musical: Making Of Special*, was also released on DVD. It is difficult to ascertain how commercially available this was. I purchased a second-hand copy from eBay but at the time of writing there are no copies available for purchase on the Internet. It was aired on Channel 10 on December 20, 2008. Philip Derriman, 'On Song: Tale of an Ordinary Aussie Bloke with a Freakish Talent,' *The Sydney Morning Herald*, December 20, 2008, https://www.smh.com.au/sport/on-song-tale-of-an-ordinary-aussie-bloke-with-a-freakish-talent-20081220-gdt77p.html.

12 A recording of the cast performing at the Gala event is available on YouTube. TheMelbComedyFest, 'Shane Warne The Musical (Eddie Perfect) – 2008 Melbourne International Comedy Festival Gala,' *YouTube*, August 4, 2015, accessed May 1, 2019, https://www.youtube.com/watch?v=J1dV6nv3f2k.

13 Louise Schwartzkoff and Bryce Hallett, 'Warne's Appeal Turned Down,' *The Sydney Morning Herald*, May 30, 2009, 19.

14 Benjamin Law, 'Eddie Perfect Unleashes the Beast,' *The Monthly*, October 2013, accessed August 25, 2022, https://www.themonthly.com.au/issue/2013/october/1380549600/benjamin-law/eddie-perfect-unleashes-beast#mtr.

15 Craig Mathieson, 'Warne Out? Not Even a Half-Chance,' *The Sydney Morning Herald*, June 14, 2013, https://www.smh.com.au/entertainment/musicals/warne-out-not-even-a-halfchance-20130613–2o6g0.html.

16 The original production concluded with the gospel ballad, 'The Ashes,' which plays on the dual meaning of the word: it refers to the revered cricket institution, but it also compares Warne to a phoenix rising from the ashes. It still appears in the 2013 production but in a different place.

17 William Mandle, 'Cricket and Australian Nationalism in the Nineteenth Century,' in *Sport in Australia: Selected Readings in Physical Activity*, ed. Trevor Jaques and G. R. Pavia (McGraw-Hill, 1976), 46–72.

18 Brett Hutchins, 'Unity, Difference and the "National Game": Cricket and Australian National Identity,' in *Cricket and National Identity in the Postcolonial Age: Following On*, ed. Stephen Wagg (Routledge, 2005), 12.

19 Hutchins, 'Unity, Difference and the "National Game",' 14.

20 Elizabeth Bernays, 'A Game of Cricket,' *Antipodes* 23, no. 2 (2009): 158, https://www.jstor.org/stable/41957804.

21 Graeme Davison, 'The Imaginary Grandstand,' *Meanjin* 61, no. 3 (2002): 9.

22 John Howard, 'Address at the Mark Taylor Tribute Luncheon,' PM Transcripts, September 12, 1997, accessed January 15, 2025, https://pmtranscripts.pmc.gov.au/release/transcript-10485.

23 Brett Hutchins, *Don Bradman: Challenging the Myth* (Cambridge University Press, 2002), 2.

24 Richard Cashman, *Paradise of Sport: A History of Australian Sport* (Walla Walla Press, 2010), 60.

25 Gill Lines, 'Villains, Fools or Heroes? Sports Stars as Role Models for Young People,' *Leisure Studies* 20, no. 4 (2001): 286, https://doi.org/10.1080/02614360110094661.

26 Douglas MacQueen-Thomson, 'The Corruption of Heroism,' *Arena Magazine* 39 (1999), 5–6.

27 It is also sometimes stated as simply 'it's not cricket.'

28 MacQueen-Thomson, 'The Corruption of Heroism,' 6.

29 Debbie Schipp, prompted by the sale of the cricket rights to another Australian television channel in 2018, recounts the history of this music and how it came to be synonymous with television broadcasts of cricket. There was great consternation from fans that they may no longer be hearing this music at the start of the broadcast. Debbie Schipp, 'What Will Happen to the Soundtrack of Summer?,' *The Daily Telegraph*, April 15, 2018, https://www.dailytelegraph.com.au/sport/cricket/what-will-happen-to-the-soundtrack-of-summer/news-story/4c7fd38e47c2dfee05a7abd5b8f5173c.

30 Scott-Norman, 'Right Note.'

31 Waleed Aly, 'Carefree Larrikin is a Myth. Australians are Obedient to Authority,' *The Sydney Morning Herald*, December 17, 2020, https://www.smh.com.au/national/carefree-larrikin-is-a-myth-australians-are-obedient-to-authority-20201217-p56oc7.html.

32 Abby Boytos, Kerry Smith and JongHan Kim, 'The Underdog Advantage in Creativity,' *Thinking Skills and Creativity* 26 (2017): 96, https://doi.org/10.1016/j.tsc.2017.10.003. Ian Menzies notes that the underdog it is a recurring and ubiquitous figure in both historical and contemporary narratives. Ian Menzies, 'Horses Down Under: The Underdog Schematic Narrative Template and Australian Nationalism,' *Journal of Australian Studies* 45, no. 1 (2021): 18–32, https://doi.org/10.1080/14443058.2021.1876137.

33 '"TJ Became My Dr Phil"–Warne, *Espncricinfo*, May 27, 2011, accessed December 1, 2024, http://www.espncricinfo.com/australia/content/story/516808.html.

34 AIS stands for Australian Institute of Sport. With headquarters in Canberra, it is the nation's premier training institute for high performance sport. The Australian Cricket Academy was formed as a partnership between the AIS and the Australian Cricket Board. It was originally based in Adelaide but since 2004 has been located in Brisbane.

35 Eddie Perfect, 'Interview – *Shane Warne: The Musical*,' *Bbmlive.com*, accessed March 23, 2019, https://bbmlive.com/interview-shane-warne-the-musical/,

36 Neil Armfield, 'Welcome from the Director,' *Shane Warne: The Musical*, theatre programme, 2008; Christine Beasley, 'Rethinking Hegemonic Masculinity in a Globalizing World,' *Men and Masculinities* 11, no. 1 (2008): 90, https://doi.org/10.1177/1097184X08315102.

37 Blake, '*Shane Warne The Musical*.' This piece has a close association with cricket, as it was the broadcast theme for Channel 7's television coverage of the sport.

38 Bruce Moore describes the term bogan as of 'unknown origin' but emerging in the 1980s. There are several regional variations. Bruce Moore, *Speaking Our Language: The Story of Australian English* (Oxford University Press, 2008), 173–174. 'Cashed up bogan' is a phrase used to describe a section of Australian society who were formerly of the working class but who greatly benefited from the resources boom of the 1990s and 2000s. Barbara Pini, Paula McDonald and Robyn Mayes, 'Class Contestations and Australia's Resource Boom: The Emergence of the "Cashed-up Bogan",' *Sociology* 46, no. 1 (2012): 142–158, https://doi.org/10.1177/0038038511419194.

39 The origin and use of the term is explored in Bert Peeters, 'Tall Poppies and Egalitarianism in Australian Discourse: From Key Word to Cultural Value,' *English World-Wide* 25, no. 1 (2004): 5–6, https://doi.org/10.1075/eww.25.1.02pee.

40 Jessica Milner Davis, '"Aussie" Humour and Laughter,' in *Serious Frolic: Essays on Australian Humour*, ed. Frances De Groen and Peter Kirkpatrick (University of Queensland Press, 2009), 38.

41 Milner Davis, '"Aussie" Humour,' 24.

42 Greg Baum, 'Warne Steals the Show as Life and Art Collide on Stage,' *The Age*, December 11, 2008, 3.

43 Harkins-Cross, *Shane Warne: The Musical.*
44 Kathy Marks, 'Shane Warne The Musical,' *The Independent*, December 3, 2008, https://www.independent.co.uk/arts-entertainment/theatre-dance/features/shane-warne-the-musical–1048567.html.
45 Milner Davis, '"Aussie" Humour,' 40.
46 Milner Davis, '"Aussie" Humour,' 40.
47 Nick Dyrenfurth, *Mateship: A Very Australian History* (Scribe, 2015), 3–4.
48 Dyrenfurth, *Mateship*, 7.
49 Varda Burstyn, *The Rites of Men: Manhood, Politics, and the Culture of Sport* (University of Toronto Press, 1999), 18.
50 Cyril Pearl, *Beer, Glorious Beer* (Thomas Nelson, 1969), 1.
51 Lawrence Wenner and Steve Jackson, *Sport, Beer, and Gender: Promotional Culture and Contemporary Social Life* (Peter Lang, 2009), 1; Diane Kirkby, '"Beer, Glorious Beer": Gender Politics and Australian Popular Culture,' *The Journal of Popular Culture* 37, no. 2 (2003): 254, https://doi.org/10.1111/1540–5931.00066.
52 Catherine Palmer and Kirrily Thompson, 'The Paradoxes of Football Spectatorship: On-Field and Online Expressions of Social Capital among the "Grog Squad",' *Sociology of Sport Journal* 24, no. 2 (2007): 187–205, https://doi.org/10.1123/ssj.24.2.187.
53 '"TJ Became My Dr Phil."'
54 'Shane Warne's Touching Tribute to Terry Jenner,' *The Adelaide Advertiser*, May 27, 2011, accessed January 28, 2020, https://www.adelaidenow.com.au/news/warnes-touching-tribute-to-jenner/news-story/107352e2e34505cf1bf357206af859d0.
55 ArtsCentreMelbourne, '*Shane Warne The Musical* – A Missing Chapter,' *YouTube*, June 10, 2013, accessed October 22, 2019, https://www.youtube.com/watch?v=SOctSEpaYX8.
56 ArtsCentreMelbourne, '*Shane Warne The Musical.*'
57 Alison Croggon, 'Review: *Shane Warne: The Musical*,' *Theatre Notes*, December 12, 2008, accessed May 15, 2019, http://theatrenotes.blogspot.com/2008/12/review-shane-warne-musical.html.
58 Fiona Gruber, 'Spin Cycle,' *The Australian*, November 21, 2008, https://www.theaustralian.com.au/arts/spin-cycle/news-story/ba6bc78f5117e01bd092542f0e4713de,
59 Gruber, 'Spin Cycle.'
60 Harkins-Cross, '*Shane Warne: The Musical.*'
61 Raymond Gill, 'With a Bit of SMSing about, It's Warney's Life in Song,' *The Sydney Morning Herald*, March 20, 2008, 3. Whether any changes to the show were made as a result is unknown. When the second production was mounted, Elizabeth Hurley, Warne's girlfriend at the time, also objected to the material. Luke Dennehy, 'Eddie Perfect Extends Invitation to Shane Warne and Elizabeth Hurley to See His Show after Hurley Slams It on Twitter,' *The Herald-Sun*, June 16, 2013, https://www.heraldsun.com.au/entertainment/eddie-perfect-extends-invitation-to-shane-warne-and-elizabeth-hurley-to-see-his-show-after-hurley-slams-it-on-twitter/news-story/67982848c7c72dc793749ec716384405.
62 Gideon Haigh, 'Warne Takes Centre Stage Again as Spinner Proves Perfect Vehicle for Satire,' *The Guardian*, December 12, 2008, https://www.theguardian.com/sport/blog/2008/dec/12/shane-warne-the-musical.
63 Katrina Strickland, 'This Spinner Will Crease You Up,' *The Australian Financial Review*, November 22, 2008, 34.
64 John Bailey, 'As Musical Fodder, King of Spin Faces the First Test,' *The Age*, October 19, 2008, 5.
65 Shane Warne, 'My Life Flashed Before My Eyes,' *The Herald-Sun*, December 10, 2008, 7.

66 Melissa Bellanta, *Larrikins: A History* (University of Queensland Press, 2012).

67 Clem Gorman, 'Round Up the Usual Suspects,' in *The Larrikin Streak: Australian Writers Look at the Legend* (Pan Macmillan, 1980), x.

68 Jo Casamento, 'Getting Warnie Down Perfect Once More,' *The Sydney Morning Herald*, September 18, 2011, style section, 5.

69 Christopher McAuliffe, 'Fair Game: Art Versus Sport in "The Lucky Country",' *Art Australia* 47, no. 4 (2010): 582.

70 McAuliffe, 'Fair Game,' 585.

71 Perfect joins a lineage of artists who love and appreciate the sport. Michael Billington recounts that Wayne Harrison, the Australian theatre director, once gifted him a copy of an anthology of cricket writing entitled *The Longest Game*, edited by another renowned dramatist, Alex Buzo. Michael Billington 'Cricket and Theatre: Australians Observed,' in *Playing Australia: Australian Theatre and the International Stage*, ed. Elizabeth Schafer and Susan Bradley Smith (Rodopi, 2003), 144–158; Alexander Buzo and Jamie Grant, *The Longest Game: A Collection of the Best Cricket Writing from Alexander to Zavos, from the Gabba to the Yabba* (Heinemann, 1990). The playwright Louis Nowra has written a biography of Warne. Louis Nowra, *Warne's World: A Personal Appreciation of Shane Warne* (Duffy and Snellgrove, 2002).

72 Jeff Turnbull, 'Warnie – the musical – has the great(ish) man stumped,' *The Sydney Morning Herald*, December 4, 2008, https://www.smh.com.au/entertainment/warnie-the-musical-has-the-greatish-man-stumped-20081204–6r9f.html.

73 Anne-Marie Peard, 'Shane Warne: The Musical,' *Sometimes Melbourne*, December 11, 2008, accessed August 18, 2022, http://sometimesmelbourne.blogspot.com/2008/12/shane-warne-musical.html.

74 Michael Ruffles, 'Bowled Over by Bogan Musical,' *The Canberra Times*, December 27, 2008, 6.

75 Raymond Gill, 'Middle Ground,' *The Sydney Morning Herald*, July 17, 2010, https://www.smh.com.au/entertainment/music/middle-ground-20100716–10e1t.html.

76 Danny Katz, 'Googly-Eyed Over Warnie's Big-Hitting Numbers,' *The Age*, December 18, 2008, 18.

77 Katz, 'Googly-eyed.'

78 Katz, 'Googly-Eyed.'

79 Nowra, *Warne's World*, 12.

80 Nowra, *Warne's World*, 18.

81 Billington, 'Cricket and Theatre,' 157, 146.

82 John Dewey, *Art as Experience* (Minton, Balch and Company, 1934), 58–81.

83 Cashman, *Paradise of Sport*, 193.

84 This line does not appear in the printed article but is in the repost on McAuliffe's personal website. One could surmise that it was cut in the editorial process. It offers an important addendum to his conception of cultural pessimism. See https://chrismcauliffe.com.au/fair-game-art-versus-sport-in-the-lucky-country-2010/.

References

Aly, Waleed. 'Carefree Larrikin Is a Myth. Australians Are Obedient to Authority.' *The Sydney Morning Herald*, December 17, 2020. https://www.smh.com.au/national/carefree-larrikin-is-a-myth-australians-are-obedient-to-authority-20201217-p56oc7.html.

Armfield, Neil. 'Welcome from the Director.' *Shane Warne: The Musical*, theatre programme, 2008.

ArtsCentreMelbourne. 'Shane Warne The Musical – A Missing Chapter.' *YouTube*, June 10, 2013. Accessed October 22, 2019. https://www.youtube.com/watch?v=SOctSEpaYX8.

Bailey, John. 'As Musical Fodder, King of Spin Faces the First Test.' *The Age*, October 19, 2008, 5.

Baum, Greg. 'Warne Steals the Show as Life and Art Collide on Stage.' *The Age*, December 11, 2008, 3.

Beasley, Christine. 'Rethinking Hegemonic Masculinity in a Globalizing World.' *Men and Masculinities* 11, no. 1 (2008): 86–103. https://doi.org/10.1177/10971 84X08315102.

Bellanta, Melissa. *Larrikins: A History*. University of Queensland Press, 2012.

Bernays, Elizabeth. 'A Game of Cricket.' *Antipodes* 23, no. 2 (2009): 158–160. https://www.jstor.org/stable/41957804.

Billington, Michael. 'Cricket and Theatre: Australians Observed.' In *Playing Australia: Australian Theatre and the International Stage*, edited by Elizabeth Schafer and Susan Bradley Smith. Rodopi, 2003.

Blake, Jason. 'Shane Warne The Musical.' *The Sydney Morning Herald*, May 22, 2009. https://www.smh.com.au/entertainment/art-and-design/shane-warne-the-musical-20090522-gdtjnk.html.

Boytos, Abby, Kerry Smith, and JongHan Kim. 'The Underdog Advantage in Creativity.' *Thinking Skills and Creativity* 26 (2017): 96–101. https://doi.org/10.1016/j.tsc.2017.10.003.

Burstyn, Varda. *The Rites of Men: Manhood, Politics, and the Culture of Sport*. University of Toronto Press, 1999.

Buzo, Alexander, and Jamie Grant. *The Longest Game: A Collection of the Best Cricket Writing from Alexander to Zavos, from the Gabba to the Yabba*. Heinemann, 1990.

Casamento, Jo. 'Getting Warnie Down Perfect Once More.' *The Sydney Morning Herald*, September 18, 2011, style section, 5.

Cashman, Richard. *Paradise of Sport: A History of Australian Sport*. Walla Walla Press, 2010.

Croggon, Alison. 'Review: Shane Warne: The Musical.' *Theatre Notes*, December 12, 2008. Accessed June 30, 2025. http://theatrenotes.blogspot.com/2008/12/review-shane-warne-musical.html.

Davis, Jessica Milner. '"Aussie" Humour and Laughter.' In *Serious Frolic: Essays on Australian Humour*, edited by Frances De Groen and Peter Kirkpatrick. University of Queensland Press, 2009.

Davison, Graeme. 'The Imaginary Grandstand.' *Meanjin* 61, no. 3 (2002): 4–18.

Dennehy, Luke. 'Eddie Perfect Extends Invitation to Shane Warne and Elizabeth Hurley to See His Show after Hurley Slams It on Twitter.' *The Herald-Sun*, June 16, 2013. https://www.heraldsun.com.au/entertainment/eddie-perfect-extends-invitation-to-shane-warne-and-elizabeth-hurley-to-see-his-show-after-hurley-slams-it-on-twitter/news-story/67982848c7c72dc793749ec716384405.

Derriman, Philip. 'On Song: Tale of an Ordinary Aussie Bloke with a Freakish Talent.' *The Sydney Morning Herald*, December 20, 2008. https://www.smh.com.au/sport/on-song-tale-of-an-ordinary-aussie-bloke-with-a-freakish-talent-20081220-gdt77p.html.

Dewey, John. *Art as Experience*. Minton, Balch and Company, 1934.

Dyrenfurth, Nick. *Mateship: A Very Australian History*. Scribe, 2015.

Eddie Perfect. *Vimeo Channel*. https://vimeo.com/eddieperfect.

Episode 1, *Sporting Nation*, ABC Television, 2012.

Gill, Raymond. 'With a Bit of SMSing about, It's Warney's Life in Song.' *The Sydney Morning Herald*, March 20, 2008, 3.

Gill, Raymond. 'Middle Ground.' *The Sydney Morning Herald*, July 17, 2010. https://www.smh.com.au/entertainment/music/middle-ground-20100716–10e1t.html.

Gorman, Clem. 'Round Up the Usual Suspects.' In *The Larrikin Streak: Australian Writers Look at the Legend*. Pan Macmillan, 1980.

Gruber, Fiona. 'Spin Cycle.' *The Australian*, November 21, 2008. https://www.theaustralian.com.au/arts/spin-cycle/news-story/ba6bc78f5117e01bd092542f0e4713de.

Haigh, Gideon. 'Warne Takes Centre Stage Again as Spinner Proves Perfect Vehicle for Satire.' *The Guardian*, December 12, 2008. https://www.theguardian.com/sport/blog/2008/dec/12/shane-warne-the-musical.

Haigh, Gideon. *On Warne*. Hamish Hamilton, 2012.

Harkins-Cross, Rebecca. 'Shane Warne: The Musical.' *The Sydney Morning Herald*, June 21, 2013. https://www.smh.com.au/entertainment/shane-warne-the-musical-20130621–2oms0.html.

Horne, Donald. *The Lucky Country*. Penguin Books, 1964.

Howard, John. 'Address at the Mark Taylor Tribute Luncheon.' *PM Transcripts*, September 12, 1997. https://pmtranscripts.pmc.gov.au/release/transcript–10485.

Hutchins, Brett. *Don Bradman: Challenging the Myth*. Cambridge University Press, 2002.

Hutchins, Brett. 'Unity, Difference and the "National Game": Cricket and Australian National Identity.' In *Cricket and National Identity in the Postcolonial Age: Following On*, edited by Stephen Wagg, Routledge, 2005.

Hutchinson, Tracee. 'Shane Warne The Musical.' *7.30 Report, ABC Television*, November 11, 2008. Accessed November 17, 2017. https://www.abc.net.au/local/videos/2008/11/12/2417241.htm.

Katz, Danny. 'Googly-Eyed Over Warnie's Big-Hitting Numbers.' *The Age*, December 18, 2008, 18.

Kirkby, Diane. '"Beer, Glorious Beer": Gender Politics and Australian Popular Culture.' *The Journal of Popular Culture* 37, no. 2 (2003): 244–256. https://doi.org/10.1111/1540–5931.00066.

Law, Benjamin. 'Eddie Perfect Unleashes the Beast.' *The Monthly*, October 2013. https://www.themonthly.com.au/issue/2013/october/1380549600/benjamin-law/eddie-perfect-unleashes-beast#mtr.

Lines, Gill. 'Villains, Fools or Heroes? Sports Stars as Role Models for Young People.' *Leisure Studies* 20, no. 4 (2001): 285–303. https://doi.org/10.1080/02614360110094661.

MacQueen-Thomson, Douglas. 'The Corruption of Heroism.' *Arena Magazine* 39 (1999): 5–6.

Mandle, William. 'Cricket and Australian Nationalism in the Nineteenth Century.' In *Sport in Australia: Selected Readings in Physical Activity*, edited by Trevor Jaques and G. R. Pavia. McGraw-Hill, 1976.

Marks, Kathy. 'Shane Warne The Musical.' *The Independent*, December 3, 2008. https://www.independent.co.uk/arts-entertainment/theatre-dance/features/shane-warne-the-musical–1048567.html.

Mathieson, Craig. 'Warne Out? Not Even a Half-Chance.' *The Sydney Morning Herald*, June 14, 2013. https://www.smh.com.au/entertainment/musicals/warne-out-not-even-a-halfchance-20130613–2o6g0.html.

McAuliffe, Christopher. 'Fair Game: Art Versus Sport in "The Lucky Country."' *Art Australia* 47, no. 4 (2010): 582–585.

McKay, Jim, et al. 'Gender Equity, Hegemonic Masculinity and the Governmentalisation of Australian Amateur Sport.' In *Culture in Australia: Policies, Publics and Programs*, edited by Tony Bennett and David Carter. Cambridge University Press, 2001.

Menzies, Ian. 'Horses Down Under: The Underdog Schematic Narrative Template and Australian Nationalism.' *Journal of Australian Studies* 45, no. 1 (2021): 18–32. https://doi.org/10.1080/14443058.2021.1876137.

Moore, Bruce. *Speaking Our Language: The Story of Australian English*. Oxford University Press, 2008.

Nowra, Louis. *Warne's World: A Personal Appreciation of Shane Warne*. Duffy and Snellgrove, 2002.

Palmer, Catherine, and Kirrily Thompson. 'The Paradoxes of Football Spectatorship: On-Field and Online Expressions of Social Capital among the "Grog Squad."' *Sociology of Sport Journal* 24, no. 2 (2007): 187–205. https://doi.org/10.1123/ssj.24.2.187.

Peard, Anne-Marie. 'Shane Warne: The Musical.' *Sometimes Melbourne*, December 11, 2008. http://sometimesmelbourne.blogspot.com/2008/12/shane-warne-musical.html.

Pearl, Cyril. *Beer, Glorious Beer*. Thomas Nelson, 1969.

Peeters, Bert. 'Tall Poppies and Egalitarianism in Australian Discourse: From Key Word to Cultural Value.' *English World-Wide* 25, no. 1 (2004): 71–92. https://doi.org/10.1075/eww.25.1.02pee.

Perfect, Eddie. 'Interview–Shane Warne: The Musical.' *Bbmlive.com*. Accessed May 14, 2025. https://bbmlive.com/interview-shane-warne-the-musical/.

Pini, Barbara, Paula McDonald, and Robyn Mayes. 'Class Contestations and Australia's Resource Boom: The Emergence of the "Cashed-up Bogan."' *Sociology* 46, no. 1 (2012): 142–58. https://doi.org/10.1177/0038038511419194.

Ruffles, Michael. 'Bowled Over by Bogan Musical.' *The Canberra Times*, December 27, 2008, 6.

Schipp, Debbie. 'What Will Happen to the Soundtrack of Summer?' *The Daily Telegraph*, April 15, 2018. https://www.dailytelegraph.com.au/sport/cricket/what-will-happen-to-the-soundtrack-of-summer/news-story/4c7fd38e47c2dfee05a7abd5b8f5173c.

Schwartzkoff, Louise, and Bryce Hallett. 'Warne's Appeal Turned Down.' *The Sydney Morning Herald*, May 30, 2009, 19.

Scott-Norman, Fiona. 'Right Note for Wronged Wife.' *The Age*, December 5, 2008. https://www.theage.com.au/entertainment/art-and-design/right-note-for-wronged-wife-20081205-ge7k1q.html.

'Shane Warne's Touching Tribute to Terry Jenner.' *The Adelaide Advertiser*, May 27, 2011. https://www.adelaidenow.com.au/news/warnes-touching-tribute-to-jenner/news-story/107352e2e34505cf1bf357206af859d0.

Strickland, Katrina. 'This Spinner Will Crease You Up.' *The Australian Financial Review*, November 22, 2008, 34.

TheMelbComedyFest. 'Shane Warne The Musical (Eddie Perfect)–2008 Melbourne International Comedy Festival Gala.' *YouTube*, August 4, 2015. Accessed June 30, 2025. https://www.youtube.com/watch?v=J1dV6nv3f2k.

'"TJ Became My Dr Phil"–Warne.' *Espncricinfo*, May 27, 2011. Accessed June 30, 2025. http://www.espncricinfo.com/australia/content/story/516808.html.

Turnbull, Jeff. 'Warnie–the Musical–has the Great(ish) Man Stumped.' *The Sydney Morning Herald*, December 4, 2008. https://www.smh.com.au/entertainment/warnie-the-musical-has-the-greatish-man-stumped-20081204-6r9f.html.

Warne, Shane. 'My Life Flashed Before My Eyes.' *The Herald-Sun*, December 10, 2008, 7.

Wenner, Lawrence, and Steve Jackson. *Sport, Beer, and Gender: Promotional Culture and Contemporary Social Life*. Peter Lang, 2009.

3

SUBURBIA AND THE BEACH IN
SONGS FROM THE MIDDLE

The distinctive landscapes of a country occupy a special place in the national imaginary. In Eddie Perfect's musical *Songs from the Middle* (2010), he draws two iconic Australian landscapes – suburbia and the beach – together. Perfect figures these landscapes as ordinary, everyday places where people live out their lives, and as catalysts for profoundly spiritual and transformative experiences. While the cycle is set in a particular place – Mentone, a beachside suburb of Melbourne where Perfect grew up – Perfect uses Mentone to represent the nation metonymically, offering a critical yet affectionate perspective on life in the Australian suburbs and on the beach. *Songs from the Middle* is a meditation on the affective dimensions of these landscapes and how they suffuse themselves into the lives of their inhabitants.

Perfect was commissioned to write *Songs from the Middle* by the Australian National Academy of Music (ANAM), a post-tertiary music institution located in Melbourne. The work, a series of themed songs performed in concert format, had its inaugural performance as part of the 2010 Melbourne Cabaret Festival. Perfect composed music and lyrics for the thirteen songs that make up the cycle, and then worked closely with arranger Iain Grandage, who took Perfect's chord charts, melodies, and lyrics, and transformed the songs into rich orchestral tapestries. The project had been timed to coincide with the visit of the esteemed Brodsky String Quartet to ANAM. The work was performed at the South Melbourne Town Hall, where Perfect was accompanied by the Brodskys as well as additional musicians from ANAM. It was later broadcast on ABC Television in 2011 and then re-staged for the 2015 Adelaide Cabaret Festival.[1]

Suburbia and the beach are examples of what geographer John Short refers to as 'national environmental ideologies': landscapes loaded with symbolic value

DOI: 10.4324/9781003590088-4

that reflect the history and character of a nation.[2] Fiske, Hodge, and Turner describe the two sites as the 'central myths' underpinning contemporary white Australian society.[3] In *Songs from the Middle*, Mentone's landscapes function metonymically. While Perfect represents the particularities of Mentone's people, places, and history, he does so indirectly. This preference for indirect reference was lamented by reviewers such as David Washington, who felt that 'Perfect has squibbed it in the storytelling. We learn little of his family or the nitty-gritty of his suburban childhood and why it repelled him, and then drew him back to reconsider the people and places of Mentone.'[4] This is because hyperlocal verisimilitude is not Perfect's goal. Rather, his metonymic representation reflects on the way these landscapes act as 'selective shorthand,' to use Tim Edensor's words, that is, as 'synecdoches through which they are recognised globally.'[5] Moreover, what iconic landscapes like suburbia and the beach do is 'stitch the local and the national together through their serial reproduction across nations.'[6] Perfect's representation of these sites strikes a balance between the particular and the generic, inviting the Australian viewer to substitute their own suburb and beach into the equation.

Perfect situates suburbia and the beach as landscapes that straddle the mythic and the ordinary. He recognises that they are 'loaded with symbolic values,' to quote Tim Edensor, and also fundamentally ordinary places where people live, work, love, laugh, and die.[7] Perfect was interested in this juxtaposition, stating that his aim was to 'find the poetry and romance in the ordinariness that I saw in Mentone.'[8] His approach, which is to render these sites through compact song-vignettes, finds beauty in the banal, elevating their everyday qualities and attenuating their mythic ones.

This sense of suburbia and the beach as landscapes characterised by their in-betweenness is encapsulated in the title of the work, with its use of the word 'middle.' It reflects Mentone's geographic position, located halfway between the city of Melbourne and the Mornington Peninsula, or halfway between the urban and the rural. Suburbia is often denoted as a middle zone: described, for instance, by Chris Healy as 'a middle landscape, as a "place" that is forever in between.'[9] 'Middle' also has a temporal resonance. In the cycle, time spent on the beach is portrayed as liminal, located between the quotidian and the transcendental. Suburbia, on the other hand, is often conceived of as a place where time is experienced as static and repetitive, an endless present. This is in contrast with the bush, which tends to symbolise a rural and/or bucolic past, and the city, which points towards modernity and the future. This sense of suburban life as stiflingly repetitive reflects Edensor's observation that the time of everyday living is interpreted as such because it is continually compared to the 'time of celebrity, of holidays, of exceptional and symbolic events.'[10]

Additionally, 'middle' signifies middle-class. Perfect has commented that so much of his work 'is about understanding what it means to be middle-class.'[11]

His early performances were marked by a denigrative treatment of the middle-classes, which he now views as a reactionary impulse to his own comfortable upbringing in Mentone as the son of teachers, taking music and ballet lessons, and attending St Bede's College.[12] His use of the song cycle format intensifies his engagement with the middle class. As musicologist Laura Tunbridge has written, the song cycle is a form that when it came to prominence as a musical genre in the nineteenth-century Europe was geared towards a 'new musical audience: the educated middle classes.'[13] It also had an explicit relationship to the expression of national identity. Tunbridge notes that it was the folk-like qualities of strophic songs, written in the local language and often with reference to environmental features and landscapes that proved so appealing to audiences. In other words, the song cycle engaged audiences in the production and reproduction of the national imaginary.

Satire and Sympathy in Suburbia

Suburbia is an ongoing concern in Perfect's work. In *Songs from the Middle*, Perfect shifts the 'stigmatise or mythologise' binary prevalent in Australian art and literature by representing suburbia both ironically and comically, sentimentally and satirically, as a place that people love, hate, and feel generally ambivalent towards.[14] The cycle reflects Chris Healy's observation that suburbia functions as a potent site of 'change, family, community, childhood, and the tenuous habits we sometimes imagine as tradition.'[15] It is thus much more than just a matter of geography. Rather, as Andrew McCann writes, suburbia is a 'neuralgic point' in the national imaginary, one that is returned to time and time again.[16]

Discussion of suburbia has tended to fall into two polarised positions: to stigmatise it or to mythologise it. Brian Kinnane submits that the anti-suburban strain 'has long been a deep current in the Australian artistic and intellectual mainstream.'[17] Graeme Davison traces this trend back to the nineteenth century, arguing that suburbia's twenty-first-century detractors – who comment on its homogeneity, its insularity, and its 'spiritual emptiness' – merely restate long-standing objections to the concept.[18] Anti-suburbanism is present across all forms of Australian art and culture. In drama, the pre-eminent example is Patrick White's *Season at Sarsaparilla* (1962), subtitled 'a charade of suburbia in two acts.' Films like *Strictly Ballroom* (1992), *The Adventures of Priscilla, Queen of the Desert* (1994) and *Muriel's Wedding* (1994) are, for Karl Quinn, premised on 'an unacknowledged loathing of suburbia.'[19] In comedy, Barry Humphries' character Dame Edna skewers suburban life, and Humphries' legacy, according to Simon Caterson and also Sue Turnbull, runs through the hit television program *Kath & Kim*.[20] In visual art, as Kinnane notes, this anti-suburban strain is evident in the work of the Heidelberg painters, the 'Heide' modernists, and Sidney Nolan.[21]

The origins of the mythologised view of suburbia lie in the colonial period. Davison demonstrates that the vision of Australia as a suburban nation was present from invasion, when two years after the founding of Sydney, Governor Phillip presented an urban design plan that suggested houses be 'laid out in such a manner as to afford free circulation of air' and that land titles should contain a clause that would 'prevent more than one house being built on the allotment.'[22] Philip's vision of Australia as a suburban society did eventuate. As Brendan Gleeson notes, by 1901, 70% of Australians were living in suburbia.[23] Suburbia was conceived of as a project that could deliver a better quality of life for Australians. This is the defence that Hugh Stretton offered in his 1970 book, *Ideas for Australian Cities*, where he wrote that 'you don't have to be a mindless conformist to choose suburban life. Most of the best poets and painters and inventors and protestors choose it too. It reconciles access to work and city with private, adaptable, self-expressive living space at home.'[24] This vision of suburbia remains a powerful ideal, as Ian Craven observes: even in the 'most critical of suburban fictions,' the potency of the suburban ideal is omnipresent.[25] This mythology has been continued in contemporary Australia through the long-running soap operas *Neighbours* and *Home and Away*. Stephen Crofts writes that *Neighbours*' idyllic Ramsay Street, where 'crime, violence, and murder – the staples of many soaps – emphatically do not occur,' is a domestic and depoliticised zone where interpersonal crises were resolved quickly and without fuss, and where wholesome suburban values prevailed.[26]

Prior to writing *Songs from the Middle*, Perfect was firmly in the stigmatise camp. He was known almost exclusively for his acerbic commentary on matters of Australian culture, and in particular, his satire of the suburban middle class. For example, his 2005 cabaret *Angry Eddie* contained a song entitled 'Suburbia' that personified the site as a woman. The female subject of the song, an 'appliance-wielding Goddess,' is constructed through products: she exists only to consume and to be consumed. Perfect here intensifies what Belinda Burns describes as the negatively tinged, 'persistent and somewhat unique coding' of Australian suburbia as 'excessively "feminine."'[27] In the song, suburbanites are cast as obsessed with the accumulation of material possessions, and suburbia is, by association, a vacuous place worthy only of derision.[28]

Songs from the Middle represents an about-face in Perfect's rhetoric. The cycle stages his acceptance of the reality that, while other artists and intellectuals have favoured the bush and the city as symbolic sites, most of the nation lives in suburbia. In a 2011 episode of the ABC television program *Artscape*, Perfect reflected on this fact when he commented that 'everyone has to live somewhere, and all places have their own unique quality and flavour and doesn't matter where you live, but amazing things, small things, exciting things, dangerous things happen, people's lives play out, millions and millions of Australians' lives play out in the suburbs.'[29] As a child, Perfect couldn't wait to get out, describing growing up in Mentone as 'like being wrapped in a beige cardigan while longing to wear something far more flamboyant,' but as he grew older, he started to see his suburb in a different light.[30] In an interview, he confessed:

> In my twenties I was running Mentone down and have always felt guilty about that because, as I came to have kids of my own, I realised that people's lives matter; the amazing, interesting heart-breaking stories of love and loss, success and failure, tragedy, wonder, and bizarreness. These things happened in all places – Mentone included.[31]

Songs from the Middle pushes back against the stigmatise or mythologise binary by portraying multivalent perspectives on suburban life. 'For much of its existence,' writes Gleeson, 'Australian suburbia has been a heartland embraced physically but denied emotionally.'[32] In *Songs from the Middle*, the emotional contours of suburban life are traced.

The cycle begins with a negative view of suburbia. 'The Way It Was,' the opening song, catalogues all the things about suburbia that are worth denigrating. It is a sardonic portrait of a fractured community, full of unhappy people with unfulfilled lives. Both the title and the music, at least initially, obfuscate the underlying critique of the song. A phrase like 'The Way It Was' suggests a nostalgic longing for the past, and this sentiment is initially conferred by the wistful and warm, yet hopeful atmosphere created by the music. Its sentimental eight-bar instrumental introduction, scored for string quartet with a sonorous melody and rich harmonies, intentionally misleads. As the verses progress, it becomes clear that the song has no intention of providing audiences with an opportunity to indulge in nostalgia about a simpler time. Each verse, which introduces us to a resident of suburbia, contains a barb that reveals no one in this suburb is living the good life. This sleight of hand is achieved through the structure of the lyrics in each verse: the first line introduces the character and the location; the second adds a complication; the third delivers the outcome; and the final line, containing the title (known as the 'hook'), draws it all together, as the first verse shows:

> Susan disappeared on the way to the shops
> Stopped to smell the roses and they called the cops
> Now she'll never know how much that new dress cost
> I think she liked it better the way it was

The unexpected demise of Susan is one example of the song's tongue-in-cheek rendering of the clichés associated with the 'suburban gothic,' a style that, as Bernice Murphy notes, exploits the lingering suspicion that even the most ordinary-looking neighbourhood, or house, or family, has something to hide, and that no matter how calm and settled a place looks, it is only ever a moment away from dramatic (and generally sinister) incident.[33]

The suburban gothic is the terrain of the middle-class, and the use of 'disappeared' as a euphemism to convey Susan's demise hints at the middle-class politeness which Perfect has so often reviled. The line also invokes the banality of 'going down the shops – always going down the shops' that, as Perfect explains in the *Artscape* program, is one of the things he found so stifling about his suburban upbringing.[34] This verse, with its imagery of consumerism, fashion, and shopping, sets up a very stereotypical image of suburbia as a feminised zone. Even in death, Susan thinks only of not having had the opportunity to buy one more item of clothing. Susan's male counterpoint, introduced in the second verse, is Mark, a depressed family man with a high-powered office job commuting long hours into the city and looking for a way out. Despite being 'rich and powerful, his life was charmed,' he is injecting drugs to ease the existential pain of his soulless office job: 'after work he still stuck a needle in his arm.' Mark's misery highlights the bleak effects of suburban sprawl and middle-class aspirations.

In the third and fourth verses, Perfect targets suburban small-mindedness, insularity, and an inability to adapt when new information presents itself. He imagines Galileo growing up in Australian suburbia, dramatising his discovery that the earth was round as being so upsetting to the townspeople – the 'angry mob' – that they have him summarily executed. Galileo mourns his decision to reveal his discovery to them and disturb the status quo: 'I think I liked it better the way it was.' Galileo's presence in Mentone draws attention to how, as Craven observes, suburbia is often represented as a place 'rocked by fears and knowledges supposedly ironed out of existence by science and rationality.'[35] The fourth verse takes the premise in a different direction, imagining if Jesus had been a boy growing up in Mentone. It evokes images of men renovating their houses with the line 'All his dad would talk about were nails and wood,' which also relays a crucifixion joke. The implication is that suburbia is a site incapable of accepting such visionaries, even if that was where they had the misfortune to be born. These verses allude to how Perfect himself felt as a young person in Mentone, like he was a Jesus or Galileo, cast out and misunderstood. It also recalls the perception of suburbia as engendering a 'living death of conformity.'[36]

In the release sections, which appear after verses two and four, Perfect implicates the audience in the horror of this suburban gothic through second person address. In the second release, which segues into the fifth verse, he sings:

It only takes one little dream to go up in smoke
Before we slam the shutters closed and give up hope

And we'll never get over that hurdle because
We think we liked it better the way it was.

While the audience has been addressed indirectly in the first release – 'don't you remember?'–this final verse is unambiguous in its interpellation. The last line, the 'hook,' has been modified slightly every verse: 'she liked it' 'he liked it' and 'I liked it' (for Jesus and Galileo). This final modification – 'we liked it' – is directed at the audience. Perfect implicates suburbanites – the vast majority of Australians – of being the ones slamming the shutters closed, of being closed to new ideas, new information, and new people, and is sceptical this can be changed. The song concludes as it began, with a short, rich passage played by a string quartet, where the beauty of the music strongly contrasts with the rather disheartening ending to the narrative.

While there is little in the lyrics to mark the song as particularly Australian, the musical idiom subtly engages the repertory of the national imaginary. In style, it appropriates many features common to standard American popular songs and, with its warm and emotive string passages, suspensions, flattened sixths, and chromatic passing notes, is reminiscent of the music of Jerome Kern. However, the song also has qualities of the narrative ballad, a form of folk music and poetry, and these two styles are not mutually exclusive: the combination has also produced 'Waltzing Matilda,' which is arguably Australia's most iconic song.[37] This affiliation with 'Waltzing Matilda' is also borne out in the music itself. The melody of the verse, with its arpeggiated tonic chords and subsequent descents towards the tonic, bears similarity to the tune of 'Waltzing Matilda.'[38] 'The Way It Was' also borrows from 'Waltzing Matilda' the juxtaposition of macabre narrative with tuneful melody. While 'Waltzing Matilda' does not have the conspicuous layer of irony of Perfect's song, there is a commonality in approach that allows Perfect to refer to drug use, execution, and crucifixion so casually, as the national citizenry is well accustomed to singing along to a tale of loneliness and suicide.[39] 'The Way It Was' is to suburbia what 'Waltzing Matilda' is for the bush. In musically appropriating 'Waltzing Matilda,' Perfect foregrounds the role of suburbia as an iconic national landscape, one that figures prominently in the national imaginary.

In 'My Sister Worked at Bunnings,' the fifth song in the cycle, Perfect reflects on how suburbia has changed with the passing of time. The song cultivates a sombre mood, steeped in nostalgia, and was described by the broadcaster and composer Andrew Ford as 'unbearably poignant.'[40] The atmosphere is prepared by Perfect's simple introduction to the song: 'This is a true story,' which is followed immediately by a plaintive, slow octave leap from the clarinet. After a short orchestral introduction, the lyrics begin with the evocation of a memory: 'When I was young, my sister worked at Bunnings.' The first verse conjures an ordinary Saturday morning spent by the young woman at her part-time job at a Bunnings hardware store, where she 'put on her uniform,' 'worked the barbecue,' and 'served sausages in bread.' But in the second verse, the subject of the song is revealed to be neither Perfect nor his sister: the story really belongs to the man who owns the local hardware store, whose store is forced to close because it can no longer compete with Bunnings. The poetic injustice of the final verse sees the man going to work for the company that has put him out of business:

> There she saw that owner of that local hardware store
> He put on their uniform
> Took orders from a young boy
> 'If you cannot beat them join them'
> This she swore he said

Perfect's performance style is grave: his face contorts with pain and his voice quavers with emotion. 'My Sister Worked at Bunnings' tells the story of a decent Aussie bloke and his family, having a go, and being defeated by the forces of neoliberalism.

The song is rendered significantly more poignant because of the special place of Bunnings in the national imaginary. Bunnings is a chain of hardware stores that were started in late nineteenth-century Western Australia by two brothers, Arthur and Robert Bunning. But the recent history of the company, and the Bunnings that exists today, begins in 1994 with the opening of the first Melbourne store and the complete acquisition of the company by the conglomerate Wesfarmers. Bunnings stores function as far more than just places to go and buy tools or garden equipment. Rather, the company is generally viewed as encapsulating something uniquely Australian. Bunnings' supposed commitment to the local renders the demise of the man's business even more heart-wrenching. This relationship between Bunnings and the community is well illustrated with a personal example. In late 2017, a new Bunnings Warehouse opened close to where I live. The news was received with great excitement, and not just because of the new jobs that it would bring to the region; its opening was produced as a community event. The store was officially opened by the former Australian cricketer Brett Lee, and it was reported in the local paper that more than 1,200 people were present.[41] The company website foregrounds their commitment to the local and Bunnings stores regularly hold other sorts of community events. In 2017, a newly married Sydney couple took their wedding party to the Bunnings carpark for a celebratory sausage sizzle: a barbecued sausage enfolded in a slice of white bread, with sauce and onions optional.[42] This 'uniquely Australian variant' of the barbecue is a staple of the Bunnings experience, where each weekend, a rotating roster of community groups use it as a fundraising opportunity.[43] In 2024, tickets sold out in just four minutes for a rave held at a Melbourne Bunnings, with DJs performing on the warehouse roof.[44] The engagement of the community with Bunnings extends into the political sphere. A striking demonstration of this occurred in 2004, when the then Minister for Multicultural Affairs Gary Hardgrave held a citizenship ceremony in a Queensland Bunnings store. Hardgrave said that he thought it was a perfect choice, remarking that 'I don't think there are many settings more Australian than a hardware store on a Sunday morning.'[45]

In order to reflect on the negative impact of the large chain store on local businesses (and communities more broadly), 'My Sister Worked at Bunnings' recalls a mythologised suburbia of tight-knit communities, populated by small businesses, and where everyone knows their neighbour. The fact that, in Perfect's song, it is Bunnings that has put the man out of business is what produces the sense of pathos. The poignancy of the song would be substantially diminished if another company were to be substituted. The song relies on the special place that Bunnings holds in the Australian national imaginary for the song to pack its affective punch.

Yet at the end of the second verse, this nostalgic vision of the past is problematised. 'My Sister Worked at Bunnings' cultivates nostalgia only to reflect on its elusiveness. Regarding the closure of the store, Perfect sings 'Some say that's sad but it's just the way it is.' The ambivalence expressed by the narrator urges us not to indulge in nostalgia's 'rebellion against the modern idea of time, the time of history and progress' and the way that it encourages our 'desires to obliterate history and turn it into private or collective mythology, to revisit time like space, refusing to surrender to the irreversibility of time.'[46] In the release section, marked on the score as 'moving forward,' the narrative is briefly suspended as the lyrics reflect upon the passage of time and the speed at which the world transforms:

Change, everything changes
The only thing that stays the same is how we hate to change
The stage transforms and rearranges
And we its weary players
Either don't give up
Or won't give up
Leap ahead
Or just pretend

On the last four lines, the tempo increases further, and the texture of the orchestral arrangement begins to thicken. A tenuto strings passage, marked accelerando, builds until the sudden pulling back of the last phrase, where Perfect sings, 'It doesn't really matter in the end,' followed by a pregnant pause. Rendered more wrenching through the tension of an extended double suspension, this is the structural climax of the song. And then, in the final verse, even the out-of-business hardware man capitulates. He puts on the Bunnings uniform and makes the choice to move forward. In doing so, Perfect problematises nostalgia for the suburban Australia of the past, asking his audience to think critically about its mythologised position in the national imaginary.

The ambivalence articulated here is germane to the choice of musical idiom. Above, I quoted Ford's remark that 'My Sister Worked at Bunnings' is 'unbearably poignant,' but this is not in fact the full quote. In its entirety, he said 'unbearably poignant when *set to music*.' This invites a consideration of the particular qualities of Perfect's music and Grandage's orchestration: how exactly do they create this poignancy? The music of 'My Sister Worked at Bunnings,' has, somewhat surprisingly, a distinctly Jewish sound. Clarinet and violin, perhaps the two instruments most affiliated with Jewish music, feature heavily. The song begins with a clarinet solo marked on the score 'molto-espressivo, quasi klezmer,' and string parts marked 'old, Polish.'

Diverse traditions of Jewish music are unified by way a common tonality – the minor mode.[47] Pertaining specifically to *Fiddler on the Roof* (the most famous musical to make use of an explicitly Jewish idiom), Joseph Swain writes that 'the alternation of parallel minor and major modes within songs, sometimes within phrases' is key to the musical construction of the work.[48] In American popular song, there is broader evidence of this as a feature of a Jewish sound. Musicologist Jeffrey Magee cites a conversation between Richard Rodgers and Cole Porter where Porter is said to have claimed that the key to writing hits was to write 'Jewish' songs. Magee suggests that what Porter is referring to is a 'mixture of major and minor modality inflected by chromaticism.'[49] Porter was not Jewish, but he certainly wrote songs that fit this description, and this is why Richard Rodgers could claim that

> it is surely one of the ironies of the musical theatre that despite the abundance of Jewish composers, the one who has written the most enduring 'Jewish' music should be an Episcopalian millionaire who was born on a farm in Peru, Indiana.[50]

All this considered, it is not as strange as it sounds to say that a song by an Australian composer, set in Bunnings, sounds Jewish.

This minor-major modality identified by Werner and Swain is present in 'My Sister Worked at Bunnings.' The tonality of the song vacillates between F minor and D-flat major (the submediant major), and the tussle between these two keys is established from the outset of the song. They are the first two chords sounded, and this equivocal sense of tonality is sustained throughout. This minor-major tonality bolsters the ambivalent nostalgia of the song. As in Jewish music, the minor mode does not necessarily evoke sadness or melancholy. Rather, as Magee notes, it '[serves] as a foundation for any kind of expression . . . just as the blues form a neutral template for a wide variety of emotions in African-American music.'[51]

This minor-major tonality has broad-ranging influences on the song. The resultant effect of the adoption of D-flat major as the secondary tonal centre is the evocative introduction of the lowered second scale degree – G-flat. This lowered second scale degree (an 'unmistakably modal reference,' according to Swain) becomes an expressive feature in both the harmony and the melody.[52] In Perfect's case, while these melodic G-flats are used as 4–3 suspensions to a D-flat major chord, they can also be interpreted as having an oblique relationship to the Freygish scale. Based on the Phrygian mode, and making use of a lowered second scale degree, the Freygish scale is a common mode in Jewish music. The song is not strictly Freygish, as the characteristic augmented second between the second and third scale degrees never used in succession in the melody. However, in 'My Sister Worked at Bunnings,' these are the only scale degrees – apart from a solitary E natural – that are altered with accidentals. It is for this reason that, while it is certainly not a textbook use of the scale, 'My Sister Worked at Bunnings' can be understood as referencing Freygish properties. This point becomes more significant when considering David Goldman's argument that in the context of Jewish religious music this Freygish movement from the flattened second to the tonic

> functions as an ironic reversal of the most characteristic gesture in Western tonal music: the ascent of the sharpened 7th degree of the ordinary Western scale, or leading tone, to the tonic. This is the most characteristic pointer to the forward motion of time in Western music.[53]

How fitting then, that Perfect alludes to this scale, and eschews 7–1 melodic movement, in a song that explicitly deals the relentless forward march of time.

Further evidence for this interpretation can be found in the harmony. Each verse ends in an imperfect cadence. The perfect cadences are in fact are displaced so that they occur *between* sections. Neither does the song conclude on a decisive perfect cadence. Rather, it closes with a dominant chord, that is eventually resolved, but most obliquely: a solitary F is sounded by a single wine glass that provides the transition from this song to the next. Through its ambivalently nostalgic music and its melancholy, conflicting narrative, 'My Sister Worked at Bunnings' asks its audiences to think critically about the role of suburbia in the national imaginary, and the way in which the suburban ideal is sustained in our lives.

The eleventh song in the cycle, 'What Are We to Do,' is a comic, affectionate take on the boredom of living in suburbia. The premise is that an alien ship has landed in Mentone in 1992. The citizens are perplexed by this: 'What Are We to Do?' they ask. They go off to alert the mayor, a rather hopeless character, who just throws his hands up in the air to ask, 'Should I issue them a fine or just arrest them? Befriend them? Lend them to the zoo? Tell me what am I to do?' The aliens are thus left to their own devices. They stroll down the main street, where they meet a young boy. He details to them all the things that he does in Mentone:

> Mostly I just ride my skateboard
> Sometimes I just watch the girls
> Avoid Patrick Charles who wants to hurt me
> Catch a bus from here to Chadstone
> Some say it's the home of fashion
> Mostly we just ride our bikes
> Buy slabs of beer and drink in parks
> Or maybe go get fish and chips
> And eat them down on Mentone beach
> We go play ten pin bowls a lot
> Some say there's drugs there but there's not
> The Edgy pub does dollar pots on Wednesday
> But you gotta wear a collared shirt have proper shoes
> Or the bouncer will not let you through
> And that's all there is to do

This collection of things to do is an attempt to constitute the ineffable experience of belonging to a place. Humorously, though, upon hearing the list, the aliens decide to pack up and leave, implying that Mentone is not interesting enough to warrant staying. But their presence in Mentone is not framed as a frightening science fiction scenario: rather, their arrival is entertaining, as is the bewilderment of the Mentonians. This is supported through the music, conveying a light-hearted, cartoon-like atmosphere through its jaunty marimba motif and *Lion King*-esque timbre and syncopated rhythm, with string tremolos and slides conveying the spookiness of the aliens. The upbeat music tempers the brief moments of critique, buried between the catchy, repetitive verses, like the first release section:

> My dog saw a cat going into a drain
> And he stared into that drain so long he was never quite the same
> Cos if you look into the void too long
> You know the void looks into you
> What are we to do?

On paper, this is a rather bleak lyric, one that hints at the mindlessness of suburban life, but the jovial music and the warmth of Perfect's delivery result in a song that is joyous rather than depressing. Overall, there is an affectionate quality present in 'What Are We to Do,' one that represents a reckoning – or at least an acceptance – with a place Perfect previously only had cause to malign.

The final song in the cycle, 'Nepean Highway,' a Jason Robert Brown-esque barcarolle that shifts between 12/8 and 9/8, reflects a different sort of ambivalence to that of 'My Sister Worked at Bunnings.' In the episode of *Artscape*, Perfect recounted how many had assumed that the creation of the show meant that he had made peace with Mentone and may even want to return. This is not the case, and he has described the cycle as 'a homage to a place you don't want to live.'[54] Perfect reflects on the contradiction that the highway is the road that brings one in and out of Mentone: simultaneously the path of escape and the path towards home, with the circular intervals of the melody musically conveying this. Perfect sings 'I came back [to Mentone] looking for answers, to dig up some mem-'ries, to feel what I felt and of course write some songs.' He recounts his time interviewing and chatting to the locals, his observations that 'these are folks who belong.' But then he reflects on his continued unease: 'what if you don't . . . feel the same? Don't need the butcher, the baker, the candlestick maker all knowing your name.' In the climactic final verse, Perfect thanks Evan Nepean, the highway's namesake, who 'helped me to realise that I left in anger'; this time, however, he's 'leaving in peace.' Some musicians begin to sing this line with Perfect, as the music grows and swells around them. The cycle closes with this calming sense of making peace with suburbia.

On the Beach: People, Time, Sensations, and Impressions

The other important landscape of Mentone is the beach. In the cycle, it is evoked through two songs. The first, 'There's a Beach Somewhere,' is a gentle meditation on the role of the beach in the Australian psyche. The second, 'The Middle of the World,' is a rumination of the passing of time and the sweetness of a life lived on the beach. These 'beach songs,' while sharing thematic ground, also bear musical and dramaturgical similarities. The orchestrations adopt similar text-painting techniques for conveying the beach, with expressive devices like trills, harmonics, and pizzicato cello basslines creating an aural continuity. For this reason, while they do not occur in sequence in the cycle, I consider them as a pair. Unlike in *Muriel's Wedding*, these depictions of the beach are devoid of clichéd signifiers, eschewing descriptions of lifesavers, surfers, tans, bikinis, ice creams, and umbrellas. Perfect focuses instead on the relationship of the beach to individuals, demonstrating the affective and spiritual qualities of the beach. The songs foreground the temporal qualities of the site, the sense of timelessness and repetition that the beach engenders. Importantly, Perfect presents the beach in its full complexity: as both a mythic site, a conduit for spiritual encounters, and also a fundamentally quotidian place.

The national anthem proclaims Australia as a land 'girt by sea,' but, since the nation boasts 36,735 kilometres of coastline, the continent perhaps is more aptly described as being girt by beach. It is a landscape considered metonymic of the nation. This is evident from its frequent reproduction in tourist campaigns, local advertisements, television programs, film, literature, and theatre – ubiquitous almost to the point of being taken for granted. But this was not always the case. Artistic depictions of the beach in the colonial period, for example, are rare as in this period the bush was omnipresent as the iconic Australian landscape. The beach operates as a 'privileged metaphor' for thinking about Australian national identity.[55] This sentiment is encapsulated by Robert Drewe's statement that 'I feel most Australian when I turn the corner on a bush track . . . and spot a patch of ocean framed in the branches of a eucalypt.'[56]

The beach rose to prominence as a cultural symbol and the subject of artistic interest in the twentieth century in tandem with the nation's rapid urbanisation. As the mythology of the bush became increasingly at odds with people's lived experience, the beach, as both 'urban *and* natural, civilised *and* primitive, spiritual *and* physical, culture *and* nature' provided an apt replacement.[57] It has been well documented that the myth of the bush was just that – a myth – and was far from 'an accurate representation of the Australian people.'[58] But as a large proportion of the Australian population is concentrated in coastal regions, many Australians do have material access to and lived experience of the beach.[59] And, while there are a wide variety of different beaches throughout Australia, there is also a sense that the beach is a 'homogenous site.'[60] It is a place of public gathering and private reflection, an egalitarian paradise, as Anne Game writes: 'no one owns the sun, sea, surf – or everyone, all Australians own it.'[61]

'There's a Beach Somewhere' acts as a meditation on the way the beach lingers in one mind's long after the actual space has been departed. It is the shortest song in the cycle, with a very brief lyric that is only sung once with no repetition:

> Old aches
> New pains
> And everything old is new again
> This thought like a chandelier hangs in my brain
> Isn't it nice to know there's a beach down there?
> Somewhere
> Anywhere
> Isn't it nice to know there's a beach?

The song is deliberately unspecific about place, with the lack of detail meaning that the song is open enough to evoke any beach. The use of the indefinite article in the title of the song explicitly invites the listener to substitute their own site. Huntsman observes that while early depictions of the beach in Australia were generally descriptive – 'that of a viewer describing a painting' – in the twentieth century, the focus shifted decisively to the '*peopled* beach.'[62] Analysis and commentary on the beach is similarly 'peopled.'[63] An expedient example of this can be witnessed in Bruce Bennett's coincidentally titled 'A Beach Somewhere: The Australian Littoral Imagination at Play,' which begins with a subheading entitled 'A Personal Response':

> We all have a beach somewhere. Mine is called City Beach. It is located some fifteen kilometres from the city of Perth and eight kilometres from my home in suburban Wembley. It is the late 1950s. As you pedal steadily up the last of the sand dunes transformed into asphalt road, you catch your first glimpse of the ocean. Although it is early afternoon, the sea breeze is already in, and beyond the gleaming white beach, the blue sea is flecked with white. Out on the horizon is your island of distant desire which the Dutch named Rottnest. The beach is now very close, as you rest on the pedals for the last downhill run, then park your bike, grab your towel, and race for the water.[64]

I, like Bennett, also have a beach, and when I listen to the song, as it reaches its structural climax on the uncomplicated pronouncement 'Isn't it nice to know that there's a beach?' I find myself nodding along: yes, it is nice to know that there's a beach.[65] This is what Perfect found when, as recounted in an interview for *The Sydney Morning Herald*, he spoke to Mentone locals 'who had never articulated what they liked about' living there, and that

> what really shone through was the importance of the beach. They live near the beach but they never go. It struck me that just the idea of something was what they carried around in their heads. It's just really nice to know it's there.[66]

Huntsman has argued that the material and emotional relationship to the beach for Australians is such that when it is invoked, little exposition or justification is required. Referring to three 1990s novels set at the beach, she remarks that there is no 'need to describe the scene for someone who has never been there, or as if seeing it for the first time' – the beach has become 'stitched' into the fabric of daily life.[67] This is the approach that Perfect adopts in *Songs from the Middle*. Through music, he shows how the landscape suffuses itself into people's lives.

'The Middle of the World' is a playful excursion to a time in the past where life is imagined as less complicated, and there is nothing but sea, sun, sand, and sky. The song takes its inspiration from the life and memories of retired schoolteacher Leo Gamble, a Mentone resident and keen local historian.[68] In the introduction to the song, Perfect tells the audience how, in researching the show, he read Gamble's history of Mentone and then conducted an interview with him. Afterwards, Gamble sent Perfect a short story that he had written entitled 'The Ducks,' set on Mentone Beach, the narrative of which tells the story of a group of young men and a group of young women meeting on the beach. A black and white photograph of Gamble and his friends in 1948 accompanied the story, and Perfect, quite taken by the image and the narrative, was inspired to write a song from Gamble's perspective.

'The Middle of the World' foregrounds the temporality of the beach experience, which is characterised by repetition and a sense of timelessness. As Mark Gibson writes that 'the significance of the beach is not as a site of escape but, on the contrary, of a certain inertia; it is a place where things can be trusted to *endure*.'[69] The song opens with a passage of rhythmically, texturally, and harmonically opaque orchestral music that gradually gives way to a steady pulse and clear tonality, where a quaver ostinato on the tonic chord (B-flat) is established conveying a constant but gentle ebb and flow of the tide.

This motif underpins the entire song, ceasing to sound only at three key points: the end of both verses, where the title of the song is sung, and the very last bar, reflecting Elizabeth Ellison and Lesley Hawkes' observation that there is a 'strong sense of repetition' embedded in the experience of the beach.[70] Structurally, while 'The Middle of the World' is just over five minutes in length, it contains only two verses – one, shown above, and a second that metamorphoses into a bridge. The song closes with an abridged third verse, where the final line is an exact repeat of the very first line of the song, thereby functioning as a sort of 'false start' by intimating that the song, or perhaps the day, will begin again. The resulting effect is that, as it contains no catchy recurring chorus, the song never quite settles into a predictable pattern. This structure can be read as a way of conveying the temporality of 'the middle.'

In *Songs from the Middle*, the beach is treated as a liminal zone, one that, like suburbia, problematises the dichotomy between city and bush. Physically, the beach is understood as a transitional landscape: an 'anomalous' zone between land and sea that provides a 'physical bridge between the city (culture) and the sea (nature).'[71] Huntsman, borrowing from Phillip Drew, who describes the veranda as a threshold, conceptualises the beach as a similarly liminal space.[72] As the first verse shows, Perfect locates the beach as existing in a temporality where, as Robert Preston-Whyte avers, 'the stress of normal working lives is suspended, cultures merge, egalitarianism flourishes, and bonds of friendship are forged.'[73] This is further intensified by the fact that the characters portrayed in the songs are adolescents, and so are also experiencing the liminal period between childhood and adulthood. This can be seen in the way that the beach is the landscape that enables the distinctly drawn groups of the 'boys' and the 'girls' to meet. The first verse establishes a distinction between the 'girls' and 'us' (the boys) and, in doing so, conveys the playfulness of the rituals of courting that often feature in representations of beach life.

Days explaining away the girls who ignore us
1948 and Port Phillip Bay stretched out before us
And when we fall we'll talk it all 'round sweet again
And when they call we'll drag our sand-burnt feet again
and after all we'll walk these tired streets again
'Til we meet again in the middle of the world

The lyrics here express the comfort of the repetitive behaviours that come with living in the same place for a long time – walking the same streets home, having the same conversations, meeting on the beach for the umpteenth time that summer. The first verse begins 'Port Phillip Bay stretched out before us,' but then transitions to future tense: 'and when we fall.' The last verse, while mainly written in present tense, suddenly, on the last line, shifts to the past, articulating the fear of the present slipping away, and the imperative to try to capture the memory before it is gone: 'Storing it up some same place in my mind again, when we were living in the middle of the world.' These choices around tense convey that the beach is not governed by clock-time. 'The Middle of the World' attempts to capture the feeling of timelessness that such a place delivers, recalling the experience of days dictated only by the sun and the tide.

In the beach songs, word-painting techniques are used as a way of musically rendering the landscape of the beach. 'There's a Beach Somewhere' evokes a tranquil atmosphere, with the opening eight bars depicting the gentle lapping of the waves through a repeated semiquaver figure on the second and third beats of the bar that tapers with a decrescendo each time. The swell of the waves is also depicted via the dynamic contour of the opening, whereby the volume increases over the first four bars, and decreases over the second. This word-painting is supported by gentle pizzicato cello bass notes at the beginning of each bar which add to the rocking motion of the rhythm.

This word-painting mirrors the nineteenth-century impressionist renderings of Mentone Beach in visual art. Mentone was established as a seaside resort for wealthy Melburnians in the 1880s, and its beach was famously rendered in the 1888 Charles Conder painting *A Holiday at Mentone* (Figure 3.1). The beach songs relocate Mentone artistically from 1888 to 1948, recasting Mentone's most iconic image. This painting has further significance to the cycle, as Iain Grandage, the arranger, has never been to Mentone, and his experience of the place is, as he writes on his website, 'entirely formed' through Perfect's lyrics and Conder's painting.[74] There are echoes of Conder's painting in Grandage's orchestral arrangement for 'There's A Beach Somewhere.' While it is unstated by Perfect and Grandage, musical references to the work of Erik Satie provide a neat (yet subtle) connection to the *A Holiday at Mentone* painting. Satie's *Gymnopédies*, although perhaps not technically examples of musical impressionism, are considered to foreshadow techniques that will

FIGURE 3.1   Charles Conder's *A Holiday at Mentone* (1888). Courtesy of the Art Gallery of South Australia

become central to the approach, while Conder's painting is an example of Australian impressionism in the visual arts.[75]

The beach songs utilise features of musical impressionism that weave subtle connections to these nineteenth-century impressionist renderings of the beach. The score is marked 'Satie-esque,' indicating that Grandage is drawing on features of Satie's compositional style in the arrangement. The triple time signature musically alludes to the *Gymnopédies* (1888) and their characteristic crotchet-minim accompaniment figure. There are also harmonic similarities between the first *Gymnopedié* and 'There's a Beach Somewhere,' with both works utilising subdominant and tonic seventh chords as fundamental harmonies. Quartal and quintal chords are also utilised, as well as frequent use of 2nds, 7ths, and 9ths in the woodwind and vibraphone parts. This choice of harmony creates quite a different sonic experience to the previous two songs. The enigmatic quality of Satie's piano pieces is appropriated by the song, and the lack of harmonic drive, particularly the absence of strong cadences – Vsus^4– IV^7 just prior to the vocal entry and at the climax of the song at the end of the verse – intensifies the contemplative nature of the lyrics.

Like the impressionists, Perfect creates an 'impression' of the beach in the mind of the listener rather than creating an explicit image of the beach or a dramatic scenario involving it. There is no plot in 'There's a Beach Somewhere,' and nothing is achieved or resolved. It foregrounds 'perspective rather than progress,' to use Mary Davis' description of Satie's music.[76] Jules-Antoine Castagnary's oft-cited definition – that impressionists 'render not the landscape, but the sensations produced by the landscape' – encapsulates Perfect's approach.[77] Richard Taruskin notes that common features of this style are 'calculated effects of spontaneity; fascination with subtle gradations in colour and texture that produced a nebulous, highly suggestive surface; and a great interest in sensuousness than in psychology or strongly declared emotion.'[78] The calculated spontaneity is evident in the fragmentary vocal line, constructed to appear improvised; the nebulousness is in the atmosphere created by the harmony, the timbre of soft mallets on the vibraphone and harmonics in the strings, the soft, swelling string figures, the pianissimo woodwind notes, the feather light pizzicato bass line of the cello, and the understated nature of the sentiment that is being expressed. The vocal line also has something of the meandering quality of Satie's melody, but while Satie's melody weaves and wanders, Perfect's presents itself in short bursts. This is enhanced through the stream-of-consciousness style of the lyrics. The words at the beginning of the verse, heightened by the vocal delivery, are soft and understated – closer to speaking on pitch than legato singing. This renders the beach as a calm, quiet place for contemplation.

The Beach as a Site of Ordinary Spirituality

Both 'The Middle of the World' and 'There's a Beach Somewhere' are what Robert Drewe describes as '[invitations] to spirituality,' catalysts for the permission to ruminate.[79] In these songs, the beach takes on divine status as a guardian – it watches over you, 'hangs' in your brain, as the lyrics of 'There's a Beach Somewhere' say. In 'The Middle of the World,' Perfect alludes to a metaphysical poetics of the beach. What is distinctive about the 'spirituality' in *Songs from the Middle* is how unremarkable – how ordinary – these pronouncements are. The spiritual quality is deliberately understated; neither song engages in explicit discourses around danger, life and death, survival, environmental threats, or the like, as is so common in other beach texts.[80] It is rendered spiritual by invoking the mythic status of beach as a national symbol.

The beach is often portrayed in art and culture as a site of healing, transcendence, escape, and spiritual connection. Robert Drewe argues that, in contrast to other comparable nations, the Australian 'spiritual consciousness draws almost totally on the elements and on our environment.'[81] For Australians, the beach is a place where significant, yet routine moments are often marked. Huntsman characterises such events – visits to the beach upon returning from overseas, the almost 'baptismal ritual' of a baby's first swim, the scattering of a loved one's ashes into the ocean – as 'invitations to spirituality.'[82]

This conception of the beach, and the act of surfing in particular (namely the 'surfing is my religion' adage), is in common parlance.[83] Ellison and Hawkes note this connection, stating that the beach is often conceived of as spiritual in that it '[becomes] a type of "heaven on earth" . . . a space that provides a connection with a higher power beyond our world.'[84]

The second verse of 'The Middle of the World' explores a potent spiritual relationship with the beach. As the song moves towards the bridge, the lyric becomes more oblique. It ceases describing the actions of the boys and the girls frolicking on the shore, and an unnamed presence, referred to only as 'it,' is introduced:

> Everyone and everything belongs to me
> Other folk hum along and it sings its quiet songs to me
> Dodging arrows and slings
> Feel the tug of its strings

The allusion to the line in Hamlet's 'To Be or Not to Be' speech – 'to suffer the slings and arrow of outrageous fortune' – further strengthens the metaphysical dimension of this lyric. This verse then spills over into the bridge, which acts as the structural climax for the song:

> And I belong here
> Heaven knows I'll still be there
> With the boys I'll be waiting
> By the shore we'll be standing in the middle of the world

The moment that 'heaven' is proclaimed is rendered significant by the introduction of a new chord (E-flat m[6]) at 'heaven knows,' a chord that has not been heard prior. This line leads to the climactic point of the song:

> And I belong here
> Heaven knows I'll still be there
> With the boys I'll be waiting
> By the shore we'll be standing in the middle of the world

Rather than read the invocation of heaven in this lyric as an offhand turn of phrase, this presence that 'sings,' and 'tugs' can be interpreted as the beach itself. The omniscient presence of the beach hints at an almost spiritual conception of the site, inviting reflection on the beach as a catalyst for such experiences.

This notion of the beach as a spiritual site for the nation flies in the face of the prevailing view of Australia as a predominantly secular society.[85] In *Beyond Belief*, a study of the relationship of Australians to religious beliefs and practices, social researcher Hugh Mackay expounds on this, devoting a chapter to a phenomenon called SBNR – spiritual but not religious. This category accounts for a growing number of Australians who wish to maintain a spiritual life but distance themselves from organised religion. Mackay writes that for these people the word spiritual signifies 'something beyond the intellectual, beyond the emotional, beyond the cultural: a heightened sense of consciousness that illuminates or enriches our human potential; a glimpse of something we might call sublime.'[86] It is this type of spiritualism that is present in the beach songs. They express that the beach is an important catalyst for such feelings as a landscape that for some engenders consideration of what lies beyond.

All these ideas – the beach, the ordinary, the spiritual and the mythic – coalesce in an essay by the cultural studies scholar Meaghan Morris, entitled 'On the Beach,' in which Morris tries to grapple with this very question: is the beach in Australia mythic, or is it ordinary?[87] She notes that when it comes to the beach, these two opposing readings are inextricably entangled. By arguing that the Australian beach is both a quotidian reality and a site of mythic significance, what Morris evinces is, as Huntsman observes, 'the complex and emotionally charged relationship with the beach that many Australians would share but find difficult to articulate.'[88]

Morris invokes the concept of the ordinary to draw attention to the quotidian, but she also uses it in a different sense – as Ordinary, with a capital letter – and when she does so, it is in reference to the notion of the Ordinary as a 'political myth.'[89] Morris regards the Ordinary as inherently bound up with the nation, asserting that the 'problem of nationality can still be framed as a scene of white, male Ordinariness.'[90] The genesis of the concept is a passage from Donald Horne's book *The Lucky Country*, which reads:

> On an Australian beach on a hot summer day people doze in the sun or shoot the breakers like Hawaiian princes on pre-missionary Waikiki. The symbol is too far fetched for Australian taste. The image of Australia is of a man in an opennecked shirt solemnly enjoying an ice-cream. His kiddy is beside him.[91]

Significantly, the location in which the Ordinary is borne out is on the beach, and from the above passage, Morris assembles the notion of the 'Great Australian Ordinary,' a 'sacred, secular value,' predicated on a conception of white masculinity.[92] The man in Horne's passage is laconic, resistant to 'symbolic excess,' for all intents and purposes an 'ordinary' Australian.[93] This concept is a fixture in the national imaginary: as Morris notes, such a figure remains 'an object of intense desire for many a man of government,' and a demographic that continues to have significant political and cultural sway. Of course, the Ordinary shifts and moves over time – it is not intractable and is also arguably at play in something like the long running Australian soap opera *Home and Away* – but it is important to note its genesis in Horne. It is interesting to note that the two key Australia soap operas of the last few decades – *Neighbours* and *Home and Away* – are set respectively in 'ordinary' suburbia and the mythic but ordinary beachside suburb, demonstrating the enduring power of these sites in the national imaginary.

We have seen versions of the Ordinary in the previous two chapters: namely in the opening number of *Muriel's Wedding*, with its 'no-worries' attitude, and in *Shane Warne* through the construction of the protagonist as an 'ordinary' Australian: 'ev'ryone's a little bit like Shane.' But for Morris, Horne's description clearly reveals a sense of white male ownership of the beach. Aileen Moreton-Robinson argues that one of the effects of colonisation was that 'in the white colonial imagination,' Indigenous 'bodies were physically erased from the beach. Over the next century the only subjects who determined which bodies mattered on the beach were almost exclusively white males.'[94]

This Ordinary operates on two levels in *Songs from the Middle* – firstly, in the construction of Leo Gamble's 1948 Mentone in 'The Middle of the World,' and secondly, in its linguistic approach. A key feature of the cycle is the un-remarkability or ordinariness of Mentone. Earlier I elucidated the 'middle' as a temporal construct, but it also perhaps functions here as a synonym for Ordinary. There is certainly something of Horne's description in 'The Middle of the World.' By locating the song in 1948, Perfect gains access to stereotypes about Ordinary Australians common in this period. As psychologist Ronald Taft queried in 1962, 'What image is conjured up by the phrase "a typical Australian"? The popular image is that of a man of 30–40 years of age, dressed indifferently, speaking with an unmistakable Australian accent, bearing himself with a casual but confident air, friendly and wearing an easy-going expression.'[95] This is certainly the image that comes to mind in 'The Middle of the World.' As noted earlier, the first verse of clearly establishes the distinction between the 'girls' and the 'boys,' proudly assuming that the girls are going to love them: 'won't they adore us?' Here Perfect explores similar terrain to *Shane Warne*, with echoes of 'mateship' throughout the song, and a fierce sense of male camaraderie: 'With the boys I'll be waiting, By the shore we'll be standing,' the lyric proclaims. There is a sense of ownership over the beach and its inhabitants: 'Everyone and everything belongs to me.' It is fun at the beach, but no one expresses too much emotion; nothing goes too wrong. Horne's description comes to life before one's eyes.

The Ordinary manifests in the way that these spiritual connections to the beach intimated in the songs are emotionally and linguistically restrained. This is the feature of the Ordinary identified by Morris as its aversion to 'symbolic excess.'[96] Huntsman echoes this, observing that while we have words with which to express our feelings towards the bush, and most Australians can sing along to 'Waltzing Matilda,' 'it seems that we have lacked the *words* with which to express our attachment to the beach.'[97] In an effort to rectify this,

Huntsman (quoting novelist Dorothy Dinnerstein) writes about the beach with fulsome prose, describing how when one moves over the threshold from the sand to the sea, what is gained is 'access, incomparably literal sensuous access to that vital level of the self which is continuous with infancy.'[98] She continues by describing how the beach offers an immersive sensory experience:

> We discover again the joy of play: of dancing through the froth, gliding up the wave face or diving through it. . . . We are enveloped in a total sensory stimulation as the cool silky water slides around our bodies, the foam fizzes over the surface of our skin, the roar of the waves fills our ears, the taste of salt in our mouth, as the body of the infant responds with ecstasy to stroking, touching, murmuring, feeding.[99]

This sort of prose could not be more different from Perfect's approach in the lyrics of the beach songs; he infers such emotions and sensations rather than stating them outright. The stereotype of the taciturn Australian man – expressed most notably in Russel Ward's *The Australian Legend* (1976) – is one that has strong reverberations in Australian culture. But this is not quite what is occurring in the cycle. Not just in the beach songs, but throughout, Perfect employs a sort of poetic 'plain speech.' Jennifer Sinclair argues that plain speech is 'valued in the (secular) Ordinary Australian imaginary, the material and literal is preferred to the symbolic and there is limited emotional or affective expression, except, perhaps, when defending the ordinary.'[100] It is not that Perfect is *unable* to express himself verbosely: it is that he often chooses not to. 'There's a Beach Somewhere' and 'The Middle of the World' navigate this cultural idiosyncrasy; they evoke the beach in all its glory without really describing it at all, avoiding effusive description without resorting to inarticulacy. The performative nature of song deliberately heightens this plain speech.

Conclusion: Music, the Ordinary, and the Dangers of Symbolic Excess

In *Songs from the Middle*, music is an important way that the dangers of 'symbolic excess' are managed. A feature of Perfect's approach in *Songs from the Middle* is that the more genuine his feeling for a topic, the less verbose, clever, and witty his language becomes – sometimes to the point of removing language altogether, as in a later song in the cycle, 'Susan Morgan.' As he explains in his introduction to the song, Susan Morgan was a girl with whom Perfect was infatuated as a child. While writing the cycle, he discovered she had passed away. His justification (as stated in the introduction to the song) for making it an instrumental is that it would have seemed presumptuous to use words. Moreover, both the beach songs have longer instrumental sections than other songs in the cycle, indicating that perhaps the music can say what the Ordinary prohibits. Across the cycle, musical idiom is used to convey an attitude to these landscapes. In my detailed analyses of six of the thirteen songs, I have demonstrated how music is integral to the representation of suburbia and the beach.

Songs from the Middle presents the iconic landscapes of suburbia and the beach as deeply lodged in the national imaginary. From the in-between space of the middle emerges multivalent readings of these sites. Suburbia is portrayed ironically, nostalgically, humorously, and ambivalently; the beach is figured as a constant companion, a liminal site of change and transformation, an invitation to spirituality, the location of the Ordinary. Perfect's approach reveals a great affection for these landscapes, and a desire to celebrate them, but equally, an imperative to look beyond their mythic representations, to understand their affective qualities and the ways in which they shape, structure, and impact upon our everyday lives. The cycle suggests that places with complex histories – like the suburbs – and precious, beloved sites – like the beach – afford rich, deep connection to a sense of national belonging and identity. *Muriel* and *Shane Warne* examined Australia through a global and a national lens. *Songs from the Middle* shifts to the level of the local, asking us to think deeply about where everyday Australians live, and more importantly, how these landscapes make us feel. The next chapter turns its attention to the traditional owners of these landscapes, the hundreds of Aboriginal nations who were displaced as a result of colonisation.

Notes

1 An album was produced from this recording, and is available on Bandcamp: https://eddieperfect.bandcamp.com/album/songs-from-the-middle-2
2 This framing is most commonly used to refer to rural landscapes, but as I have articulated, suburbia and the beach are contemporary manifestations of this phenomenon. In the course of his chapter on Australia, Short moves from the bush to the suburbs. John Short, *Imagined Country: Society, Culture and Environment* (Routledge, 1991).
3 John Fiske, Bob Hodge and Graene Turner, *Myths of Oz: Reading Australian Popular Culture* (Allen & Unwin, 1987), 54.
4 David Washington, 'Eddie Perfect: *Songs from the Middle*,' *InDaily*, June 16, 2015, accessed March 3, 2025, https://indaily.com.au/arts-and-culture/festivals/2015/06/16/eddie-perfect-songs-from-the-middle/.
5 Tim Edensor, *National Identity, Popular Culture and Everyday Life* (Berg, 2002), 39–40.
6 Edensor, *National Identity*, 53.
7 Edensor, *National Identity*, 40.
8 Catherine Blanch, 'Eddie Perfect Sings "Songs from the Middle" and Stories from His Life – Adelaide Cabaret Festival Interview,' *The Clothesline*, May 27, 2015, accessed March 3, 2025, http://theclothesline.com.au/eddie-perfect-middle-cabaret-festival-interview/.
9 Chris Healy, 'Introduction' in *Beasts of Suburbia: Reinterpreting Cultures in Australian Suburbs*, ed. Sarah Ferber, Chris Healy and Chris McAuliffe (Melbourne University Press, 1994), xvii.

10 Edensor, *National Identity*, 18.
11 Mary O'Brien, 'Eddie Perfect's Secret Melbourne: An Exploration of Middle-Class Life,' *The Sydney Morning Herald*, June 12, 2015, https://www.smh.com.au/entertainment/eddie-perfects-secret-melbourne-an-exploration-of-middleclass-life-20150607-ghh9ns.html.
12 Benjamin Law, 'Eddie Perfect Unleashes the Beast,' *The Monthly*, October 2013, https://www.themonthly.com.au/issue/2013/october/1380549600/benjamin-law/eddie-perfect-unleashes-beast.
13 Laura Tunbridge, *The Song Cycle* (Cambridge University Press, 2010), 3.
14 Andrew McCann, ed. *Writing the Everyday: Australian Literature and the Limits of Suburbia* (University of Queensland Press, 1998), viii.
15 Healy, 'Introduction,' xvii.
16 McCann, *Writing the Everyday*, vii.
17 Brian Kinnane, 'Shopping at Last!; History, Fiction and the Anti-Suburban Tradition,' in *Writing the Everyday: Australian Literature and the Limits of Suburbia*, ed. Andrew McCann (University of Queensland Press, 1998), 41.
18 Graeme Davison, 'The Suburban Idea and Its Enemies,' *Journal of Urban History* 39, no. 5 (2013): 829, https://doi.org/10.1177/0096144213479307.
19 Karl Quinn, 'Drag, Dags, and the Suburban Surreal,' *Metro Magazine* 100 (1994): 24.
20 Simon Caterson, 'A Preposterous Life,' *Griffith Review* 8 (2005): 57–63; Susan Turnbull, 'Mapping the Vast Suburban Tundra: Australian Comedy from Dame Edna to *Kath and Kim*,' *International Journal of Cultural Studies* 11, no. 1 (2008): 15–32, https://doi.org/10.1177/136787790708639.
21 Kinnane, 'Shopping At Last!,' 41–42.
22 Graeme Davison, 'Australia: The First Suburban Nation?,' *Journal of Urban History* 22, no. 1 (1995): 42.
23 Brendan Gleeson, *Australian Heartlands: Making Space for Hope in the Suburbs* (Allen & Unwin, 2006), 9.
24 Hugh Stretton, *Ideas for Australian Cities*, 3rd edn (Transit Australia, 1989), 21.
25 Ian Craven, '"Emoh Ruo" – The Suburbanization of Australia Cinema,' *Antipodes* 11, no. 5 (1997): 30.
26 Stephen Crofts, 'Global Neighbours?,' in *To Be Continued: Soap Operas Around the World*, ed. Robert C. Allen (Routledge, 1994), 100–101.
27 Belinda Burns, 'Made in Suburbia: Intra-suburban Narratives in Contemporary Australian Women's Fiction,' in *Claiming Space for Australian Women's Writing*, ed. Davaleena Das and Sanjukta Dasgupta (Palgrave Macmillan, 2017), 163.
28 A comparable critique of middle-class consumerism is also present in 'I Wanna Go Home (The IKEA Song),' a song that originally appeared in his cabaret *Drink Pepsi, Bitch!* (2006) but is also included in *Songs from the Middle*.
29 'Artscape: Eddie Perfect,' *ABC Television*, episode 7, 20 Nov. 2012.
30 Kathy Evans, 'Comedy Offensive,' *The Sydney Morning Herald*, March 19, 2011, https://www.smh.com.au/entertainment/comedy/comedy-offensive-20110318-1c0dg.html.
31 Blanch, 'Eddie Perfect Sings "Songs from the Middle".'
32 Gleeson, *Australian Heartlands*, 12.
33 Bernice Murphy, *The Suburban Gothic in American Popular Culture* (Palgrave Macmillan, 2009), 2.
34 'Artscape: Eddie Perfect.' This, of course, is also the position of the artist in Patrick White's *Season at Sarsaparilla*.
35 Craven, '"Emoh Ruo,"' 29.
36 Kinnane, 'Shopping at Last!,' 42.
37 Musicologist Jon Stratton has argued that while 'Waltzing Matilda' is generally considered to be a folk song, this characterisation is not entirely accurate. Stratton

states that while the song was most probably not 'written self-consciously as a piece of commercial, popular music, and while its lyrical form is an imitation of an oral ballad, popular music it is.' Jon Stratton, 'Producing an Australian Popular Music: From Stephen Foster to Jack O'Hagan,' *Journal of Australian Studies* 31, no. 90 (2007): 157.

38 There are two different versions of 'Waltzing Matilda,' with different melodies – the original, with words by Banjo Patterson and music by Christina Macpherson (1895), and Marie Cowan's arrangement for the Billy Tea Company to use as an advertising jingle. The melodic material I am referring to is common across both versions.

39 For the history of the song and its use over the centuries, see Therese Radic, 'The Song Lines of Waltzing Matilda,' in *The Australian Legend and Its Discontents,* ed. Richard Nile (University of Queensland Press, 2000), 105–116.

40 'Eddie Perfect and His Suburban Song Cycle,' *ABC Radio National,* July 24, 2010, accessed March 3, 2025, https://www.abc.net.au/radionational/programs/musicshow/eddie-perfect-and-his-suburban-song-cycle/3015342.

41 Greg Ellis, 'Bellambi Bunnings Officially Opened by Brett Lee,' *Illawarra Mercury,* October 27, 2017, accessed February 25, 2022, https://www.illawarramercury.com.au/story/5018051/what-its-like-to-work-at-the-new-bellambi-bunnings/

42 Peter Devlin and Sam McPhee, 'Bride and groom presented with a SNAG wedding cake on the Today Show after holding their reception at a Bunnings sausage sizzle,' *Daily Mail Australia,* August 29, 2017, accessed June 30, 2025, https://www.dailymail.co.uk/news/article-4831824/Australian-bride-groom-sausage-cake-Today-Show.html.

43 Barbara Santich, *Bold Palates: Australia's Gastronomic Heritage* (Wakefield Press, 2012), 146. The sausage sizzle also has a particular relationship to Australian democracy. The 'democracy sausage' is an Australian tradition that on election days, citizens enjoy a sausage sizzle at polling places when they cast their vote. See Melissa Zappavigna, 'Enjoy Your Snags Australia . . . Oh and the Voting Thing Too #ausvotes #auspol: Iconisation and Affiliation in Electoral Microblogging,' *Global Media Journal–Australian Edition* 11, no. 2 (2014), https://www.hca.westernsydney.edu.au/gmjau/?p=1139.

44 Shivaune Field, 'How Bunnings, a sausage sizzle, and Aussie DJs are raving to support the music industry,' *Forbes Australia,* September 1, 2024, https://www.forbes.com.au/life/entertainment/inside-bunnings-warehouse-carpark-rave-with-peking-duk/.

45 Chris Jones, 'Welcome Mat Out to Ocker Tradition,' *The Courier Mail,* March 10, 2004, 1.

46 Svetlana Boym, *The Future of Nostalgia.* (Basic Books, 2001), xv.

47 Eric Werner in Joseph Swain, *The Broadway Musical: A Critical and Musical Survey* (Oxford University Press, 1990), 251.

48 Swain, *The Broadway Musical,* 253.

49 Jeffrey Magee, 'Irving Berlin's "Blue Skies": Ethnic Affiliations and Musical Transformations,' *The Musical Quarterly* 84, no. 4 (2000): 540, https://doi.org/10.1093/mq/84.4.537.

50 Richard Rodgers, *Musical Stages: An Autobiography* (Da Capo Press, 1995), 88.

51 Magee, 'Irving Berlin's "Blue Skies",' 547.

52 Swain, *The Broadway Musical,* 257. As Swain notes, this feature is integral to the tune that symbolises the fiddler in *Fiddler on the Roof.*

53 David Goldman, 'How Time's Arrow and the Phrygian Half-Step Make Jewish Music Holy,' *Tablet,* accessed May 20, 2018, http://www.tabletmag.com/jewish-arts-and-culture/music/184773/jewish-music-holy.

54 'Eddie Perfect and His Suburban Song Cycle.'

55 Frances Bonner, Susan McKay and Alan McKee, 'On the Beach,' *Continuum: Journal of Media and Cultural Studies* 15, no. 3 (2001): 273, https://doi.org/10.1080/10304310120086768.

56 Robert Drewe, *The Beach: An Australian Passion* (National Library of Australia Publishing, 2015), 1.

57 Fiske, Hodge and Turner, *Myths of Oz*, 55, original emphasis.

58 Craig McGregor, 'The Beach, the Coast, the Signifier, the Feral Transcendence and Pumpin' at Byron Bay,' in *The Abundant Culture: Meaning and Significance in Everyday Australia*, ed. David Headon, Joy W. Hooton and Donald Horne (Allen & Unwin, 1994), 52.

59 Elizabeth Ellison and Donna Lee Brien, eds., *Writing the Australian Beach: Local Site, Global Idea* (Springer International Publishing, 2020), 1.

60 Elizabeth Ellison, 'Badland Beach: The Australian Beach as a Site of Cultural Remembering,' *International Journal of Media and Cultural Politics* 12, no. 1 (2016): 116.

61 Anne Game, 'Nation and Identity: Bondi,' *New Formations* 11 (1990): 115.

62 Leone Huntsman, *Sand in Our Souls: The Beach in Australian Cultural History* (Melbourne University Press, 2001), 45, 153, original emphasis.

63 In addition to those cited, see James Skinner, Keith Gilbert and Allan Edwards (eds.), *Some Like It Hot: The Beach as a Cultural Dimension* (Meyer and Meyer, 2003) and Ann Game, Andrew Metcalfe and Demelza Martin (eds.), *On Bondi Beach* (Arcadia 2013). Huntsman's book also grants its author the right of first-person address.

64 Bruce Bennett, 'A Beach Somewhere: The Australian Littoral Imagination at Play,' in *Littoral Zone: Australian Contexts and their Writers*, ed. C. A. Cranston and Robert Zeller (Rodopi, 2007), 31.

65 I have published previously on 'my beach,' Thirroul Beach. Mara Davis, 'Feeling Good? Pride, Shame, and Being Australian,' *Antithesis* 28 (2018): 46–77.

66 Clara Iaccarino, 'For Old Time's Sake,' *The Sydney Morning Herald*, July 30, 2010, 12.

67 Huntsman, *Sand in Our Souls*, 153.

68 Gamble has written a history of Mentone. Leo Gamble, *Mentone Through the Years* self-published, 2003.

69 Mark Gibson, 'Myths of Oz Cultural Studies: The Australian Beach and "English" Ordinariness,' *Continuum* 15, no. 3 (2001): 282, https://doi.org/10.1080/10304310120086777.

70 Elizabeth Ellison and Lesley Hawkes, 'Australian Beachspace: The Plurality of an Iconic Site,' *Borderlands: E-Journal* 15, no. 1 (2016): 7, https://www.jstor.org/stable/48782565.

71 Fiske, Hodge and Turner, *Myths of Oz*, 59.

72 Huntsman, *Sand in Our Souls*, 183.

73 Robert Preston-Whyte, 'The Beach as a Liminal Space,' in *A Companion to Tourism*, ed. Alan A. Lew, C. Michael Hall and Allan W. William (Blackwell Publishing, 2004), 349.

74 'Eddie Perfect – *Songs from the Middle*,' *Iaingrandage.com*, accessed January 20, 2018, http://www.iaingrandage.com/work-categories/eddie-perfect/.

75 I am cognisant of the fact that Satie was an eccentric figure who tried to eschew categorisation and that terming him an impressionist is therefore somewhat tenuous. However, the *Gymnopédies* do contain compositional features than will later appear in impressionist works. Barbara Kelly recounts that Ravel credited Satie as 'the precursor' to musical impressionism but Satie 'was not content to remain' as such. Barbara Kelly, 'Ravel's Timeliness and His Many Late Styles,' in *Late Style and Its Discontents: Essays in Art, Literature, and Music*, ed. Gordon McMullan and Sam Smiles (Oxford University Press, 2016), 160.

76 Mary Davis, *Erik Satie* (Reaktion Books, 2007), 33–34.

77 Jules-Antoine Castagnary cited in Mary Tompkins-Lewis, ed. *Critical Readings in Impressionism and Post-Impressionism: An Anthology* (University of California Press, 2007), 2.

78 Richard Taruskin, *The Oxford History of Western Music,* vol. 4 (Oxford University Press, 2004), 78.
79 Drewe, *The Beach,* 1.
80 Bennett, 'A Beach Somewhere,' 32–33; Ellison, 'Badland Beach'; Ellison and Brien, *Writing the Australian Beach;* Huntsman, *Sand in Our Souls,* 148–152.
81 Robert Drewe, 'Australia's Cultural Identity Now,' *New Literatures Review* 44 (2005): 24.
82 Huntsman, *Sand in Our Souls,* 187.
83 While this quote was coined by the American surfer Kelly Slater, it is ubiquitous enough among surfing communities that its sentiment is well-understood. There is even a genuinely religious offshoot of this phenomenon in Christian Surfers International, founded in the late 1970s by Australian Brett Davis.
84 Ellison and Hawkes, 'Australian Beachspace,' 8.
85 Malcolm Wood argues that this view originated in the colonial period. Malcolm Wood, *Australia's Secular Foundations* (Australian Scholarly Publishing, 2016).
86 Hugh Mackay, *Beyond Belief* (Macmillan, 2016), 101.
87 Meaghan Morris, 'On the Beach,' in *Cultural Studies,* ed. Lawrence Grossberg, Cary Nelson, and Paula A. Treicher (Routledge, 1992), 450–478. This question is also addressed by Ellison and Hawkes, who argue that it is both. Borrowing from Roja's idea of thirdspace, they develop the concept of *beachspace* to suggest that the beach is 'simultaneously a real and imagined space' that moves between the mythic and the ordinary. Ellison and Hawkes, 'Australian Beachspace,' 3.
88 Huntsman, *Sand in Our Souls,* 169.
89 Morris, 'On the Beach,' 470. The Ordinary is also the prompt for Jennifer Sinclair's work; while her research is not actually about the beach, she takes up Morris' coupling of the sacred and secular and, in doing so, argues that conceptions of spirituality in Australia are often framed in terms of the Ordinary, explicating how it is frequently mobilised by politicians. Sinclair builds on the work of Judith Brett, who has argued that Howard skilfully moved the conversation from the world stage back to the Ordinary. Jennifer Sinclair, 'Spirituality and the (Secular) Ordinary Australian Imaginary,' *Continuum* 18, no. 2 (2004): 279–293, https://doi.org/10.1080/1030431042000215059
90 Morris, 'On the Beach,' 452.
91 Donald Horne cited in Morris, 'On the Beach,' 451.
92 Morris, 'On the Beach,' 462.
93 Morris, 'On the Beach,' 466.
94 Aileen Moreton-Robinson, *The White Possessive: Property, Power, and Indigenous Sovereignty* (University of Minnesota Press, 2015), 36.
95 Jonathan Bollen, Adrian Kiernander and Bruce Parr, *Men at Play: Masculinities in Australian Theatre since the 1950s* (Rodopi, 2008), 34.
96 Morris, 'On the Beach,' 466.
97 Huntsman, *Sand in Our Souls,* 2.
98 Dinnerstein in Huntsman, *Sand in Our Souls,* 8.
99 Huntsman, *Sand in Our Souls,* 8.
100 Sinclair, 'Spirituality and the (Secular),' 281.

References

'Artscape: Eddie Perfect.' *ABC Television*, episode 7, November 20, 2012.
Bennett, Bruce. 'A Beach Somewhere: The Australian Littoral Imagination at Play.' In *Littoral Zone: Australian Contexts and their Writers*, edited by C.A. Cranston and Robert Zeller. Rodopi, 2007, 31–44.

Blanch, Catherine. 'Eddie Perfect Sings "Songs from the Middle" and Stories from His Life–AdelaideCabaretFestivalInterview.' *TheClothesline*,May27,2015.AccessedMarch3, 2025. https://theclothesline.com.au/eddie-perfect-middle-cabaret-festival-interview/.

Bollen, Jonathan, Adrian Kiernander, and Bruce Parr. *Men at Play: Masculinities in Australian Theatre Since the 1950s.* Rodopi, 2008.

Bonner, Frances, Susan McKay, and Alan McKee. 'On the Beach.' *Continuum: Journal of Media and Cultural Studies* 15, no. 3 (2001): 269–274. https://doi.org/10.1080/10304310120086768

Boym, Svetlana. *The Future of Nostalgia.* Basic Books, 2001.

Burns, Belinda. 'Made in Suburbia: Intra-suburban Narratives in Contemporary Australian Women's Fiction.' In *Claiming Space for Australian Women's Writing*, edited by Davaleena Das and Sanjukta Dasgupta. Palgrave Macmillan, 2017.

Caterson, Simon. 'A Preposterous Life.' *Griffith Review* 8 (2005): 57–63.

Craven, Ian. '"Emoh Ruo" – The Suburbanization of Australia Cinema.' *Antipodes* 11, no. 5 (1997): 25–31.

Crofts, Stephen. 'Global *Neighbours*?' In *To Be Continued: Soap Operas Around the World*, edited by Robert C. Allen. Routledge, 1994, 98–121.

Davis, Mary. *Erik Satie.* Reaktion Books, 2007.

Davis, Mara. 'Feeling Good? Pride, Shame, and Being Australian.' *Antithesis* 28 (2018): 46–77.

Davison, Graeme. 'Australia: The First Suburban Nation?' *Journal of Urban History* 22, no. 1 (1995): 40–74.

Davison, Graeme. 'The Suburban Idea and Its Enemies.' *Journal of Urban History* 39, no. 5 (2013): 829–847. https://doi.org/10.1177/0096144213479307.

Devlin, Peter, and Sam McPhee. 'Bride and Groom presented with a SNAG Wedding Cake on the Today Show After Holding their Reception at a Bunnings Sausage Sizzle.' *Daily Mail Australia*, August 29, 2017. Accessed June 30, 2025. https://www.dailymail.co.uk/news/article-4831824/Australian-bride-groom-sausage-cake-Today-Show.html.

Drewe, Robert. 'Australia's Cultural Identity Now.' *New Literatures Review* 44 (2005): 23–31.

Drewe, Robert. *The Beach: An Australian Passion.* National Library of Australia Publishing, 2015.

'Eddie Perfect – *Songs from the Middle*.' *Iaingrandage.com.* Accessed March 3, 2025. http://www.iaingrandage.com/work-categories/eddie-perfect/.

'Eddie Perfect and His Suburban Song Cycle.' *ABC Radio National*, July 24, 2010. Accessed March 3, 2025. https://www.abc.net.au/radionational/programs/musicshow/eddie-perfect-and-his-suburban-song-cycle/3015342.

Edensor, Tim. *National Identity, Popular Culture and Everyday Life.* Berg, 2002.

Ellis, Greg. 'Bellambi Bunnings Officially Opened by Brett Lee.' *Illawarra Mercury*, October27,2017.https://www.illawarramercury.com.au/story/5018051/what-its-like-to-work-at-the-new-bellambi-bunnings/.

Ellison, Elizabeth. 'Badland Beach: The Australian Beach as a Site of Cultural Remembering.' *International Journal of Media and Cultural Politics* 12, no. 1 (2016): 115–127.

Ellison, Elizabeth, and Donna Lee Brien, eds. *Writing the Australian Beach: Local Site, Global Idea.* Springer International Publishing, 2020.

Ellison, Elizabeth, and Lesley Hawkes. 'Australian Beachspace: The Plurality of an Iconic Site.' *Borderlands: E-Journal* 15, no. 1 (2016): 1–20. https://www.jstor.org/stable/48782565.

Evans, Kathy. 'Comedy Offensive.' *The Sydney Morning Herald*, March 19, 2011. https://www.smh.com.au/entertainment/comedy/comedy-offensive-20110318-1c0dg.html.

Ferber, Sarah, Chris Healy, and Chris McAuliffe, eds. *Beasts of Suburbia: Reinterpreting Cultures in Australian Suburbs.* Melbourne University Press, 1994.

Field, Shivaune. 'How Bunnings, a sausage sizzle, and Aussie DJs are raving to support the music industry.' *Forbes Australia*, September 1, 2024. https://www.forbes.com.au/life/entertainment/inside-bunnings-warehouse-carpark-rave-with-peking-duk/.

Fiske, John, Bob Hodge, and Graeme Turner. *Myths of Oz: Reading Australian Popular Culture.* Allen & Unwin, 1987.

Gamble, Leo. *Mentone Through the Years.* Self-published, 2003.

Game, Anne. 'Nation and Identity: Bondi.' *New Formations* 11 (1990): 105–121.

Game, Anne, Andrew Metcalfe, and Demelza Martin, eds. *On Bondi Beach.* Arcadia, 2013.

Gibson, Mark. 'Myths of Oz Cultural Studies: The Australian Beach and "English" Ordinariness.' *Continuum* 15, no. 3 (2001): 275–288. https://doi.org/10.1080/10304310120086777.

Gleeson, Brendan. *Australian Heartlands: Making Space for Hope in the Suburbs.* Allen & Unwin, 2006.

Goldman, David. 'How Time's Arrow and the Phrygian Half-Step Make Jewish Music Holy.' *Tablet.* Accessed May 20, 2018. http://www.tabletmag.com/jewish-arts-and-culture/music/184773/jewish-music-holy.

Huntsman, Leone. *Sand in Our Souls: The Beach in Australian Cultural History.* Melbourne University Press, 2001.

Iaccarino, Clara. 'For Old Time's Sake.' *The Sydney Morning Herald*, July 30, 2010, 12.

Jones, Chris. 'Welcome Mat Out to Ocker Tradition.' *The Courier Mail*, March 10, 2004, 1.

Kelly, Barbara. 'Ravel's Timeliness and His Many Late Styles.' In *Late Style and Its Discontents: Essays in Art, Literature, and Music*, edited by Gordon McMullan and Sam Smiles. Oxford University Press, 2016, 158–173.

Law, Benjamin. 'Eddie Perfect Unleashes the Beast.' *The Monthly*, October 2013. https://www.themonthly.com.au/issue/2013/october/1380549600/benjamin-law/eddie-perfect-unleashes-beast.

Mackay, Hugh. *Beyond Belief.* Macmillan, 2016.

Magee, Jeffrey. 'Irving Berlin's "Blue Skies": Ethnic Affiliations and Musical Transformations.' *The Musical Quarterly* 84, no. 4 (2000): 537–579. https://doi.org/10.1093/mq/84.4.537.

McCann, Andrew, ed. *Writing the Everyday: Australian Literature and the Limits of Suburbia.* University of Queensland Press, 1998.

McGregor, Craig. 'The Beach, the Coast, the Signifier, the Feral Transcendence and Pumpin' at Byron Bay.' In *The Abundant Culture: Meaning and Significance in Everyday Australia*, edited by David Headon, Joy W. Hooton and Donald Horne. Allen & Unwin, 1994.

Moreton-Robinson, Aileen. *The White Possessive: Property, Power, and Indigenous Sovereignty.* University of Minnesota Press, 2015.

Morris, Meaghan. 'On the Beach.' In *Cultural Studies*, edited by Lawrence Grossberg, Cary Nelson, and Paul A. Treicher. Routledge, 1992.

Murphy, Bernice. *The Suburban Gothic in American Popular Culture.* Palgrave Macmillan, 2009.

O'Brien, Mary. 'Eddie Perfect's Secret Melbourne: An Exploration of Middle-Class Life.' *The Sydney Morning Herald*, June 12, 2015. https://www.smh.com.au/entertainment/eddie-perfects-secret-melbourne-an-exploration-of-middleclass-life-20150607-ghh9ns.html.

Preston-Whyte, Robert. 'The Beach as a Liminal Space.' In *A Companion to Tourism*, edited by Alan A. Lew, C. Michael Hall and Allan W. William. Blackwell Publishing, 2004, 349–359.

Quinn, Karl. 'Drag, Dags, and the Suburban Surreal.' *Metro Magazine* 100 (1994): 23–26.

Radic, Therese. 'The Song Lines of Waltzing Matilda.' In *The Australian Legend and Its Discontents*, edited by Richard Nile. University of Queensland Press, 2000, 105–116.

Rodgers, Richard. *Musical Stages: An Autobiography*. Da Capo Press, 1995.

Santich, Barbara. *Bold Palates: Australia's Gastronomic Heritage*. Wakefield Press, 2012.

Short, John. *Imagined Country: Society, Culture and Environment*. Routledge, 1991.

Sinclair, Jennifer. 'Spirituality and the (Secular) Ordinary Australian Imaginary.' *Continuum* 18, no. 2 (2004): 279–293. https://doi.org/10.1080/1030431042 000215059.

Skinner, James, Keith Gilbert, and Allan Edwards, eds. *Some Like It Hot: The Beach as a Cultural Dimension*. Meyer and Meyer, 2003.

Stratton, Jon. 'Producing an Australian Popular Music: From Stephen Foster to Jack O'Hagan.' *Journal of Australian Studies* 31, no. 90 (2007): 153–165.

Stretton, Hugh. *Ideas for Australian Cities*, 3rd edition. Transit Australia, 1989.

Swain, Joseph. *The Broadway Musical: A Critical and Musical Survey*. Oxford University Press, 1990.

Taruskin, Richard. *The Oxford History of Western Music*, volume 4. Oxford University Press, 2004.

Tompkins-Lewis, Mary, ed. *Critical Readings in Impressionism and Post-Impressionism: An Anthology*. University of California Press, 2007.

Tunbridge, Laura. *The Song Cycle*. Cambridge University Press, 2010.

Turnbull, Susan. 'Mapping the Vast Suburban Tundra: Australian Comedy from Dame Edna to *Kath and Kim*.' *International Journal of Cultural Studies* 11, no. 1 (2008): 15–32. https://doi.org/10.1177/1367877907708639.

Washington, David. 'Eddie Perfect: *Songs from the Middle*.' *InDaily*, June 16, 2015. Accessed March 3, 2025. https://indaily.com.au/arts-and-culture/festivals/2015/06/16/eddie-perfect-songs-from-the-middle/.

Wood, Malcolm. *Australia's Secular Foundations*. Australian Scholarly Publishing, 2016.

Zappavigna, Melissa. 'Enjoy Your Snags Australia . . . Oh and the Voting Thing Too #ausvotes #auspol: Iconisation and Affiliation in Electoral Microblogging.' *Global Media Journal – Australian Edition* 11, no. 2 (2014). https://www.hca.westernsydney.edu.au/gmjau/?p=1139.

4

FEELING BAD, FEELING GOOD: RECONCILIATION, APOLOGY, AND WHITE WITNESSING IN *THE RABBITS*

In 1788, eleven British ships known as the First Fleet arrived on the shores of Sydney Cove to colonise the land before them, subjecting the Indigenous inhabitants of the continent to a brutal invasion and decimating a culture that had thrived in this place for more than 40,000 years. Over 200 years later, the legacy of invasion continues to have broad-ranging consequences for contemporary Australian society. Colonisation remains a deep wound, one that pervades the national imaginary. *The Rabbits* (2015) is a musical that wrestles with this history, engaging in the ongoing conversation about how Australia can find a way, as Penelope Edmonds avers, to 'hold this enduring violence in our consciousness and yet continue to live together.'[1] It contemplates where we have come from, and how we move forward.

The Rabbits, based on John Marsden and Shaun Tan's 1998 award-winning picture book of the same name, has music by the Australian pop artist Kate Miller-Heidke and libretto by playwright Lally Katz.[2] It was a multi-organisation collaboration, co-commissioned by Perth and Melbourne International Arts Festivals, and co-produced by Barking Gecko Theatre Company (a Western Australian company who specialise in children's theatre) with Opera Australia (the national opera company). Barking Gecko's Artistic Director, John Sheedy, was the director on the production, which premièred at the 2015 Perth International Arts Festival before transferring to Melbourne later that year, and then played seasons in both Sydney and Brisbane in 2016. Additional music was composed by Iain Grandage, who also acted in the role of orchestrator and conductor. The esteemed Indigenous theatre maker and director Rachael Maza was employed as an artistic consultant on the production. In 2016, a performance was recorded at the Roslyn Packer Theatre in Sydney, which was then released on CD.[3]

DOI: 10.4324/9781003590088-5

The Rabbits makes an anthropomorphic allegory of colonisation, where the British colonisers are represented as rabbits and the Indigenous population represented as a kind of native marsupial. In this chapter, I jettison claims about the universality of the allegory to argue that *The Rabbits* reflects a uniquely Australian socio-political context. I argue that the production's use of stratified musical genres for different groups of characters instructs the audience on how to read the power dynamics of the plot, reinforcing the pejorative distinction between coloniser and colonised. I conceptualise *The Rabbits* as part of a broader movement of performances of reconciliation and apology, and analyse how it stages the utopian aspirations of reconciliation through its anthemic finale, 'Where?' these utopian aims are undermined by the way that the character of the Bird mirrors the subject position of the audience, creating 'white witnesses' who observe the events of colonisation, full of settler shame but powerless to intervene. Finally, I examine how the production induces 'feeling bad' and then, through the utopian reconciliatory finale, transforms this into 'feeling good,' constituting its audience as 'sorry people,' 'white witnesses,' who can go on home, purged of their shame and their faith in reconciliation renewed. Ultimately, *The Rabbits* conceptualises the theatre as a site where a national citizenry can gather to have their shame transformed and the wounds in the national imaginary healed.

Representing Colonisation: From Picture Book to Musical Adaptation

Narrated by the Marsupials, the picture book details the speed with which the Rabbits plundered their new land; the foreign animals, crops, and customs that they introduced; and the incongruity of the two cultures. Tan's evocative and idiosyncratic illustrations are inspired by a range of visual sources, including several Australian landscape painters. The front cover, for example, is a recasting of a colonial painting by E. Phillips Fox.[4] Pictorially, the angular, menacing Rabbits with their long probing ears, spindly legs, and full bellies dominate the smaller, rounder Marsupials. The illustrations depict environmental devastation and violence, evocatively conveying the profound sense of loss experienced by the Indigenous population as a consequence of colonisation.

The stage adaptation largely follows its source text, with one significant change: the creation of a new character, the Bird, played by Miller-Heidke. The scenography of the production borrows heavily from the picture book, and the lighting design, costumes, and set pieces mimic the colour scheme, geometric shapes, and uncanny bodies of Tan's illustrations. The narrative plotting of the book is followed on stage, and the events of colonisation it depicts are dealt with episodically: arrival, first encounter, transformation of the landscape, proliferation of the Rabbits, conflict, removal of children, possibility of reconciliation. Marsden's pithy text is carried over in its entirety, but as the picture book is fewer than 250 words long, Katz was called upon to write additional material: a most unusual situation for a librettist whose work is generally an exercise in reduction. Her lyric additions capture and extend the terse poeticism of the original text.

In relation to both the picture book and the musical, the purported universality of the allegory, rather than its specific depiction of the Australian experience of colonisation, was foregrounded. Shaun Tan remarked in an interview that he deliberately '[avoided] any specific cultural reference to an Aboriginal experience' as it was 'an obviously charged and problematic issue,' while John Marsden noted that he sought to portray the 'universal experience of colonisers consuming everything they encounter.'[5] John Sheedy, director of the musical adaptation, similarly maintained that the production should not be read as purely about the Australian situation: 'We are presenting this on a much bigger, universal level, about any indigenous culture around the world that has been colonised by Europeans.'[6]

While the picture book may be regarded as 'universal' (or, at least, ambiguous in its message) the stage adaptation cannot sustain such ambiguity. The casting of five Indigenous actors to play the Marsupials, and five white actors to play the Rabbits, adds a layer of corporeality that is impossible to ignore. The sequence entitled 'Kitesong,' explicitly stages a shameful period in Australian history between 1910 and 1970 when as many as one in three Aboriginal children were removed from their families. Another song, the 'Seasick Waltz,' features a character who represents a convict, a figure particular to Australian history. Throughout, the Rabbits sing in British accents, while the Marsupials sing in Australian accents, and the colour scheme of the set, with its ochres, red, and browns, borrows the palette of the Australian desert. Even if Sheedy's statement about universality is to be taken at face value, the production displays only minor attempts to minimise references to the Australian context. These attempts – like when flags resembling the Union Jack are brought out on stage with a red rather than blue colour scheme – are rather perfunctory, and the relevance of the work to other colonised societies is unable to be determined, as to date *The Rabbits* has only played seasons in Australia.

Both stage adaptation and picture book are products of fraught debates about how to reconcile Australia's colonial past. The reception of the picture book reflected the polarised political climate of the 1990s known as the 'history wars.'[7] On one hand, it was praised for its role in promoting reconciliation and was named 1999 Picture Book of the Year by the Australian Children's Book Council. On the other hand, commentator and journalist Andrew Bolt, a tenacious critic of the book, repeatedly attacked it for its depiction of colonisation.[8] He was similarly displeased with the stage adaptation, terming it a 'taxpayer-funded vilification of Australia.'[9] Bolt's interpretation is reminiscent of the (highly contested) conservative view that the way forward is to focus on positivity rather than dwelling on the nation's violent past.

Critiques of the picture book have centred on its colonialist thinking and conciliatory approach. Clare Bradford argues that the false binary created by the history wars meant that the picture book was exempted from criticism by left-leaning scholars and critics. She is critical of the anthropomorphism, stating that casting Indigenous people as native animals does little more than '[reinscribe] colonial discourses,' privileging the binaries of nature and culture, coloniser and colonised, primitive, and civilized.[10] Brooke Collins-Gearing and Dianne Osland make a similar argument, that the portrayal of Indigenous society in the book harks back to a pre-Mabo 'psychological *terra nullius*.'[11] The picture book, they suggest, is characterised by passivity of language and the insistent drive of the master narrative of white colonisation, and that while it attempts to convey the 'horrors of colonial exploitation,' it ultimately upholds the status quo.[12]

Michael Halliwell argues that the musical adaptation ameliorates some of the problematic tendencies of the book identified by scholars. In his book *National Identity in Contemporary Australian Opera: Myths Reconsidered*, Halliwell notes that while the illustrations in the picture book were criticised for placing the Marsupials on the periphery of the images, the set design of the musical – a conical structure resembling a tree that houses the Marsupials – redresses this by placing the Marsupials at the centre of the action-space.[13] He contends that the amplification of the voices acts as an equalising force, ensuring the voices of the Marsupials are heard as commensurate to those of the Rabbits. While there has been criticism of the ending of the book, Halliwell argues that the final number of the musical, where the Rabbits and Marsupials join together to sing in harmony, the 'Marsupials have reclaimed their land through their song, and the Rabbits, by joining in and singing the same words and music, could be seen symbolically as finally becoming part of this land.'[14] Through music, he suggests, the characters become 'somewhat more multi-dimensional' than they appear in the book, and that the immediacy of live performance heightens an understanding of the socio-political context of the work, by demanding their 'engagement and empathy.'[15]

In what follows, I address and challenge several of these points. I analyse the 'hopeful outlook' of the finale as a performance of reconciliation and tacit apology and offer a counterargument to Halliwell's assertion that the Marsupials' agency is augmented in the musical adaptation. While I concur that the production is a moving experience, Halliwell's analysis only gestures at its affective power; he does not explain *how* this is achieved. I address this through my discussion of the transformation of settler shame and the healing of the national imaginary and, also, through attention to the role that music plays in cultivating this. Central to my analysis is how *The Rabbits* employs different musical styles. This strategic use of genre shapes how spectators interpret the musical's portrayal of colonisation.

Playing With Genre: Musical Style as Dramaturgical Device

The three groups of characters in *The Rabbits* are represented with different styles of music: opera for the Rabbits, pop for the Marsupials, and a hybrid of the two for the Bird. This stratified use of genre is a dramaturgical device designed to shape the audience's perception of the events, engendering a sympathetic representation of Indigenous Australians and a negative one of the colonisers. This distinction is important for the impact of the utopian reconciliatory ending.

In pursuing this hybridity, Opera Australia cultivated both a new sound and a new audience. Sandra Willis, executive producer for touring and outreach, stated that the company was aiming for 'a contemporary Australian musical theatre sound' and that they had engaged Kate Miller-Heidke as composer in the hope that the production could 'resonate in a new way with a 21st century audience.'[16] Miller-Heidke's successful career as a contemporary musician held the promise that her name would attract a broader audience than could be expected otherwise, but her background in classical voice (having studied opera at the Queensland Conservatorium) provided assurance that she was familiar with the parameters of working in an operatic context.

Miller-Heidke was a pivotal part of the strategy that would see Opera Australia not only attract a broader and younger audience for new Australian work but also record a commercial success. *The Rabbits* was the first new commission for the company since their 2010 production of Brett Dean's *Bliss* which, while critically acclaimed, had not performed well at the box office. Since assuming the leadership of Opera Australia in 2009, then Artistic Director Lyndon Terracini had made a range of inflammatory comments about contemporary Australian opera. In 2011, he articulated the 'biggest challenge' for Australian opera as being to produce 'new work that the public will actually like. It's all very well for the critics to say "oh this is magnificent, it's a work of genius," and no one buys a ticket.'[17] He went on to say that popular, commercially successful production must become 'one of our primary imperatives' and that the company wouldn't any longer be 'commissioning composers that are writing music that will alienate the public.[18] *The Rabbits* fulfilled this goal and, according to Willis, 'was everything we'd hoped for,' selling out its performances at the Perth Festival three months before the festival began.[19]

The clear demarcation of musical styles instructs audiences how to read the dynamics of the plot. The stuffy Rabbits, deceitful and stuck in the past, are presented as overblown operatic caricatures, while the pop idiom of the music of the Marsupials presents them as modern, authentic, and relatable. While this musical signification is somewhat problematic in that it underscores the nature/culture dualism in the picture book that has been criticised, it is effective in differentiating the two groups on stage. The distinction between coloniser and colonised affords the possibility of a greater level of empathy to the Marsupials. Miller-Heidke spoke to this decision-making process in an interview when she noted that deciding on an idiom for the Rabbits was a simple process and that there was no question that they would sing

> straight-down-the-line, fuddy-duddy opera. But with the marsupials, we were asking ourselves: how do they sound? Do we even give them words to sing? And Rachael [Maza, the Indigenous consultant on the production] said: 'That's absolute bullshit. They just sound normal. They sound like people.'[20]

The designation of operatic music as anachronistic, formal, and stuffy is presented in stark contrast to the 'normal' music of the Marsupials, which reference pop textures, colours, and structures.

Vocally, the Marsupials sing in keeping with conventions of popular music performance. They use unambiguously Australian accents, in contrast to the Rabbits' pseudo-British ones. Their voice types are less clearly demarcated and the orchestrations for their songs are more dominated by guitars and keyboard than by the strings and brass of the Rabbits. The performers avoid the crisp articulation and elongated vowels characteristic of operatic singing. They also use vibrato sparingly. The Marsupials make use of chest-voice dominant timbres, rather than head-dominant operatic sound of the Rabbits. 'Kitesong,' for instance, a slow song in 12/8 time, has a gospel-soul feel and is performed by an ensemble of women, providing a counterpoint to the all-male Rabbit troupe. The melodies stick closely to the rhythm of speech, making ample use of syncopation. The singers riff freely at the climax, producing a sound reminiscent of crying out in pain. This is a world away from the cultivated, trained sound produced by the Rabbits. In 'Watching from Trees,' during which the Marsupials rally each other to defend their kind against the Rabbits, they belt out their objections to invasion, riffing and singing in harmony to a rhythmic pulse. The tension produced by the cross-rhythms – quadruplets against the 5/4-time signature – mimics the rhythm of speech.

In comparison, the music of the Rabbits adopts an operatic performance style. Their music is scored for standard operatic voice ranges: bass-baritone, baritone, tenor, and countertenor. The countertenor role is often used for comic relief. Kanen Breen, the singer playing this part, employs an overly shrill, mannered timbre, drawing attention to the anachronistic nature of this voice type. The parodic use of operatic conventions is used to signify falseness and convey that the Rabbits are not to be trusted. The performance of 'The Seasick Waltz,' for example, features excessive vibrato and over-enunciated diction. In this song, all of the Rabbits – the Captain, the Scientist, a Society Rabbit (a member of the upper class), a French Lieutenant, and finally, the Convict – introduce themselves to the audience with a verse apiece. The

Captain is a doddering a bass-baritone with a pompous British accent. The opening phrases of the song depict the feeling of being seasick. The melody weaves and wobbles through the singer's range, allowing the grace notes to mimic an out-of-control vibrato. These compositional features are accentuated by the singer in performance, who plays this effect up, pushing these stylistic devices to their extreme. Casting operatic music as both comedic and the preserve of the villains of the piece underscores Terracini's remarks about the continuing relevance and economic performance of new Australian opera. It also links opera to colonisation, suggesting that both need their place in the national imaginary rethought and revised.

The music of the Bird uses a hybrid style, somewhere between pop and classical music, demonstrating that she moves between worlds. Her music is written in the soprano register, but the high tessitura is tempered through the clear articulation of text which Miller-Heidke maintains throughout. The chorus of 'Electric Light,' written in the style of a pop song, is an apt demonstration of the hybrid style that she cultivates throughout the performance. Techniques from contemporary music production are utilised, like the loop pedal in 'Watching from Trees.' The flexibility of the Bird's music not only highlights the way that this figure can move between worlds but also reflects her position as the supposedly impartial narrator.

These three musical idioms are an effective method of rendering the power dynamics of the plot unambiguous, affording greater empathy to the Marsupials and priming audiences for the reconciliatory ending. Having established this, I now turn to how *The Rabbits* performs reconciliation and apology.

Towards Apology: Performing Reconciliation

The Rabbits is part of a broader movement that views performances of apology as important symbolic gestures towards achieving reconciliation. The stage adaptation takes the 'sorry business' of the picture book further by bringing an audience together for a public performance of truth-telling, apology, and reconciliation.[21]

Reconciliation is a common concept across settler colonial and postcolonial societies. In Australia, it is the dominant social, educational, and legal framework through which the possibility of improved relationships between settlers and Indigenous peoples has been conceived. It was adopted as an Australian Government policy in 1991 in response to increased awareness and pressure around ideas of Aboriginal sovereignty, land rights, and status in the community. For Pat Dodson, Yawuru elder and former Chairman of the Council for Aboriginal Reconciliation (CAR), the promise of reconciliation was its potential to 'recognise the traditional ownership status of Indigenous people and unravel the historical layers of colonial legacy that continue to determine contemporary relationships between Indigenous communities and

Australian governments and other institutions.'[22] While it has yet to live up to this aim and has been much criticised for its failure to deliver legal and constitutional redress for Indigenous peoples, it is nevertheless an important framework for understanding symbolic efforts towards change. Penelope Edmonds notes that for many Indigenous people, reconciliation and 'its associated performances, can be repressive and reinforce colonial hegemonies as a poor symbolic substitute for actual and substantive reparations.'[23] At the same time, she suggests that perhaps performances of reconciliation are of great importance in a place like Australia: as 'one of the few settler nations without a formal treaty process, perhaps invented handshakes are all we have.'[24] Alongside its legal and constitutional aims, reconciliation has an important educative function. Miller-Heidke addressed this in a newspaper article, where she stated that her aim had been to

> present these very difficult issues, this awful chapter of Australia's history, in a way that does make it really approachable and hopefully fills everybody in the audience with empathy . . . and the feedback I've had from a lot of families is that they had amazing discussions with their kids afterwards.[25]

In support of this aim, Opera Australia produced an educational resource pack for use in primary and secondary schools.[26]

Performances of apology and reconciliation proliferated after the *Bringing Them Home* report, which examined the separation of Aboriginal and Torres Strait Islander children from their families, was tabled in the Australian Parliament in 1997. After *Bringing Them Home*, as Celermajer and Moses note, 'saying sorry and performing repentance became a national motif.'[27] In other words, it became part of the repertory of the national imaginary. The focus on apology was due to the fact that *Bringing Them Home* had made several key recommendations, one of which was for an apology to be made to the victims of the policy. However, Prime Minister John Howard, bolstered by the groundswell in conservative thinking, refused to offer one throughout his tenure as Prime Minister. When the election of Kevin Rudd removed Howard from office in late 2007, the new Labor Government mobilised quickly, and in early 2008, Rudd delivered the long-awaited Apology to the Stolen Generations in the Parliament. This was widely viewed as a deeply symbolic act, one that, as Anne Boyd suggests, 'signalled the possibility of re-setting the start button in Australia's troubled relations with its Indigenous population.'[28]

Characteristic of such performances of apology and reconciliation are their utopian aspirations. Artists involved in *The Rabbits* referred to its potential for such a utopian moment to occur. One of the Marsupials, Hollie Andrew, reflected on her personal experience of the reconciliatory effects of performing in the production, remarking that 'I love that this show says what has happened and then poses the question, "where do we go from here?" We need to own what has happened and together find a way to move forward. That's the beauty of this story.'[29] Here, Andrew's remarks emphasise that the production seeks to bring people together, not drive them apart. In a newspaper interview, director John Sheedy also foregrounded the work's engagement with reconciliation when he stated that 'the important thing at the end is that the rabbits realise they have gone too far. . . . At the end you have a rabbit and a marsupial coming together. It's about reconciliation: How do we fix this? How do we find a common voice?'[30] Sheedy's remarks demonstrate an optimism that there is a resolution to the situation. This 'coming together' of Indigenous and coloniser onstage asks an audience to entertain the idea of doing so offstage. For such a transformative moment to take effect, performances of apology and reconciliation often require their audiences to recall the violence, trauma, and suffering of colonisation. As Edmonds notes, in these performances Indigenous and non-Indigenous people often 'stand in for their own ancestors as they face past violence together,' and in doing so, take on the associated burdens of these subject positions.[31] Hollie Andrew reflected this from an Indigenous perspective when she remarked that while performing, 'I'm singing on behalf of my ancestors . . . I imagine my ancestors are calling out to me.'[32]

For settler Australians, who must place themselves in the role of the colonisers, this process often elicits feelings of shame. Sarah Kizuk describes this 'settler shame' as

> an experience that destabilizes a settler's sense of self through the recognition of unearned advantage over and systemic harm done to Indigenous peoples. In this sense, it is the emotional response to seeing one's culpability and feeling it as reflective of *who we are*.[33]

Kizuk draws on the work on Sara Ahmed, who argues that in the Australian context, shame has functioned as 'a form of nation building,' and that this, somewhat paradoxically, rather than undermining a sense of national or collective identity actually strengthens it.[34] Ahmed notes the public dimension of shame, that it is not 'just about feeling bad *for* others' but 'about feeling bad *about* oneself before others.'[35] When we witness past injustice together, and feel shame, this reaffirms us as well-meaning citizens who can go forth and 'work to reproduce the nation as an ideal.'[36] To mitigate the effects of settler shame, performances of apology and reconciliation frequently choose, as Rosanne Kennedy notes, aesthetic modes that foreground suffering rather than injustice. Kennedy describes the reconciliation movement as having deliberately promoted 'non-confrontational strategies and modes of engagement' that encouraged the 'concept of reconciliation as a unifying ideal for the nation.'[37]

The finale of *The Rabbits*, 'Where?,' embodies the non-confrontational, utopian aspirations and aesthetics of reconciliation. 'Where?' exemplifies the utopian aspirations of the reconciliation project by staging the Marsupials and the Rabbits joining together to sing as a united force. It amalgamates the final three pages of the book into an anthemic performance of tacit apology. In the picture book, as the narrative progresses the illustrations become more and more monochrome: colour is 'leeched from the palette,' as Rebecca-Anne Do Rozario describes.[38] On the final page, a thick black border encloses a much smaller rectangular drawing of a deserted blue landscape and a night sky littered with stars, where a single Rabbit and Marsupial are staring into a water hole. While the rest of the book is narrated from the perspective of the Marsupials, the text on this page draws invader and invaded together, culminating in the final line: 'Who will save us from the rabbits?'

Anthropomorphism in *The Rabbits* creates a mythic space where the violent past is recalled in a stylised manner. The utopian aspiration of the finale is strengthened through the dystopic nature of the previous song, 'Millions of Rabbits.' The Rabbits, holding representations of the British flag, stand in a military-style formation around the tree that has been the home of the Marsupials but from where they are now absent. The lieutenant, the leader of the Rabbits, enters from stage right and makes his way to the centre of the stage where he plants his flag in the ground. Smoke billows from chimney-like poles that have also been erected on the stage, representing industrialisation. The menacing rhythmic vamp of offbeat cluster chords drawn from D minor is accompanied by the staccato phrase 'Rabbits, millions, everywhere we look.' Both 'rabbits' and 'millions' are extended melismatically far beyond their two syllables, illustrating the dominance of the Rabbits. Here and throughout, the use of an excessive amount of tongue-trilled 'r' on words that begin with this letter – most notably 'rabbits' – emphasises the belligerence of the colonisers. In 'Millions of Rabbits,' this is further accentuated by the timbre of flutter-tongue trumpet and distorted electric guitar. After two verses, the Marsupials, huddled together and looking frightened, enter this Rabbit-dominated environment. In a contrasting legato style, they echo the words that have been sung by the Rabbits before adding some of their own thoughts:

Rabbit tails in the clouds
Lost and caught in a rabbit crowd
Rabbit ears listenin'
Red rabbit eyes glistenin'

As they continue to sing, set pieces painted as clock towers descend from the fly rails, suddenly drawing clarity to the incessant cowbell crotchet beat that was established in the first bar of the song: it represents the ticking of a clock, the passing of time, the permanence of their dispossession. The Rabbits exit the stage as the Marsupials sing, 'And there are more to come . . . Millions and millions.' They inspect the intrusions the Rabbits have made to their landscape before taking refuge in their home once more. When the Rabbits re-emerge, they stand in a line at the front of the stage, marching. They are singing a new tune: 'Tock tick tick tock, progress o'clock, tick tock tock tick, build it up, stick it in its place.' This section builds in intensity, with both groups singing their respective melodies before, in the last verse, the Marsupials finally succumb to the music of the Rabbits. Suddenly, sharp beams of green light appear all over the stage; the sky turns red, then blue, as the music starts to disintegrate into anarchy. A low, rumbling drone sound accompanies the appearance of a large, imposing building on the downstage right. Invasion is complete.

'Where?' emerges out of this desolation, with the Marsupials forced to contemplate the irreversibility of colonisation. All the actors come to stillness, and into their tableau sounds a tinkling piano arpeggio. A gentle waltz in D-flat major ensues. Flinch, one of the Marsupials, comes to the front of the stage to sing the first verse solo. In a pure, clear tone, with little vibrato, she laments the intrusion of the Rabbits and their objects:

> Now the land is bare and brown
> And the wind blows empty 'cross the plain
> I have walked these plains for the whole mem'ry of my soul

The second verse develops this simple melody, adding a harmony, and splitting the material between three Marsupials: Roxie, Three Stripe, and Two Stripe, adding melodic interest by way of a harmony line and timbral variety through the different voices of the Marsupials. The lyrics assert the long history Indigenous custodianship of this land: its status as the oldest continuous culture in the world.

The music continues to build in intensity as we arrive at the pre-chorus, where new melodic material is sung by Flinch and the Bird in counterpoint, with the chorus taken by the Bird alone. Miller-Heidke's fulsome soprano rings out through the auditorium as she melancholically asks, 'Where is the rich dark earth, brown and moist? Where is the smell of rain dripping from gum trees?' to a one-in-the-bar chordal accompaniment. The Marsupials descend from their tree, as they contemplate the destruction of the land and lament their powerlessness: 'I can't run, I can't swim away from this land.' From here, the texture thickens as all the voices combine to sing the chorus in harmony. All performers make their way to the front of the stage, with the Bird high in the Marsupials' tree. The rich and sonorous ten-part choral arrangement, with Miller-Heidke singing the melody is repeated several times, with a modulation one tone higher midway through the second iteration, adding to the intensity of their plea.

In the short coda that rounds off 'Where?,' soaring high in the soprano register, Miller-Heidke sings 'Who will save us' as the music gradually dies away. Into this quiet, she slowly whispers 'from the rabbits,' drawing out all the unvoiced consonants, particularly the final 's' sound. The orchestra gently replay material from 'Where?' as one by one several performers leave the stage. As the lights begin to dim, a circular beam of shimmering blue light materialises on the front of the stage, mimicking a pool of water. A single Rabbit and Marsupial approach the waterhole from opposite sides of the stage. Simultaneously, they crouch down to take a closer look, representing the theatrical rendering of the final page of the picture book. The two performers make eye contact, and then simultaneously, slowly rise as the lights fade to black.

The utopian final tableaux conveys that we are all in this together: Marsupial and Rabbit, Indigenous and non-Indigenous, and rhetorically gestures towards a path forward. While the work has depicted an allegorical Australian past – a history of colonial violence and dispossession – at its conclusion, *The Rabbits* transports us into the present. When the Bird asks, 'Who will save us from the Rabbits?' she looks towards the audience, implicating them directly. The performers are still standing on stage in costume, granted. But by the end of the song, the allegory has slipped away, and the audience are left to contemplate the questions that the song has posed. With its chorus of rhetorical questions, 'Where?' reflects the view that there is still much 'unfinished business' when it comes to reconciliation.[39]

White Witnesses

Having established how *The Rabbits* stages reconciliation through its anthemic finale, I now turn to what I identify as the production's fundamental contradiction: that the central figure at this climactic moment, the one leading the chorus of rhetorical questions, is the Bird, who does not represent an Indigenous character. During the last section of the song, the performers all move to the very front of the stage and stand in a straight line, singing together in harmony; however, the Bird is the dominant figure, both visually and vocally, in this staging of reconciliation. In her analysis of the picture book, Bradford is critical of the final line – 'who will save us from the rabbits?' – because she argues that it 'constructs an alliance between indigenous and non-indigenous' and that 'this sleight of hand' produces a 'dehistoricised domain in which "we are all victims together"' and we all suffer from the effects of colonisation.[40] Through its elevation of the Bird, the stage adaptation certainly does little to circumvent Bradford's criticism. In asking 'who will save us from the rabbits?' it is she who draws audience, Marsupials, and Rabbits together. In occupying this reconciliatory position, the Bird displaces the agency from the Indigenous characters, thereby privileging white settler subjectivity.

The Bird never interacts directly with the Marsupials or the Rabbits; she is merely an observer, a witness to the events that take place. Freddie Rokem, writing about performing history, makes the broad assertion that an 'actor performing a historical figure on the stage in a sense also becomes a witness of the historical event.'[41] For the audience, this creates a dynamic that Caroline Wake terms 'tertiary witnessing' whereby a spectator watches a character in the process of witnessing. Quoting Rokem, Wake suggests that spectating characters, embedded in the action of the drama, '[serve] as a mirror image, a kind of filter or lens, or focalizer for the real spectators watching the performance.'[42] Witnessing is an established modality in the process of reconciliation. Rosanne Kennedy describes it as 'a process of national and personal healing, facilitated by a dialogic model of testimony and witnessing.'[43] In her capacity as witness, the Bird functions as a bridge between the world of the play and the world of the spectators. She provides them a figure with which they can identify, a representative from within the world of the play who can feel guilt, shame, and sorrow with them in real time.

The costuming codes the Bird as white, making her not just a witness to the events of colonisation, but a 'white witness.' Dressed in a resplendent white feathered costume, with her face also painted white, the symbolism of her face and costume is difficult to ignore; after all, Australian birds come in a wide variety of colours. As such, she acts as a representative for other white witnesses: those of us sitting in the theatre. Importantly, she is as powerless to stop the atrocities as the spectator, unable go back in time and change history. This identification between the Bird and the audience is a strategy that ultimately mitigates the impact of the settler shame cultivated throughout the production.

Visually, spatially, and aurally, the Bird dominates the stage. The tessitura of her vocal part, high in the soprano range, means it soars high above the other singers, commanding aural attention. Much of the writing is virtuosic, which draws further attention to her. This, combined with her placement at the apex of the structure occupied by the Marsupials, recalls the music of Queen of the Night from Mozart's *The Magic Flute*, and positions her as the diva, the star of the production. When she first appears, she emerges at the top of a billowing blue cloth (Figure 4.1). Her voice is amplified throughout and the atmospheric reverb effects on the microphone create a fulsome, ethereal sound. This all problematises Halliwell's argument that the transposition of the story from page to stage 'serves to even out the balance between the two groups, so that there is no one point-of-view that is dominant and both groups have equal agency.'[44] While the balance between the Marsupials and the Rabbits may have been addressed, the centrality of the Bird, as an innovation in the stage adaptation, results in the dominant viewpoint being that of the white witnessing settler audience.

As the narrator, the Bird exerts control over the narrative. Her dominance is not confined to the finale: it is she who makes the first appearance on stage and, while she is not the last figure to exit, she speaks the last line. Information

FIGURE 4.1   Kate Miller-Heidke in *The Rabbits.*

Photo: Alex Coppel ©

is almost always filtered through her consciousness, and often this leaves the Marsupials to echo or reinforce her sentiments. A notable example of this is in the scene of first contact, early in the performance. The Rabbits assert their presence musically before they arrive, with a staccato, syncopated musical accompaniment that is used as a leitmotif throughout the work. They trundle onto the stage on a strange, wheeled contraption, from which smoke is emitting. There are only two of them at this point, and they are identifiable as scientists by the smoke and the test-tube that one of them is holding (Figure 4.2). They

FIGURE 4.2 The arrival of the Rabbits.

Photo: Jeff Busby ©

take a lizard – the animal that has been used as a metaphor for Indigenous people in Flinch's previous song – and over a suspended chord decorated with a trill, plop it into a tube, taking it as a specimen. In a free, *Sprechstimme* style, the Bird offers the commentary that:

> The Rabbits came many grandparents ago
> At first the Marsupials didn't know what to think
> They looked a bit like them

These are the first lines of the picture book, but in the stage adaptation, this final sentiment is extended. Two of the Marsupials, Coda and Flinch, expand on this observation:

Flinch:	They look like us
Coda:	No they don't
Flinch (spoken):	They do a bit.

The Marsupials do not get first right of response to the arrival of the Rabbits – they echo what the Bird has told us, which is what the audience already know. We have been expecting the arrival of the Rabbits. In these cases, the privileging of the Bird's perspective is a surreptitious (perhaps unintentional) strategy that weakens the agency of the Marsupials. It reflects what Kizuk describes as 'the over-privileged recognition of the self within the experience of settler shame.'[45]

The Bird represents the hesitancy of the well-meaning settler audience to fully accept responsibility for the harms of colonial dispossession. While the Bird is omniscient, able to tell us what will happen before the Marsupials can, she is unable to intervene and assist the Marsupials. This can be seen in her two solos, 'My Sky' and 'Electric Light. In 'My Sky,' the domain of the Bird is conceived as neutral territory. 'From this distance I don't cry, I don't have to feel for you,' she sings. The Bird is not at fault; she is not culpable for the sins of the Rabbits, and by association, neither are we. We are separated in time and place from the atrocities – 'Far away in air, far away in time' – and we are fundamentally different – 'Your world is not the same as mine.' Towards the end, as the song begins to build to a climax, the lyrics depict how when she does 'fly closer' to the Marsupials, she can suddenly 'smell the sickness,' and 'hear your calls.' But it ends with the quite disarmingly dispassionate statement 'I can't help you. Sorry.' This is the only explicit statement of apology in the production. Danielle Celemajer notes that in the public debate about the apology there was a tension between wanting to find 'some way in which to acknowledge that the violation of the rights of Indigenous peoples was part of the nation's past, while simultaneously resisting being blamed for actions they did not *personally* take.'[46] This feeling is palpable in the Bird's songs.

'Electric Light,' the second solo for the Bird, again, insinuates that she and the audience are also victims of colonisation. 'Electric Light' is a short number that alternates between sections of recitative and a section marked as a chorus. The lyrics cultivate an enigmatic quality, using electricity as emblematic of the intrusive technology brought over by the colonisers: 'Flickering, blinding electric light burns bright but it burns cold. . . . Even birds couldn't find their way home.' In the second recitative section, alone on the stage, as Miller-Heidke vocally mimics the sound of a bird by pulling off the notes, she sings:

I am the fluorescent beam
I cannot change anything
Mountains fall, mountains rise
Swallowed by the fire of electric light

This foregrounding of the Bird's incapacity through first-person address seems somewhat tone-deaf, particularly for this moment in the work, as what has preceded it is 'Kitesong,' a wrenching gospel-style song for the three female Marsupials who have wailed as their children, represented by box-kites, have been removed from them. The cultivation of sympathy for the Bird's position is augmented by the quality of the music of the two songs. Both 'My Sky' and 'Electric Light' are slow, sombre songs that cultivate a sorrowful atmosphere. In the main chord progression of 'My Sky' the second chord utilised is an E-flat major chord. This decision creates the interval of a tritone between this chord and the preceding one, A minor, turning what could have been a predictable pop chord progression into one brimming with pathos.

Feeling Bad, Feeling Good: Transforming Settler Shame

The Rabbits, for many, was a profoundly moving performance that produced intense feelings of settler shame. It was also a euphoric experience. When I attended a performance of the production in the Heath Ledger Theatre in Perth on February 16, 2015, I found 'Where?' overwhelming in its pathos. At the final curtain, the audience collectively jumped to their feet, and I spotted tears in many eyes. They were also in my own. I left feeling intensely sad about the dark and violent history I had witnessed. I listened, acknowledged, and accepted the trauma that this nation had exacted on Aboriginal people. Raimond Gaita defines reconciliation as 'the name given to the acknowledgment that past and present injustices committed against the Aboriginal peoples generated for the non-Aboriginal inhabitants a sense of collective responsibility for the wrong committed by their political ancestors.'[47] After *The Rabbits*, I felt I had undergone an experience that had brought this into stark relief.

But I also felt good. I felt exhilarated by the music, the singing, the theatrical experience. Then I felt bad about feeling good: Is not this letting a white audience off far too easily? Three-and-a-half years later, sitting in the DVD room at Opera Australia watching the archival footage, I found myself welling up once again. 'Where?' was no less powerful; the guilt, shame, and sorrow that I experienced were no less palpable. This contradiction between emotional catharsis and political accountability highlights the central tension performances of reconciliation grapple with.

The intense emotional effect of the production was both lauded and criticised. There is not a review of the production that does not mention the word emotion (or one of its synonyms), indicating that the affective pull of *The Rabbits* was commonly experienced. Van Badham's review describes a similar reaction to my own, praising the production's treatment of these difficult ideas and foregrounding its emotional potency:

> At a time when theatre made about Australia continues to grapple with the culturally unavoidable narrative of white invasion and black dispossession, this sophisticated reduction of historical detail into tropes and characters both accessible to children and recognisable to anyone delivers an unambiguous emotional experience that I can only compare to a walloping.[48]

Badham's 'walloping' to describe the impact of the production is well chosen. This is a version of the 'empathetic and emotional response' identified by Halliwell in his analysis.[49]

A notable exception to the overwhelmingly positive consensus was Christopher Johnstone, whose review is critical of the Bird in line with the arguments I have outlined above. Writing for the *Melbourne Review of Books*, Johnstone argued that 'whereas the focus of the story should be on the tragedy of the marsupials, The White Bird of Spiritual Whiteness ends up with her own narrative arc, being flashed with electric lights and tragically not able to find her way home.'[50] He then went onto say that

> what *The Rabbits* teaches us is that the true victims of the genocide of Aboriginal peoples of Australia are not the Aboriginal people themselves. No, the true victims are enlightened white people who are forced to feel very bad and very disorientated by all that bad history. I for one feel such a deep and abiding sorrow for the white people who are forced to feel guilt that I . . . no, actually I can't even finish the sentence.

He also addresses the question that I asked myself: Isn't this letting us off far too easily? On this matter, Johnstone emphatically says yes:

> In the end, *The Rabbits* got a resounding ovation and applause. To every one of those people who applauded, it might behoove [sic] you to consider why it was that you didn't actually notice that it is not exactly racially enlightened to uncritically watch a group of modern Aboriginal people pretending to be a neutered, tamed and Disneyfied White Australian ideal of ancient Aboriginal people.

Johnstone's critique resonates with an oft-cited article that gives 'those people who applauded' a name: 'sorry people.' Haylie Gooder and Jane Jacobs' 'On the Border of the Unsayable: The Apology in Postcolonizing Australia' considers this prospective act in line with Judith Butler's work on speech acts, drawing out how the act of apology would have 'the power to form and reform what and who is considered to be legitimate within the reconstituting national imaginary. It is an utterance, therefore, which has immense potential as a redistributive force, both material and symbolic.'[51] But they are primarily concerned with how such acts are already occurring in unofficial capacities, and that what they are doing is 'reconstituting' the subjectivities of white settlers. For Gooder and Jacobs, these 'sorry people' have

> assumed not only feelings of guilt but also the mantle of responsibility for assuaging such feelings. They do so on behalf of themselves and of the nation. These guilt-afflicted settler Australians feel the legitimacy of their

national subjectivity to be compromised. They begin to experience a form of settler melancholia. The proliferation of apologies from settler 'sorry people' is a symptom of this melancholia and testifies to the strange (and estranging) rewirings of circuits of power in postcolonizing settler contexts like Australia.[52]

This reflects the tension that *The Rabbits* produces. Gooder and Jacobs' evocation of 'settler melancholia' is redolent of my experience of 'feeling bad.' At the performance of *The Rabbits* that I attended, we became 'sorry people' at the finale: watching and listening to the actors perform an apology on our behalf.

It is in the transformation of 'feeling bad' to 'feeling good' at the conclusion of *The Rabbits* that its utopian aspirations are most potently realised. As Ahmed and Kizuk have identified, shame plays a key role in strengthening national and collective identity. However, as Gaita observes in his critique of reconciliation, shame is only available to those to whom the nation is a potent concept: 'Only as an Australian citizen whose identity has to some extent been shaped by Australia, by attachment to this country, can I feel ashamed of what was done by my political ancestors.'[53] In other words, there needs to be some 'good feeling' attached to nation for the 'bad feeling' to be able to take hold. Feeling bad is thus only ever temporary, and a necessary part of the restoration of faith in the concept of the nation. As Kizuk writes, settler shame 'desperately seeks resolution, preferring to re-establish the self as good, or worthy of pride, rather than respond to other-oriented concerns of justice.[54] *The Rabbits* provided such a resolution, transforming feelings of settler shame into a buoyant, hopeful optimism. The production acknowledges the wound of colonisation but, ultimately, aims to heal it.

Conclusion: Healing the National Imaginary

In staging a utopian performance of reconciliation and apology, *The Rabbits* conceptualises the theatre as a powerful site in which the wounds of the national imaginary can be healed. Under the banner of our national opera company, *The Rabbits* invites us to come together in the auditorium to grapple with Australia's status as a settler colony. It elicits our empathy for the Marsupials and amplifies our antipathy to the Rabbits through its stratified use of musical genre. The staging of the violent colonial past calls upon audiences to witness suffering, feel shame and grief, mourn, recognise, and admit collective wrongs. The production casts us as 'white witnesses,' 'sorry people,' who after witnessing utopian staging of reconciliation between the Rabbits and the Marsupials can then go on home, buoyed by the belief – the hopeful wish – that forgiveness is possible. In the next chapter, we will see Indigenous politics embodied through an alternative emotional and affective tenor and musical genre – anger as expressed through rock music.

Notes

1 Penelope Edmonds, *Settler Colonialism and (Re)Conciliation: Frontier Violence, Affective Performances, and Imaginative Refoundings* (Palgrave Macmillan, 2016), 2.

2 John Marsden and Shaun Tan, *The Rabbits* (Hachette, 1998). I attended a performance live at the Heath Ledger Theatre, Perth, on 16 February 2015. The analysis in this chapter was greatly assisted by access to a score, provided by Iain Grandage, and to archival recordings viewed in Opera Australia's Surry Hills office in early 2019. The recordings I accessed were of performances given on October 12, 2015 in the Playhouse at the Arts Centre Melbourne, and in March 2016 at QPAC, Brisbane.

3 Kate Miller-Heidke and Lally Katz, *The Rabbits (Live Original Cast Recording)*, ABC Classics, 2016. It is also available on Spotify: https://open.spotify.com/album/4OtnOXhblByWEH2qGNoabd?si=asGJamO_TKayqbgX4yCMvg

4 In 2001, Tan gave a paper at a conference that provides a detailed account of his eclectic visual source material. Shaun Tan, 'Originality and Creativity,' in *Joint National Conference of the Australian Association for the Teaching of English and the Australian Literacy Educators' Association*, Hobart, July 12–15, 2001, 5–6, https://files.eric.ed.gov/fulltext/ED458582.pdf

5 Shaun Tan, 'Rabbiting On: A Conversation about *The Rabbits*,' accessed November 1, 2018, http://www.shauntan.net/images/essay%20Rabbits%20interview.html; John Marsden, 'From Bestselling Book to Opera: The Rabbits Are Unleashed on Stage,' *The Sydney Morning Herald*, August 18, 2015, https://www.smh.com.au/entertainment/from-bestselling-book-to-opera-melbourne-festival-2015-unleashes-the-rabbits-20150814-giyz10.html.

6 Matthew Westwood, 'The Rabbits' Den,' *The Australian*, February 7, 2015, 3.

7 The 'history wars' is a term that reflects the cultural battle about how the events of colonisation should be interpreted. It operated on both political, historical, and social fronts, and is an ideological battle that arguably continues to be waged up to the present day. It is present in the conflict around the celebration of Australia Day, a public holiday that commemorates the arrival of the First Fleet. The 'Change the Date' movement calls on the Government to move the celebration to an alternate date, arguing that it shows great disrespect to Indigenous peoples and a lack of understanding of the violent history of colonisation.

8 Andrew Bolt, 'More Shame and Guilt to Heap on our Kids,' *The Herald-Sun*, August 23, 1999, 18. Bolt is surprisingly fixated on *The Rabbits* as emblematic of an approach that he finds distasteful and has continued to write about it long after its publication: Andrew Bolt, 'Remember Who We Are,' *The Herald-Sun*, November 12, 2010, 34; Andrew Bolt, 'Why Do We Preach This Hatred of Our Country?,' *The Advertiser*, February 26, 2015, 13.

9 Andrew Bolt, 'Prizes for Singing about How Awful the Colonisers Were,' *The Herald-Sun*, August 1, 2015, https://www.heraldsun.com.au/blogs/andrew-bolt/prizes-for-singing-about-how-awful-the-colonisers-were/news-story/17b75cbbb21ca2a9a824cf616c75217c.

10 Clare Bradford, 'There's No Place Like Home: Unhomely Moments in Three Postcolonial Picture Books,' in *Cinderella Transformed: Multiple Voices and Diverse Dialogues in Children's Literature*, ed. Doreen Darnell, John McKenzie and Anna Smith (Centre for Children's Literature, 2003), 107.

11 The struggle to undo racist policies and laws had come to a head in 1992 when the landmark Mabo decision was passed by the High Court of Australia. Mabo led to legislation that eventually undid the colonial doctrine of *terra nullius*, heralding a new era in Indigenous relations, and facilitated the traditional owners to make native title claims for land that had been taken from them. Brooke Collins-Gearing and Dianne Osland, 'Who Will Save Us from the Rabbits?: Rewriting the Past

Allegorically,' *The Looking Glass: New Perspectives on Children's Literature* 14, no. 2 (2010), https://ojs.latrobe.edu.au/ojs/index.php/tlg/article/view/227

12 Brooke Collins-Gearing and Dianne Osland, 'Who Will Save Us from the Rabbits?: Rewriting the Past Allegorically,' *The Looking Glass: New Perspectives on Children's Literature* 14, no. 2 (2010), https://ojs.latrobe.edu.au/ojs/index.php/tlg/article/view/227

13 Michael Halliwell, *National Identity in Contemporary Australian Opera: Myths Reconsidered* (Routledge, 2018), 178.

14 Halliwell, *National Identity,* 179.

15 Halliwell, *National Identity,* 179.

16 Michaela Boland, 'A Little Bird Told Us,' *The Australian,* October 2, 2015, Wish magazine, 72.

17 Gabriella Coslovich, '"Whiteley," the Opera, Bets Big on Attracting a Large Audience,' *The Australian Financial Review,* February 20, 2019, https://www.afr.com/brand/afr-magazine/whiteley-the-opera-bets-big-on-attracting-a-large-audience-20190103-h19o7e. Terracini's arguments are outlined in detail in his 2011 Peggy Glanville-Hicks lecture. Transcript available at: Melissa Leslie, 'Lyndon Terracini: The 2011 Peggy Glanville-Hicks Address,' *Limelight,* November 3, 2011, https://limelightmagazine.com.au/features/lyndon-terracini-the-2011-peggy-glanville-hicks-address/.

18 Coslovich, '"Whiteley," the Opera.'

19 Coslovich, '"Whiteley," the Opera.'

20 Nancy Groves, 'Kate Miller-Heidke: Opera's Former "Bratty Upstart" Tackles a Tragic Australian Story,' *The Guardian,* January 5, 2016, https://www.theguardian.com/culture/2016/jan/05/kate-miller-heidke-operas-former-bratty-upstart-tackles-a-tragic-australian-story.

21 Sorry business is a term used by Indigenous people to refer to the 'mutually binding, ritual obligations' prompted by the death of a family member. Cohen, Dwyer, and Ginters extend the term to discuss a process whereby through performance, Indigenous and non-Indigenous work together to promote truth-telling and reconciliation. Michael Cohen, Paul Dwyer and Laura Ginters, 'Performing "Sorry Business": Reconciliation and Redressive Action,' in *Victor Turner and Contemporary Cultural Performance,* ed. Graeme St John (Berghahn Books, 2008), 76.

22 Patrick Dodson, 'Whatever Happened to Reconciliation?,' in *Coercive Reconciliation: Stabilise, Normalise, Exit Aboriginal Australia,* ed. Jon Altman and Melinda Hickson (Arena Publications Association, 2007), 21.

23 Edmonds, *Settler Colonialism,* 8.

24 Edmonds, *Settler Colonialism,* 15.

25 Chris Hook and Clare Morgan, 'Creatures of Havoc,' *The Courier Mail,* March 5, 2016, 4.

26 'The Rabbits Learning Resource Pack,' *QPAC,* accessed February 13, 2025, https://www.qpac.com.au/resources/images/160203_The_Rabbits_Education_Kit.pdf.

27 Danielle Celemajer and A. Dirk Moses, 'Australian Memory and the Apology to the Stolen Generations of Indigenous People,' in *Memory in a Global Age: Discourses, Practices and Trajectories,* ed. Aleida Assman and Sebastian Conrad (Palgrave Macmillan, 2010), 38.

28 Anne Boyd, '"To Didj or Not To Didj": Exploring Indigenous Representation in Australian Music Theatre Works by Margaret Sutherland and Andrew Schultz,' in *Opera Indigene: Re/Presenting First Nations and Indigenous Cultures,* ed. Pamela Karantonis and Dylan Robinson (Ashgate, 2011), 93.

29 Elissa Blake, 'How Pregnancy Has Changed Kate Miller-Heidke's Performance in *The Rabbits,' The Sydney Mornings Herald,* January 11, 2016, https://www.smh.com.au/entertainment/the-rabbits-20160111-gm3ea2.html.

30 Westwood, 'The Rabbits' Den.'

31 Edmonds, *Settler Colonialism*, 25.

32 Blake, 'How Pregnancy has Changed Kate.'

33 Sarah Kizuk, 'Settler Shame: A Critique of the Role of Shame in Settler–Indigenous Relationships in Canada,' *Hypatia* 35 (2020): 162, original emphasis, https://doi.org/10.1017/hyp.2019.8

34 Sara Ahmed, 'The Politics of Bad Feeling,' *Australian Critical Race and Whiteness Studies* 1 (2005): 73.

35 Ahmed, 'The Politics of Bad Feeling,' 75.

36 Ahmed, 'The Politics of Bad Feeling,' 77.

37 Rosanne Kennedy, 'An Australian Archive of Feelings: The Sorry Books Campaign and the Pedagogy of Compassion,' *Australian Feminist Studies* 26, no. 69 (2011): 261, https://doi.org/10.1080/08164649.2011.606603

38 Rebecca Do Rozario, 'Australia's Fairy Tales Illustrated in Print Instances of Indigeneity, Colonization, and Suburbanization,' *Marvels & Tales* 25, no. 1 (2011): 26, https://www.jstor.org/stable/41388975

39 Unfinished business' is a term coined by the Council for Aboriginal Reconciliation in its final report in 2000 before the organisation was discontinued. It was also invoked by Kevin Rudd in the Apology to the Stolen Generations. The term in is common parlance in contemporary Australia to describe how the campaign for constitutional recognition has stalled.

40 Bradford, 'There's No Place Like Home,' 107.

41 Freddie Rokem, *Performing History: Theatrical Representations of the Past in Contemporary Theatre* (University of Iowa Press, 2000), 9.

42 Caroline Wake, 'The Accident and the Account: Towards a Taxonomy of Spectatorial Witness in Theatre and Performance Studies,' *Performance Paradigm* 5, no. 1 (2009): 92, https://www.performanceparadigm.net/index.php/journal/article/view/68

43 Rosanne Kennedy, 'Reflections on Post-Apology Australia: From a Poetics of Reparation to a Poetics of Survival,' in *Breaking Intergenerational Cycles of Repetition: A Global Dialogue on Historical Trauma and Memory*, ed. Pumla Gobodo-Madikizela (Barbara Budrich Publishers, 2016), 196–197.

44 Halliwell, *National Identity*, 178.

45 Kizuk, 'Settler Shame,' 162.

46 Danielle Celemajer, *The Sins of the Nation and the Ritual of Apologies* (Cambridge University Press, 2009), 171–172, original emphasis.

47 Raymond Gaita, 'The Moral Force of Reconciliation,' in *Coercive Reconciliation: Stabilise, Normalise, Exit Aboriginal Australia*, ed. Jon Altman and Melinda Hickson (Arena Publications Association, 2007), 300–301.

48 Van Badham, '*The Rabbits* Review – Triumphant Adaptation of a Deeply Tragic Story,' *The Guardian*, February 18, 2015, https://www.theguardian.com/music/2015/feb/18/the-rabbits-review-triumphant-adaptation-of-a-deeply-tragic-story.

49 Halliwell, *National Identity*, 179.

50 Christopher Johnstone, '*The Rabbits* (Opera),' *Melbourne Review of Books*, October 13, 2015, accessed January 15, 2019, http://melbournereviewofbooks.com/the-rabbits-opera/.

51 Haydie Gooder and Jane Jacobs, '"On the Border of the Unsayable": The Apology in Postcolonizing Australia,' *Interventions* 2, no. 2 (2000): 231, https://doi.org/10.1080/136980100427333

52 Gooder and Jacobs, '"On the Border",' 232.

53 Gaita, 'The Moral Force of Reconciliation,' 301

54 Kizuk, 'Settler Shame,' 162.

References

Ahmed, Sara. 'The Politics of Bad Feeling.' *Australian Critical Race and Whiteness Studies* 1 (2005): 72–85.

Badham, Van. '*The Rabbits* Review – Triumphant Adaptation of a Deeply Tragic Story.' *The Guardian*, February 18, 2015. https://www.theguardian.com/music/2015/feb/18/the-rabbits-review-triumphant-adaptation-of-a-deeply-tragic-story.

Blake, Elissa. 'How Pregnancy Has Changed Kate Miller-Heidke's Performance in *The Rabbits.*' *The Sydney Mornings Herald*, January 11, 2016. https://www.smh.com.au/entertainment/the-rabbits-20160111-gm3ea2.html.

Boland, Michaela. 'A Little Bird Told Us.' *The Australian*, October 2, 2015, Wish magazine, 72.

Bolt, Andrew. 'More Shame and Guilt to Heap on our Kids.' *The Herald-Sun*, August 23, 1999, 18.

Bolt, Andrew. 'Remember Who We Are.' *The Herald-Sun*, November 12, 2010, 34.

Bolt, Andrew. 'Why Do We Preach This Hatred of Our Country?.' *The Advertiser*, February 26, 2015, 13.

Bolt, Andrew. 'Prizes for Singing about How Awful the Colonisers Were.' *The Herald-Sun*, August 1, 2015. https://www.heraldsun.com.au/blogs/andrew-bolt/prizes-for-singing-about-how-awful-the-colonisers-were/news-story/17b75cbbb21ca2a9a824cf616c75217c.

Boyd, Anne. '"To Didj or Not To Didj": Exploring Indigenous Representation in Australian Music Theatre Works by Margaret Sutherland and Andrew Schultz.' In *Opera Indigene: Re/Presenting First Nations and Indigenous Cultures*, edited by Pamela Karantonis and Dylan Robinson. Ashgate, 2011.

Bradford, Clare. 'There's No Place Like Home: Unhomely Moments in Three Postcolonial Picture Books.' In *Cinderella Transformed: Multiple Voices and Diverse Dialogues in Children's Literature*, edited by Doreen Darnell, John McKenzie and Anna Smith. Centre for Children's Literature, 2003.

Celermajer, Danielle. *The Sins of the Nation and the Ritual of Apologies.* Cambridge University Press, 2009.

Celermajer, Danielle, and A. Dirk Moses. 'Australian Memory and the Apology to the Stolen Generations of Indigenous People.' In *Memory in a Global Age: Discourses, Practices and Trajectories*, edited by Aleida Assman and Sebastian Conrad. Palgrave Macmillan, 2010.

Cohen, Michael, Paul Dwyer, and Laura Ginters. 'Performing "Sorry Business": Reconciliation and Redressive Action.' In *Victor Turner and Contemporary Cultural Performance*, edited by Graeme St John. Berghahn Books, 2008.

Collins-Gearing, Brooke, and Dianne Osland. 'Who Will Save Us from the Rabbits?: Rewriting the Past Allegorically.' *The Looking Glass: New Perspectives on Children's Literature* 14, no. 2 (2010). https://ojs.latrobe.edu.au/ojs/index.php/tlg/article/view/227.

Coslovich, Gabriella. '"Whiteley," the Opera, Bets Big on Attracting a Large Audience.' *The Australian Financial Review*, February 20, 2019. https://www.afr.com/brand/afr-magazine/whiteley-the-opera-bets-big-on-attracting-a-large-audience-20190103-h19o7e.

Dodson, Patrick. 'Whatever Happened to Reconciliation?' In *Coercive Reconciliation: Stabilise, Normalise, Exit Aboriginal Australia*, edited by Jon Altman and Melinda Hickson. Arena Publications Association, 2007.

Do Rozario, Rebecca. 'Australia's Fairy Tales Illustrated in Print Instances of Indigeneity, Colonization, and Suburbanization.' *Marvels & Tales* 25, no. 1 (2011): 13–32. https://www.jstor.org/stable/41388975.

Edmonds, Penelope. *Settler Colonialism and (Re)Conciliation: Frontier Violence, Affective Performances, and Imaginative Refoundings.* Palgrave Macmillan, 2016.

Gaita, Raymond. 'The Moral Force of Reconciliation.' In *Coercive Reconciliation: Stabilise, Normalise, Exit Aboriginal Australia*, edited by Jon Altman and Melinda Hickson. Arena Publications Association, 2007.

Gooder, Haydie, and Jane Jacobs. '"On the Border of the Unsayable": The Apology in Postcolonizing Australia.' *Interventions* 2, no. 2 (2000): 229–247. https://doi.org/10.1080/136980100427333.

Groves, Nancy. 'Kate Miller-Heidke: Opera's Former "Bratty Upstart" Tackles a Tragic Australian Story.' *The Guardian*, January 5, 2016. https://www.theguardian.com/culture/2016/jan/05/kate-miller-heidke-operas-former-bratty-upstart-tackles-a-tragic-australian-story.

Halliwell, Michael. *National Identity in Contemporary Australian Opera: Myths Reconsidered*. Routledge, 2018.

Hook, Chris, and Clare Morgan. 'Creatures of Havoc.' *The Courier Mail*, March 5, 2016, 4.

Johnstone, Christopher. '*The Rabbits* (Opera).' *Melbourne Review of Books*, October 13, 2015. Accessed January 15, 2019. http://melbournereviewofbooks.com/the-rabbits-opera/.

Kennedy, Rosanne. 'An Australian Archive of Feelings: The Sorry Books Campaign and the Pedagogy of Compassion.' *Australian Feminist Studies* 26, no. 69 (2011): 257–279. https://doi.org/10.1080/08164649.2011.606603.

Kennedy, Rosanne. 'Reflections on Post-Apology Australia: From a Poetics of Reparation to a Poetics of Survival.' In *Breaking Intergenerational Cycles of Repetition: A Global Dialogue on Historical Trauma and Memory*, edited by Pumla Gobodo-Madikizela. Barbara Budrich Publishers, 2016.

Kizuk, Sarah. 'Settler Shame: A Critique of the Role of Shame in Settler–Indigenous Relationships in Canada.' *Hypatia* 35 (2020): 161–177. https://doi.10.1017/hyp.2019.8.

Leslie, Melissa. 'Lyndon Terracini: The 2011 Peggy Glanville-Hicks Address.' *Limelight*, November 3, 2011. https://limelightmagazine.com.au/features/lyndon-terracini-the-2011-peggy-glanville-hicks-address/.

Marsden, John. 'From Bestselling Book to Opera: The Rabbits Are Unleashed on Stage.' *The Sydney Morning Herald*, August 18, 2015. https://www.smh.com.au/entertainment/from-bestselling-book-to-opera-melbourne-festival-2015-unleashes-the-rabbits-20150814-giyz10.html.

Marsden, John, and Shaun Tan. *The Rabbits*. Hachette, 1998.

Miller-Heidke, Kate, and Lally Katz. *The Rabbits (Live Original Cast Recording)*. ABC Classics, 2016.

'*The Rabbits* Learning Resource Pack.' *QPAC*. Accessed February 13, 2025. https://www.qpac.com.au/resources/images/160203_The_Rabbits_Education_Kit.pdf.

Rokem, Freddie. *Performing History: Theatrical Representations of the Past in Contemporary Theatre*. University of Iowa Press, 2000.

Tan, Shaun. 'Originality and Creativity.' In *Joint National Conference of the Australian Association for the Teaching of English and the Australian Literacy Educators' Association*. Hobart, July 12–15, 2001. https://files.eric.ed.gov/fulltext/ED458582.pdf.

Tan, Shaun. *Rabbiting On: A Conversation about The Rabbits*. Accessed November 1, 2018. http://www.shauntan.net/images/essay%20Rabbits%20interview.html.

Wake, Caroline. 'The Accident and the Account: Towards a Taxonomy of Spectatorial Witness in Theatre and Performance Studies.' *Performance Paradigm* 5, no. 1 (2009): 82–100. https://www.performanceparadigm.net/index.php/journal/article/view/68.

Westwood, Matthew. 'The Rabbits' Den.' *The Australian*, February 7, 2015, 3.

5

ARTISTIC AGENCY, ANGER, AND PUB ROCK IN *BARBARA AND THE CAMP DOGS*

In the National Institute of Dramatic Arts' (NIDA) inaugural NAIDOC week lecture, given in November 2020, Ursula Yovich described theatre as 'an integral and vital part of any culture. It reflects back at us what's happening in our societies, in our communities, in our families, our homes, our politics.'[1] She stressed the need for contemporary performance to adequately reflect the diversity of Australian society and importantly, to represent Indigenous Australians in a meaningful way. Yovich's tour-de-force rock musical, *Barbara and the Camp Dogs* (2017), written in collaboration with Alana Valentine, is a perfect example of her vision. *Barbara*'s defining feature is its depiction of unbridled, profound anger, intensified through rock music. Staged as a rock gig in a pub, the musical idiom and setting supply the energy that supports the production's critique of the social conditions of contemporary Australia. It is a work where, through story and song, the ongoing effects of colonial racism are painfully exposed, highlighting how the history of violence and dispossession of Indigenous communities continues to ripple through to the present day. In doing so, it is firmly focused on the present, asking: 'Where are we now?' as a settler-colonial nation.

Barbara and the Camp Dogs was produced by Belvoir in conjunction with Vicki Gordon Music Productions in 2017. The production opened on December 2, 2017, and played a three-week season. In 2019 it toured to Melbourne, Brisbane, and Wollongong before returning to Belvoir. It was also performed in Yovich's hometown in North-West Arnhem land for an Aboriginal audience.[2] The production garnered a range of accolades, including being shortlisted for the Nick Enright Prize for Playwriting and the Victorian Premier's Prize for Drama, and subsequently attracted funding from Screen Australia for adaptation as a film.[3]

DOI: 10.4324/9781003590088-6

This chapter analyses the way that rock music, humour, and anger coalesce in *Barbara*. Through analysis of process and playscript, I demonstrate how *Barbara* makes use of features of the monodrama, a form that promotes artistic agency and privileges Indigenous perspectives. *Barbara*'s use of the rock musical form extends the aesthetic boundaries of the Indigenous musical established in landmark productions like *Bran Nue Dae* and *The Sapphires*. I argue that situating the production as a live music gig performed in a pub is a subversive move that reclaims a space from which Aboriginal women have been historically excluded. The pub setting also facilitates a meta-commentary on the place of women in the Australian music scene. Finally, I turn to the coexistence of humour and anger in the work, demonstrating how this combination operates as a coping mechanism for intergenerational trauma. The final song, 'Let in the Love,' dispenses with anger to offer a sense of hope and the possibility of future healing. In contrast to *The Rabbits*, however, the way forward is on Aboriginal terms.

The plot tells the story of two women: Barbara and her cousin René, both of whom were raised by René's mother, Mum Jill, after Barbara's mother left. In the opening scene, René says, 'These people,' gesturing to the audience, 'would say your adopted mother,' to which Barbara replies, 'I don't give a bag full of smashed arseholes what these gangstas would call her, if I call her my mother then she's my mother.'[4] The narrative is a journey-back-home road-trip, prompted by the impending death of a family member, a structural device identified by Susanne Thurow as functioning as a catalyst for 'communal realignment, bringing dispersed and estranged families back together to enact a catharsis from long-held resentments and the trauma emanating from buried family secrets.'[5] Both women are singers, subsisting by playing gigs around Sydney. When René discovers that their mother is unwell and that they need to urgently get home to see her, she insists that they find the funds to get back to Darwin. While at first Barbara is reluctant to make the journey home, she eventually procures them a gig that earns them just enough money to buy the plane tickets. On arrival at the hospital in Darwin, they discover that their mother has been taken three hours south to Katherine, their hometown. Over the course of their journey home, Barbara's trepidation about the act of returning home and revisiting her past becomes palpable. When they arrive in Katherine, she orchestrates a fight with René outside the hospital that gives her an excuse to leave, avoiding the painful experience of having to say goodbye to her mother. Fuelled by alcohol, a series of events ensue that result in her being arrested, spending the night in gaol, and thus missing out on seeing Mum Jill one last time. René is furious with her: 'Don't come anywhere near me, ever again.'[6] Consumed with grief, Barbara travels east to the small Indigenous community of Bulman, where she locates her long-estranged brother Joseph, thereby fulfilling her mother's final wish. Barbara returns to Katherine to reconcile with René – 'you might want to record this, 'cause it's only going to happen once' – and finally finds the courage to tell her sister how much she loves her.[7] The production ends how it began, with Barbara, René, and Joseph united in song.

The Road to *Barbara*

The eponymous Barbara of the title is Yovich's alter-ego. The character began as a running gag between Yovich and her friend Stephen Page (Artistic Director of Bangarra Dance Theatre, the pre-eminent Indigenous dance company) about Yovich 'being the lead singer of an all-girl Aboriginal band.' Page named her Barbara: 'he thought the band should be called *Barbara and the Camp Dogs*.'[8] The character came to serve as an outlet for Yovich, allowing her to express her frustrations and affording her the 'permission to say what I want to say.'[9] The impetus for creating the musical arose out of Yovich's anger at the entertainment industry, namely that she was only being considered for roles marked as Indigenous when she felt she had so much more to offer as an actor – 'you have to be in the race to be able to win it, but if you're not allowed to race you've got no chance of winning it, which is how I felt about auditions.'[10] But as the idea developed, she gravitated towards an exploration of more systemic issues:

> It's not just theatre or film or television, it's actually the way the rest of Australia perceives Aboriginal people and it's not always in a positive light, or it's in a two-dimensional light, where you don't actually understand where that anger comes from . . . well, there are reasons behind why people kinda lash out, people don't just lash out for nothing and so, that's where it's coming from . . . it's my own frustrations.[11]

Her desire was to create the kind of character that she was impatient to perform: one who was angry, vulnerable, funny, and complex. Receiving the Balnaves Foundation Indigenous Playwright's Award in 2016 provided Yovich with the opportunity to develop the character of Barbara into the protagonist of her first play.

Theatrical representations of Indigenous lives and stories which, like *Barbara*, often involve representations of violence and intergenerational trauma, present significant challenges for artists and companies alike. Helena Grehan argues that 'performance and theatre by and about Indigenous people carries a complex burden,' because it is 'concerned with sharing stories that have been silenced, rendered invisible or left untold. This means that the work is always, at some level, political: it is informed by the often-fraught cultural, social, and political conditions within which it is situated.'[12] In Susanne Thurow's account of Indigenous identities in Australian theatre, the rehearsal room becomes a 'laboratory' for the exploration of 'questions of power and colonial legacy.'[13] For Indigenous artists the lack of agency they are afforded when collaborating with mainstream, white-dominated theatre companies can be a source of frustration. As Liza-Mare Syron argues, this is often because the artistic authority in these cases 'lies explicitly with those who finance commercial productions, and or with the director's "vision."'[14] As a collaboration with a mainstage theatre company that featured both a white director and a white co-author, *Barbara* could easily have run into difficulties.

The artists and companies involved in *Barbara*, Indigenous and non-Indigenous, developed an appropriate working model that was ultimately successful. In a 2018 radio interview, when asked what the key factors for a successful collaboration with white artists were, Yovich emphatically responded with 'respect.'[15] Yovich and co-writer Alana Valentine had an existing artistic relationship, having worked together on *Barefoot Divas*, an Indigenous musical revue presented as part of the 2012 Sydney Festival. Yovich valued Valentine's experience and mentorship, expressing in the programme note her 'love and appreciation to Alana for guiding and nurturing me as a new writer.'[16] The process of writing the script was highly collaborative, as Valentine detailed:

> During rehearsals Ursula and I would sit next to each other and pass the laptop literally back and forth, as she wrote a section or revised a lyric and then passed it back to me to augment and write more. I can honestly say that it was a bizarre and wonderful experience of having two brains synchronised to one voice.[17]

Director Leticia Cáceres described the process as a 'fruitful and robust collaboration' and offered the following description of her approach to the theatrical process:

> I tried very hard to exercise deep listening, and not impose. I've been invited into a process of telling a story that is culturally and politically very personal and sensitive. I'm here to support a vision and to craft the story; my ownership over this work is only earned by the respect and trust I have gained in this process of collaborating with these artists.[18]

Cáceres also noted that Yovich and Valentine had a tight partnership and that she had to 'learn their way of working and my place within that relationship.' Yovich and Valentine in turn thanked Cáceres for the 'incredible care, passion, and vision' she brought to the project, indicating the positive working relationship among the three.[19]

Yovich saw *Barbara* as an opportunity not only to write herself a bespoke character but also to express herself through music by writing her own songs. As well as her extensive work in theatre, television, and film, Yovich has maintained a parallel career as a musician and songwriter.[20] Her love of music was fostered through listening to the radio and through voracious consumption of the iconic Australian television programme *Rage*. Yovich held ambitions of being a singer but struggled to see a career in the performing arts as a viable option for a young Aboriginal woman.[21] The turning point was the Saturday morning when, as per usual, she turned on the television to see Whitney Houston sing for the first time:

> She was someone that I could relate to because her dark skin matched mine and she was in this position of power that I hadn't seen my own mob, or anyone of my colour in before. . . . That there was when I knew I was going to be a professional singer.[22]

In 2009, she performed a solo cabaret entitled *Magpie Blues*, which contained a mix of original songs and covers, interspersed with stories of her experience of navigating her mixed heritage. The music of *Magpie Blues* ranged from soul-inspired originals to a medley of 1980s hits to a cover of Andrea Boccelli's version of 'Caruso.' The final song she performed, a version of 'Somewhere over the Rainbow,' was sung in a combination of three languages: English, Serbian, and, her mother tongue, Bararra.[23]

Drawing on Yovich's experience as a songwriter, and with the assistance of musician Adam Ventoura, Yovich and Valentine composed the music and lyrics for the sixteen songs that are interspersed into the play.[24] The songs traverse a range of contemporary genres: rock, blues, soul, funk, and more. A record of five of the songs was produced and sold in limited release.[25] The production featured an onstage band to accompany the singers, comprised of three women on guitar, bass, and drums. These are the 'Camp Dogs' and the band are intermittently included in the narrative. Barbara formally introduces them in performance as 'the magnificent Camp Dogs. They got their name from being mangy, pasty bitches, and as musicians they're used to being offended, insulted, humiliated and ignored, so they fit right in with us.'[26] 'Camp' in this context has a double meaning, referring to both 'camp' as queer sensibility and to the wild dogs found in the bush 'that actually don't belong to anybody; they just belong to the community,' as Yovich explained.[27]

Joining Yovich/Barbara and the Camp Dogs onstage were performers Elaine Crombie and Troy Brady. Crombie was brought on-board to play the role of René, a character who was modelled on her. Crombie is a Pitjanjtajtarra, Warrigmal, South Sea Islander woman with German ancestry on her father's side. Yovich and Crombie have known each other for decades. 'We understand each other,' says Yovich, while Crombie describes their relationships as being like sisters.[28] Crombie's career spans music, comedy, theatre performance, and television, and she is an advocate for Indigenous representation in the arts industry, working as a First Nations Organiser for the Media Entertainment and Arts Alliance (MEAA). Brady, who appears on stage ostensibly as a sound technician for much of the work, makes a surprise transition at the end of the production to play the role of Barbara's brother Joseph. He is a Western GuGuYalanji and Birri Gubba musician who was a member of the Black Arm Band, an Aboriginal and Torres Strait Islander music theatre organisation that was active from 2005 to 2017, and with which Yovich was also involved. This account of the key artists and the process of developing *Barbara* foregrounds how mutual trust, listening, respect, and artistic agency are essential components for a fruitful collaboration between Indigenous and white artists. This is particularly vital when a work has a relationship to lived experience, as *Barbara* does.

Barbara strategically employs dramaturgical conventions of the monodrama, a form of dramatic storytelling featuring a single performer. With a focus on personal stories, it has, and continues, to be used to great effect by Aboriginal women as a 'powerful vehicle for talking back.'[29] Monodramas incorporate multiple modes of performance, including but not limited to song, dance, and traditional Aboriginal performance. They often feature use of Indigenous languages. They can be autobiographical, semi-autobiographical, or can 'combine details from many lives into a representative central character or characters.'[30] *Barbara* takes some of its inspiration from Yovich's life. For example, like Barbara, Yovich's mother left when she was young, meaning that Yovich has had to wrestle with '[feelings of] abandonment, you know, I didn't grow up with my mother and yet I still have a connection with her.'[31] Valentine's experience with verbatim theatre meant that part of the writing process involved working with Yovich's stream-of-consciousness: 'I would spew out all this stuff that Alana would record, and she turned my words into this wonderful monologue about not being seen.'[32] However, the distance created through the character device of the alter-ego allowed the production to include a wider range of perspectives: 'There are experiences I have seen, parts of my family in there. I'm sure parts of Alana are in there too.'[33] These aspects of the monodrama strengthen the agency of the protagonists, ensuring their perspectives are privileged.

Barbara uses a form of first-person storytelling to re-enact past events in present tense. While many monodramas are polyvocal, involving the performer embodying a series of characters in addition to themselves, in *Barbara* the supporting characters are conjured indirectly through recount. The one exception to this is her brother Joseph (played by Brady), who only appears in the penultimate scene. This is a mode of storytelling seen frequently in stand-up comedy. In *Barbara*, it operates as a particularly important strategy because many of these unnamed characters are white and commit acts of racism. These figures have no voice, allowing Barbara/Yovich to retain full agency of the narrative, as it is told entirely through their perspective. Writing about Tammy Anderson's monodrama *I Don't Wanna Play House*, Alison Lyssa makes a similar observation, noting that:

> Because in performance, Anderson is prey and predator, child and attacker, female and male, black and white, she enacts the pain inflicted, but the agonistic element cannot triumph. Because the attacker is only present when brought into being by the body of his survivor, the usual power dynamic . . . cannot be reinscribed as unchangeable reality. Where their might have been a 'victim,' there is a self . . . the destroyer in *I Don't Wanna Play House* has no physical presence with which to gloat.[34]

Likewise, in *Barbara*, other characters have a limited verbal presence. When René reluctantly invites Barbara to attend her regular gig singing at the casino, Barbara ends up in a fistfight with another patron, after drinking a 'couple of beers. No more than two.'[35] While René is singing, Barbara notices a 'room full of dickheads' talking through the performance, with one man 'yelling at the top of his lungs.' She goes over to him to ask him to be quiet: 'If you kept the noise down, mate, you might be able to actually hear what she's tryin' to sing to you,' to which he replies, 'Fuck off, you stupid black bitch. Who let you in?' Barbara immediately springs into action: 'I looked at him and I smile and I say, "Dickhead, you just made my day," and I thumped him – *poom*, one to the face; *poom*, one to the groin.' After she attacks the man, a security guard 'the size of the Big Banana' approaches Barbara, so she ups the ante – 'I headbutt him and I fucking cut.' René turns to the audience and remarks: 'See, when Barbara headbutts anyone she has to jump. Like a soccer player heading the ball. It's quite a picture.'[36] Yovich is small in stature, and Barbara as a character has such energy that the image of her jump-head-butting someone is extremely humorous. It almost certainly would not have been as funny to watch the racist encounter unfold in real-time and to witness the aggression and vitriol of the man first-hand. This present-tense re-enactment storytelling device is used for all the violent encounters in the production, and its effect that Yovich/Barbara's perspective on the encounter is the only perspective that is heard; the only perspective that matters.

Indigenous Rock Musical

Barbara forms part of a rich tradition of musicals authored by Indigenous Australians. A landmark moment for the field was *Bran Nue Dae* (1990), written by the late Jimmy Chi with his band Kuckles. The joyous road trip story, set in Western Australia, is an eclectic celebration of music, dance, comedy and Indigenous language.[37] It was highly acclaimed at the time and its success has endured, having enjoyed several repeat productions in the intervening decades. Other significant works are Wesley Enoch's *The Sunshine*

Club (1999), a story about an Aboriginal serviceman returning home after the Second World War and Tony Briggs' *The Sapphires* (2004), loosely based on the story of a family of Aboriginal women who sang for troops on the frontlines of the Vietnam War. Yovich performed in the inaugural seasons of both *The Sunshine Club* and *The Sapphires*.[38] *The Sapphires*, like *Bran Nue Dae*, was also adapted for the screen in recent years. These are significant works of musical theatre that are critically acclaimed and have attracted broad audiences, building the public's appetite for Indigenous musical theatre.

A shared feature of these Indigenous musicals is that the music is drawn more from popular music genres rather than adopting the transnational style of Broadway musical theatre.[39] This is the case whether the music is composed specifically for the narrative, as in the case of *Barbara*, or drawn from popular music repertoire, like the soul songs in *The Sapphires*.[40] The predominance of popular music genres in Indigenous musical theatre mirrors the adoption of these genres in Aboriginal music more broadly. As Peter Dunbar-Hall and Chris Gibson note, Aboriginal musicians in contemporary Australia have engaged with a wide range of musical genres, including folk music, gospel, and country, which have 'become Indigenous musical languages in their own right.'[41]

What distinguishes *Barbara* from these other Indigenous musicals is the predominance of rock in its musical palette. The production was characterised as and compared to other rock musicals. Cáceres drew a comparison with *Once* (2012), while Belvoir's marketing material contained the tag line 'They will rock you' (a clear allusion to the Queen musical, *We Will Rock You*).[42] Yovich and Valentine's remarks were more protean. In *The Guardian*, Valentine averred that 'Ursula hates musicals! But we both had a bit of difficulty with the emotional structure of musicals.'[43] Yovich said that she 'wouldn't say it's a musical but wouldn't say it's a play with songs' either.[44] She contradicted this by saying in a separate interview 'we [Yovich and Valentine] both love singing so we knew it was going to be a musical.'[45]

Emphasis was placed on the fact that the music was not tethered to the narrative as in a standard integrated musical. The songs function like an album, and while only a handful were recorded, the music could easily have been released in its entirety. Yovich illustrated this when she said that 'these are actual songs that you'll probably see me perform as Ursula.'[46] Valentine, acknowledging it was a rock musical, was also careful to distinguish it for other examples of the form:

> What we found, when it was on in Sydney is that a lot of people who would, not to mince words, 'diss' the music that happens in a rock musical[–] they were coming to the show and saying 'wow, this is really legitimately good music.' We were really proud of that.[47]

This act of setting *Barbara* apart reflects the discourse of inauthenticity that plagues the rock musical. Elizabeth Wollman attributes the 'uneasy relationship' between rock and the musical to rock's emphasis on the notion of authenticity, and the way in which rock positions itself as a 'transgressive, rebellious genre' that is 'ideologically superior' to its counterpart, pop music, which is tarnished by its flagrant commercialism.[48] Musical theatre and pop are equivalents here in the sense that the musical too 'is not particularly preoccupied with notions of authenticity' and 'celebrates the self-conscious blend of high and low cultures, revels in artifice and kitsch, and has been closely and comparatively unflinchingly associated with commercialism from its inception.'[49] As Valentine's comments suggests, the sticking point has often been to do with the quality of the music.

While their stories are distinct, I identify similarities between *Barbara* and the rock musical *Hedwig and the Angry Inch* (2001). Both works display what Dominic Symonds terms as a formal 'inbetweenness': a cross between a drag act and a rock gig in the case of *Hedwig*, a cross between a rock gig and a monodrama in *Barbara*.[50] The titles of the two works are structured similarly – protagonist and their band, and the character of Hedwig was also the alter ego of creator John Cameron Mitchell. Like *Barbara*, *Hedwig*'s music was praised. 'In the whole long, sorry history of rock musicals, *Hedwig and the Angry Inch* is the first one that truly rocks,' wrote David Fricke in *Rolling Stone*.[51] There is also a connection between rock music, marginality, and anger in both works.

Barbara, like Hedwig, ensures that its music 'rocks' by closely emulating rock instrumentation and song structures. The music is scored for what Susan Fast describes as the 'ur-ensemble' of rock: a vocalist with drums, bass, and guitar.[52] Most of the songs are short in length, using simple two- or three-part forms. Melodies are often broken into short fragments that are frequently repeated. For example, René's song 'Fury Street,' which expresses her view that Barbara has spent too much of her life wallowing in anger, uses a standard verse-chorus structure. The song begins with a rhythmic two-bar riff where the female electric guitarist descends from the rostrum to swagger around the stage. This riff, which underpins the song, is constructed with six beats of pulsed eight-notes on the tonic pitch, subtly accented on the second, fourth and sixth beat, followed by two resounding power chords on beats seven and eight. The song begins with two identical strophic verses: three lines of lyrics sung to an identical melody, followed the hook: 'now it's time to put it down, time to put it down, time to put it down, down, down.' The hook line adds backing vocals to the texture of the song. The second verse is immediately followed by a virtuosic electric-guitar solo, and in the final verse Crombie lets loose with the vocals, improvising and embellishing the melodic material established earlier, making use of her upper range and a grungy, powerful timbre.

The lyrics in *Barbara* privilege emotion over character development, which is characteristic of rock music. Simon Frith articulates that rock performance is not concerned with 'pleasing an audience (pop style) nor representing it (folk style) but, rather, displaying desires and feelings rawly, as if to a lover or friend.'[53] According to Yovich, the songs do not 'carry the story lyrically' but rather provide 'an emotional journey for the characters, so you get a sense of what the characters are feeling at any given moment.'[54] This is another way in which *Barbara* distinguishes itself from the standard musical. One model for the lyrics of *Barbara* was the song 'Don't Dream It's Over' by the Australian rock band Crowded House. Valentine commented that she was inspired by the way that 'you sort of know what it means but you also don't, and there's heaps of space for *you*. And in the play, you think you know how the lyrics emotionally connect to the story, but it's not a direct line. And we wanted that. That was really deliberate.'[55] These comments indicate their desire to forego the specificity of character and narrative cultivated by musical theatre lyrics, positing the lyrics of Crowded House against the artful, self-aware theatrical style of lyrics.

The song 'Out of Sight, Out of Mind' provides an apt example. The song follows a scene outside the hospital where Barbara tries to stall having to go in and face the confronting reality of her dying mother. She tries to convince René to go to the pub, to the supermarket, and to the chemist. René calls her on this tactic, but Barbara takes off to the chemist anyway, leaving René to deliver a monologue that contextualises Barbara's reluctance. She explains that when Barbara's mother left her with Mum Jill, Barbara's father came around and promised to come and take her away, but he never did. Consequently,

> when it feels too good to be true, [Barbara] pushes. She pushes me away. She'll jump ship before she gets hurt . . . because feeling abandoned, left behind, that's the most real connection to them she can get. In the chaos she shines, in the chaos she knows herself. So now Mum's sick and it's bad, we both know it . . . I think she's probably dying and it's the only thing Barbara can't argue with, challenge, challenge. She just has to face it. And yeah. She's not. She's waiting for me to abandon her.[56]

René decides not to wait for her and to go into the hospital to see her mother. When Barbara returns with a packet of cigarettes, she is visibly hurt by René's absence. She asks the audience – addressed as if they were passers-by – if 'any of you mob have a light?'[57] 'Out of Sight, Out of Mind' begins in the silence formed by the lack of response to her request:

> Wrap me up and ship me out
> On a boat that's sinking fast
> Out of sight, out of mind
> Out of mind, out sight

Simple metaphors, restrained language, repetition, and short syllables characterise the lyrics of 'Out of Sight, Out of Mind.' In the second verse, the focus shifts outwards: 'you pick me up then you push me down, you fill my head with crazy doubt.' While in the context of the dramatic scene, the 'you' is most likely René, this device is ubiquitous in popular music, where the 'casual use of the second person "you" is substituted for "I," deliberately or coincidentally implicating the listener.'[58] While there is a correlation to the scene that preceded it, the connection is continually understated. For example, the subtle link between René's use of 'jump ship' in the above monologue and the image of the sinking ship in the lyrics of the song. The lyrics are careful to remain suitably vague, to not mention names, places, or circumstances associated with the narrative, but rather to explore the broad emotional spectrum of loss, resentment and abandonment felt by Barbara. In the chorus, Barbara gathers her strength and belts out:

Who are you to tell me
That I gotta, gotta play nice
And who are you to tell me
I'm a slave to sacrifice

The absence of rhyme in the verses, and this only very simple use in the chorus (nice/sacrifice), further differentiates the lyric from musical theatre style. The lyrics become a vehicle for the emotion brimming in Yovich's voice. Similar techniques are used in the song 'Brushing the Dust,' sung by Barbara and René. In the chorus of 'Brushing the Dust,' words are absent, and the melody is sung only on the vowel 'ah.'

In the musical, Barbara becomes more than an alter-ego: she is also a rock persona. Philip Auslander, following Simon Frith, identifies three layers of performance in popular music: the real person, the performance persona, and the character.[59] He states that, in autobiographical popular music, the 'line between real person and performance persona and the line between persona and character may be blurry and indistinct,' citing David Bowie as an example.[60] This mimics the way that in the monodrama writers often take inspiration from the experiences of a range of people and combine them into one voice. Cáceres used musicians as models for the character when she described Barbara as 'that kind of classic tortured artist figure that we love, like Amy Winehouse or Courtney Love.'[61] The slipperiness between these three layers – Yovich as actor and singer, Barbara as rock performance persona, and Barbara as dramatic character – means that the songs have equal functions as rock songs *and* musical theatre songs. Valentine gestured at this when she remarked that the songs in *Barbara* have a 'relationship to the characters like rock singers' songs have a relationship [to their singers].'[62] This layer of rock authenticity protects the songs from becoming self-consciously corrupted by character or story.

Rock Music in the Pub

In this section, I analyse how *Barbara* pursued an authentically rock atmosphere through its *mise en scène*. Stephen Curtis' set design recreates a live music gig in an Australian pub. The pub (public bar) is an iconic locale where drinking culture, live music, and Australian national identity have coalesced. As Shane Homan writes, 'the rich history of Australian drinking laws and practices provide a social memory, a collective bedrock of sorts' that render the pub a site of national significance.[63] It is a location that has been instrumental in the development and promotion of the Australian popular music scene, though in recent years the pub's role as a venue for live music has been in decline as it adapts and gentrifies.[64]

Recreating the pub is a strategy that cultivates a performance atmosphere that is more casual and less staged than the standard theatrical experience. As Steve Feffer argued in relation to *Hedwig*, the 'site specificity of the show's production and this location's relationship to the title character's performance' is key to its production of authenticity.[65] Setting *Barbara* in the pub also solves the dilemma of finding a suitable justification for the characters to sing. In this context, music is always diegetic: Barbara, like Hedwig, 'always has a fully naturalistic reason for singing – she's performing a concert for us.'[66] According to Wollman, the fundamental point of divergence between rock and musical theatre is that in the musical 'there is ultimately more emphasis on accuracy and precision – and thus, less on spontaneity.'[67] She goes on to note that rock gigs are crafted as 'ecstatic events: performers exert and emote; audience members cheer, applaud, dance, and otherwise commune emotionally with the performers and one another.' Musical theatre audiences, on the other hand, are expected to be more subdued and to behave with decorum. Staging *Barbara* as a rock gig assists the production in cultivating an atmosphere of raw, unmediated expression of emotion.

The stage is furnished with a garish pink carpet and a rostrum with a small stage where the musicians sit, and the women sing. A large chalkboard at the back of the stage advertises happy hour and upcoming gigs. The chalkboard evokes the 'comparative ephemerality' of the rock gig that moves from one venue to the next each day, rather than the staid theatrical experience of each performance in the season occurring in the same venue.[68] Karen Norris' lighting design is replete with vibrant red and blue washes, which shine through plenty of haze, evoking the once-smoky atmosphere of a pub. Belvoir offered various seating options for the performances; while individual seats were unreserved, spectators could choose between couches, chairs at low tables, or bar stools at high tables around the stage, or the standard fixed seating in the raked auditorium, when purchasing tickets. Drinks from the bar were permitted in the theatre, and this, combined with the seating arrangements, encouraged the audience to behave socially, more as if they would at a concert. The production begins as a rock gig. When the women enter to sing the opening number, 'Look at the Sun,' they are dressed in 'rock chick' attire: Yovich in a pair of tight leather pants, Crombie in a shaggy fluoro pink jacket (Figure 5.1).

Setting *Barbara* in the pub is more than a gesture towards rock authenticity. It is also a subversive act that highlights the historical exclusion of Indigenous people from this arena. The pub, a space 'deeply entwined with the history of colonisation,' is a place from which Indigenous Australians have been systematically excluded.[69] From 1830 there were laws in place that prohibited alcoholic consumption by Indigenous Australians, and Aboriginal people have been refused service in pubs.[70] While most of these laws were officially repealed by 1972, a range of official and unofficial prohibitions remain in place. For Aboriginal people, the right to drink liquor was, like so many other things, hard won.[71] Ann McGrath notes that, for Indigenous men, 'open drinking was the most clearly identifiable evidence of parity with white Australians,' while women, unsurprisingly, were generally excluded from drinking rituals.[72] The women of *Barbara* reclaim this space as their own, commanding it with their bodies and voices.

I identify the relationship between whiteness, rock music, and the pub as another holy trinity like that of beer, sport, and masculinity identified in relation to *Shane Warne*. In Australia, whiteness, rock music and the pub converge in the genre known as 'pub rock,' an amorphous style understood to

FIGURE 5.1   Rene Crombie and Ursula Yovic in *Barbara and the Camp Dogs*.
Photo: Pia Johnson ©

be prototypically Australian, as its other title, 'Oz rock,' indicates. It has been described by Tony Mitchell as a 'white Anglo-Australian, male-dominated, nationalist tradition.'[73] For Jon Stratton, it is notable that Oz rock 'privilege[s] elements drawn from the white, European musical tradition over influences from African-American, and other Black musics.'[74] The sound of the genre is described by David Nichols as 'thunderous music with chanted vocals and catchy choruses.'[75] Paul Oldham attributes these musical features in part to the role of alcohol in the pub experience, citing evidence that publicans valued bands whose audiences consumed lots of alcohol, and that audiences that consumed lots of alcohol tended to prefer 'increasingly basic, loud rock music.'[76] The music of *Barbara* deliberately eschews this sound in order to revision the kind of music, voices, and stories associated with this space.

Yovich also subverts the traditional audience dynamics of pub rock. Doc Neeson, the vocalist from the band *The Angels*, used remarkably theatrical language in describing what kind of experience audiences are seeking at a pub gig:

> You hear guys talking at the bar, and they're always saying they've come for a rage . . . or . . . a sort of catharsis. We always feel that there's this implied confrontation between band and audience. They're saying, 'Lay it on! Do it to us!,' and it's like a veiled threat that if you don't, you'll get canned.[77]

In *Barbara*, this audience/performer dynamic is reversed. Through her anger, Yovich creates a confrontational atmosphere puts the audience, rather than the performers, in the firing line. This dynamic is explored in the opening number, 'Look at the Sun.' The two women saunter onto the stage from opposite sides of the theatre to the sound of a quiet, funky, seductive double bass riff, turning towards each other as they approach the microphones. To this simple accompaniment, Barbara grabs the microphone stand with two hands, feet wide apart in a power stance, stares down the crowd and begins to sing, 'Look at the sun, And do not even flinch,' to which René responds, 'Look at the sun, And never give an inch.' The pauses between the paired vocal lines strengthen the sense of the title as a command, and the women augment this by staring intensely into the eyes of individual audience members as they call out these opening lines. Images of heat and fire appear throughout the lyric, reinforcing the implicit heat of the sun: boiling liquid, 'ash and aggravation.' This is intensified by the electric guitar, which, as the song progresses, increasing fills the gaps between the vocal phrases with short squeals or grungy chords. Its piercing timbre adds to the imagery of the sharp heat of the sun. When the opening section returns at the end (the song uses a loose ABA structure, with a coda), there are new lyrics prior to the restating of the flinch/inch rhyme that suggest that the pain of looking into the sun is 'nothing new' and that Indigenous communities can only rely on each other – 'there's only me and you.' From its sparse opening, the volume and texture of the song gradually builds until we reach the climactic final section, where the women riff freely on the lyric 'You got to fight it, fight it, fight it,' before descending for the emphatic final line: 'and destroy hypocrisy when she comes.' 'Look at the Sun' commands the audience to look into the sun and not to look away – a metaphor for what the work as a whole will ask them to do.

Finding a Way: Humour, Anger, Love, and Hope

This final section of the chapter examines how in *Barbara*, anger, humour, and hope coalesce. Anger delivers the message, entreating audiences to sit up and pay attention, while humour provides points of connection, empathy, and understanding. Both anger and humour demonstrate the steadfast resilience of Indigenous Australians. Finally, the hopeful finale of the production points towards the glimmer of a way forward.

As a coping mechanism for her pain and anger, Barbara often turns to humour. The production's combination of comedy and trauma is common to the monodrama and Indigenous theatre more generally, where, as Adam Shoemaker describes, 'scenes of hardship, misery, poverty, discrimination and even death' are rarely 'unrelievedly sombre in tone.'[78] A good example of this is a scene on arrival in Darwin, where Barbara is pushed aside on a footpath by a couple of white tourists. She accosts them for 'taking up the whole fucking path,' prompting René to advise her not to get so worked up 'over their bad manners.'[79] Barbara retorts, refusing to put the encounter down to this, saying: 'They don't see people like you and me.' René, exasperated, accuses her of using racism as a catch-all. Barbara explodes:

> These dickheads don't see us 'cause we're shit to them. The only time they ever see us is when we break the illusion of their so-called perfect lives. They even bitch about having to pay to lock us up. I sit on a bus and the woman next to me suddenly zips up her handbag and pulls it closer to her chest . . . 'I'm not going to steal your fuckin' handbag, bitch. I might take it if it wasn't a fucking replica Prada!' Why do you think you see us mob yelling and screaming on the streets. 'Cause it's the only way they notice us long enough to give us some space. *[To the audience]* You ever seen birds flying into a window? Nobody told them that there are windows in the world. Nobody. So I fuckin' tell 'em. 'Move out of the fucking way! Faark!' They just take up all the space. Fucking colonial cunts. The footpath has original owners, you know!

This scene demonstrates, as Lillian Holt argues, that for Indigenous people humour is a 'tool of everyday existence . . . and survival.'[80] Barbara recasts the racist encounter on the bus by turning the tables on the woman, criticising her knock-off handbag and rendering her the butt of the joke. The situational comedy of taking something as serious as native title legislation to claim priority standing on a city footpath operates similarly.

Barbara is full of what Karen Austin terms 'blak humour,' a 'form of comedy tinged with morbidity, often lacking in "taste," and almost always crossing the virtual line that determines what is and what is not socially appropriate.'[81] Blak humour is on show when, en route to Katherine, the women stop at the Adelaide River Inn. Barbara panics, realising that an old nemesis, Stella Cole, might be in there:

Barbara: When I was going out with, what was his name, Cake Boy, from Alice Springs, she stole him from me.
René: Cake boy?
Barbara: Yeah. . . . He could make me cream up, that one!
René: Barbara!
Barabra: It's true! Anyways. . . . She stole him from me and then came round to Mum's place with a spear and she was saying, 'Don't let that cunt near me because I'll fuckin' spear her. Try and take my man!'
René: [*realising*] Stella Cole, with the stellar hole.[82]

The combination of the lewd description of orgasm and female sexual organs, the possibility of being speared, and the swearing, all over a man known only as 'Cake Boy,' renders a heated and potentially violent situation extremely humorous.

While the production contains many such comedic moments, *Barbara* is a distinctively angry work. Other Indigenous musicals, like *Bran Nue Dae*, *The Sapphires*, and *The Sunshine Club*, are markedly different. Anna Haebich describes *Bran Nue Dae* as 'gentle and disarming' and describes it as a 'child of the 1990s – that decade of hope for Aboriginal rights and national reconciliation.'[83] It offered white audiences, as Helen Gilbert avers, 'something more than absolution for the sins of colonization: a sense of "indigenous" national belonging.'[84] *Barbara*'s anger means it offers no such comfort. As Cassie Tongue wrote

The Australian theatrical canon sometimes feels like we've run the national identity through Instagram; we put the filtered, carefully curated version of ourselves on display, keeping our mess neatly cropped out of frame. But *Barbara and the Camp Dogs* . . . rips away the strategically placed curtain of performative Australian identity to reckon with the country's true nature: an open wound, raw and angry-red. Still weeping.[85]

'I am angry,' Barbara tells us within minutes of encountering her.[86] René evocatively describes her as 'the arse-burning, eye-watering fart you do in a room full of strangers,' 'the face-filling burp you make in a room full of haters,' the 'long streak of piss that dribbles out of you when you're so scared of what might happen that you can barely control your bladder.'[87] In a later scene, René explains that Barbara uses anger as a coping mechanism: 'She needs to be fighting and hating things, she gets her energy from being pissed off.'[88] In the story, anger has come to define Barbara and her interactions with the world. She actively rejects politeness, refusing to play a game where the rules have been set by someone else.

In this sense, Barbara occupies a position as an 'angry black woman.' Yovich explicitly referred to her as such, reclaiming a term that has frequently been used to malign and silence women of colour who have complained about the conditions that contribute to their systemic oppression. In an impassioned piece for the website *IndigenousX*, the Munanjali and South Sea Islander woman Chelsea Watego defended anger as both a natural emotion and a vital strategy: 'I reckon being angry is the only thing that has got Black people anything, either locally or globally.'[89] Watego argued that the fight against racism requires ferocity – 'we simply cannot outthink or outrun it' – and, detailing several instances where the anger of Aboriginal women has been either disregarded or met with an equally angry backlash, she asserted that the trope of the angry black women perniciously continues to suggest 'that our emotional responses are irrational and unregulated, which then makes the oppression we experience seem like a rational outcome of *our* behaviour.'[90]

Yovich made the character of Barbara angry because she had observed that female Indigenous characters who were afforded permission to express rage were few and far between. She remarked that

> in my twenty years of working and doing Indigenous plays, I've not come across a female character that was complex and also full of anger. Because we're going through the same things as our black men are, but it always felt like we were this kind of side story and I didn't want that.[91]

One of Yovich's objectives in portraying anger was to demonstrate causation. She stated that she wanted to show that 'people aren't angry for no reason. There's always a reason.'[92] Using *Barbara* as a prototypical example, Thurow argues that

> narrativising dysfunctionality (i.e. placing it in a logical structure of cause and effect) . . . reverts agency back to Indigenous subjects because emotional struggles are no longer exclusively presented as a psychological instability but mainly as a logical outcome of systemic oppression that continues to undermine Indigenous communal relations, and which forestalls cultural sovereignty.[93]

Yovich stages Barbara's angry reactions to the racist encounters represented in the story in this context. When René and Barbara are performing for the Indian party on the yacht, Barbara has an altercation with one of the attendees: a white woman scornfully described as a 'Barbie cunt.' When one of the waiters refuses to give Barbara a free drink (the bar tab has inconveniently ended just before they finished their set), she leans over and helps herself to one. The white woman objects, provoking the following diatribe from Barbara:

> She looks at me like I'm a piece of shit. Like I'm a piece of filth on the bottom of her shoe. And I'm like, 'What, you pissed that you didn't think of doing that yourself, bitch? Like, the bottle was there and you just politely stood there with your finger up your arse waiting to be served? Why are you all so compliant, you complacent fucks, that's what's wrong with this country. You want us all to wait in line, but I never agreed to the line and when I stand in it I never get served anyway.'[94]

Rather than framing Barbara's reaction at the party on the yacht as an irrational outburst, the production frames the explosiveness of Barbara's rage as part of the wide-reaching implications of colonisation. As Aileen Moreton-Robinson explains:

> The very existence of white women and men is thus a constant reminder that our lands were invaded and stolen, our ancestors massacred and enslaved, our children taken and our rights denied and that these acts of terror forged white identity in this country. The presence of white bodies is connected to invasion, theft, murder and domination. White corporeality is thus one of the myriad ways in which relations between the colonising past and present are omnipresent.[95]

Musical numbers render Barbara's angry reactions to her encounters with colonial racism viscerally. Rock supports the deep sense of rage underpinning the show, and the connection between the two is offered explicitly in the opening scene, when Barbara explains that 'that's what rock is supposed to be. Angry, full of pain.'[96] Music often functions in the production as a way to express what Sonali Chakravarti describes as the 'kinetic' dimension of anger: anger that is not connected to notions of redress or confrontation but that 'operates on the level of visceral experience and the recognition of shared humanity.'[97] After the above diatribe on the yacht, Barbara launches into the song 'Betty Boo,' the title indicating her derisive nickname for the woman who criticised her taking the drink from behind the bar. This fast rock number with a hint of punk has short, punchy rhythmic lines. It is sung predominantly on one pitch with a vocal pull off at the end of the line, which amplifies the anger of the text:

> I will not be reduced by you
> Your narrow, shallow, muddy view
> The labels and abuse you spew
> I'll never be seduced by you
> I will not be defamed by you
> Not ever play the games you do
> You just don't have any clue[98]

The metamorphosis from scene into song lifts the encounter to a new level. The final verse descends into manic nonsense syllables as Yovich writhes on the floor of the stage. She sings, screams, and dances her anger, but it is not exorcised. It is subdued only temporarily until the next outburst.

The most arresting moment of anger occurs in the absence of music. When Barbara storms out of the hospital in Katherine after fighting with René, she tells us that she is 'like a fire out of control, consuming everything in its path, ready to swing, lash out.' She comes across some Indigenous people drinking outside a pub and makes contact with them, addressing them as 'Aunty' and 'Unc.' They welcome her. She sits down and drinks with them for so long that she passes out. She wakes up to a police boot kicking her side. The police officers are arresting the older woman Barbara has been drinking with. The woman has been 'stripped down to her skirt, her breast exposed, and she's thumping at her chest. . . . "You fucking take everything! I know you, you fuckin' shit! I know you. It's you mob, took my kids."' At this point in the monologue, Yovich also removes her own shirt to reveal her bra. She tells us that the police officer throws the woman into the paddy wagon so hard that she becomes unconscious. Barbara tries to spring into action: 'I manage to get up and I'm spewing hatred at this man.' She tells him she needs to go to the hospital but she is so drunk that she cannot stand. Next thing she knows, she too has been shoved into the back of the paddy wagon. She puts up a fight, so as they drive, the cops deliberately slam the brakes on at unexpected moments in order to injure her. She is crying, begging, telling them she needs to see her mother. At this point, Yovich lets out a primal scream and then explodes:

> You hate us 'cause we're black or pity us 'cause we're black. Which is worse? You whitefellas have an infection that makes you think that I really am different. Shit, you get crazy with hatred or crazy with guilt, one minute we're more real and the next we're primitive natives. This is the meanest, pettiest, most ungenerous country in the world. Because at the heart of this country is a theft, and now the whole place crouches, waiting, calculating about when it is going to be stolen back from them. Because nobody fears

being thieved from as much as a pack of thieves, a gang, a group. A nation. And I understand theft. Of community, of culture, of language, of family. Belonging. I wanted to belong somewhere, and I never belonged here.[99]

Standing before us in her underwear, Yovich's voice is raw with emotion. The characterisation of white Australians as thieves who are crouching and waiting to have to defend themselves from other thieves is searing. This scene is a painful and blunt reminder that the realities of racism and the trauma of dispossession are profound and ongoing.

The final scene and song display a way through the anger, hurt, and pain, to something resembling peace and acceptance. 'Sometimes in order to heal you have to allow people to love you,' remarked Yovich.[100] Reviewer John Shand noted that 'for all its anger, ultimately [*Barbara*] is a play about healing,' going on to clarify that 'without the songs this might not be so.'[101] The final song, 'Let in the Love,' illustrates this powerfully. The lights change to a smoky blue wash, and the three performers – Yovich, mascara staining her cheeks, Crombie and Brady, line up together, one microphone apiece, to the sound of a simple two-chord acoustic guitar progression in G major (Figure 5.2). Each verse describes the plight of an unnamed Indigenous person: Barbara sings of a man 'sitting at the station with a cup in his hand, begging for the coins for the theft of his land,' who could be her brother Joseph; René sings of a woman

FIGURE 5.2 The cast of *Barbara and the Camp Dogs* performing 'Let in the Love.'
Photo: Pia Johnson ©

'taken from family at an early age, Singing a story to push down the rage,' who could be Barbara; Joseph sings of 'the next generation' who 'can't stay in this fog.' The final iteration of the chorus is performed in *a cappella* harmony, where the performers sing once more:

> We are bringing the steady
> We are bringing the sure
> We are finding a way to let ourselves be more
> We are naming the troubles to keep our heads above
> We are finding a way now to let in the love

After which, the lights fade to black. It is an ending that conveys both resilience, strength, and hopefulness.

These lyrics echo the words of the Uluru Statement from the Heart, which had been released earlier in 2017, the same year *Barbara* was produced. At the time of its release, the statement represented an extraordinary coalition of Indigenous nations and elders coming together to call for the establishment of a First Nations Voice to Parliament, one that would be enshrined in the Constitution. After much stalling and reluctance, this notion was eventually repudiated via an unsuccessful referendum in 2023. Thus 'we' in this context is not inclusive of the audience; 'we' means Indigenous Australians who, time after time, are having to find the strength to chart a path forward. All the issues that *Barbara* has raised are left unsolved, but 'Let in the Love' shows the resilience of Indigenous Australians who continue to fight for recognition. The song also evinces the power of music as a tool for personal healing, reflecting Streit-Warburton's assertion that '[f]or Aboriginal women, music is like a raft that ferries them through the hazards of the mainstream. For many, it has also been a lifesaver, keeping alive important knowledge and raising spirits.'[102] Music is Barbara, René, and Joseph's comfort on their journey. Unlike in *The Rabbits*, the finale is not there to make us feel better. Rather, it belongs to the three of them. *Barbara* asks its audience first and foremost to listen.

Conclusion: Listening from the Heart

The rock music-fuelled anger of *Barbara and the Camp Dogs*, I argue, lacerates the national imaginary. Unlike the reconciliatory ending of *The Rabbits* examined in the previous chapter, *Barbara*'s uncompromising stance urges audiences to listen from the heart to Indigenous perspectives on the ongoing effects of colonisation.

Earlier in this chapter, I cited Leticia Cáceres' remark that she embarked upon a process of 'deep listening' when working with the Indigenous artists on *Barbara*. Her words evoke the concept of *dadirri*, described by Ngangiwumirr woman Miriam Rose Ungunmerr as 'inner, deep listening and quiet, still awareness,' 'our most unique gift . . . perhaps the greatest gift we can give to our fellow Australians.'[103] In Judy Atkinson's work on transgenerational trauma in Indigenous communities, she offers this evocative description of the process of *dadirri*:

> The result of *dadirri's* profound, non-judgemental watching and listening is insight and recognition of the responsibility to act with fidelity in relationship to what has been heard, observed, and learnt. *Dadirri* listens and knows, witnesses, feels, empathises in the pain under the anger, and, if the anger is accompanied by action, seeks to understand the thoughts and feelings behind the action. *Dadirri* then seeks to find the source of that pain in knowledge-building for a deepening understanding of the more complete story of the person. *Dadirri* is the stillness and contemplation, in the confusion of chaos as actions of violence are witnessed. *Dadirri* can also be, however, the chaos of feelings and actions as pain-anger-grief is articulated in processes of relating to the group which is in stillness and listening.[104]

In *Barbara*, the audience have been asked to listen, witness, feel, and empathise with the characters' anger and to understand the genesis of their frustration. Yovich and Valentine have presented three-dimensional Indigenous characters who have asked us to sit in stillness and contemplation. More than this, though, they have asked us to listen not only to their pain, anger, grief, and chaos but also to their profound statements of love. As Atkinson goes on to say, 'at its deepest level [*dadirri*] is the search for understanding and meaning. It is listening and learning at its most profound level – more than just listening by the ear, but listening from the heart.'[105]

While Yovich, Valentine, and Cáceres do not link the process or the production to the concept of *dadirri*, I was struck with how much this description spoke to my experience of *Barbara* in the theatre and how it encapsulated the relationship between the characters, the narrative, and the audience. For much of the performance, I sat in stillness and contemplation, watching Barbara and René move through pain, anger, grief, and hope. Without expectations of solutions or answers, I listened – heart open, ready to understand. In the next chapter, we are called to action through different means, through satire.

Notes

1 NAIDOC stands for National Aborigines and Islanders Day of Observance. It is celebrated in the first week of July each year and honours the achievements of Aboriginal and Torres Strait Islander people. NIDA, 'Inaugural NAIDOC Week Lecture with Ursula Yovich,' *YouTube*, November 16, 2020, accessed February 18, 2025, https://www.youtube.com/watch?v=YFHcZ08nR_w.

2 Ursula Yovich and Alana Valentine, 'Writing and Performing *Barbara and the Camp Dogs*,' *TEXT Special Issue* 62 (October 2021): 13.

3 It received $35,000 for Indigenous Feature development in the 2018–19 funding round, and the same amount again in 2019–2020. It is to be produced by Sweet Country Films, but at the time of writing, has not been released. Screen Australia, *Annual Report 2018–19*, accessed February 18, 2025, https://www.screenaustralia.gov.au/getmedia/98d29914-2704-4c9b-aab2-ae6fc9ee0b68/SA-Annual-Report-2018-2019.pdf?ext=.pdf; Screen Australia, *Annual Report 2019–20*, accessed February 18, 2025, https://www.screenaustralia.gov.au/getmedia/29a3dc12-fd97-492c-890a-c75b2ff27bfa/SA-Annual-Report-2019–2020.pdf?ext=.pdf.

4 Ursula Yovich and Alana Valentine, *Barbara and the Camp Dogs* (Currency Press, 2017), 3.

5 Susanne Thurow, *Performing Indigenous Identities on the Contemporary Australian Stage* (Taylor and Francis, 2020), 60.

6 Yovich and Valentine, *Barbara and the Camp Dogs*, 37.

7 Yovich and Valentine, *Barbara and the Camp Dogs*, 42.

8 Elissa Blake, 'Ursula Yovich Rocks out Belvoir's *Barbara and the Camp Dogs*,' *The Sydney Morning Herald*, November 14, 2017, https://www.smh.com.au/entertainment/ursula-yovich-rocks-out-belvoirs-barbara-and-the-camp-dogs-20171114-gzl6xl.html.

9 'Unleashing Barbara,' *Belvoir*, podcast, accessed April 2, 2021, https://belvoir.com.au/news/barbara/.

10 'Barbara and the Camp Dogs Backstage,' *Belvoir*, November 28, 2017, podcast, accessed February 18, 2025, https://open.spotify.com/episode/0wz0b8nD85rmK0n5X7jqUW?si=Wtww0BTvQa2ZExbtbcu3Y.

11 'Barbara and the Camp Dogs Backstage.'

12 Helena Grehan, 'Aboriginal Performance: Politics, Empathy and the Question of Reciprocity,' *Australasian Drama Studies* 56 (2010): 39–40.

13 Thurow, *Performing Indigenous Identities*, 2.

14 Liza-Mare Syron, 'Afterword: Contemporary Indigenous Theatre and Performance Practice in Australia: Cultural Integrity and Historical Significance,' in *Telling Stories: Aboriginal Australian and Torres Strait Islander Performance*, ed. Maryrose Casey (Australian Scholarly Publishing, 2012): 146.

15 'Who's Telling Indigenous Australian Stories on Stage?,' *ABC Radio National*, October 29, 2018, accessed June 30, 2025. https://www.abc.net.au/radionational/programs/the-stage-show/whos-telling-indigenous-australian-stories-on-stage/10433140. An interview with Yovich that discusses theatrical process and Indigenous ways of working can be found in Camilla Sobb Ah Kin, '*A Chance Gathering of Strays: The Australian Theatre Family*,' (Masters diss., University of Sydney, 2010): 73–81.

16 Ursula Yovich and Alana Valentine, 'Co-Writer's Note,' *Barbara and the Camp Dogs* (Currency Press, 2017).

17 Yovich and Valentine, 'Co-Writer's Note.'

18 '"Barbara and the Camp Dogs" Is Passionate, Soulful, and Deeply Affecting,' *The Music*, February 5, 2019, accessed February 18, 2025, https://themusic.com.au/features/barbara-the-camp-dogs-is-passionate-soulful-deeply-affecting/-PLg6u3s7-4/05-02-19/.

19 Yovich and Valentine, 'Co-Writer's Note.'

20 A discography of Yovich's work up until 2002 can be found in Katelyn Barney, '"Women Singing Up Big": The Growth of Contemporary Music Recordings by Indigenous Australian Women Artists,' *Australian Aboriginal Studies* 1 (2006): 44–56.

21 NIDA, 'Inaugural NAIDOC Week Lecture.'
22 NIDA, 'Inaugural NAIDOC Week Lecture.'
23 Ursula Yovich, *Ursula Yovich Live*, MGM Music, sound recording, 2010.
24 Belvoir's website offers additional attributions for additional songs. Vicki Gordon contributed music to 'Tick Sista,' Merenia Gillies to 'Chained to You' and James Warwick Shipstone to 'Pieces.' A wonderful account of the songwriting process can be found in Yovich and Valentine, 'Writing and Performing,' 9–10.
25 I purchased the CD at the Hal Bar after the show. The recording is not currently available to purchase online, although two songs are available on *Soundcloud*. Queensland Theatre, *Soundcloud* channel, accessed January 15, 2025, https://soundcloud.com/user–874518784.
26 Yovich and Valentine, *Barbara and the Camp Dogs*, 8.
27 Yovich and Valentine, 'Writing and Performing,' 3.
28 'Ursula Yovich Unleashes Her Inner Diva,' *ABC Radio National*, December 2, 2017, accessed June 30, 2025. https://www.abc.net.au/listen/programs/awaye/ursula-yovich-gives-voice-to-her-alter-ego/9211870.
29 Maryrose Casey and Cathy Craigie, *A Brief History of Indigenous Australian Contemporary Theatre* (Australian Script Centre, 2011), 5. See Hilary Glow, 'Recent Indigenous Theatre in Australia: The Politics of Autobiography,' *International Journal of the Humanities* 4, no. 1 (2007): 71–77 for a catalogue of examples up until 2007. More recent examples include Dalisa Pigram's *Gudirr Gudirr* (2018), Ghenoa Gela's *My Urrwai* (2019), and Henrietta Baird's *The Weekend* (2019). There are also many monodramas by Aboriginal men, as detailed in Maryrose Casey, 'Bold, Black, and Brilliant: Aboriginal Australian Drama,' in *A Companion to Australian Aboriginal Literature*, ed. Belinda Wheeler (Camden House, 2013), 162.
30 Casey, 'Bold, Black, and Brilliant,' 162.
31 'A Mother's Funeral and Identity: Ursula Yovich's Story Wins Playwright Award,' *NITV*, June 15, 2016, accessed March 12, 2021, https://www.sbs.com.au/nitv/nitvnews/article/2016/06/15/mothers-funeral-and-identity-ursula-yovichs-story-wins-playwright-award.
32 Blake, 'Ursula Yovich Rocks Out.'
33 Gabriella Beaumont, 'The Origin Story of Acclaimed Rock Musical "Barbara and the Camp Dogs," *Beat.com.au*, February 13, 2019, accessed February 21, 2025, https://beat.com.au/the-origin-story-of-acclaimed-rock-musical-barbara-and-the-camp-dogs/.
34 Alison Lyssa, 'Black and White: Australia's History on Stage in Four Plays of the New Millennium,' *Australasian Drama Studies* 48 (2006): 215.
35 Yovich and Valentine, *Barbara and the Camp Dogs*, 4.
36 Yovich and Valentine, *Barbara and the Camp Dogs*, 5.
37 After the success of *Bran Nue Dae*, Chi developed a second musical, *Corrugation Road* (1996), based on his personal experiences and which explored mental illness, sexuality, and religion.
38 She can be heard on the demo recording made on *The Sunshine Club* held by the State Library of NSW. Wesley Enoch and John Rodgers, *The Sunshine Club*, Sydney Theatre Company, sound recording, 2000. The question of Yovich's involvement in *Bran Nue Dae* is unclear. While Thurow describes *Bran Nue Dae* as a 'launching pad' for her career (*Performing Indigenous Identities*, 49), my calculations put Yovich at just thirteen years old when *Bran Nue Dae* premièred, which would mean she had not yet left the Northern Territory for Perth. Penny Durham, '*Barbara and the Camp Dogs* and Me,' *The Australian*, November 17, 2017, https://www.theaustralian.com.au/life/weekend-australian-magazine/ursula-yovich-barbara-and-the-camp-dogs-and-me/news-story/112a22f45c1b0ab1ed58a54b88d370ce.

39 This is also a feature of black musical theatre in America. While some, like Warren Hoffman, have argued that the Broadway musical is largely by, for, and about white people, there is a significant canon of black music theatre. Allen Woll traces the history of the form through minstrel shows and coon songs, to shows from the 1920s (the 'golden age' of the black musical) through to hits of the 1970s like *The Wiz* (1975), *Ain't Misbehavin'* (1978) and *Dreamgirls* (1981). Allen Woll, *Black Musical Theatre: From Coontown to Dreamgirls* (Da Capo Press, 1989); Warren Hoffman, *The Great White Way: Race and the Broadway Musical* (Rutgers University Press, 2014). Moving forward from Woll's book, we could add works such as *Jelly's Last Jam* (1992), about the famous jazz musician Jelly Roll Morton, *Bring in 'da Noise, Bring in 'da Funk* (1996), a revue about African American history, Stew's *Passing Strange* (2008), and *A Strange Loop* (2020), which won the Pulitzer Prize for Drama, to the black musical theatre canon.

40 The soundtrack for the movie did include one original song, 'Gotcha,' composed by Jessica Mauboy, Ilan Kidron, and Louis Schor, and 'Ngarra Burra Ferra,' a song in Yorta Yorta language with a fascinating history. ABC Indigenous, 'One Song's 130-Year Impact on Australian Music,' *YouTube*, August 8, 2018, accessed February 18, 2025, https://www.youtube.com/watch?v=vDZ2NQkkOAk.

41 Peter Dunbar-Hall and Chris Gibson, *Deadly Sounds, Deadly Places: Contemporary Aboriginal Music in Australia* (University of New South Wales Press, 2004), 17, 132.

42 Stephen Russell, 'Rock-N-Roll Spirit Meets Indigenous Experience in Ursula Yovich's *Barbara and the Camp Dogs*,' *The Music*, November 3, 2017, accessed February 21, 2025, https://themusic.com.au/features/ursula-yovich-barbara-and-the-camp-dogs-belvoir-theatre-stephen-a-russell/r0Cgo6KlpKc/03-11-17/; Yovich and Valentine, 'Writing and Performing,' 9.

43 Cassie Tongue, '*Barbara and the Camp Dogs*: How One Woman's Anger Became a Rock Show,' *The Guardian*, December 18, 2017, https://www.theguardian.com/stage/2017/dec/18/barbara-and-the-camp-dogs-how-one-womans-anger-became-a-rock-show.

44 'Ursula Yovich Unleashes Her Inner Diva.'

45 Michelle Bessley, '#SheInspires Ursula Yovich,' *SheSociety*, May 17, 2019, accessed September 24, 2021, https://shesociety.com.au/news/sheinspires-ursula-yovich/.

46 '*Barbara and the Camp Dogs* Backstage.'

47 Hayden Fritzlaff, '*Barbara and the Camp Dogs* Blurs the Lines Between Theatre and Rock,' *Riot Act*, May 24, 2019, accessed March 1, 2020, https://the-riotact.com/barbara-and-the-camp-dogs-blurs-the-lines-between-theatre-and-rock/303869.

48 Elizabeth Wollman, 'Much Too Loud and Not Loud Enough: Issues Involving the Reception of Staged Rock Musicals,' in *Bad Music: The Music We Love to Hate*, ed. Christopher J. Washburn and Maiken Derno (Routledge, 2004), 311.

49 Wollman, 'Much Too Loud,' 312.

50 Dominic Symonds, 'Drag, Rock, Authenticity and In-Betweenness: *Hedwig and the Angry Inch*,' in *Twenty-First Century Musical Theatre: From Stage to Screen*, ed. George Rodosthenous (Routledge, 2017), 25.

51 David Fricke, 'Sex & Drag & Rock & Roll,' *Rolling Stone*, December 10, 1998, accessed February 21, 2025. https://www.rollingstone.com/music/music-news/sex-drag-rock-roll-188691/.

52 Susan Fast, 'Rock,' *Grove Music Online*, January 31, 2014, accessed February 21, 2025, https://doi.org/10.1093/gmo/9781561592630.article.A2257208.

53 Simon Frith, 'Rock and the Politics of Memory,' *Social Text* 9–10 (1984): 66, https://doi.org/10.2307/466535.

54 Ursula Yovich Unleashes Her Inner Diva.'

55 Tongue, '*Barbara and the Camp Dogs*.'

56 Yovich and Valentine, *Barbara and the Camp Dogs*, 28–29.

57 Yovich and Valentine, *Barbara and the Camp Dogs*, 29.

58 Keith Negus, 'Authorship and the Popular Song,' *Music and Letters* 92, no. 4 (2011): 617, https://doi-org.ezproxy.uow.edu.au/10.1093/ml/gcr117

59 Philip Auslander, 'Performance Analysis and Popular Music: A Manifesto,' *Contemporary Theatre* 14, no. 1 (2004): 6, https://doi.org/10.1080/10267160 32000128674.

60 Auslander, 'Performance Analysis,' 7.

61 Russell, Spirit.'

62 '*Barbara and the Camp Dogs* Backstage.'

63 Shane Homan, 'Losing the Local: Sydney and the Oz Rock Tradition,' *Popular Music* 19, no. 1 (2000): 33.

64 Ben Gallan and Chris Gibson, 'Mild-Mannered Bistro by Day, Eclectic Freak-Land at Night: Memories of an Australian Music Venue,' *Journal of Australian Studies* 37, no. 2 (2013): 174, https://doi.org/10.1080/14443058.2013.781051

65 Steve Feffer, '"Despite All the Amputations, You Could Dance to the Rock and Roll Station": Staging Authenticity in *Hedwig and the Angry Inch*,' *Journal of Popular Music Studies* 19, no. 3 (2007): 241, https://doi.org/10.1111/ j.1533-1598.2007.00126.x.

66 Scott Miller, *Sex, Drugs, Rock and Roll, and Musicals* (Northeastern University Press, 2011), 207.

67 Wollman, 'Much Too Loud,' 315–316.

68 Wollman, 'Much Too Loud,' 316.

69 Diane Kirkby, Tanja Luckins and Chris McConville, *The Australian Pub* (University of New South Wales Press, 2010), 1.

70 Maggie Brady, *Teaching 'Proper' Drinking? Clubs and Pubs in Indigenous Australia* (ANU Press, 2017), xvii.

71 Brady, *Teaching 'Proper' Drinking?*, xvii–xviii.

72 Ann McGrath, '"Beneath the Skin": Australian Citizenship, Rights and Aboriginal Women,' *Journal of Australian Studies* 37, no. 99 (1993): 107–108, https://doi. org/10.1080/14443059309387144.

73 Tony Mitchell, *Popular Music and Local Identity: Rock, Pop and Rap in Europe and Oceania* (Leicester University Press, 1996), 204.

74 Jon Stratton, 'Whiter Rock: The "Australian Sound" and the Beat Boom,' *Continuum* 17, no. 3 (2003): 343, https://doi.org/10.1080/10304310302732. There is also a white/black split in the rock musical that is worth noting. See Elizabeth Wollman, 'Review,' *Theatre Journal* 60, no. 4 (2008): 635, https:// www.jstor.org/stable/40211203.

75 David Nichols, *Dig: Australian Rock and Pop Music 1960–1985* (Verse Chorus Press, 2016), 154.

76 Paul Oldman, '"Suck More Piss": How the Confluence of Key Melbourne-Based Audiences, Musicians, and Iconic Scene Spaces Informed the Oz Rock Identity,' *Perfect Beat* 14, no. 2 (2013): 129, https://doi.org/10.1558/prbt.v14i2.120.

77 James Cockington, *Long Way to the Top: Stories of Australian Rock and Roll* (ABC Books, 2001), 188.

78 Adam Shoemaker, *Black Words, White Page: Aboriginal Literature 1929–1988* (University of Queensland Press, 1989), 234.

79 Yovich and Valentine, *Barbara and the Camp Dogs*, 16.

80 Lillian Holt, 'Aboriginal Humour: A Conversational Corroboree,' in *Serious Frolic: Essays on Australian Humour*, ed. Fran De Groen and Peter Kirkpatrick (University of Queensland Press, 2009), 81.

81 Karen Austin, '*Talkin' Blak*: Humour in Indigenous Australian Theatre, 1970–2000,' *Philament* 20 (2015): 136.

82 Yovich and Valentine, *Barbara and the Camp Dogs*, 25.

83 Anna Haebich, 'On "Bran Nue Dae," by Jimmy Chi,' *Griffith Review*, accessed February 21, 2025, https://www.griffithreview.com/bran-nue-dae-jimmy-chi/.

84 Helen Gilbert and Jacqueline Lo, *Performance and Cosmopolitics: Cross-Cultural Transactions in Australia* (Palgrave Macmillan, 2007), 59.

85 Tongue, '*Barbara and the Camp Dogs*.'

86 Yovich and Valentine, *Barbara and the Camp Dogs*, 3.

87 Yovich and Valentine, *Barbara and the Camp Dogs*, 4.

88 Yovich and Valentine, *Barbara and the Camp Dogs*, 28.

89 Chelsea Watego, 'The Audacity of Anger,' *IndigenousX*, January 29, 2018, accessed February 21, 2025, https://indigenousx.com.au/chelsea-bond-the-audacity-of-anger/.

90 Watego, 'The Audacity of Anger,' original emphasis.

91 Matt Abotomey, 'A Bluffer's Guide to the Belvoir's Latest Play Featuring a Live Band on Stage,' *Concrete Playground*, December 8, 2017, accessed February 21, 2025, https://concreteplayground.com/sydney/arts-entertainment/stage-arts-entertainment-2/bluffers-guide-belvoirs-latest-play-featuring-live-band-stage.

92 Kerrie O'Brien, '"They're Bad Women, in the Best Sense of That Word; They Won't Conform",' *The Sydney Morning Herald*, January 30, 2019, https://www.smh.com.au/entertainment/theyre-bad-women-in-the-best-sense-of-that-word-they-wont-conform-20190129-h1alrn.html.

93 Thurow, *Performing Indigenous Identities*, 61.

94 Yovich and Valentine, *Barbara and the Camp Dogs*, 12.

95 Aileen Moreton-Robinson, 'Tiddas Talkin' Up to the White Woman: When Huggins et al. Took on Bell,' in *Blacklines: Contemporary Critical Writing by Indigenous Australians*, ed. Michelle Grossman (Melbourne University Press, 2003), 67.

96 Yovich and Valentine, *Barbara and the Camp Dogs*, 3.

97 Sonali Chakravarti, *Sing the Rage: Listening to Anger after Mass Violence* (University of Chicago Press, 2014), 149–150.

98 Yovich and Valentine, *Barbara and the Camp Dogs*, 13.

99 Yovich and Valentine, *Barbara and the Camp Dogs*, 35.

100 '*Barbara and the Camp Dogs* Take Us on a Rock-Fueled Road Trip,' *ABC Radio National*, February 5, 2019, accessed February 21, 2025, https://www.abc.net.au/radionational/programs/the-stage-show/barbara-and-the-camp-dogs-take-us-on-a-rock-fueled-road-trip/10780058.

101 John Shand, '*Barbara and the Camp Dogs* Review: Rock Music Erupts from the Mouth of a Volcano,' *The Sydney Morning Herald*, December 7, 2017, https://www.smh.com.au/entertainment/theatre/barbara-and-the-camp-dogs-review-rock-music-erupts-from-the-mouth-of-a-volcano-20171207-h00aka.html.

102 Jilli Streit-Warburton, 'Craft, Raft and Lifesaver: Aboriginal Women Musicians in the Contemporary Music Industry in Australia,' in *Sounding Off: Music as Subversion/Resistance/Revolution*, ed. Ron Salolsky and Fred Wei-Han Ho (Autonomedia, 1995), 307.

103 Miriam Rose Ungunmerr, 'Dadirri: Inner Deep Listening and Quiet Still Awareness,' *EarthSong Journal: Perspectives in Ecology, Spirituality and Education* 3, no. 4 (2017): 14. While *dadirri* is an Ngangikurungkurr word, it has equivalents in several other Indigenous language groups.

104 Judy Atkinson, *Trauma Trails, Recreating Song Lines: The Transgenerational Effects of Trauma in Indigenous Australia* (Spinifex Press, 2002), 18.

105 Atkinson, *Trauma Trails*, 18.

References

ABC Indigenous. 'One Song's 130-Year Impact on Australian Music.' *YouTube*, August 8, 2018. Accessed February 21, 2025. https://www.youtube.com/watch?v=vDZ2NQkkOAk.

Abotomey, Matt. 'A Bluffer's Guide to the Belvoir's Latest Play Featuring a Live Band on Stage.' *Concrete Playground*, December 8, 2017. Accessed February 21, 2025. https://concreteplayground.com/sydney/arts-entertainment/stage-arts-entertainment-2/bluffers-guide-belvoirs-latest-play-featuring-live-band-stage.

Atkinson, Judy. *Trauma Trails, Recreating Song Lines: The Transgenerational Effects of Trauma in Indigenous Australia.* Spinifex Press, 2002.

Auslander, Philip. 'Performance Analysis and Popular Music: A Manifesto.' *Contemporary Theatre* 14, no. 1 (2004): 1–13. https://doi.org/10.1080/10267 16032000128674.

Austin, Karen. '*Talkin' Blak*: Humour in Indigenous Australian Theatre, 1970–2000.' *Philament* 20 (2015): 129–163.

'"Barbara and the Camp Dogs" Is Passionate, Soulful, and Deeply Affecting.' *The Music*, February 5, 2019. Accessed February 18, 2025. https://themusic.com.au/features/barbara-the-camp-dogs-is-passionate-soulful-deeply-affecting/-PLg6u3s7-4/05-02-19/.

'*Barbara and the Camp Dogs* Take Us on a Rock-Fueled Road Trip.' *ABC Radio National*, February 5, 2019. Accessed February 21, 2025. https://www.abc.net.au/radionational/programs/the-stage-show/barbara-and-the-camp-dogs-take-us-on-a-rock-fueled-road-trip/10780058.

'Barbara and the Camp Dogs Backstage.' *Belvoir*, podcast, November 28, 2017. Accessed February 18, 2025. https://open.spotify.com/episode/0wz0b8nD85rm K0n5X7jqUW?si=Wtww0BTvQa2ZExbtbcu3Y.

Barney, Katelyn. '"Women Singing Up Big": The Growth of Contemporary Music Recordings by Indigenous Australian Women Artists.' *Australian Aboriginal Studies* 1 (2006): 44–56.

Beaumont, Gabriella. 'The Origin Story of Acclaimed Rock Musical "Barbara and the Camp Dogs."' *Beat.com.au*, February 13, 2019. Accessed February 21, 2025. https://beat.com.au/the-origin-story-of-acclaimed-rock-musical-barbara-and-the-camp-dogs/.

Bessley, Michelle. '#SheInspires Ursula Yovich.' *SheSociety*, May 17, 2019. Accessed February 21, 2025. https://shesociety.com.au/news/sheinspires-ursula-yovich/.

Blake, Elissa. 'Ursula Yovich Rocks out Belvoir's *Barbara and the Camp Dogs*.' *The Sydney Morning Herald*, November 14, 2017. https://www.smh.com.au/entertainment/ursula-yovich-rocks-out-belvoirs-barbara-and-the-camp-dogs-20171114-gzl6xl.html.

Brady, Maggie. *Teaching 'Proper' Drinking? Clubs and Pubs in Indigenous Australia.* ANU Press, 2017.

Casey, Maryrose. *Telling Stories: Aboriginal Australian and Torres Strait Islander Performance.* Australian Scholarly Publishing, 2012.

Casey, Maryrose. 'Bold, Black, and Brilliant: Aboriginal Australian Drama.' In *A Companion to Australian Aboriginal Literature*, edited by Belinda Wheeler. Camden House, 2013, 155–172.

Casey, Maryrose, and Cathy Craigie. *A Brief History of Indigenous Australian Contemporary Theatre.* Australian Script Centre, 2011.

Chakravarti, Sonali. *Sing the Rage: Listening to Anger after Mass Violence.* University of Chicago Press, 2014.

Cockington, James. *Long Way to the Top: Stories of Australian Rock and Roll.* ABC Books, 2001.

Dunbar-Hall, Peter, and Chris Gibson. *Deadly Sounds, Deadly Places: Contemporary Aboriginal Music in Australia.* University of New South Wales Press, 2004.

Durham, Penny. '*Barbara and the Camp Dogs* and Me.' *The Australian*, November 17, 2017. https://www.theaustralian.com.au/life/weekend-australian-magazine/ursula-yovich-barbara-and-the-camp-dogs-and-me/news-story/112a22 f45c1b0ab1ed58a54b88d370ce.

Enoch, Wesley, and John Rodgers. *The Sunshine Club.* Sydney Theatre Company, sound recording, 2000.

Fast, Susan. 'Rock.' *Grove Music Online*, January 31, 2014. Accessed February 21, 2025. https://doi.org/10.1093/gmo/9781561592630.article.A2257208.

Feffer, Steve. '"Despite All the Amputations, You Could Dance to the Rock and Roll Station": Staging Authenticity in *Hedwig and the Angry Inch*.' *Journal of Popular Music Studies* 19, no. 3 (2007): 239–258. https://doi.org/10.1111/j.1533-1598.2007.00126.x.

Fricke, David. 'Sex & Drag & Rock & Roll.' *Rolling Stone*, December 10, 1998. Accessed February 21, 2025. https://www.rollingstone.com/music/music-news/sex-drag-rock-roll-188691/.

Frith, Simon. 'Rock and the Politics of Memory.' *Social Text* 9–10 (1984): 59–69. https://doi.org/10.2307/466535.

Fritzlaff, Hayden. '*Barbara and the Camp Dogs* Blurs the Lines Between Theatre and Rock.' *Riot Act*, May 24, 2019. Accessed February 21, 2025. https://the-riotact.com/barbara-and-the-camp-dogs-blurs-the-lines-between-theatre-and-rock/303869.

Gallan, Ben, and Chris Gibson. 'Mild-Mannered Bistro by Day, Eclectic Freak-Land at Night: Memories of an Australian Music Venue.' *Journal of Australian Studies* 37, no. 2 (2013): 174–193. https://doi.org/10.1080/14443058.2013.781051.

Gilbert, Helen, and Jacqueline Lo. *Performance and Cosmopolitics: Cross-Cultural Transactions in Australia*. Palgrave Macmillan, 2007.

Glow, Hilary. 'Recent Indigenous Theatre in Australia: The Politics of Autobiography.' *International Journal of the Humanities* 4, no. 1 (2007): 71–77.

Grehan, Helena. 'Aboriginal Performance: Politics, Empathy and the Question of Reciprocity.' *Australasian Drama Studies* 56 (2010): 38–52.

Haebich, Anna. 'On "Bran Nue Dae," by Jimmy Chi.' *Griffith Review*. Accessed February 21, 2025. https://www.griffithreview.com/bran-nue-dae-jimmy-chi/.

Hoffman, Warren. *The Great White Way: Race and the Broadway Musical*. Rutgers University Press, 2014.

Holt, Lillian. 'Aboriginal Humour: A Conversational Corroboree.' In *Serious Frolic: Essays on Australian Humour*, edited by Fran De Groen and Peter Kirkpatrick. University of Queensland Press, 2009.

Homan, Shane. 'Losing the Local: Sydney and the Oz Rock Tradition.' *Popular Music* 19, no. 1 (2000): 31–49. https://doi.org/10.1017/S0261143000000040/.

Kirkby, Diane, Tanja Luckins, and Chris McConville. *The Australian Pub*. University of New South Wales Press, 2010.

Lyssa, Alison. 'Black and White: Australia's History on Stage in Four Plays of the New Millennium.' *Australasian Drama Studies* 48 (2006): 203–227.

McGrath, Ann. '"Beneath the Skin": Australian Citizenship, Rights and Aboriginal Women.' *Journal of Australian Studies* 37, no. 99 (1993): 99–114. https://doi.org/10.1080/14443059309387144.

Miller, Scott. *Sex, Drugs, Rock and Roll, and Musicals*. Northeastern University Press, 2011.

Mitchell, Tony. *Popular Music and Local Identity: Rock, Pop and Rap in Europe and Oceania*. Leicester University Press, 1996.

Moreton-Robinson, Aileen. 'Tiddas Talkin' Up to the White Woman: When Huggins et al. Took on Bell.' In *Blacklines: Contemporary Critical Writing by Indigenous Australians*, edited by Michelle Grossman. Melbourne University Press, 2003.

'A Mother's Funeral and Identity: Ursula Yovich's Story Wins Playwright Award.' *NITV*, June 15, 2016. Accessed March 12, 2021. https://www.sbs.com.au/nitv/nitvnews/article/2016/06/15/mothers-funeral-and-identity-ursula-yovichs-story-wins-playwright-award.

Negus, Keith. 'Authorship and the Popular Song.' *Music and Letters* 92, no. 4 (2011): 607–629. https://doi.org.ezproxy.uow.edu.au/10.1093/ml/gcr117.

Nichols, David. *Dig: Australian Rock and Pop Music 1960–1985.* Verse Chorus Press, 2016.

NIDA. 'Inaugural NAIDOC Week Lecture with Ursula Yovich.' *YouTube*, November 16, 2020. Accessed February 18, 2025. https://www.youtube.com/watch?v=YFHcZ08nR_w.

O'Brien, Kerrie. 'They're Bad Women, in the Best Sense of That Word; They Won't Conform.' *The Sydney Morning Herald*, January 30, 2019. https://www.smh.com.au/entertainment/theyre-bad-women-in-the-best-sense-of-that-word-they-wont-conform-20190129-h1alrn.html.

Oldman, Paul. '"Suck More Piss": How the Confluence of Key Melbourne-Based Audiences, Musicians, and Iconic Scene Spaces Informed the Oz Rock Identity.' *Perfect Beat* 14, no. 2 (2013): 120–139. https://doi.org/10.1558/prbt.v14i2.120.

Queensland Theatre, *Soundcloud* channel. Accessed January 15, 2025. https://soundcloud.com/user-874518784.

Russell, Stephen. 'Rock-N-Roll Spirit Meets Indigenous Experience in Ursula Yovich's *Barbara and the Camp Dogs.*' *The Music*, November 3, 2017. Accessed February 21, 2025. https://themusic.com.au/features/ursula-yovich-barbara-and-the-camp-dogs-belvoir-theatre-stephen-a-russell/r0Cgo6KlpKc/03-11-17/.

Screen Australia, *Annual Reports.* Accessed February 18, 2025. https://www.screenaustralia.gov.au/about-us/corporate-documents/annual-reports.

Shand, John. '*Barbara and the Camp Dogs* Review: Rock Music Erupts from the Mouth of a Volcano.' *The Sydney Morning Herald*, December 7, 2017. https://www.smh.com.au/entertainment/theatre/barbara-and-the-camp-dogs-review-rock-music-erupts-from-the-mouth-of-a-volcano-20171207-h00aka.html.

Shoemaker, Adam. *Black Words, White Page: Aboriginal Literature 1929–1988.* University of Queensland Press, 1989.

Sobb Ah Kin, Camilla. '*A Chance Gathering of Strays: The Australian Theatre Family.*' Masters diss., University of Sydney, 2010.

Stratton, Jon. 'Whiter Rock: The "Australian Sound" and the Beat Boom.' *Continuum* 17, no. 3 (2003): 331–346. https://doi.org/10.1080/10304310302732.

Streit-Warburton, Jilli. 'Craft, Raft and Lifesaver: Aboriginal Women Musicians in the Contemporary Music Industry in Australia.' In *Sounding Off: Music as Subversion/Resistance/Revolution*, edited by Ron Salolsky and Fred Wei-Han Ho. Autonomedia, 1995.

Symonds, Dominic. 'Drag, Rock, Authenticity and In-Betweenness: *Hedwig and the Angry Inch.*' In *Twenty-First Century Musical Theatre: From Stage to Screen*, edited by George Rodosthenous. Routledge, 2017.

Thurow, Susanne. *Performing Indigenous Identities on the Contemporary Australian Stage.* Taylor and Francis, 2020.

Tongue, Cassie. '*Barbara and the Camp Dogs*: How One Woman's Anger Became a Rock Show.' *The Guardian*, December 18, 2017. https://www.theguardian.com/stage/2017/dec/18/barbara-and-the-camp-dogs-how-one-womans-anger-became-a-rock-show.

Ungunmerr, Miriam Rose. 'Dadirri: Inner Deep Listening and Quiet Still Awareness.' *EarthSong Journal: Perspectives in Ecology, Spirituality and Education* 3, no. 4 (2017): 14–15.

'Unleashing Barbara.' *Belvoir*, podcast. Accessed April 2, 2021. https://belvoir.com.au/news/barbara/.

'UrsulaYovich Unleashes Her Inner Diva.' *ABC Radio National*, December 2, 2017. Accessed June 30, 2025. https://www.abc.net.au/listen/programs/awaye/ursula-yovich-gives-voice-to-her-alter-ego/9211870.

Watego, Chelsea. 'The Audacity of Anger.' *IndigenousX*, January 29, 2018. Accessed February 21, 2025. https://indigenousx.com.au/chelsea-bond-the-audacity-of-anger/.

'Who's Telling Indigenous Australian Stories on Stage?' *ABC Radio National*, October 29, 2018. Accessed June 30, 2025. https://www.abc.net.au/radionational/programs/the-stage-show/whos-telling-indigenous-australian-stories-on-stage/10433140.

Woll, Allen. *Black Musical Theatre: From Coontown to Dreamgirls*. Da Capo Press, 1989.

Wollman, Elizabeth. 'Much Too Loud and Not Loud Enough: Issues Involving the Reception of Staged Rock Musicals. In *Bad Music: The Music We Love to Hate*, edited by Christopher J. Washburn and Maiken Derno. Routledge, 2004.

Wollman, Elizabeth. 'Review.' *Theatre Journal* 60, no. 4 (2008): 635–637. http://www.jstor.org/stable/40211203.

Yovich, Ursula. *Ursula Yovich Live*. MGM Music, sound recording, 2010.

Yovich, Ursula, and Alana Valentine. *Barbara and the Camp Dogs*. Currency Press, 2017.

Yovich, Ursula, and Alana Valentine. 'Writing and Performing *Barbara and the Camp Dogs*.' *TEXT Special Issue* 62 (October 2021): 1–16.

6

CLIMATE CHANGE AND SOFT-CLOSE DRAWERS: THE LOCAL MEETS THE GLOBAL IN *VIVID WHITE*

The desire to own one's own home in Australia is so deeply entrenched in the national imaginary that it is often referred to as the Australian Dream. In her book *Renovation Nation,* Fiona Allon described it as an obsession, one that 'extends to everything to do with home and housing: house prices and property values, interest rates and mortgages, investment properties and, of course, home renovations.'[1] *Vivid White* (2017) is a musical that engages critically with this aspect of Australian culture. While the production promoted itself as a satire on the state of the Australian housing market – a rollicking evening of funny songs and witty comedy peppered with familiar tropes from the national repertory – the work's social commentary on property ownership disguised a much deeper engagement with an issue of global proportions: climate change. Ultimately, the production stages a dystopic world in which climate change has resulted in the extinction of humanity.

Like *Muriel, Vivid White* engages with the national imaginary as contained within a wider frame: the global imaginary. Perfect's transmutation of the narrative from home ownership (the national) to climate change (the global) is achieved by stealthily moving the frame of the narrative outwards. For Australian theatre scholar Denise Varney, the theatre is an art form that can effectively navigate this local/global divide. Theatre, with its capacity for 'meta-theatrical and other frame-breaking moves across time and space,' both 'localises and situates the global in a designated place, while keeping an eye of the wider frame.'[2] In *Vivid White*, climate change is framed, as Una Chaudhuri conceptualises it, as a 'post-national' problem.[3] However, by grounding the narrative in the local, in the repertory of the national imaginary, Perfect acknowledges what philosopher Nancy Tuana describes as the 'affective dimension of loss of home.'[4] In *Vivid White*, a loss of home operates on multiple

DOI: 10.4324/9781003590088-7

levels. Some characters lose a home at auction, others to invasion, and they all lose their lives in the end as humanity cedes its home to another species. By constructing the loss of home as both local and global, Perfect demonstrates the limits of the national imaginary in the face of climate catastrophe.

In problematising the desire for home ownership by staging the loss of home, *Vivid White* recasts the Australian dream as the Australian nightmare. In this chapter, I demonstrate how the production reflects on conceptions of land, property, and home as they relate to colonisation and dispossession of Indigenous Australians. By outlining the importance of home ownership and the associated practice of renovation to Australian culture, I elucidate how home renovations function as 'performances of property' that are available solely to owners.[5] The musical intensifies existing tensions between renters and owner-occupiers by staging a dystopian Melbourne in which renters have become second-class citizens. The deus ex machina ending that sees giant, sentient squids take over the earth transposes the local crisis of the housing market onto the global crisis of climate change, bringing together a highly secure, most deeply held figment of the national imaginary with a reality that is both contested and frightening. I then argue that, through its pastiche of musical theatre styles and conventions, *Vivid White* subverts the musical's 'middlebrow horizon of expectations' to offer a politically charged satire.[6] Finally, I demonstrate how Vivid White debates its own efficacy as a piece of satire, dramatising Perfect's insecurity about this mode means for changing hearts and minds on these most prescient of issues.

The Melbourne Theatre Company commissioned Perfect to write *Vivid White* on the back of the success of his first play, *The Beast* (2013). It was the final performance in the company's 2017 season, and the first new Australian musical produced by the company since their production of Tony Briggs' *The Sapphires* in 2004. The plot of the musical follows two couples – Liz and Ben and Cynthia and Evan – living in present-day Melbourne. Ben and Evan are friends who, as younger men, had attempted to forge careers as satirical comedians. The stark reality of making a living from this endeavour meant that they have since parted ways professionally. Evan has become a reality television star and is now earning a sizeable income, while Ben is still trying to catch his big break on the comedy circuit. Both couples decide they want to buy a house. Independently, they find the perfect home, which ironically turns out to be the same property. Of course, only one couple can be successful at the auction: Evan and Cynthia, who have more capital available to them and have hired a smarmy real estate agent, are ultimately victorious. Liz and Ben are forced to retreat, representing the group of Australians who have been effectively priced out of the housing market. But from here, things start to take a strange turn. By the end of the musical, we have witnessed the complete disintegration of the society, the death of all four protagonists, and a triumphant takeover of the planet and the nation by giant squids.

Vivid White's engagement with climate change received scant mention in critical reviews, promotional material, and interviews with the cast and production team. The only explicit remark made on the subject of climate change was in an interview for *Limelight* magazine, when Verity Hunt-Ballard (who played Liz) commented that *Vivid White* is about 'climate change and the way we turn on our back on the big world issues because we get obsessed with our own situations, choosing colours for the walls and home renovations.'[7] It is possible that others remained silent in order to preserve the surprise of the *coup de théâtre* at the end of the second act: the reveal of the giant squid in the form of an inflatable puppet. An alternative possibility is that, given the fraught politics of discussion of climate change in Australia, this aspect of the musical was deliberately sidelined. In Australia, as in many other countries, climate change policy has proved a polarising and intractable issue, one that has been the undoing of several governments.[8]

In lieu of assessing *Vivid White*'s provocations regarding climate change, reviewers focused their critiques on the quality of the satire being presented. For *The Sydney Morning Herald*, Cameron Woodhead wrote that 'satire requires a scalpel to cut through to uncomfortable truths. *Vivid White* opens a soft-closing drawer of butter knives and throws them distractedly around the room.'[9] Kate Herbert, for *The Herald-Sun*, commented that if the aim of satire is to 'mercilessly flay its targets, then Perfect misses an opportunity to attack significant impediments to home ownership: investors, developers, banks, and government. The hapless, single homebuyer seems a soft target.'[10] Tim Byrne, writing for *Timeout*, was particularly excoriating:

> Perfect spends half the play 'mansplaining' the concept of satire – which is presumably meant as an in-joke but is actually just eye-rollingly tedious. If he'd created real recognisable characters and slowly turned up the heat on them, this might have worked. As it stands, it's rather like our property market: extortionate, and ludicrous.[11]

A likely explanation for why reviewers tended to focus on the satirical qualities of the work is that the *Vivid White* programme contained an essay by Perfect that framed the performance in this way. However, in the essay, which offers a view of satire's efficacy and debates its value as an artistic practice, Perfect deliberately avoids explaining his intentions, omitting clear explication of *Vivid White*'s 'satiric purpose,' to use Robert Phiddian's term.[12] Perfect writes that 'satire is best served without a wink or a nudge. To let an audience in on the joke is unforgivable; to give an audience an "out," cowardly,' and moreover, that 'the act of an author laboriously penning an explanation of his or her intentions' is most unseemly.[13] It is plausible that this open-ended statement diverted reviewers' attention from climate change onto *Vivid White*'s more obvious satirical engagement with the property market.

A different reading of the work emerges if the target of the satire is conceptualised in this way. Rather than satirising the vagaries of Australian housing market, what emerges if Perfect's 'satiric purpose' is to encourage audiences to seriously contemplate the realities of the impacts of changes to the climate on life as they know it? Home ownership in *Vivid White* acts as a smokescreen behind which to introduce ideas about climate change and human culpability in the destruction of the planet. This destruction only becomes possible because of the national obsession with home ownership.

The Australian Dream: Owner-Occupiers as Good Citizens

The idea of owning one's home is deeply lodged in the national imaginary. In the preface to *Australia's Home*, Robin Boyd wrote in 1961 that 'Australia is one small house' and that acquisition of a 'fenced allotment' is an 'inevitable and unquestionable goal.'[14] To this day, Australia continues to boast one of the highest rates of home ownership in the developed world. Housing scholar Richard Ronald writes that even when compared with the United States and Britain, Australians exhibit the strongest preference for private housing.[15] In recent history, this is in no small part due to the influence of former Prime Minister John Howard, who, as Allon reminds us, 'urged us to be not only a nation of shareholders, but a nation of homeowners too.'[16]

The second song of the musical, 'A House Is More,' is a clear statement of the value of home in Australian culture.[17] After a gentle piano introduction, Ben appears on stage to sing,

> A house is more than bricks and mortar
> More than carpets and running water
> It's more than floorboards, supporting walls, and natural light

In the meantime, other cast members have rolled onto the stage on rostra with musical instruments in hand. Wearing colourful 1980s style tracksuits, and enthusiastically playing their instruments, their demeanour suggests the atmosphere of a jam session at a barbecue. They join Ben to sing the last line of the verse: 'A house is so much more.' The word 'more' underscores, as Carole Després has catalogued, that home is a bastion of security and control, a reflection of one's identity, a conduit for family and relationships, a refuge, and so on.[18] The song also reflects that a home is a place to fill with things, acknowledging the materialism that goes hand in hand with contemporary home ownership. The first two verses list a plethora of things that are to be acquired and installed in the home: bathroom fixtures, children's pictures, foldable doors, polished concrete floors, and so forth. The latter half of the song shifts from detailing lists of items that fill the home to intimate something beyond materialism. At the climax of the song, the now well-established tune is harmonised by the company *a cappella*, punctuated with accented chords and reinforced by a key change, up a semitone from E-flat to E major. They conclude that 'whatever it is, it's yours,' reflecting Ronald's observation that a 'home of one's own' refers less to the idea of 'living in a self-contained dwelling but rather being an owner-occupier.'[19] Purchasing a home affords one the status of an owner-occupier and all the privileges that go with it.

Vivid White continually emphasises the perception that to be an owner-occupier is to be a good citizen. As Louise Crabtree outlines, the 'dominant Australian property narrative rests on an unconscious assertion of owner occupation as a signifier of individual and financial success and worthiness.'[20] That owners are 'hardworking, rate-paying citizens' or, as Susan Smith puts it, 'responsible' and 'risk-averse' has been a powerful narrative in the national imaginary.[21] Unlike the productivity and good citizenship vested in the owner-occupier, as Cheshire, Walters, and Rosenblatt describe, renters in Australia are constructed as inadequate on three levels:

aesthetics, and the perceived failure of renters to meet prevailing standards of home design and maintenance; ethics, whereby rental tenants are viewed not only as aesthetically, but ethically, deficient by virtue of their lack of care for the self and the home; and finally, community, through a lack of moral compunction to consider the impacts of their conduct upon the value of other people's property.[22]

Owner-occupiers, this suggests, are the best sort of neighbours. Jennifer Rutherford writes that the 'code of neighbourliness is immediately recognisable; it is the touchstone of Australianness.'[23] This 'moral code,' described by Rutherford as the 'Australian good,' is a potent force in the national imaginary, one that, as she notes, is intrinsically linked to white Australia.[24]

Vivid White presents the pursuit of home ownership as only possible due to the dispossession of First Nations people from their land. It acknowledges that the idea of owner-occupiers as good citizens conflicts with the facts of Indigenous dispossession of land and property. As Aidan Davison writes, 'the boundaries of the private home' have been key to the attempt 'to live at a safe distance from the profitable but disturbing realities of technological domination and colonial dispossession.'[25] *Vivid White* draws attention to this from the first moment of the production. As is customary in Australian theatre, it begins by acknowledging the traditional owners of the land, who at the Sumner Theatre in Melbourne, are the Boon Wurrung people of the Kulin nation. Emerging out of pitch-black darkness, and spoken in a low, gravelly voice with a Scandinavian accent, the acknowledgment of country, rather than acting as a discrete prelude to the show, marks the beginning of the show proper. This unusual voice addresses the audience directly: 'We would also like to acknowledge you guys. White people.' It continues to prosecute the whiteness of the audience by sardonically commenting that 'You're good people. Not even your murderous, land-thieving ancestors can change that.' A second acknowledgment of country is performed at the fateful scene where the two couples go head-to-head at the auction. The auctioneer begins the proceedings with the following statement:

> Ladies and Gentlemen, before the auction gets under way I'd like to first acknowledge the traditional owners of the land that I am about to sell today; the Boon Wurrung people of the Kulin Nation. A big shout out to them. I didn't steal it. You didn't steal it. Let's get over it together! Go Australia!

The crowd that has accumulated for the auction respond in kind with 'Go Australia!' The perfunctory acknowledgment of country, the absolution of responsibility, and the jingoistic cheers cumulatively reflect the schism between these platitudes and the reality of Indigenous dispossession.

The title of the musical can similarly be read as a gesture towards a critical politics of settler-colonial race relations in Australia. In the scene after Evan and Cynthia have purchased their house, they employ a pretentious interior designer to assist them in choosing a paint colour. They are asked to choose between two almost identical shades of white.

Colour Consultant: The colour you are holding is not really a colour. It's called Vivid White. It's the most white you can get; there's no blue, no red . . . no warmth or coolness . . . it's just . . . white. It's Vivid White.

They are then asked to compare this to another colour, about which Evan remarks 'It's white,' and to which the Colour Consultant retorts: 'It's a kind of white. This is White On White.' 'White?' says Evan; 'on white,' responds the consultant. The incessant and pronounced repetition of the word white in this scene crudely draws attention to the whiteness of the pursuit of home ownership. The image of a white couple plastering their walls with the whitest paint possible is further intensified by the way Gillian Cosgriff, the actress playing the Colour Consultant, pronounces the word white with an affected, aspirated 'h' sound at the beginning of each utterance. In doing so, she makes the whiteness of the audience visible rather than invisible.

After becoming an owner-occupier in Australia, the next step is often to embark upon a process of renovation. The plot of *Vivid White* shows Evan and Cynthia following this familiar script. Once the couple have been successful at auction, they begin to renovate. Renovations are, to use Nicholas Blomley's term, 'performances of property' that are citational, reiterative, and continually 'remade and re-enacted.'[26] Elaborating Blomley's concept, Davison argues that such performances 'demarcate public and private realms, allocate civic responsibilities and rights, establish social conditions of belonging and exclusion, confer economic advantages and disadvantages and distribute environmental goods and bads.'[27] In Australia, renovation is a potent example of how such performances of property are the exclusive preserve of owners.

The renovation-themed humour in *Vivid White* relies on the audience identifying as either renovators or potential renovators, and most importantly, as not (or no longer) renters. Some of these jokes are intended as light commentary, like Evan's job as the host of a reality television series called *Humiliating Houses* – a play on television programs like *The Block* that have enjoyed extraordinary popularity among Australians.[28] Another example – and the moment that earned the biggest laugh at the performance I attended – was a joke about Bunnings, the chain of hardware stores discussed in relation to *Songs from the Middle*, beloved by renovators. In the scene, Cynthia and Evan are discussing the prospective renovations to their new property:

Cynthia: Might call the electrician.
Evan: Good idea. I might head to Bunnings.
Cynthia: Do we need anything?
Evan: No. I feel like a sausage.

Bunnings stores are renowned for their provision of a sausage sizzle, a 'uniquely Australian variant' of the barbecue, which acts as a fundraising opportunity for a rotating roster of community groups.[29] While this humour masquerades as benign social commentary, underlying it is an exclusionary dynamic. As Hazel Easthope outlines, Australian renters are beholden to much stricter conditions than in other countries, like fixed-term leases, short termination periods and frequent rent increases.[30] Tenants also have few rights to make changes to properties, and many avoid asking landlords to undertake repairs for fear of retaliation. In NSW, it was only in 2020 that legislation enshrined it as unreasonable for landlords to refuse tenants the right to make small modifications to properties, like hanging picture frames and planting vegetables. Nevertheless, renovation remains an exclusive zone, one that is unavailable to renters. Bunnings' appeal to renovators, therefore, associates it more with homeowners than with renters. After all, what business does a renter have in Bunnings with their limited capacity to make modifications?

This kind of exclusivity is on show in 'They Come (Or Not at All),' an exuberant, mostly spoken 1950s style rock 'n' roll number. In the second verse, Cynthia laments the unreliability of 'tradies,' the Australian moniker for tradesmen like plumbers, electricians, builders, and so on:

Cynthia: I called a sparky [an electrician] up on Sunday
Ensemble: Emergency, Emergency!
Cynthia: He said I'll be there right away, babe

Ensemble: Ain't that what they all say?
Cynthia: Four hours later in he came
Ensemble: Four hours? What'd ya say?
Cynthia: Well, nothing 'cos he fixed it
Ensemble: Right
Cynthia: But it was inconvenient!

Cynthia's inconvenience is performative, no more than a chance to brag that she has both the home and the disposable income to be able to execute the renovations she desires. In response, the ensemble *ad lib* in general agreement about the truth of what she has said, conferring the ubiquity of the problem, and demonstrating that they are in on the joke.

These allusions to middle-class anxieties about renovations underscore that underneath these performances of property are deep-set fears: fears around the impacts of globalisation, migration, economic insecurity. Allon contends that what renovations do is bring our focus inwards:

> They focus our concentration on the here and now, the little details, and they appear to bring everything under our control. When so much else around us seems complex and difficult and unmanageable, home renovations provide the pleasure of small choices, satisfying decisions.[31]

She also argues that the retreat into the home at the turn of the twenty-first century should be read as symptomatic of a post-9/11 retreat to the domestic. In this period of

> anxiety and insecurity, the domestic realm provided a clear and uncomplicated sense of secure moorings and a reassuring confirmation of identity and purpose. . . . But what are the consequences of a culture preoccupied with hibernation or in the grip of isolationism? What happens when a society disengages, turns inwards and obsessively monitors the property index?[32]

Vivid White addresses this question by staging a class conflict between owners ('good' citizens) and renters that divides and distracts a society, setting the scene for the dystopian take-over of the earth by the giant squids.

The Impossible Dream: Renters as Persecuted Underclass

While the owner-occupied home continues to be a fixture in the national imaginary, the nature of the Australian property markets means that, for Australians, the acquisition of property has become exponentially more difficult. In *Vivid White*, Liz and Ben represent the section of Australian society for whom this is the case. In 2017, when the production premièred, the situation around housing was at a crisis point. After the 2008 Global Financial Crisis, the Australian property market had become increasingly more bloated and volatile than the situation Allon documented in *Renovation Nation*. In a 2018 report published by the Grattan Institute, John Daley and Brendan Coates described the contemporary Australian housing market as 'a perfect storm of rising incomes and falling interest rates, rapid migration, tax and welfare settings feeding demand, and planning rules restricting supply,' citing figures that showed in the period since 2012, house prices in Melbourne and Sydney rose by 50% and 70%, respectively.[33] Since that time, housing conditions have been further exacerbated by high-interest rates, the COVID-19 pandemic, and several years of inflationary conditions. One significant consequence of this has been that amongst younger Australians, home ownership rates have fallen substantially. Home ownership is no longer the inevitable and unquestionable goal that Robin Boyd described in the 1950s. In 2014, writer and journalist Gillian Terzis, reflecting on her own inability to access the housing market, had recast home ownership as 'the impossible dream.'[34]

Vivid White magnifies the pre-existing and intense undercurrents of the debate around housing by situating renters as a persecuted underclass. The performance stages what geographer Susan Smith observes to be the status quo in housing policy, namely that it operates through the juxtaposition of a 'mainstream ownership ideal with its marginalised "Other," renting.'[35] In *Vivid White*, the 'Othering' of the renter is established through the strange, sinister, and apocalyptic atmosphere that is cultivated in the opening scene. In the opening monologue, the faceless voice that chastises the audience for their white privilege also attacks their class status. It then condescendingly asks the audience, 'Are you renting?' and then proceeds to perniciously stoke middle-class anxieties around socio-economic status. It tells us that Steve, who earns less than you, has managed to buy a house, and Sonja and her husband, who are younger than you, are already renovating theirs. The tone of the monologue becomes gradually more sinister, until suddenly a soundscape of multiple, overlapping voices booms throughout the auditorium:

You should buy
You should renovate
You should secure an investment property
You should negatively gear
This is not enough

This continues until, as the stage directions state, 'the cacophony of overlapping voices abruptly stops.' With contempt, the voice says:

You are a renter
You disgust me.
Buy or die. Buy or
die. Buy or die.

This is followed by an 'unearthly shriek,' a flash of light, and then two shadows shaped like tentacles twist across the stage. Immediately after, to the sound of chaos and drums, silhouetted human figures appear one by one, voicing fragments of information that fade in and out, as if one is tuning into a radio. This assemblage of news fragments and eyewitness accounts indicates that there has been an invasion. We are told that it has 'left officials baffled and local residents disturbed,' that the invader is killing animals, that it has something to do with creatures that 'fall outside the category of any known oceanic species,' and that these creatures should not be approached. Red emergency-lights beam across the stage and two groups of performers, playing musical instruments, are illuminated. 'What the Fuck Was That?' they exclaim in song, confirming the uncertainty that surrounds the attack. In the next scene, this strange, unnamed voice is heard again. It spooks Liz in her kitchen, probing her and pressuring her to buy a house. It reveals its name to be Guus, and throughout the first act, Guus spiritually possesses various characters, causing them to involuntarily spout the 'buy or die' rhetoric from the opening scene. The initial apocalyptic event is periodically alluded to as the narrative progresses. Midway through the auction, a bleeding man runs down the street shouting, 'Help me! Somebody help me!! They're everywhere!'

The divide between renters and homeowners invoked in the opening scene becomes progressively actual rather than satirical. In the scene with the Colour Consultant, in a bizarre turn of events, as she makes a sweeping movement with her arm, a spray of blood spatters across the wall. It turns out that she is one of 'them': a renter. After Liz and Ben lose the auction, things get progressively worse for the renting class and things come to a head in the final scene of Act One, when Liz observes that renters are rapidly disappearing while homeowners seem unaffected. Emergency warnings begin to sound, advising renters to report to controlled facilities with curfews. Liz and Ben realise that no one is coming to rescue them from the threat, still at this point unknown, resulting in a reprise of 'They Come Late (Or Not at All).' This slower, heavier, and more ominous rendition of the earlier song concludes the first act. The drums beat a martial rhythm as the company sing in layers of harmony:

> They come late or not at all
> They tell us help is on its way
> And yet it's always one more day
> And we pray inside our walls
> Ever helplessly awaiting our fate

In the first rendition of this song, 'they' referred to a group of unreliable tradesmen. In the reprise, it has shifted in meaning: it now refers to the owning class, who have abandoned and forsaken renters, allowing a stratified society to emerge. Following this, several chorus members who represent renters are pulled off stage one at a time by snaking tentacles.

Enter the Squids: Climate Change, the Local, and the Global

In Act Two, the thematic threads of home, nation, and renovation are drawn together as the narrative of *Vivid White* shifts towards its destination: climate change. By transposing the local crisis of the housing market onto the global crisis of climate change, *Vivid White* brings together a highly secure, most deeply held fixture of the national imaginary with a reality that is both contested and frightening. The takeover of the home, and by extension Australia and the world, by squids invokes anxieties around national borders, sovereignty, and the possibility of invasion. When Guus is unexpectedly revealed to be a giant squid, everything changes. The characters' obsession with home ownership and renovation has blinded them to the existential threat that is right on their doorstep. In doing so, the production mounts the argument that it is only through attention to the consequences at the local level that the problem of climate change can be fully grasped.

As the situation in Melbourne deteriorates further for renters, Liz and Ben end up at Cynthia and Evan's door begging for sanctuary. After being accosted and pinned down by the armed private security guard whom Evan and Cynthia have hired to protect their property, Liz and Ben are granted entry. Upon entry, the conversation turns to the subject of renovation, and after a long, drawn-out scene where the tension gradually escalates, Evan angrily hacks down his newly erected dividing wall with an axe. Suddenly the sofa starts to move and within five seconds, the stage has been engulfed by a giant inflatable puppet: Guus, a giant cephalopod, combination of squid, octopus, and cuttlefish (Figure 6.1).[36]

The fact that Guus is a cephalopod is significant, as in recent years there has been much discussion of how these 'fast-growing, adaptable creatures are perfectly equipped to exploit the gaps left by extreme climate changes.'[37] Guus announces to the humans that the squids are taking over, admonishing them for their role in their own demise:

We've been waiting for decades . . .
Strolling around the living room.
. . . we nearly invaded in the 90s, but you were building all
those *town houses* . . . I mean, what *are* they? They're not *houses*.
They're not *apartments*. All those stairs? Marching up and
Down. Up and down. No thank you. We called off the attack . . .
we waited. . . . You spent the noughties developing telepathy!
And then you finally discovered OPEN PLAN LIVING. Your

FIGURE 6.1   Guus inflates onto the stage in *Vivid White*.

Photo: Jeff Busby ©

> OPEN PLAN LIVING would provide us with the PERFECT
> CONDITIONS to sustain our civilization. Bravo, fools! You
> architecturally designed yourselves TO DEATH!

The seemingly innocuous jokes about colours of paint, tradies, and soft-close
drawers were in fact leading to this moment. Renovation has been the death
knell; home ownership the insidious cancer that led to the demise of the humans.
Within a few minutes of Guus' arrival, all four protagonists have been slaughtered.
Cynthia is taken first, and then Guus turns to the remaining protagonists. They
try to hold the cephalopod off but are ultimately unsuccessful. After a brief
reprieve, Guus breaks their necks simultaneously; all three are killed in one fell
swoop. Then, just as in the beginning, Guus turns to the audience:

> This is the end. Do not be afraid. People are too quick to fear the end.
> It is the reason they rush out and purchase new rolls of the gladwrap
> although the current one is still going. Two hundred thousand years. That's
> all you get. We cephalopods, on the other tentacle, have been here for
> 500 million years. I'd love to say it's not a competition, but it so is.

The rendering of Guus as a giant squid calls attention to Australian anxieties
around the security of the Australian coastline as our national border. As

Suvendrini Perera writes, in the twenty-first century the water has been the primary site where 'Australian sovereignty and territoriality [are] exercised . . . and where the limits of the national [are] performed and tested.'[38] Perfect has staged a narrative in which it is a cruel and tragic twist of fate that a nation so proud of its coastline, yet so obsessed with protecting its borders, has been infiltrated by invaders from the sea. *Vivid White* suggests that, had Australians been less insular, less concerned with the domestic, the everyday, the material, then such a demise would not have been possible. Perera argues that insularity is 'Australia's defining characteristic,' a proposition with which Allon agrees, averring that 'agonising over whether to go with the teal or bunt orange tiles for the new kitchen floor' promotes an insular world view.[39] Echoes of this are present in Cynthia's swan song, 'Vivid White,' which sees her reflect on the myopia of contemporary Australian society. She sings how 'we just take the past and paint it Vivid White,' white-washing history by 'changing things we can't stand facing.' She realises the futility of this approach all too late: 'but now I see the light,' and then she dies.

The transposition of the local crisis of the housing market onto the global crisis of climate is particularly potent because in Australia, home ownership has functioned as a national source of 'ontological security,' while climate change, on the other hand, functions resolutely as a source of 'ontological anxiety.'[40] Indeed, in terms of comparable developed nations, Australia has been at the forefront of an asset-based approach to welfare whereby the acquisition of property has been seen as the best way to ensure a comfortable retirement. Housing has been considered a prudent investment that would act as a social safety net, decreasing one's reliance on government payments and improving the quality of retirement.[41] Homes were meant to be, as Yates and Bradbury observe, 'islands of sanctuary and refuge (for ourselves, not for others) where we could retreat, and once there look inward and get on with the renovations.'[42] *Vivid White* exposes the frailty of this national source of ontological security, and actively asks it audience it to reconsider its own culpability and responsibility.

Vivid White counters the assumption that homeowners are good citizens, arguing that these good burghers – the renovators – are responsible for the destruction of society. These assumptions are problematised further through the invocation of climate change. The ending insinuates that it is humanity's arrogance regarding its longevity and singularity that leads to its demise. This line of argument is pursued in the final song of Act One, where Ben braves the renter's curfew to go and perform his regular gig at the Rec Centre. In this song, 'Hands,' a gentle pop song sung by mobile phone light due to a power blackout at the Rec Centre, the conclusion of the plot was foreshadowed:

It's a wonder of evolution
That the right conditions made us the chosen species

> That we'd stand, walk upright and take command
> So nothing else would eat me
> Here on Earth, a third of it is land
> The other two's where life began, deep within the ocean
> Down there there's evidence of equal intelligence

This ocean theme is continued through the choreography, where the chorus are placed around Ben like a pod of dolphins, with their movement mimicking the graceful movement of these animals through the water. They sing 'if we found life like ours, how it would surprise us' in warm harmony. Audiences and characters alike experience this surprise in real time when the sentient, gigantic Guus inflates onto the stage.

In positing that the colour of the paint will no longer matter if we are not around to choose it, *Vivid White* urges us to think beyond the confines of the quarter-acre block. After all the protagonists have been killed, Guus announces that they will sing a song to mark the extinction of humanity: 'This one goes out to you – so fragile. So . . . temporary. Ubiquitous . . . then nothing. Like snowflakes. . . . Precious little snowflakes.' In the first half of the song, entitled 'Precious Little Snowflake,' Guus sings a number that mocks the human fixation with the uniqueness of the individual.

> No more looking out for number one
> Only here a moment, then you're done
> Precious Little Snowflake
> Here comes the sun

In this soft-shoe number, which parodies the Broadway song convention of a leading lady surrounded by a dancing chorus who echo her (in the manner of *Hello, Dolly!*), the metaphor of the snowflake is employed to critique the Western proclivity towards self-interest and individualism. In the finale sequence, which also encompasses the curtain call, the company form a chorus line at the front of the stage, and dressed in glittering gold tracksuits and top hats, they dance in unison, singing, 'Here comes the sun' repeatedly in harmony. The title of the well-known Beatles song is given a sinister twist in a context where 'here comes the sun' now means 'here comes the inescapable warming of the planet.' Two curtains that have sectioned the stage lift to allow the choreography to gradually fill more and more of the now empty stage. In this first half of the number, the lighting state was a deep oceanic blue, but as the song progresses, the colour of the stage gradually starts to brighten. As the last curtain lifts, the stage becomes saturated with brilliant gold light. This transition visually mimics the warming of the ocean and the melting of the snow invoked in the lyrics. In these conditions, while humans struggle, squids will multiply and prosper. Eventually, each unique human, or 'precious little snowflake,' will be subsumed back into the earth. Humans will just 'go ahead and melt,' as Guus says. On the one hand, this scene makes for an intensely pleasurable musical theatre send-off; on the other, this stage, flooded with gold, represents the end of the Anthropocene.

Vivid White's contention is that it is only through attention to the local – to the home – that the consequences of climate change can be comprehended. In *Renovation Nation*, Allon made an off-hand comment linking home ownership and climate change when she observes:

> We are all now more connected than ever in all kinds of intimate and entangled ways: through telecommunications, though financial networks and not least environmentally, through the effects of climate change. Yet we still maintain the illusion that by closing the front door we can shut the world out, that what we do *here* doesn't have any bearing on what happens *there*, when what we should be doing is recognising the conditions of interconnectedness and the new obligations this entails.[43]

Vivid White stages this interconnectedness by showing that Australian homeowners will not be able to barricade themselves inside their houses forever, and that what happens to the renters, to 'other' people, will eventually happen to them. It advocates, to quote Doreen Massey, for 'a global sense of the local, a global sense of place.'[44] As Smith and Howe outline, many environmentalists feel that the only way that meaningful action on climate change will be achieved is through attention to the local:

> In their darker hours, environmentalists often say that apathetic members of affluent societies will only take climate change seriously when it starts to 'hit home' – when they and their families and friends start to suffer from unmistakable, localized changes. As long as she sees it as somebody else's problem, the argument goes, the average member of the middle class will find other issues to worry about.[45]

But they then go on to outline the inverse of this narrative, describing how

> in more optimistic moments, the same environmentalists tell a different version of this story. Individuals, they say, will band together to fight climate when they feel they are fighting for home, when concrete, meaningful place – not abstract, global space – becomes the focus on their shared concern.[46]

Perfect's assumption is that for the middle class, the battleground upon which climate change is fought will be the home. It is through linking the two that *Vivid White* makes its argument most potently.

Parodying the Canon: *Vivid White* as Political Musical Satire

Vivid White makes many musical, choreographic, narrative, and stylistic allusions to other musicals, as indicated through the above reference to *Hello, Dolly!* Another obvious example is Guus itself, with the giant squid puppet recalling the Audrey II plant from *Little Shop of Horrors*. But far from benign pastiche, *Vivid White* very consciously parodies the tropes, conventions, and song forms of the musical theatre canon to make biting – and sometimes subtle – political statements about class and community. In this section, I turn my attention to the music of *Vivid White* by analysing three song parodies: 'Soft-Close Drawers,' a Weill-Brecht appropriation; 'Taking Out the Bins,' a parody of a Rodgers and Hammerstein ensemble number; and 'Here Comes the Sun,' a parody of the finale from *A Chorus Line*, 'One.' These parodies demonstrate how Perfect mobilises the conventions and iconic moments of musical theatre history for political ends.

The production deliberately and pointedly figures its audience as part of a middle-class, middlebrow milieu. Middlebrow, a term that developed in the 1920s as an 'elastic' category for cultural products, described a kind of aesthetic which 'emulated highbrow forms while attempting to make them more accessible.'[47] The middlebrow consumer is one who is 'traditional at heart yet striving to be *au courant*, a middle-class man or woman with education and social aspirations.'[48] This is precisely the class of Australians that Perfect fixes his gaze on in *Vivid White*. Intertextual references to other musicals, including parodies of well-known Broadway conventions, are a way of reinforcing the class-conflict dynamic established in the plot. It is a way of giving audiences what they are presumed to want: the hits of the canon they know and love, but with a parodic twist of the knife. Discussing the 2001 musical *Urinetown*, a work with many resonances with *Vivid White*, Anne Beggs writes that it successfully '[delivered] provocative material within a middlebrow horizon of expectations.'[49] She argues that it is remarkable in that it deliberately 'withholds the satisfaction of redemption and personal triumph, and that its narrative extends past the liberal sentiments of tolerance, freedom, and equality' common across the musical theatre canon.[50] *Vivid White*, in its stark treatment of the realities of climate change, is a similar case.

In pursuing this aim, *Vivid White*, like *Urinetown*, draws on techniques of Brechtian theatre. With Guus' opening monologue, the fourth wall is broken before it even has a chance to be erected. Without exception, all the songs are implicitly addressed to the audience: not one is sung for the benefit of another character. Many of the jokes are highly didactic, some so obvious that they may as well have been introduced with a placard.

One song, 'Men's Rights Activist,' which satirises performances of white middle-class masculinity, is extremely didactic, with deliberately blunt lead in dialogue:

Evan: We *are* men. We are *very much* men.
Ben: So much Men.
Evan: Did you know that almost HALF THE POPULATION are men?
Ben: Half men.
Evan: And yet almost 99.9% of all women are NOT men.
Ben: Not men.
Guus: That's true!
Evan: That's a scientific fact, ladies and gentlemen. And you all know who invented science . . .
Evan/Ben: Men!

The plot also concludes in Brechtian style. In describing *Urinetown*'s relationship to Brechtian theatre, Beggs argues that 'in the best tradition of [this style], the extreme failures of social, political, and economic structures are incorporated into a dramatic fable, and, ultimately, the narrative withholds resolution.'[51] Eric Bentley writes that 'Brecht saw the humaneness in human nature swamped out by inhumanity, by the cruelty of what he at first thought of the universe and later as capitalist society. The standard ending of Brecht plays is the total victory of this cruelty.'[52] In *Vivid White*, decades of stagnation and failure to address the root economic problems underpinning the inflated housing market are collapsed into a dystopian narrative that sees Australians turning against one another. Regarding the finale of *Urinetown*, Beggs writes that 'the real conclusion to the story, in Brechtian fashion, must be worked out after the performance: what happens next is up to you, the spectator.'[53] This is also true of *Vivid White:* at the conclusion of the work, with the death of the protagonists, the only thing that is clear is that the current situation is unsustainable and that something has to be done.

The number 'Soft-Close Drawers' is the most overtly Brechtian musical parody in the production.[54] The song acts a response to the scene that immediately precedes it, in which Evan broadly shows off his new soft-close drawers to an unimpressed Ben. 'Soft-Close Drawers' is a comic song about finding the sound of a drawer closing so obscene that an alternative must be invented. A patent critique of the middle class, it adopts the style established by Brecht and Weill in their works produced in 1930s Weimar German and that was then mimicked by Kander and Ebb in *Cabaret* (1966). The texture of the accompaniment and its minor tonality is characteristic of this period. The tessitura of the melody, written for a female voice, is very low, and the speech-like vocal timbre that this engenders also distinctly conveys this style.

Kim Kowalke pithily describes this sound as 'the Brechtian bark,' although it must be said that Virginia Gay's low register is of such quality that the bark in this case is much less pronounced than it could be.[55] 'Soft-Close Drawers' invokes a Brechtian-style class struggle dynamic in its dismissive characterisation of the 'wealthy': the lyrics disparagingly state that 'the wealthy are stealthy, they're quiet that's for sure.' The emphatic final lines are acerbic in their condemnation of the divide between rich and poor.

> If you hear that rattling, that skittering, that scattering
> The clinking and the clattering
> Then you are poor
> Oh, the rich will live forever with their soft-close drawers

The cruel irony is that the characters are about to find out that such modern comforts like soft-close drawers are about to bring them all undone.

At other points, Vivid *White* engages in more subtle critique of Broadway conventions. Perfect's parody of a classic Broadway ensemble number, 'Taking Out the Bins,' subverts conventions about the role of community in the musical. The Act Two opening number is, as Reuben Liverside observes, a 'Rodgers and Hammerstein-esque wheelie bin ballet' (Figure 6.2).[56] It functions, to use Scott McMillin's term, as a 'Clambake' ensemble number, meaning that it has the same function as the Act Two opening number of *Carousel* (1945), 'This Was a Real Nice Clambake.'[57] The 'Clambake' number is a form 'perfected' by Rodgers and Hammerstein, one where 'groups of fellow citizens get together and demonstrate through singing and dancing that a community spirit prevails.'[58] While McMillin describes the innovation of the 'Clambake' number as a 'defining achievement in the genre,' he also notes that many subsequent musicals of note 'have placed it under ironic examination, turned it inside out, disbelieved it.'[59] In *Vivid White*, Perfect does both. 'Taking Out the Bins' is both ironic and sincere. It also shares with 'Clambake' simple, folksy lyrics and a triple metre time signature. 'Clambake' adopts a unique vernacular in its depiction of the citizens of Maine siting around a fire contemplating the end of the clambake (a regular ritual in this part of northeast America). *Vivid White* engages in a similar type of localised vernacular in its title: 'taking out the bins' is, it seems, a uniquely Australian phrase. 'Clambake' also has a further synergy in that is depicts a postcolonial society, built on the exploitation of marine resources for the benefit of a settler community.

As Mark Steyn observes, the chorus in *Carousel* functions as 'an expression of community values. Not in a signposted, didactic sort of way, but unobtrusively.'[60] 'Taking Out the Bins' is an ironic staging of a community coming together through the weekly ritual of wheeling the rubbish bin to the curb. This rallying of the community through song around the weekly garbage

FIGURE 6.2 The cast of *Vivid White* performing 'Taking Out the Bins.'

Photo: Jeff Busby ©

collection operates in stark contrast to the divided renters-versus-owners dystopia that concluded Act One. It is an appropriately humorous Australian interpretation of the 'Clambake' number where a sense of community, rather than being found in the ritual of a wholesome communal meal, is fostered through something so mundane. Steyn describes 'Clambake' as being 'about ritual and sacrament and a secular Yankee communion.'[61] 'Taking Out the Bins' is framed as a quiet moment to stop, think, and reset: 'There is relief in routine, there is a peace in-between,' 'a pause out of doors before all the disorder begins.' The act is another 'performance of property' from which renters are excluded. In the song, it is only rate-paying homeowners who can bring their bins to the curb and experience this moment of community. Choreographically they weave in and around each other, as do the vocal lines. While they do not communicate with each other directly, the simultaneous singing of these temporarily connected neighbours portrays a sense of unity in time and space: 'It's just me and my bin,' they all sing in unison. The removal of waste is used as a cleansing metaphor: the garbage man 'takes all your waste and he weighs your mistakes.' We will soon learn that much bigger, broader mistakes have been made.

The finale rejects the (ironic) sense of community established in 'Taking Out the Bins.' It appropriates the trademark gold costumes and glittering top hats of 'One,' the famous finale of *A Chorus Line*. In *Vivid White*, as the actors take their bows, the piano vamps some music that, at first, is almost identical to that of 'One.' It then gradually develops this basic motif, modulating to different keys and eventually segueing into the second half of the song, 'Here Comes the Sun.' Andrew Hallsworth's choreography is highly reminiscent of Michael Bennett's iconic steps: moving the gold hats up and down, forward and back; sharp turns that traverse diagonally across the stage; and the step-touch pattern with the popped knee that is so identifiable. The formation of the performers in evenly spaced lines is also mimicked in *Vivid White*. Additionally, *A Chorus Line* is a concept-musical that celebrates the stories and lives of the dancers whose job it is to be inconspicuous, identical members of a dance chorus. 'One' celebrates the singularity, the uniqueness of each of these dancers; 'Precious Little Snowflake' ironically subverts this in its send-off of the human race, thereby recasting this celebrated musical theatre moment in dystopic light.

Changing Hearts and Minds: The Value of Satire

Vivid White's parodic musical numbers are part of the work's broader aim, which is to question the effectiveness of satire as an agent of political change. Satire is not just the mode in which *Vivid White* has been created, but it also has an important narrative function. Dialogues about the nature of satire occur both in the intra-scenic dialogue between characters and in direct address to the audience. The primary vehicle for this is through the narrative sub-plot about Evan and Ben's musical comedy act. In doing so, the production assesses its own efficacy as a piece of satire, staging Perfect's anxieties about whether it can have a material impact on hearts and minds.

This metatheatrical consideration of the efficacy of satire is conveyed through Evan and Ben's professions. The protagonists, Evan and Ben, are musicians, who, along with Liz, their accompanist, formed the satirical comedy act known as Random Axe of Kindness. Ben and Evan are constructed as opposites: one the ideological and impassioned failing artist; the other the commercially successful sell-out. In a flashback scene in Act Two, we witness how he break-up of Random Axe of Kindness was due to artistic differences about the effectiveness of satire. They have just claimed the trophy for Best Comedy Act at the Edinburgh Fringe Festival, when Evan introduces Ben and Liz to Cynthia. Not yet his girlfriend, she has attended the festival as part of her job in production management. Ben, the principled artist reluctant to sell out, rudely dismisses her suggestions for their act outright:

Cynthia: Hey, Ben? Some advice. The audience love Evan. Random Axe works because of him. Do you want to know why? The satire is bitter, but cuts through because he likes them. I don't think you like your audience and it reads.

Ben: Of course I don't. What the fuck do you think we do? We literally tell people things they don't want to hear.

After this, Ben and Evan have an argument that results in the breakup of their act. Ben, however, still clings on to the hope that there can be a professional reconciliation. Throughout *Vivid White* he is trying to convince Evan that they should get the act back together. Early in the piece, when Ben is invited to meet Evan at his office, Ben naively thinks it might be to pick up where they left off. Evan's intention is entirely different; it is to inform Ben that he and Cynthia will try to outbid them at the auction. To add insult to injury, Evan then proceeds to wound Ben's pride, belittling his continued faith in satire as a practice:

Evan: You're still doing the satirical thing, right? You know you'll never rake it in with satire, mate. People don't understand it.

Ben: You don't give people enough credit. They understand it.

Evan: No, they don't. They spend all night thinking you're tearing strips off someone else.

Ben: They might not get it right away, but satire takes time to gestate. You plant the seed and it grows . . . down the line . . . at home.

Evan: And then what?

Ben: And then what? It fundamentally changes their personal perspective. For the better.

Evan: We're still talking about *human beings*, right? *Audiences?*

Ben: You don't think human beings are capable of change?

Evan: Oh my God, Benno. You still believe satire can change the world? That's adorable.

Ben maintains this faith in satire until the bitter end. When he and Liz arrive at Cynthia and Evan's newly renovated house, they try to convince the other couple to join them in their plight to bring meaning to the lives of renters like themselves: 'Once upon a time, you and I believed in satire,' Ben implores, 'We are asking you to believe again.' He then launches into 'One Satirical Song,' a folk-rock ballad that espouses the virtues of such music:

> One sweet refrain for ending pain and righting ev'ry wrong
> Some witty rhyming couplets and the tyrant's on his knees
> Sing vocal social justice and the whole world will be free
> A tune to hear the wounded make 'em strong
> All it takes is one, one, one, one, one satirical song

By halfway through, despite his wife's obvious disdain (Cynthia struts around in the background as they sing, deliberately ignoring the performance) Evan bursts into song, joining Liz and Ben:

> With citizens divided they'll destroy us one by one
> But our satire will unite us if we sing it they will come
> And soon ev'ry broken heart will sing along

At the conclusion of the song, Cynthia gets in the way yet again, demanding that Liz and Ben leave. Following this, a series of violent events distracts the protagonists – two minor characters are killed – and then Guus appears. Cynthia is the first of the four to be murdered by Guus, and it is only after her death that Ben's desire can finally come to fruition. In the throes of imminent death, Evan capitulates, crying 'Now we'll never get to do that reunion tour.' This piques Guus' interest, and they demand to see some of this supposed 'award-winning satire.' Random Axe of Kindness sing one of their hit songs and, upon its conclusion, exhilarated from the performance, the three remaining protagonists embrace. 'We're going on tour,' Ben exclaims, 'And this time, we're going to save the human race!' to which Evan responds, 'I'm sorry I doubted you. Satire *can* change the world.' But the euphoria of this moment is quickly undercut. While they are rejoicing, Guus has snuck up behind them, ensnaring each character with one of its tentacles. As they choke to death, Guus scornfully says, 'Did you really think *satire* would change anything? Satire can't *hurt* me. Satire is confusing to the audience and only makes me stronger!'

The scene and song recounted here functions as a metacommentary on *Vivid White*'s own efficacy as a piece of satire. It dramatises Perfect's own consternations about the potential impotence of the form, expressed in the program note, where he wrote that

> What is satire but the art of making the middle class (of which I am a card-carrying member) feel bad about themselves in a manner entertaining enough to avoid been lynched when the curtain comes down? What is satire but the promise of a better way to exist? A more compassionate way to act? Satire is form of exposure therapy; it confronts us with the worst of ourselves in order to inspire change. But can satire change us? If we are unable or unwilling to change, has satire *failed*? Since the world we inhabit is objectively unhinged, can we expect satire to really work anymore? Did it *ever*?[62]

The question of whether satire is an effective agent of political change is one that has been much debated. As Dustin Griffin writes, satire 'comes in so many different forms . . . and often seems a "mode" or a "procedure" rather than a single "genre."'[63] He argues that this fact makes satire a form that is 'problematic, open-ended, essayistic, ambiguous in its relationship to history, uncertain in its political effect, resistant to formal closure, more inclined to ask questions than to provide answers, and ambivalent about the pleasures it offers.'[64] This open-endedness means that is not uncommon, as Robert Phiddian notes, for 'people with competent contextual knowledge' to arrive at 'quite contradictory interpretations' of the same satiric text.[65] As a result, it is more prudent to acknowledge that the 'actual effects of satire [are] often limited or hit-and-miss, often counterproductive, seldom directly successful, sometimes little more than a consolation for the defeated or merely grumpy.'[66] This 'hit-and-miss' quality explains why the reviewers quoted at the outset struggled to see how Perfect was using satire to assess his own intervention into the climate debate.

Despite his reservations, Perfect retains an optimistic view of the role of satire. The programme note concludes with his assertion that 'the belief that we can change the world, even just a bit,' is at the core of satirical work. 'I'm an optimist,' he writes, 'I don't think I'd bother with satire otherwise,' reflecting Ruben Quintero's assertion that it is requisite for the satirist to be a 'true believer, a practicing humanitarian.'[67] This optimism notwithstanding, Perfect places the power for change firmly in the audience's hands. In the programme note, he comments:

> Unlike any other theatrical form, audiences are left at the conclusion of a satirical work thinking 'Yes, but what is it all *for*? How are we supposed to *live*?' That's a terrific question. When you find the answer, be a dear and let the rest of us know, will you?[68]

Quintero observes that the satirist bears no such obligation to solve the problem that they expose. He states that the satirist is like the watchdog, and after all, 'no one expects a watchdog to do the double duty of alarming others that the barn is on fire and of putting out the blaze'; rather, what satirists do is 'rouse *us* to put out the fire.'[69] Perfect's satirist is one who sounds the alarm. *Vivid White* does not pretend to have the answers or solutions to the wicked problem of climate change. Its brand of satire tries to force a conversation, to spur an audience to action, even in some local way.

Conclusion: The Australian Nightmare

Vivid White ends with the Australian colonial dream of property ownership in tatters. It leaves its audience shell-shocked. The ontological security of home, so carefully established in the early part of the musical, has been destroyed on a local, national, and global level. Liz and Ben lose a home at the auction, Evan and Cynthia have their house invaded by Guus, and they all lose their lives, as do (presumably) all the other Australians homeowners. By the conclusion of the narrative, humanity as a whole has ceded its home to the squids. By constructing the loss of home as simultaneously local and global, Perfect illuminates how profound a disruption climate change will wreak on the national imaginary. *Vivid White* uses the local as a strategy with which to emphasise the immediacy and materiality of the current climate, hoping that through humour, music, and satire, change is possible.

While interpreted as farraginous by some critics, *Vivid White*'s sprawling nature in fact offers an ideal vantage to survey the ruins of the national imaginary. So many of the questions and concerns raised in previous chapters are also explored in this musical. We can see *Muriel*'s concern with 'what is our place in the world?'; *Shane Warne*'s focus on masculinity and cultural norms; a deep interrogation of 'where we are,' like in *Songs from the Middle*; and an acute awareness of the burden of living in a settler-colony, as in *The Rabbits* and *Barbara and the Camp Dogs*. In this sense, it is the perfect place to end this book's enquiry into the multivalent national imaginaries of Australian musical theatre.

Notes

1 Fiona Allon, *Renovation Nation* (University of New South Wales Press, 2008), 1.
2 Denise Varney, 'Perfect Unhappiness: Globalisation in the Suburbs,' in *The Local Meets the Global in Performance*, ed. Pirkko Koski and Melissa Sihra (Cambridge Scholars Publishing, 2010), 112.
3 Una Chaudhuri, 'Climate Lens: Birth of a Post-Nation!,' *Howlround Theatre Commons,* April 21, 2017, accessed February 28, 2025, https://howlround.com/climate-lens.
4 Nancy Tuana, 'Climate Change and Place: Delimiting Cosmopolitanism,' in *Cosmopolitanism and Place*, ed. Jessica Wahlman, Jose M. Medina and John J. Stuhr (Indiana University Press, 2017), 187.
5 Nicholas Blomley, 'Performing Property: Making the World,' *Canadian Journal of Law and Jurisprudence* 26, no. 1 (2013): 25, https://doi.org/10.1017/S0841820900005944.
6 Anne Beggs, '"For Urinetown Is Your Town . . .": The Fringes of Broadway,' *Theatre Journal* 62, no. 1 (2010): 51, https://www.jstor.org/stable/40587441.
7 Jo Litson, 'Catch Verity Hunt-Ballard in a Perfect Show,' *Limelight,* November 19, 2017, https://www.limelightmagazine.com.au/features/catch-verity-hunt-ballard-perfect-show/.
8 Annabel Crabb's 2018 article argued that there had been seven such casualties of the climate change debate to that point. Annabel Crabb, 'Recent Climate Change Policy: A Brief History of Seven Killings,' *ABC News,* August 23, 2018, accessed September 26, 2018, http://www.abc.net.au/news/2018-08- 23/climate-change-policy-a-brief-history-of-seven-killings/10152616.
9 Cameron Woodhead, '*Vivid White* Review: Satirical Musical Fails to Gel,' *The Sydney Morning Herald,* November 23, 2017, https://www.smh.com.au/entertainment/vivid-white-review-satirical-musical-fails-to-gel-20171123-gzrpsn.html. In a wrap-up of a year of theatre performances in Melbourne, Woodhead panned the show, writing that 'Eddie Perfect's musical *Vivid White* was a travesty, clearly not stage-worthy despite a talented cast.' Cameron Woodhead, 'The Stage's Rainbow Connection,' *The Age,* January 3, 2018, 24.
10 Kate Herbert, 'Eddie Perfect's *Vivid White* is Clever but Could Develop Further,' *The Herald-Sun,* November 27, 2017, http://www.heraldsun.com.au/lifestyle/melbourne/eddie-perfects-vivid-white-is-clever-but-could-develop-further/news-story/7bc0b47daf304a2586d896a0d6eaf1dc.
11 Tim Byrne, '*Vivid White*,' *Timeout,* accessed February 28, 2025, https://www.timeout.com/melbourne/theatre/vivid-white. For an additional negative review, see Chris Boyd, 'Eddie Perfect's *Vivid White* is Less Than Ideal Look at Near Future,' *The Australian,* November 26, 2017, https://www.theaustralian.com.au/

arts/stage/eddie-perfects-vivid-white-is-less-than-ideal-look-at-near-future/news
story/812cab5b05cc9c30b1af7eda880c0e2c.

12 Robert Phiddian, 'Satire and the Limits of Literary Theories,' *Critical Quarterly* 55, no. 3 (2013): 50, https://doi-org.ezproxy.uow.edu.au/10.1111/criq.12057. Phiddian argues that this term is preferable to either intention or frame of mind.

13 Eddie Perfect, 'Walking the Line,' *Vivid White,* theatre programme, 2017, accessed February 28, 2025 http://www.mtc.com.au/backstage/2017/11/ programme-vivid-white/.

14 Robin Boyd, 'Preface,' *Australia's Home* (Melbourne University Press, 1961).

15 Richard Ronald, *The Ideology of Home Ownership: Homeowner Societies and the Role of Housing* (Palgrave Macmillan, 2008), 152–153.

16 Allon, *Renovation Nation*, 3.

17 Shelley Mallett observes that in the terms 'house' and 'home' are regularly conflated, noting that this is particularly so in popular media, but that they are in fact quite distinct concepts. Shelley Mallett, 'Understanding Home: A Critical Review of the Literature,' *The Sociological Review* 52, no. 1 (2004): 62–89, https://doi-org. ezproxy.uow.edu.au/10.1111/j.1467-954X.2004.00442.x. I suggest that *Vivid White* similarly conflates the terms in this way; that they are used interchangeably. In this song, it may be for very practical reasons: 'A House Is More' is a superior lyric than a 'home is more.' Additionally, using house but meaning home allows for a heightened awareness of the materialistic qualities of homemaking.

18 Carole Després, 'The Meaning of Home: Literature Review and Directions for Future Research and Theoretical Development,' *Journal of Architecture and Planning Research* 8, no. 2 (1991): 98–99, https://www.jstor.org/stable/ 43029026.

19 Ronald, *The Ideology of Home Ownership*, 50.

20 Louise Crabtree, 'Unbounding Home Ownership in Australia,' in *Housing and Home Unbound: Intersections in Economics, Environment and Politics in Australia,* ed. Nicole Cook, Aidan Davison and Louise Crabtree (Routledge, 2016), 174.

21 Crabtree, 'Unbounding Home Ownership,' 174; Susan Smith, 'Owner Occupation: At Home in a Spatial, Financial Paradox,' *International Journal of Housing Policy* 15, no. 1 (2015): 62, https://doi.org/10.1080/14616718.2014.997432.

22 Lynda Cheshire, Peter Walters and Ted Rosenblatt, 'The Politics of Housing Consumption: Renters as Flawed Consumers on a Master Planned Estate,' *Urban Studies* 47, no. 12 (2010): 2602, https://doi-org.ezproxy.uow.edu.au/ 10.1177/0042098009359028.

23 Jennifer Rutherford, *The Gauche Intruder: Freud, Lacan, and the White Australian Fantasy* (Melbourne University Press, 2000), 7.

24 Rutherford, *The Gauche Intruder*, 7.

25 Aidan Davison, 'Secure in the Privacy of Your Own Nature: Political Ontology, Urban Nature and Home Ownership in Australia,' in *Housing and Home Unbound: Intersections in Economics, Environment and Politics in Australia,* ed. Nicole Cook, Aidan Davison and Louise Crabtree (Routledge, 2016), 106.

26 Blomley, 'Performing Property,' 25.

27 Davison, 'Secure in the Privacy,' 104.

28 Allon discusses *The Block* in Chapter 2 of *Renovation Nation*. See also Buck Clifford Rosenberg, 'Property and Home-Makeover Television: Risk, Thrift and Taste,' *Continuum: Journal of Media and Cultural Studies* 22, no. 4 (2008), 505–513, https://doi.org/10.1080/10304310802189980.

29 Barbara Santich, *Bold Palates: Australia's Gastronomic Heritage* (Wakefield Press, 2012), 146.

30 Hazel Easthope, 'Making a Rental Property Home,' *Housing Studies* 29, no. 5 (2014): 579–596, https://doi.org/10.1080/02673037.2013.873115.

31 Allon, *Renovation Nation*, 13.

32 Allon, *Renovation Nation*, 37.

33 John Daley and Brendan Coates, 'Housing Affordability: Re-Imagining the Australian Dream,' *The Grattan Institute*, March 4, 2018, accessed February 28, 2025, https://grattan.edu.au/report/housing-affordability-re-imagining-the-australian-dream/, 3.

34 Gillian Terzis, 'The Impossible Dream?,' *Meanjin* 73, no. 3 (2014): 32–41.

35 Smith, 'Owner Occupation,' 62.

36 This puppet was designed by Joe Blanck from the Melbourne company A Blanck Canvas. melbtheatreco, 'Vivid White | Meet Guus,' *YouTube*, December 20, 2017, accessed March 3, 2025, https://www.youtube.com/watch?v=bx1L2gxAedA.

37 Alexander Arkhipkin, 'Octopus and Squid Populations are Booming – Here's Why,' *The Conversation*, May 25, 2016, https://theconversation.com/octopus-and-squid-populations-are-booming-heres-why–59830.

38 Suvendrini Perera, *Australia and the Insular Imagination: Beaches, Borders, Boats, and Bodies* (Palgrave Macmillan, 2009), 4.

39 Perera, *Australia and the Insular Imagination*, 10; Allon, *Renovation Nation*, 13.

40 Davison, 'Secure in the privacy,' 109–110.

41 Smith, 'Owner occupation,' 66–67.

42 Judith Yates and Bruce Bradbury, 'Home ownership as a (crumbling) fourth pillar of social insurance in Australia,' *Journal of Housing and the Built Environment* 25, no. 2 (2010), 193–211, https://doi-org.ezproxy.uow.edu.au/10.1007/s10901-010-9187-4; Allon, *Renovation Nation*, 2.

43 Allon, *Renovation Nation*, 15, original emphasis.

44 Doreen Massey, *Space, Place, and Gender* (University of Minnesota Press, 1994), 156.

45 Philip Smith and Nicholas Howe, *Climate Change as Social Drama: Global Warming in the Public Sphere* (Cambridge University Press, 2015), 166–167.

46 Smith and Howe, *Climate Change*, 167.

47 David Savran, 'Class and Culture,' in *The Oxford Handbook of the American Musical*, ed. Raymond Knapp, Mitchell Morris and Stacy Wolf (Oxford University Press, 2011), 242.

48 Savran, 'Class and Culture,' 242.

49 Beggs, '"For Urinetown Is Your Town . . .": 51.

50 Beggs, '"For Urinetown Is Your Town",' 43.

51 Beggs, '"For Urinetown Is Your Town",' 43.

52 Eric Bentley, *Bentley on Brecht*, 3rd edn (Northwestern University Press, 2008), 85.

53 Beggs, '"For Urinetown Is Your Town",' 44.

54 'Soft-Close Drawers' is the only song from the production available on YouTube. melbtheatreco, 'Soft-Close Drawers | *Vivid White*,' *YouTube*, November 16, 2017, accessed March 3, 2025, https://www.youtube.com/watch?v=Gm6AU-jmJIE.

55 Kim Kowalke, 'Brecht and Music: Theory and Practice,' in *The Cambridge Companion to Brecht*, ed. Peter Thomson and Glendyr Sacks (Cambridge University Press, 1994), 231.

56 Reuben Liverside, 'Vivid White,' *ArtsHub*, November 27, 2017, accessed March 3, 2025, https://performing.artshub.com.au/news-article/reviews/performing-arts/reuben-liversidge/vivid-white–254845. A parallel intertextual reference can also be read into 'Taking Out the Bins.' It is a quintet, scored for three men and two women, which is remarkably like the makeup of the *Night Music* quintet (or Liebeslieders, as they are commonly known) – three women and two men – of Stephen Sondheim's *A Little Night Music*. Act Two of *A Little Night Music* begins with a piece for the quintet entitled 'Night Waltz I (The Sun Won't Set)' in which the singers obliquely converse with one another about the liminal qualities of dusk. 'Taking Out the Bins' is also set at dusk but depicts a much more ironic liminal space.

57 Scott McMillin, *The Musical as Drama* (Princeton University Press, 2006), 81. This technique of borrowing not only the style and structure of the song, but also placing the parody in the same position, also occurs in *Urinetown*. Beggs identifies *Urinetown's* 'Run, Freedom, Run!' and its parallel, 'Sit Down You're Rockin' the Boat' from *Guys and Dolls* as one example. Beggs, '"For Urinetown is your town"', 45.

58 McMillin, *The Musical as Drama*, 81. For consideration of the role of community in Rodgers and Hammerstein musicals see Kati Donovan, 'No One Walks Alone: An Investigation of the Veteran and the Community in Rodgers and Hammerstein's *Carousel*,' *Studies in Musical Theatre* 5, no. 3 (2012): 287–295, https://doi.org/10.1386/smt.5.3.287_1. Derek Miller, 'Underneath the Ground: Jud and the Community in *Oklahoma!*' *Studies in Musical Theatre* 2, no. 2 (2008): 163–174, https://doi.org/10.1386/smt.2.2.163_1; Andrea Most, '"We Know We Belong to the Land": The Theatricality of Assimilation in Rodgers and Hammerstein's *Oklahoma!*,' *PMLA* 113, no. 1 (1998): 77–89, https://doi.org/10.2307/463410; Katie Welsh and Stacy Wolf, 'Interrogating America's National Myth Onstage: Case Studies on the Individual and the Community in U.S. Musical Theatre,' in *The Routledge Companion to Musical Theatre*, ed. Laura MacDonald and Ryan Donovan (Routledge, 2022).

59 McMillin, *The Musical as Drama*, 82.

60 Mark Steyn, *Broadway Babies Say Goodnight* (Faber and Faber, 1997), 97.

61 Steyn, *Broadway Babies*, 97.

62 Perfect, 'Walking the Line,' original emphasis.

63 Dustin Griffin, *Satire: A Critical Reintroduction* (University of Kentucky Press, 1994), 4.

64 Griffin, *Satire*, 5.

65 Phiddian, 'Satire and the Limits of Literary Theories,' 48.

66 Phiddian, 'Satire and the Limits of Literary Theories,' 53.

67 Ruben Quintero, *A Companion to Satire: Ancient and Modern* (Blackwell Publishing, 2007), 3.

68 Perfect, 'Walking the Line,' original emphasis.

69 Quintero, 'Introduction: Understanding Satire,' 4, my emphasis.

References

Allon, Fiona. *Renovation Nation*. University of New South Wales Press, 2008.

Arkhipkin, Alexander. 'Octopus and Squid Populations are Booming – Here's Why.' *The Conversation*, May 25, 2016. https://theconversation.com/octopus-and-squid-populations-are-booming-heres-why–59830.

Beggs, Anne. '"For Urinetown Is Your Town . . .": The Fringes of Broadway.' *Theatre Journal* 62, no. 1 (2010): 41–56. https://www.jstor.org/stable/40587441.

Bentley, Eric. *Bentley on Brecht*, 3rd edition. Northwestern University Press, 2008.

Blomley, Nicholas. 'Performing Property: Making the World.' *Canadian Journal of Law and Jurisprudence* 26, no. 1 (2013): 23–48. https://doi.org/10.1017/S0841820900005944.

Boyd, Chris. 'Eddie Perfect's *Vivid White* is Less Than Ideal Look at Near Future.' *The Australian*, November 26, 2017. https://www.theaustralian.com.au/arts/stage/eddie-perfects-vivid-white-is-less-than-ideal-look-at-near-future/newsstory/812cab5b05cc9c30b1af7eda880c0e2c.

Boyd, Robin. *Australia's Home*. Melbourne University Press, 1961.

Byrne, Tim. '*Vivid White*.' *Timeout*. Accessed February 28, 2025. https://www.timeout.com/melbourne/theatre/vivid-white.

Chaudhuri, Una. 'Climate Lens: Birth of a Post-Nation!,' *Howlround Theatre Commons*, April 21, 2017. Accessed February 28, 2025. https://howlround.com/climate-lens.

Cheshire, Lynda, Peter Walters, and Ted Rosenblatt. 'The Politics of Housing Consumption: Renters as Flawed Consumers on a Master Planned Estate.' *Urban Studies* 47, no. 12 (2010): 2597–2614. https://doi.org.ezproxy.uow.edu.au/10.1177/0042098009359028.

Clifford Rosenberg, Buck. 'Property and Home-Makeover Television: Risk, Thrift and Taste.' *Continuum: Journal of Media and Cultural Studies* 22, no. 4 (2008): 505–513. https://doi.org/10.1080/10304310802189980.

Cook, Nicole, Aidan Davison, and Louise Crabtree, eds. *Housing and Home Unbound: Intersections in Economics, Environment and Politics in Australia*. Routledge, 2016.

Crabb, Annabel. 'Recent Climate Change Policy: A Brief History of Seven Killings.' *ABC News*, August 23, 2018. Accessed September 26, 2018. http://www.abc.net.au/news/2018-08-23/climate-change-policy-a-brief-history-of-seven-killings/10152616.

Daley, John, and Brendan Coates. 'Housing Affordability: Re-Imagining the Australian Dream.' *The Grattan Institute*, March 4, 2018. Accessed February 28, 2025. https://grattan.edu.au/report/housing-affordability-re-imagining-the-australian-dream/.

Després, Carole. 'The Meaning of Home: Literature Review and Directions for Future Research and Theoretical Development.' *Journal of Architecture and Planning Research* 8, no. 2 (1991): 96–115. https://www.jstor.org/stable/43029026.

Donovan, Kati. 'No One Walks Alone: An Investigation of the Veteran and the Community in Rodgers and Hammerstein's *Carousel.' Studies in Musical Theatre* 5, no. 3 (2012): 287–295. https://doi.org/10.1386/smt.5.3.287_1.

Easthope, Hazel. 'Making a Rental Property Home.' *Housing Studies* 29, no. 5 (2014): 579–596. https://doi.org/10.1080/02673037.2013.873115.

Griffin, Dustin. *Satire: A Critical Reintroduction*. University of Kentucky Press, 1994.

Herbert, Kate. 'Eddie Perfect's *Vivid White* is Clever but Could Develop Further.' *The Herald-Sun*, November 27, 2017. http://www.heraldsun.com.au/lifestyle/melbourne/eddie-perfects-vivid-white-is-clever-but-could-develop-further/news-story/7bc0b47daf304a2586d896a0d6eaf1dc.

Kowalke, Kim. 'Brecht and Music: Theory and Practice.' In *The Cambridge Companion to Brecht*, edited by Peter Thomson and Glendyr Sacks. Cambridge University Press, 1994.

Litson, Jo. 'Catch Verity Hunt-Ballard in a Perfect Show.' *Limelight*, November 19, 2017. https://www.limelightmagazine.com.au/features/catch-verity-hunt-ballard-perfect-show/.

Liverside, Reuben. '*Vivid White.' ArtsHub*, November 27, 2017. Accessed March 3, 2025. https://performing.artshub.com.au/news-article/reviews/performing-arts/reuben-liversidge/vivid-white–254845.

Mallett, Shelley. 'Understanding Home: A Critical Review of the Literature.' *The Sociological Review* 52, no. 1 (2004): 62–89. https://doi.org.ezproxy.uow.edu.au/10.1111/j.1467-954X.2004.00442.x.

Massey, Doreen. *Space, Place, and Gender*. University of Minnesota Press, 1994.

McMillin, Scott. *The Musical as Drama*. Princeton University Press, 2006.

melbtheatreco. 'Soft-Close Drawers | *Vivid White.' YouTube*, November 16, 2017. Accessed March 3, 2025. https://www.youtube.com/watch?v=Gm6AU-jmJIE.

melbtheatreco. 'Vivid White | Meet Guus.' *YouTube*, December 20, 2017. Accessed March 3, 2025. https://www.youtube.com/watch?v=bx1L2gxAedA.

Miller, Derek. 'Underneath the Ground: Jud and the Community in *Oklahoma!' Studies in Musical Theatre* 2, no. 2 (2008): 163–174. https://doi.org/10.1386/smt.2.2.163_1.

Most, Andrea. '"We Know We Belong to the Land": The Theatricality of Assimilation in Rodgers and Hammerstein's Oklahoma!' *PMLA* 113, no. 1 (1998): 77–89. https://doi.org/10.2307/463410.

Perera, Suvendrini. *Australia and the Insular Imagination: Beaches, Borders, Boats, and Bodies*. Palgrave Macmillan, 2009.

Perfect, Eddie. 'Walking the Line.' *Vivid White*, theatre programme, 2017. Accessed February 28, 2025. http://www.mtc.com.au/backstage/2017/11/programme-vivid-white/.

Phiddian, Robert. 'Satire and the Limits of Literary Theories.' *Critical Quarterly* 55, no. 3 (2013): 44–58. https://doi.org.ezproxy.uow.edu.au/10.1111/criq.12057.

Quintero, Ruben, ed. *A Companion to Satire: Ancient and Modern*. Blackwell Publishing, 2007.

Ronald, Richard. *The Ideology of Home Ownership: Homeowner Societies and the Role of Housing*. Palgrave Macmillan, 2008.

Rutherford, Jennifer. *The Gauche Intruder: Freud, Lacan, and the White Australian Fantasy*. Melbourne University Press, 2000.

Santich, Barbara. *Bold Palates: Australia's Gastronomic Heritage*. Wakefield Press, 2012.

Savran, David. 'Class and Culture.' In *The Oxford Handbook of the American Musical*, edited by Raymond Knapp, Mitchell Morris and Stacy Wolf. Oxford University Press, 2011.

Smith, Philip, and Nicholas Howe. *Climate Change as Social Drama: Global Warming in the Public Sphere*. Cambridge University Press, 2015.

Smith, Susan. 'Owner Occupation: At Home in a Spatial, Financial Parado.' *International Journal of Housing Policy* 15, no. 1 (2015): 61–83. https://doi.org/10.1080/14616718.2014.997432.

Steyn, Mark. *Broadway Babies Say Goodnight*. Faber and Faber, 1997.

Terzis, Gillian. 'The Impossible Dream?' *Meanjin* 73, no. 3 (2014): 32–41.

Tuana, Nancy. 'Climate Change and Place: Delimiting Cosmopolitanism.' In *Cosmopolitanism and Place*, edited by Jessica Wahlman, Jose M. Medina and John J. Stuhr. Indiana University Press, 2017.

Varney, Denise. 'Perfect Unhappiness: Globalisation in the Suburbs.' In *The Local Meets the Global in Performance*, edited by Pirkko Koski and Melissa Sihra. Cambridge Scholars Publishing, 2010.

Welsh, Katie, and Stacy Wolf. 'Interrogating America's National Myth Onstage: Case Studies on the Individual and the Community in U.S. Musical Theatre.' In *The Routledge Companion to Musical Theatre*, edited by Laura MacDonald and Ryan Donovan. Routledge, 2022.

Woodhead, Cameron. '*Vivid White* Review: Satirical Musical Fails to Gel.' *The Sydney Morning Herald*, November 23, 2017. https://www.smh.com.au/entertainment/vivid-white-review-satirical-musical-fails-to-gel-20171123-gzrpsn.html.

Woodhead, Cameron. 'The Stage's Rainbow Connection.' *The Age*, January 3, 2018, 24.

Yates, Judith, and Bruce Bradbury. 'Home Ownership as a (Crumbling) Fourth Pillar of Social Insurance in Australia.' *Journal of Housing and the Built Environment* 25, no. 2 (2010), 193–211. https://doi.org.ezproxy.uow.edu.au/10.1007/s10901-010-9187-4.

CONCLUSION

The Australian Musical Arrives

In this book, I have argued that Australian musical theatre produces and reproduces a repertory of themes, tropes, characters, places, stories, fixations, and myths that form a national imaginary for Australia. I have articulated the connections between musical theatre and the nation and, in doing so, have positioned Australian musical theatre as a vibrant, affective, and thoughtful site for the production and reproduction of national imaginaries. Cumulatively, the analysis of each musical makes a strong case against the rhetoric of crisis that has plagued discussion of Australian musical theatre. This has been demonstrated by the formal breadth and thematic depth of these musicals: how they paint with a diverse musical palette with musical theatre, opera, rock, and pop all variously representing the 'sound' of Australia, and how they take a variety of forms, from large-scale productions to small, intimate works. The method that has supported these findings – both careful attention to the dramaturgy and the points of connection drawn from research in sociology, cultural studies, geography, history, politics, and so on – has revealed that, far from frivolous forms of commercial entertainment, Australian musicals are sophisticated renderings of the national imaginary that parallel research and findings identified in these other fields. The book has shown that musicals and the national imaginary are deeply embedded within Australian culture, not set apart from it. Ultimately, in showing how these musicals engage with the questions most central to the national imaginary – who we are and where we are, where we have come from and where we are going – I have foregrounded how Australian musicals engage with the nation in exciting, arresting, confronting, and playful ways.

The musicals considered have expanded and transformed the repertory of the national imaginary. The book has drawn out recurrent and neuralgic points

DOI: 10.4324/9781003590088-8

in the national imaginary, such as the wounds of colonisation (*The Rabbits, Barbara, Vivid White*), national approaches to humour (*Shane Warne, Barbara, Vivid White*), the role of landscapes, cities, and suburbs (*Muriel's Wedding, Songs from the Middle, Vivid White*), and meta-discourses concerning the place of art in Australian society and culture (*Shane Warne, The Rabbits, Vivid White*). It has also accounted for the affective impact of each musical.

Muriel's Wedding represents an attempt to grapple with Australia's place in the world. By contextualising the work as a transnational, 'Broadway-style' musical, I demonstrated how it appeals to both an actual domestic and a prospective international audience, simultaneously representing and advertising Australia. *Muriel's Wedding* binds the national citizenry together by asking us to barrack for 'our' Muriel as she prepares to represent us abroad. We watch in anticipation from afar, wishing and wanting her to succeed. *Muriel* takes recurrent anxieties about Australia's place in the world and transforms them by representing a modern, outward-looking nation, open for business and ready to participate on the world stage. The fact that in 2025 she made it to the UK is the icing on the cake.

Shane Warne approaches this anxiety about 'who we are' from a different angle, using the life of the late cricketer as a mechanism by which to look inward. The musical interrogates the interplay between nation, sport, and masculinity in the national imaginary. I argued that by aestheticising the moment that Warne bowled the 'ball of the century,' Perfect rejects the crude binary between art and sport in Australian culture. In *Shane Warne*, art and sport meet in the middle in its response to the question of 'who we are.' By the end, the musical manages the feat of binding the national citizenry closer together: the sport lovers and the artistic types, the intellectuals, and the working class, even Warne himself, are all brought together in the theatre. In asking us to take the repertory of the national imaginary – battlers and underdogs, cricket players and 'taking the piss' – seriously, the musical instils a sense of pride, and the belief that the national imaginary is worth celebrating. We're not perfect, but we're ok.

Songs from the Middle moves us further inward still. By foregrounding the affective dimensions of the iconic Australian landscapes of suburbia and the beach, the cycle demonstrates the mythic role of these sites in the national imaginary. Equally, it explores their status as everyday places where ordinary people live out their lives. While *Shane Warne* centres on a national celebrity, in *Songs from the Middle* the focus is on the ordinary Australian, those people sitting beside you in the auditorium. In *Muriel* the beach is iconised, represented stereotypically through the tourist gaze, while in *Songs from the Middle* it is not described but experienced. The cycle is about what it feels like to live in contemporary Australia: not in the mythologised rural past or the exciting cosmopolitan city, but in the banality and ordinariness of beachside suburbia. It dispels anxieties about our place in the world altogether, saying:

this is where we live, and this is how it makes us feel, how these landscapes shape the lives of the national citizenry.

In my discussion of *The Rabbits*, I articulated how, through a utopian performance of reconciliation and apology, the theatre becomes a place in which a national citizenry can gather to have their faith in the nation restored. Its anthropomorphic allegory allows it to tread lightly, with the Bird guiding the national citizenry, supporting them and addressing their concerns. But it also actively reopens the wounds of colonisation in order to heal them, positing that there can and will be a better future together.

Barbara and the Camp Dogs offers a counterpoint to this version of the national imaginary, painting a portrait of a nation struggling to manage the ongoing effects of colonisation. *Barbara* urges us to listen from the heart to Indigenous perspectives on colonisation. In making the voices and stories of Indigenous Australians central, it transforms the national imaginary. Unlike in *The Rabbits*, in *Barbara* there is no Bird to guide, mediate, translate, and support us. *Barbara* is testimony, truth-telling in the here and now. Ultimately, it represents a nation that is moving imperfectly, incrementally towards repairing its relationship with First Nations people.

These five musicals all ended with some sense of hope and optimism. *Vivid White* is the outlier. By its conclusion, the Australian dream of property ownership is in tatters. In *Muriel, Shane Warne*, and *Songs from the Middle*, the repertory of the national imaginary is celebrated. *The Rabbits* and *Barbara* both depict a reconciled national imaginary, one in which colonial violence can be repaired. *Vivid White* does not hold out such hope. The climate catastrophe is coming, and the production asks us: What are we going to do about it? Despite its big musical theatre finale, the national citizenry is left fractured, rather than bound together. Underlying this, though, is the sense that the idea of the nation is worth saving – but it is not going to be easy, and we are going to have to work together.

In the introduction, I positioned this study's aim as being to reframe the discourse surrounding the Australian musical. However, the book has also borne witness to, and documented, the profound transformation that the Australian musical has undergone this century. Since I commenced this research, the discourse has genuinely shifted, so much so that I would argue that the Australian musical is no longer seen as being at the margins of the culture. In 2022, Ben Neutze published an article in *Limelight*, proffering that, given the great number of new Australian musicals to be produced that year, 'if there was ever going to be a golden age of new Australian musicals, then surely we're on the cusp.'[1] The writer and composer Laura Murphy, whose musical *The Lovers* was staged by Bell Shakespeare in late 2022, also noted a transformation in the landscape:

> I didn't really know that somebody could write musicals in Australia [. . .] I saw jukebox musicals like *The Boy from Oz* and *Priscilla*, but because I was

coming at it as the author of the music and lyrics, I just thought, 'Well I guess we don't do that here.' And that has changed dramatically over the last five years.[2]

In 2023, *The Guardian* published an article entitled 'The 15 Greatest Australian Musicals on Stage and Screen – sorted.'[3] All this marks a stark contrast to the rhetoric of crisis that I outlined in the introduction. My analysis of how Australian musicals produce and reproduce national imaginaries through inventive combinations of drama, dance, and song represents the most significant and substantial counter argument to the crisis rhetoric and has contributed to the changed discourse surrounding new Australian musicals.

The Hayes Theatre in Sydney's Potts Point deserves a great deal of the credit for cultivating this groundswell over the last decade. The theatre has become a hub for new Australian work. Emblematic of their approach is their Festival of New York, a two-week event, which features concert presentations, script-in-hand readings, masterclasses, panels, networking and social events, development showings, and cabaret performances. In July 2025, in the midst of writing this conclusion I attended the special Festival edition of Home Grown, an organisation I mentioned in the introduction, who champion emerging writers and composers. The event I was in the audience for was vibrant evening of new work, with a supportive audience, and a wonderful mix of both experienced and emerging performers and writers. Home Grown's tagline, projected onto the upstage wall for everyone to see as we waited for the performance to begin, is 'Not Grease. Not Cats. Not Sorry.' More than anything, I was struck by the confidence in this statement, and how emblematic it is of the shift that this book has documented. Fifteen years ago, when I started university, and my interest in the Australian musical became serious, I could not have conceived that in 2025, every major theatre company in Australia would have produced an original musical, and that musicals would now feature as a regular part of their programming.

A great deal has changed. What has not shifted is the Australian musical's focus on the national imaginary. To conclude, I offer some thoughts about the directions in which the Australian musical seems to be moving, and the ways in which the national imaginary continues to be revised and reproduced. While there are many directions this enquiry could take, I want to focus on just one, what I have termed the 'female turn' – an observable trend towards musicals about and for young women.

The Female Turn

The influence of *Muriel's Wedding* on subsequent Australian musicals is significant, and the musical's focus on young women as its target audience has continued emphatically in subsequent years. As Stacy Wolf has demonstrated, female fans are a key demographic for musical theatre internationally.[4] What is notable post-*Muriel* is how the prominence of female writers and composers, and the female protagonists they create, is further transforming the national imaginary.

Yve Blake's *Fangirls* (2019) explores the passionate devotion of a group of adolescent girls to their favourite boy band. Part pop concert, part thriller, part musical, *Fangirls* was co-produced by Queensland Theatre, Brisbane International Arts Festival, and Belvoir, and then toured nationally, before returning to Sydney for a repeat season at the Sydney Opera House in 2022. A cast recording was also produced.[5] It follows the story of Edna, a fourteen-year-old mega fan of the band True Connection (an obvious play on the name of the band One Direction). Edna hatches an outlandish plan to meet Harry, her favourite band member, which results in her drugging and kidnapping him, and then hiding him in her bedroom. Eventually, with the help of her mother and her friends, they set Harry free, and Edna realises that the value of her obsession with him was the sense of community and absolute devotion rather than the man himself.

Fangirls has an explicitly feminist agenda, one that offers an alternative to the exploration of masculinity on display in *Shane Warne*. By building on the narrative of female friendship established in *Muriel*, the musical demonstrates that the stories of young women form a vital part of the national imaginary. It also diversifies the national imaginary: the 2022 production, for example, featured a gender-diverse cast. Rita Bratovich wrote that '[w]hat's notable and truly refreshing is the diversity of people on stage. It's a cast that defies the homogeny of type that usually dominates this kind of theatre, and . . . is much more representative of the real world.'[6] The resources that accompany the published playscript, intended for high school students, note that '*Fangirls* is grounded in contemporary Australia, echoing the need to lean on the internet for connection due to our geographical distance from pop culture centres like the US and UK.'[7] The same resource explicitly invokes Blake's debt to '[m]usicals like *Muriel's Wedding*, that embrace an Australian sensibility and lean heavily into our long vowels.' And, while in some ways *Muriel* leant into the homogenising aspects of internet culture, Blake wanted to draw out the Australian features of the teenage experience, desiring to

> work against the image of a 'perfect' American teenager that has been presented in popular culture for years. Being a teenager in Australia does not feel as manicured, with sweaty school uniforms due to our extreme weather; often accompanied with feelings of isolation from the rest of the world.

Blake, following in the footsteps of all the musicals examined in this book, is at the vanguard of producing musical theatre that is unashamedly Australian.

Like *Muriel*, *Fangirls* had ambitions to play beyond Australian shores – and remarkably, it made it there first. In 2024, a year before *Muriel*, *Fangirls* had its international premiere, playing a season at the Lyric Hammersmith theatre in London. At the time of writing, it has been reported that a screen adaptation is also in the works. Blake's career is ascendant: her new play-with-songs, *Mackenzie*, a retelling of Macbeth with a young female protagonist and Lady Macbeth as nightmarish stage mum, had a London reading in July 2025.

In 2021, The Australian Theatre for Young People (ATYP) produced *The Deb*, a comedy musical conceived and written by Hannah Reilly, who had received the 2019 Rebel Wilson Comedy Commission from the organisation. With music by the pop star Megan Washington, similarities between *The Deb* and *Muriel* were also remarked upon, with Jason Blake commenting that '[f]or a company of ATYP's scale to realise something that rivals *Muriel's Wedding* is no small feat.'[8] The musical stages the schism between rural and urban Australia that increasingly plays a significant role in politics and the national imaginary. The musical is set in rural Australia, in the fictional drought-ravaged town of Dunburn. The young people of Dunburn, including protagonist Taylah, are looking forward to their debutante ball ('deb') an antiquated tradition whereby teenage girls make their society debut. The arrival of Maeve, Taylah's city-living, woke cousin, casts the beloved traditions of rural Australia in a new light. In 2024, the screen adaptation, directed by Wilson herself, premiered at the Toronto International Film Festival. While the film has been embroiled in controversy and legal disputes, and thus hasn't been publicly released, it is nonetheless remarkable that an Australian musical that began at this small scale has so quickly been adapted to film.[9]

In 2024, Melbourne Theatre Company presented *My Brilliant Career*, a new musical by Matthew Frank, Dean Bryant, and Sheridan Harbridge. Based on the novel of the same name by the turn of the century Australian writer and feminist Miles Franklin, it was the second original Australian musical produced by the company since *Vivid White*. Harbridge commented that what she found so 'exciting about adapting the book' was that it was so 'distinctively Australian.'[10] The score had an eclectic variety of musical styles and genres (in keeping with the phenomenon I have identified earlier) and boasted an actor-musician cast.[11] The review in *The Sydney Morning Herald* noted that 'an original homegrown musical that could smash it on the West End or Broadway is the holy grail of Australian musical theatre. This is it. This is the one.'[12] Due to excellent ticket sales, the season was briefly extended and a tour is planned for 2026.

There are many more new Australian musicals I could have profiled in this conclusion that pick up on the themes explored in this book. There's Nicholas Christo and Johannes Luebbers' portrayal of the life of Dame Nellie Melba with *Melba: A New Musical* (2017); Naomi Livingston and Hugo Chiarella's *Evie May: A Tivoli Story* (2018), which explored the history of Australian variety performance; *Dubbo Championship Wrestling* (2022), by James and

Daniel Cullen, which along with *The Deb* represents a shift from the suburbs to the region; Vidya Makan's song cycle *The Lucky Country* (2023); *Zombie! The Musical* (2023), set in a post-apocalyptic Sydney (a la *Vivid White)* by Laura Murphy; Squabbalogic's *The Dismissal* (2023), a musicalisation of the 1975 constitutional crisis; Conor Neylon and Jackson Peele's *The Beep Test* (2025), celebrating an Australian primary school rite of passage. As is evident from these titles, the 'taking this piss' approach to humour remains a feature of new Australian work. It is significant how many of these works also feature women writers and protagonists. This focus is sure to continue in the short, and perhaps the long term.

Waiting in the Wings

While this book has focused on professional productions of new Australian musicals, there is a substantial infrastructure and ecology of independent, semi-professional and community organisations that sustain these performances. It is in these companies that the next generation of artists, writers, and performers are cutting their teeth. There is much scope to consider the role that community, independent, and semi-professional organisations play in producing Australian musical theatre. The aim of this final foray is not only to highlight the contributions of a little explored theatrical ecosystem but also to consider how the grassroots feeds the professional and vice versa: that is to say, how someone like Eddie Perfect, for example, might have got from Mentone to Broadway.

The community theatre network in Australia has a long history. It is extensive and extremely well organised. The community theatre is, as Stacy Wolf observes in relation to the United States, 'a folk practice,' one 'handed down from one generation to the next.'[13] Multiple generations of a family often work on the same production together. Directors, musical directors, and choreographers train their successors. Many are prolific and tireless in their pursuits, embodying, as Wolf notes, that 'community musical theatre defies the opposition between work and leisure.' The people involved in these organisations pour their time, money, and energy into these productions and, in some cases, are able to stage professional-level work. In the organisations I know well, I have observed hives of activity, full of passionate and committed musical theatre artists who genuinely problematise the distinction between amateur and professional. But so much of this labour occurs under the radar that it can be difficult, especially for an outsider, to find out how these companies operate and exactly how they do what they do. None of this information is readily available and can only be obtained via an ethnographic 'boots on the ground' approach, travelling around the country spending time with these organisations, understanding how they operate, and the communities that they service.

If Australian musicals as an artistic form are to continue to occupy a more central role in the national imaginary, the community, independent, and semi-professional organisations will be key. This conclusion demonstrates the beginnings of what we might call the 'trickle-down' effect, whereby, as the rhetoric of crisis dissipates, and Australian musicals begin to be programmed more frequently, this will eventually flow through to the grass roots level. The future of Australian musical theatre – and its continued production and reproduction of the national imaginary – rests with those young people sitting in the audience at a local community theatre hearing those first glorious notes of an overture, marvelling at the wonder of the musical, and who will go on to start their own companies and forge professional careers.

My first experience of musical theatre was when, for my tenth birthday, I was gifted tickets to a production of *Oklahoma!* I can still vividly remember the feel of the red velvet upholstery; the way my breath caught as the curtains came up on those glorious first notes of the overture; how at the finale, as they sang 'You're doing fine, Oklahoma, Oklahoma, Ok!' I felt like I might cry, not from sadness but from the fast-approaching reality that the magic was about to end. From that moment, I was hooked. It was a life-changing experience and one that I have never forgotten.

The company that presented this production, which spawned my passion for musical theatre, was called The Guild Theatre. It was a semi-professional company that operated in Wollongong, a regional city on the New South Wales coast, and my hometown, in the 1980s and 1990s. In writing this book, I felt compelled to find out something more about this organisation, which no longer exists. I started searching for traces of it on Google, Trove, and academic databases. Nothing could be found, so I started working my way through my community theatre contacts, trying to find out if anyone in current organisations had any information. Steve Sanders, current president of the Arcadians Theatre Group, a community theatre based in Wollongong, gave me an email address for one Bob Peet. I had heard this name before, because in in the Illawarra Performing Arts Centre (IPAC), the venue at which I saw *Oklahoma!* there is a studio, used for rehearsals, developments, and small-scale performance, named after one such Bob Peet. I emailed with a series of questions, to which he was most kind to respond. He told me that he was 'indeed the Bob Peet of the Bob Peet Studio fame' and that 'as the person who instigated the Guild Theatre,' he was happy to provide me with a 'potted history of the venture.'[14] Peet's brief but generous account of the circumstances that led to formation of the Guild indicates that in Wollongong the creation of a professional theatre company and the development of high-quality performance venues ran parallel with the work of the community theatre and the university where I work. It illustrates one way in which community musical theatre organisations are inextricable from the history and life of a city. In Peet's account, we see power tussles between different community groups, adjustments made to seasons due to the preferences of audiences, and interactions between the local council, the arts organisations, and the passionate amateurs and the aspiring professionals. The community theatres have and continue to be an important part of Australian artistic culture.

Given the strength and breadth of the musicals analysed in this book, and those that have emerged since, I have confidence that future ten-year-olds will not just be in attendance at productions of *Oklahoma!* but also at a wide variety of Australian musicals, ones that produce and reproduce the national imaginary in new and exciting ways. When such works emerge, they will no longer be received in a critical vacuum. This study has laid the foundations for Australian musicals to be understood, interpreted, and, most importantly, valued for their significant contribution to the national imaginary.

Notes

1 Ben Neutze, 'The New Musicals from Oz,' *Limelight,* June 20, 2022, https://limelightmagazine.com.au/features/new-australianmusicals.
2 Neuzte, 'The New Musicals.'
3 Cassie Tongue and Ben Neuzte, 'The 15 Greatest Australian Musicals on Stage and Screen – Sorted,' *The Guardian,* August 8, 2023, https://www.theguardian.com/stage/2022/aug/08/the-15-greatest-australian-musicals-on-stage-and-screen-sorted.
4 Stacy Wolf, '"It's All About Popular": Wicked Divas and Internet Girl Fans,' *Changed for Good: A Feminist History of the Broadway Musical* (Oxford University Press, 2011), 219–235.
5 Yve Blake, *Fangirls (World Premiere Cast Recording),* accessed July 11, 2025, https://open.spotify.com/album/0ec6rirgVGksSIMtpDINJy?si=KEAUJ-2eTkWc5rk5dTNxUQ
6 Rita Bratovich, 'Fangirls – REVIEW,' *City Hub Sydney,* August 2, 2022, accessed July 17, 2025, https://cityhubsydney.com.au/2022/08/fangirls-review/.
7 'Teachers' Notes: Fangirls by Yve Blake,' *Currency Press,* 3, accessed July 21, 2025, https://www.currency.com.au/wp-content/uploads/Fangirls-HSC-Resources_FIN.pdf.
8 Jason Blake, 'The Deb,' *Audrey Journal,* April 25, 2022, accessed August 23, 2022, http://www.audreyjournal.com.au/arts/the-deb-atypreview/.
9 Tatiana Siegel, 'Rebel Wilson Escalates Battle with 'The Deb' Producers in 'Bizarre Outburst of Jealous' After Cannes Yacht Party,' *Variety,* May 20, 2025, https://variety.com/2025/film/festivals/rebel-wilson-escalates-deb-producers-battle-cannes-party-1236403316/
10 Dean Bryant, Mathew Frank, and Sheridan Harbridge, 'Writer's note: From page to stage,' *My Brilliant Career,* theatre programme, accessed July 24, 2025, https://www.mtc.com.au/discover-more/backstage/my-brilliant-career-programme/.
11 Dean Bryant and Mathew Frank, *My Brilliant Career (Original Cast Recording),* Bryant & Frank Productions, accessed July 24, 2025, https://open.spotify.com/album/0CGhWXzmDcQrzCi3nHygkg?si=duW-uIXtRMGxvDLP6IADHA.
12 Will Cox, Tony Way, and Cameron Woodhead, 'Rebellious, big-hearted: This show is the holy grail of Australian musical theatre,' *The Sydney Morning Herald,* November11,2024,https://www.smh.com.au/culture/live-reviews/this-is-serious-fun-tism-deliver-a-welcome-blast-from-the-past-20241110-p5kpd6.html

13 Stacy Wolf, *Beyond Broadway: The Pleasure and Promise of Musical Theatre Across America* (Oxford University Press, 2019), 5.
14 Bob Peet, personal communication, November 23, 2021.

References

Blake, Jason. 'The Deb.' *Audrey Journal*, April 25, 2022. Accessed August 23, 2022. http://www.audreyjournal.com.au/arts/the-deb-atypreview/.

Blake, Yve. *Fangirls (World Premiere Cast Recording)*. Accessed July 11, 2025. https://open.spotify.com/album/0ec6rirgVGksSIMtpDINJy?si=KEAUJ-2eTkWc5rk5dTNxUQ.

Bratovich, Rita. 'Fangirls – REVIEW.' *City Hub Sydney*, August 2, 2022. Accessed July 17, 2025. https://cityhubsydney.com.au/2022/08/fangirls-review/.

Bryant, Dean, and Mathew Frank. *My Brilliant Career (Original Cast Recording*. Bryant & Frank Productions. Accessed July 24, 2025. https://open.spotify.com/album/0CGhWXzmDcQrzCi3nHygkg?si=duW-uIXtRMGxvDLP6IADHA.

Bryant, Dean, Mathew Frank, and Sheridan Harbridge. 'Writer's Note: From Page to Stage.' *My Brilliant Career*, theatre programme. Accessed July 24, 2025. https://www.mtc.com.au/discover-more/backstage/my-brilliant-career-programme/.

Cox, Will, Tony Way, and Cameron Woodhead. 'Rebellious, Big-Hearted: This show is the Holy Grail of Australian Musical Theatre.' *The Sydney Morning Herald*, November 11, 2024. https://www.smh.com.au/culture/live-reviews/this-is-serious-fun-tism-deliver-a-welcome-blast-from-the-past-20241110-p5kpd6.html.

Neutze, Ben. 'The New Musicals from Oz.' *Limelight*, June 20, 2022. https://limelightmagazine.com.au/features/new-australianmusicals.

Siegel, Tatiana. 'Rebel Wilson Escalates Battle with 'The Deb' Producers in 'Bizarre Outburst of Jealous' After Cannes Yacht Party.' *Variety*, May 20, 2025. https://variety.com/2025/film/festivals/rebel-wilson-escalates-deb-producers-battle-cannes-party-1236403316/.

'Teachers' Notes: Fangirls by Yve Blake.' *Currency Press*. Accessed July 21, 2025. https://www.currency.com.au/wp-content/uploads/Fangirls-HSC-Resources_FIN.pdf.

Tongue, Cassie, and Ben Neutze. 'The 15 Greatest Australian Musicals on Stage and Screen – Sorted.' *The Guardian*, August 8, 2023. https://www.theguardian.com/stage/2022/aug/08/the-15-greatest-australian-musicals-on-stage-and-screen-sorted.

Wolf, Stacy. *Changed for Good: A Feminist History of the Broadway Musical*. Oxford University Press, 2011.

Wolf, Stacy. *Beyond Broadway: The Pleasure and Promise of Musical Theatre Across America*. Oxford University Press, 2019.

INDEX

For Product Safety Concerns and Information please contact our EU
representative GPSR@taylorandfrancis.com
Taylor & Francis Verlag GmbH, Kaufingerstraße 24, 80331 München, Germany